Th

(Ratings ac

Average rating 4.1 out of 5 stars

"I really enjoyed reading this story and getting to know the characters. In a very short time, I found myself caring what happened to them. I am a mystery fan, and this definitely was a fun ride."

—*Mountain Mom*

"Quill Gordon courts trout, a lady, and justice, and there's a little 'catch and release' applied to all three in this most entertaining murder mystery."

—*Edan D. Cassidy*

"Well written good story. Ready for next book about these people. Could be a start to a fun set of books."

—*Tim Smith*

Wash Her Guilt Away

Average rating: 4.7 out of 5 stars

"The characters are so well drawn, each one seemed to be plucked from real life and placed into the story."

—*Sentia*

"As languid and dark as a quiet trout stream on an overcast day, the second Quill Gordon novel is a pleasure to read ... even the weather has a plot twist."

—*Judy Parrish*

"The fly-fishing descriptions were amazing. I was thoroughly engaged. I couldn't figure out who dunnit until the very end ... Great story."

—*Lovedrama*

Not Death, But Love
Average rating: 4.8 out of 5 stars

"This is my third Michael Wallace/Quill Gordon book, and I enjoyed this as much as the other two."

—*Steve Reese*

"Perfect for summer vacation reading. Good character development and plot, with some nice surprises."

—*Doug Simmons*

"Enjoyed very much. Fast read."

—*T. Mitchell*

Also by Michael Wallace

Quill Gordon Mysteries

The McHenry Inheritance
Wash Her Guilt Away
Not Death, But Love

Nonfiction

The Borina Family of Watsonville (California history)

The Daughters Of Alta Mira

A Quill Gordon Mystery

Michael Wallace

ISBN: 978-0-9903871-2-1

Cover Design: Deborah Karas, Karas Technical Services

In the spirit of Rex Stout

For Kathe and Susan,
My father's daughters

Logging Road, Dusk

"Take off your clothes."

"You're kidding me, right?"

"Does this gun look like a joke?"

They stared at each other, five feet apart in the fading light. He gestured with the gun.

"Come on," he said. "I mean it."

"You're crazy," she said. "It's fricking cold out here."

"Once we get going, you won't feel the cold."

"Who said anything about getting going? You were just giving me a ride."

"Maybe half an hour ago, but as you can see, the situation has changed. Now *move!* Blouse first. I'm losing my patience."

She looked at him, looked at the gun, and unbuttoned the top button of her pink blouse. A gust of cold autumn wind came up, rattling through the treetops. It knifed through her thin blouse, and she shivered.

"It's cold," she said.

"Honey, that's the least of your problems."

"I can't believe you think you're going to get away with this."

"Why not? I have so far."

Then she *knew*, and a stab of fear went through her, colder and deeper than the gust of wind.

There was no chance of anyone coming along this deserted logging road at sunset. Her only hope was to take matters into her own hands.

She looked at his eyes, which to her advantage, were fixed on her breasts. *He's behaving like a man,* she thought. *Maybe I can use that against him.*

"All right, then," she said, unbuttoning the blouse slowly for deliberate effect. She wished that today, of all days, she hadn't worn the Victoria's Secret bra she'd bought last summer in Sacramento. He noticed it immediately.

"I see you're dressed for this," he said. "I like that. Now let's see your panties."

As she unbuttoned the last button, she pulled the blouse open, showing off her torso and the bra. The cold air stung her skin, but she saw he was looking at her breasts and took a half step forward. She was about three and a half feet from him. Not as close as she would have liked, but she didn't feel she could move any closer.

"All in good time," she said. She slid her right arm out of the blouse, then reached across her front and grabbed the collar with it, pulling the left sleeve down over the arm. When she was done, she stood looking at him.

"Take off the jeans," he said.

Now or never. To make him think she was complying, she reached down and touched her belt buckle. Suddenly, with a quick, backhand motion, she swung the blouse as though snapping a towel in the locker room and hit him across the side of the head.

He wasn't expecting it. The others had gone along meekly, so he'd been looking at her crotch, waiting for her to pull the jeans down. When the blouse hit the side of his head, he started and took a step backward, inadvertently lowering the gun. She lunged forward and grabbed his hand.

She was five-nine and fit from playing on the volleyball team, but he still had the physical edge. They grappled awkwardly for several seconds, as she put both her hands on his right wrist, trying to turn the gun away. Using both hands, he gave her a hard shove backwards.

As he did, the gun went off.

The velocity of the bullet gave her an additional impetus that sent her over the edge of the road. He saw, as a quick flash, the wound near her heart, then she was out of sight.

He stood shaking and panting. It had all gone spectacularly wrong.

They had been in a turnout on a logging road several miles from the state highway and the nearest paved county road. At this point, the road had a nearly sheer dropoff of about 75 feet. Nervously, he walked to the edge and looked down.

She had ended up caught in the branches of a pine tree, 20 feet below the road and 50 feet up from the base of the tree. She was still. From the quick glimpse of her wound, he guessed she was either dead or bleeding out and soon would be. There was no way he could get down to the body. Recovering it would be a major effort, even for the professionals on the Search and Rescue team.

He walked up and down the road in either direction and concluded that she couldn't readily be seen by a passing driver. Not that there were many of those at this time of year. There would be no logging operations on this road until spring, and deer-hunting season had concluded last weekend. He walked back to the turnout and looked down. Her white torso stood out against the tree branches, but in the growing darkness, the jeans blended into the background.

Then he heard the sound of the stream running through the gorge below and realized there were nearly two weeks left in the fishing season. There was a chance a fisherman in the gorge might spot her in the tree. He squinted to try to see what the sight lines from the creek would be, but it was getting too dark to tell.

Still, he thought, calming himself, the odds were in his favor. Most people here stopped fishing when deer hunting season began and didn't start again until spring. No, there was a pretty good chance that the body wouldn't be found until next spring, if at all. Who could say what animals might get at it? And if it should be found sooner, there would be nothing to connect it to him.

Moving to his vehicle, he stopped to pick up the pink blouse, which was lying on the ground. He sniffed it, opened one of the doors, unzipped a duffel bag and put the blouse inside. He started the engine and began driving back down the hill, thinking that, unlike her, he had dodged a bullet. Even so, he was displeased.

I got careless, he thought. *It won't happen next time.*

Thursday November 6, 1997

RESTING HIS FOREHEAD on top of the steering wheel, hands at ten and two o'clock, Quill Gordon squeezed his eyes tightly shut – as if that might make it go away. The ignition of his Cherokee was switched off, but the reassuring, folksy baritone on the radio was still coming through loud and clear.

"And it looks like this beautiful Indian Summer weather we've been having will last through the weekend, though it'll be getting a bit cooler and breezier. Deer season is over, but if you wanna get out and enjoy it, remember trout season in the streams is still open until November 15th, and the fish'll be eating up to get fat for winter. Now this just in during our last song: John Davidson, wherever you are on the Lower Forty, your wife, Martha, wants to remind you that she's leaving for her bridge game at one o'clock, so if you want lunch, you need to be home by noon.

"But if you miss lunch at home, you might want to go to Danny's Diner at Second and Chaparral, serving breakfast and lunch from 6 to 2:30 seven days a week. This week's breakfast special is chicken-fried steak, three eggs cooked any style, home-fried potatoes and a biscuit with gravy, only $4.95 at Danny's Diner – where the elite meet to eat.

"Four minutes to the hour, so just enough time for a little Barbara Mandrell. This is her big hit from 1978, and it's probably a classic by now. 'Sleeping Single in a Double Bed.' You're listening to Morning Coffee with Mountain Bob on Radio KNEP, Alta Mira, the Voice of the High Desert."

The spiel was followed by a coyote howl, which tailed off into the percussive first notes of the song. Gordon sat up, opened his eyes, and turned off the radio. Glancing at the rear-view mirror, he saw that the Highway Patrol car was still parked behind his on the side of the state highway, across from the county airport. He sighed and leaned toward the glove compartment to retrieve his registration.

It was his own fault and he knew it. He was scheduled to meet his friend Sam Akers at eleven o'clock for the beginning of a 10-day late-season fishing trip. Sam was flying in from Summit County, far to the south, Gordon was particularly eager for any news he might be bringing. Yet he had become distracted in town (not an easy thing in a place with fewer than 4,000 residents) and was rushing to the airport when he saw the flashing lights in his mirror.

The officer appeared by the passenger window, and Gordon lowered it. The name above his badge said Armstrong, and he looked every bit the fit and clean-cut athlete in his late twenties or early thirties.

"Do you know why I pulled you over?" the officer asked, as if he wasn't quite sure himself.

"I was in a hurry to meet a friend who's flying in," Gordon said. "Guess I lost track of how fast I was going."

The officer nodded. "Seventy-four in a 55 zone. We don't like to give tickets to visitors, cause we don't get enough of them. But 19 over the limit is a bit more than we can ignore. You staying here long?"

"Through next Saturday. We're here for a little late-season fishing."

"Should be good, especially if the weather holds. The creeks are still running pretty well, and I hear the lakes have been producing. Let me see your license and registration please, so we can get on with this, and you can go fishing."

He went back to the patrol car, and Gordon sat fuming. It was his first moving violation in nine years, so the damage would be slight. But as the son of a judge, he was acutely embarrassed to run afoul of the law in any way. He heard the drone of an engine overhead, and looked up to see a small plane circling to land at the airport. Could be Sam's, he thought. If it is, he'll see me for sure.

Gordon watched the plane land, and Officer Armstrong returned as it touched down.

"I wrote you up for 65 instead of what you were actually doing," he said. "That's a bit of a break. And if you go to a driver safety class, they'll wipe this off the record and your insurance shouldn't go up. I see you're from San Francisco. I hear they have some pretty good comedy driving classes there. If you can get into one of those, it shouldn't be too painful." He handed the citation to Gordon. "Sign here, and you can get on to your fishing."

"Thank you." Gordon scribbled his signature at the bottom and the officer gave him a copy.

"Drive careful the rest of the trip, and good luck fishing. Have a nice day now."

Gordon folded the citation and put it in his shirt pocket. Double-checking the roadway, he pulled out and drove slowly to the airport entrance, nervously checking the speedometer every five seconds.

THAT LOOKED LIKE Gordon's Cherokee across from the airport as I came in, with the Highway Patrol car right behind it. Can't say I'm surprised. It's not that he's a bad driver as a rule, but he loses track of things sometimes and goes faster than he realizes.

On the other hand, he was right about the weather. It's much better than I would have expected this late in the season. He knows the mountains and the fishing conditions really well. Going with him is almost like hiring a guide – except the guide doesn't generally make a point of out-fishing you.

He knows I've just been to Summit County, and he probably wants the news from there. I hope that's not why he was speeding. He's not going to like what I have to report, and there was no sense rushing to hear it. Oh, well. His problem, not mine.

THE NOON RUSH, such as it was, had not yet kicked in at the Danube Hotel's Vienna Café. Gordon and Sam arrived at quarter to noon and were quickly seated at a booth. Eager to begin fishing, they ordered sandwiches and iced tea.

The five-story hotel building was the tallest structure in the town of Alta Mira (unless you counted the water tower) and had been built in 1907. A bit frayed at the edges, but still clean and comfortable, it had a superb central heating system, which was why Gordon chose it for a late-season trip.

"Where are we fishing today?" said Sam.

"Where do you want to fish?" asked Gordon. "I mean, what type of fishing?"

Sam thought for a moment. "Small or medium-size stream if you know of one. That'd suit me."

"Then let's do Powder Creek — the upper part of it in the mountains behind the community college."

"I defer to your judgment."

The waitress brought their tea, and they each took a sip.

"How are Nancy and the kids?" Gordon asked.

"Still doing well."

Gordon took another sip of tea, followed by a deep breath. "So how was Summit County?"

"Beautiful as ever. We really should go back sometime soon."

"Not me. Not for a while. Did you get a chance to talk to anybody when you were there?"

"As a matter of fact, I caught Sheriff Mike in the office yesterday afternoon. He filled me in pretty well."

Gordon raised his eyebrows.

"He's finally going to hang it up next year," Sam continued. "He's not running for re-election."

"He'll be dead a year and a half after he quits. That job is his life."

"Maybe. Anyway, he's already hand picked his successor. A woman he brought in from San Jose not long after the last time we were there."

"If he's behind her, she'll probably win. What else?"

"Some bad news. Remember Kitty, who owned the café where we ate?" Gordon nodded. "Well, she has ovarian cancer. Probably won't make it through the month."

"That's a shame. She's not that old."

"Sixty, according to Sheriff Mike."

"Too damn bad." Gordon took another sip of tea and stared at the faded mural of old Vienna on the far wall.

"And how about…?" his voice trailed off.

Sam also took a sip of tea, followed by a deep breath.

"She's engaged, Gordon. To an undertaker in Carson City. If it makes you feel any better, Sheriff Mike thinks it's a case of settling for Mr. Good Enough."

Gordon sat motionless for a minute, staring into his tea, while Sam grew increasingly jittery.

"You could always kidnap the bride," Sam said. "But whenever the wedding is, I'm already busy that weekend."

"No, Sam. It's been over for almost four years, and this just makes it final. I hope he makes her happy. She deserves it, and that wasn't something I could do."

"How old are you, Gordon? Thirty-seven?"

"Thirty-eight."

"Even in San Francisco, that's pretty old to still be a bachelor. I think this has been holding you back way too long."

He didn't immediately answer, and finally said, "Let's talk about fishing." Lunch arrived, and he took a bite from his sandwich, chewing it slowly. "But before we head to the creek, there's one little thing I'd like to do."

THANK GOD THAT'S OVER WITH. I don't know why I was so nervous about this. I mean, I knew it would affect him, but whatever Gordon's failings are, blaming the messenger isn't one of them. And maybe now he can really move on. I'm not the only friend who's been worried about him in that regard.

Now he's saying he wants to go to an art gallery after lunch. An art gallery! In this town! At least it shouldn't take very long.

THE DANUBE HOTEL occupies one of the corners at Fourth Street and Chaparral Boulevard, the north-south highway through Alta Mira. Gordon and Sam emerged into autumn sunlight, rendered slightly hazy by the smoke from ranches and homeowners burning debris and yard waste at the end of the season. They walked up Chaparral a block to Third Street, crossed it, and turned right. Halfway down the block was a two-story, turn-of-the-century brick office building. The upper story had been vacant since 1973, but the windows weren't boarded up because it hadn't yet occurred to anyone to break them. At street level were two working storefronts, separated by an empty one. The one on the right housed Merton's Print and Copy, while the one on their left was home to the High Desert Artists Co-Operative. Gordon stopped in front of it and pointed to the watercolor in the window. It showed a solitary angler fishing in a mountain stream.

"Caught my eye when I was out for a walk this morning," he said. "They're only open noon to four Thursday through Sunday, so I thought we'd drop in now."

They stepped inside. A severe-looking woman, with no-nonsense glasses and hair so firmly in place that a gale wouldn't move it, eyed them warily from a desk in the back corner.

"Feel free to look around," she said grudgingly. "I'm here to answer questions." Her tone indicated she wouldn't be distressed if they didn't have any.

With Sam following, Gordon moved to the left of the space and began circulating clockwise, looking at the paintings on the walls. Most of them were earnest representations of local scenes, lacking the sense of light, color, texture and composition that make a good painting. Gordon gave them a quick glance and moved on.

At the back wall he stopped longer in front of a 3-by-4-foot landscape. Done in a bold, impressionistic style, it showed a small mountain lake on what appeared to be a stormy day. Where the other paintings were light with gay colors, this one was a study in black, brown, gray and deep blue, except for a shaft of light, vivid white with a tinge of yellow, that broke through the clouds and illuminated a jagged rock jutting from the water and reflecting on its surface. The tag by the lower right corner of the frame said the painting was called "Reflection Lake" and its price was $950. The artist's signature on the painting read simply, "Macondray."

Gordon stood in front of it for three minutes before moving on. At the front of the gallery, he looked at the fishing painting for only 15 seconds. There were a half-dozen sculptures scattered around the middle of the room. Out of curiosity, more than anything else, they paused in front of a wood carving that looked like a pile of dog feces. The tag by it was labeled "Bear Scat," and the price had been reduced from the original $400 to $300, then again to $250.

"You must admit," said Sam, finally breaking the silence, "it tells the story."

Without replying, Gordon moved to the back and stood in front of "Reflection Lake," tapping his right foot nervously. Finally, he turned to the woman at the desk.

"Excuse me," he said. "What can you tell me about Macondray?"

She frowned. "Teaches at the community college," she said. "Full of airs, if you ask me. Has the most expensive painting in here, and it isn't even pretty."

"Ah, but it has style. It's kind of dark back here. Would it be possible to take it up to the front where the light's better?"

Her expression froze, the rictus of the bureaucrat who doesn't know what to do with a request not covered by the formal rules.

"I suppose so," she said warily. "But you need to carry it yourself, and if you break it, you have to pay for it."

"Fair enough." Gordon, just under 6-5, with an athletic build and long arms, gracefully lifted it from the wall and carried it to the front. Ever vigilant, the woman at the desk jumped up and moved to the front door, ready to block his path if he tried to make a run for it with the merchandise.

The low November sun flooded the front of the gallery with light, and in that light, the rich palette of the painting's dark hues showed its true vibrancy. Gordon looked at it for ten seconds and made a decision.

"I'll take it," he said. "I see you accept credit cards."

Stunned, she nodded. When Gordon picked up the painting and headed toward the desk, she meekly followed.

Gordon had already set his VISA card on the desk. After rummaging through its drawers, she found the card machine. Carefully she ran an impression of his card and handed him a triplicate receipt.

After signing it, he said, "Would it be possible to get this wrapped?"

This time she knew the rule.

"What do you think this is – San Francisco?" she snapped. "If you want it wrapped, take it to Merton's next door and he'll do it for three dollars."

Which was what they did. As they were Merton's only customers, it didn't take long, and they were soon on the way to Powder Creek.

THE TIME-AND-TEMPERATURE SIGN at Great Northeast Bank showed 71 degrees at 1:14 p.m. as they drove by. A few blocks from the Danube, the north-south highway heading toward Oregon met the east-west highway heading toward Nevada. They became the same road for about ten miles, before the east-west highway broke off, crossed a mountain range and entered Serendipity Valley, running through the town of Big Piney (slogan: "Last stop before legal gambling").

Two miles outside Alta Mira, on the left side of the highway, stood Homestead Community College. Finished in 1969, at the end of California's postwar education boom, it had the unadorned look of government buildings of its era – greatly improved, however, by the planting of numerous trees, which had flourished in the three decades since. The evergreens were ready to take on the coming winter, and the deciduous trees showed signs of late fall color. Between the highway and the college proper was 150 yards of dirt, stone and sagebrush, with several large boulders breaking up the barrenness.

Halfway between the college and the point where the highways diverged, a road ran into the mountains on the left. The sign marking it read, "Wappinger Lake," and, as Gordon explained, the lake was the source of Powder Creek.

"Will there be any water this late in the year?" asked Sam.

Gordon nodded. "The lake's fed by several large springs, year-round. The creek should be fine."

The road forked a few miles from the highway. The fork leading right to the lake remained paved. Going left to Powder Creek, it turned to well-packed dirt, along which the Cherokee bounced jauntily. They went down a long grade, passed two logging roads rising to the left, and stopped when the road ended at a primitive Forest Service campground with ten campsites and two outhouses. It was closed for the winter, and Gordon parked by the gate that blocked vehicles, but not pedestrians, from getting through. With the car windows down, they could hear the sound of the rushing creek.

"What fly should I use?" asked Sam as they were pulling on their waders.

"I'm starting with attractors," Gordon replied. "Royal Wulffs and Humpys size 12 and 14. The fish are loading up for winter, and a big bug floating by should look good. Where there's a grassy bank you might even want to use a hopper imitation."

"Let's start with that," said Sam. "We can always try something else if it doesn't work."

It worked. They fished their way a mile downstream, savoring the day. The creek was 20 to 30 feet wide and looked fishy, with numerous riffles, pools and undercut banks The cool water glistened in the afternoon sun, and when they cast their flies to a likely spot, a fish rose to them as often as not. Most were Rainbow Trout in the 10 to 12 inch range, but there were also a few Brook Trout (one a surprising 13 inches) and a couple of Browns. Sam, making a perfect cast to the current at the edge of an undercut bank, caught the largest fish of the day, a 16-inch Rainbow, with a Yellow Humpy. As always, they released all the fish back to the creek.

For the first two hours the weather was perfect – warm enough to be comfortable, but not too hot. At four o'clock, the sun went behind the mountains. In half an hour the temperature dropped from 70 to 50, and eased into the high 40s from there. The wind picked up too, blowing more steadily, rattling the tops of the pine trees, and foretelling the winter in its chill. It was 4:45 when they got back to the campground and already noticeably darker, almost twilight.

They took off their waders and put the fly rods in the back of the Cherokee. Gordon donned a light windbreaker over his flannel shirt and got behind the wheel. Sam stood by the passenger door several seconds longer, looking up through the tree branches at dusk's fading light, listening to the sounds of the wind and creek, breathing the pure mountain air. That was when he heard a sharp crack in the distance, like a whip snapping.

"Did you hear that?"

"Hear what?" Gordon said.

"It sounded like a gunshot."

Gordon nodded. "A lot of guns around here. Was it close by?"

"No. A ways off."

"Then probably nothing to worry about. Let's get going. I don't know about you, but I'm getting hungry, and we're meeting my friend Bob Hastings in an hour."

GORDON'S TRYING NOT TO SHOW IT, but I know he's not happy about the fact I caught the biggest fish this afternoon. That doesn't happen very often but he is *such* a competitor he can't stand it when it does. Come to think of it, he was a bit off this afternoon. He made several bad casts, and a few times he wasn't paying attention when a fish rose to his fly. It isn't like him.

We're supposed to have dinner at some Basque restaurant tonight with an old college friend of his. Should be interesting. I'm pretty hungry, too, and one nice thing about traveling with Gordon is he's a good guide. Another nice thing is that this late in the year, we can fish until dark and still have dinner at a civilized hour.

I swear that was a gunshot I heard.

MOUNTAIN BOB HASTINGS had scheduled dinner for 6:30 out of consideration for Gordon's fishing plans. By then, Elizalde's Basque restaurant was busy – surprisingly so for a small-town establishment on a Thursday night, with winter drawing near. The bar was nearly full, and three-quarters of the red-covered tables were occupied. Bob was at a table near a large stone fireplace, in full use now that the evening chill had descended. He was wearing worn jeans, running shoes, and a flannel shirt of dark green and gold. He had mousy brown hair that sprung out from the sides of his head, a face that looked happy and honest, and a pair of glasses with thick black rims. As Gordon and Sam walked past several historical ranching photos to his table, he rose to greet them.

"Flyboy!" he said enthusiastically, grasping Gordon's right hand in his and giving it a strong shake, while slapping Gordon's shoulder with his left hand. "Good to see you again. It's been a long time."

"Too long," Gordon said. "This is my friend Sam."

"You have a last name, Sam?" Bob said as they shook hands.

"Akers," Sam said.

"Akers and Pains," Bob ad-libbed.

"You'll get used to it, Sam," Gordon said. "He calls me Flyboy because I taught him fly fishing. He was a worm and lure guy before."

"And I'm in your debt, Gordon. Welcome to our little town, Akers and Pains. This your first time here?" Sam nodded. "I hope you'll like it. And I hope you're both hungry and decisive. At my house, if you get to the dinner table this late in the day, the food's all gone."

"How's Brenda?" asked Gordon.

"Doing great. She's with the kids at a school dance rehearsal, so it worked out well for this little stag night."

"And Eileen? She must be 13 now."

"Fourteen in September."

"Fourteen! Where did the time go?"

"And Sarah'll be 12 in February."

"Both doing well in school?"

"Pretty good. Eileen's the better student, but Sarah has the personality. We're gonna have our hands full when she starts dating."

A waitress who must have been at least 70, with gray frizzy hair, materialized at their table, pad in hand.

"Can I get you boys something to drink?" She looked at Bob. "Pretty late for you to be here."

"Had to wait for my friends here to wrap up their fishing. Ruby, my friends Gordon and Sam."

"Pleased to meetcha. What are you having?" She looked at Gordon.

"Dos Equis for me."

"I'll have the same," said Sam.

"The usual," Bob said.

She moved off toward the bar with a surprising spring in her step.

"She looks pretty spry for her age," Sam ventured.

Bob nodded. "That's what 50 years of eating red meat and inhaling second-hand smoke will do for you. If she ate fruits and salads, she'd be in a nursing home now." He turned to Sam. "I know what Gordon's ordering, and I hope you like beef and lamb, 'cause that's what they do right here. A lot of Basques settled in these parts a century ago, and old man Elizalde finally figured it was easier to make money cooking beef than raising it. Ruby's his daughter. Rest his soul."

Sam opened his menu, scanned it briefly, and closed it.

"I'm really glad to see you here, Gordon," said Bob. "Always good to see you, but there's something going on here that just might be in your line."

"What – tax-free municipals? Short sales?"

"Naw. I thought you were getting out of that stuff, anyway. I mean your next line." He looked quickly around the room and lowered his voice to a whisper.

"Crime."

Gordon nodded his head slightly and looked at Bob out of his right eye. "What do you mean, Bob? Somebody been vandalizing the tractors at the local farm supply?"

"Not so loud," Bob said in a hoarse whisper. "This is really serious, though I don't think it's made the San Francisco papers yet. In the last month, two students from the community college have gone missing. Both attractive women."

Ruby returned with two Dos Equis and a Budweiser for Bob. She took their orders (lamb chops for Gordon, Santa Maria tri-tip for Bob, and sirloin for Sam) and scooted off to the kitchen.

"I don't suppose," Gordon said quietly, "that there's any chance they just ran away."

"That's what everybody's hoping," Bob said, "but I think it's a pretty slim chance. They'd have called someone by now."

"Not necessarily," Sam said. "I serve on a board for a group in San Francisco that works with runaways. Some of them had something really bad to run away from."

"I hear what you're saying, but I don't think so. They were both girls who got good grades, never got in trouble. Seemed like normal, happy kids."

"When did this happen?" Gordon asked.

"The first one was Jennifer McCall. On October third she was working at a writing lab at the college, helping students with their papers. She walked out the door at 3:30, waving goodbye to the other tutor and three students like she didn't have a care in the world. That's the last time anyone saw her for sure."

"For sure?"

"Well, a couple of people thought they might have seen her, but by the time they were asked, a few days had gone by and they couldn't be positive it was that day."

"And the second?"

"Michelle Robertson. She vanished October 24th, also late afternoon. She had a part-time job at the school library, and when it closed at three, she was out the door like a shot. Her boyfriend's on the football team, and they were playing at home that night. She wanted to get pretty for him for after the game."

"Doesn't sound like someone who was about ready to bolt," Sam said.

"Not at all. This is really bothersome."

"The thing that strikes me," said Gordon, "is that both disappearances were at about the same time on the same day of the week – a Friday. Does the sheriff – or whoever's investigating – have any thoughts about that?"

"Haven't asked, but I doubt it. No one seems to have any idea what's going on. The sheriff – Chris Huntley – is new to the job, and I'd say pretty competent, but there just isn't much to go on." Bob looked over Gordon's shoulder and waved. "Well, look who's here."

Gordon and Sam turned to see two young women, drinks in hand, leaving the bar and heading for the table. One was five-nine, slender, with raven-black hair cut short and designer glasses that accentuated her angular features and knowing eyes. The other woman was an inch shorter, with a stocky build that suggested muscularity, not flabbiness, and light brown hair pulled up in a bun.

"What brings you here on a weeknight?" Bob said. "Gordon, Sam, this is Elizabeth Macondray," he gestured to the woman with glasses, "who teaches at Homestead College, and Sandy Steadman of the Highway Patrol."

"We're celebrating," Elizabeth said. "I got a call from the gallery this afternoon. Some sucker finally bought my painting."

HERE WE GO AGAIN. I can tell she's checking Gordon out. Women seem to do that. I don't think he's particularly handsome, but I'm a man, so what do I know? He does have that honest face that makes people think they can trust him. But if she gets his attention, I can say sayonara to fishing with him. And whatever else you can say about Gordon, he knows where and how to fish.

Only one thing to do. If we're going to get any fishing done this trip, I've got to nip this in the bud.

"DIDN'T YOU BUY a painting today?" Sam said to Gordon.

Elizabeth froze. Gordon stared daggers at his friend. Bob picked up on the tension and tried to move forward.

"Well, Flyboy. I didn't know you're an art collector. Elizabeth here does really nice work. Why don't you ladies sit down?"

"No one here appreciates it," said Sandy, pulling up a chair. "In this town, a painting without animals doesn't sell."

"I can believe that," Gordon said.

"I'm so sorry," said Elizabeth. "But Sandy's right. It makes you cynical when you put out something you think is really good and it doesn't sell, but other things do. If you bought my painting, I'm very appreciative that you saw something in it."

"You have an eye, and an ability to express what you see. I can't explain it technically, but I can recognize it."

"How about joining us for dinner?" Bob said. "We just ordered, and we were talking about the case."

"Which one?" Elizabeth said.

"There's more than one?" Sam asked.

"The missing students," Bob said. "Gordon has a little history of doing investigations, and he was asking about the sheriff's take on it."

"I was wondering," Gordon said, "if he had any theories or is seeing a pattern."

The silence that greeted the remark was telling. Bob, Elizabeth and Sandy looked at each other, and Sandy finally spoke.

"Sheriff Christina Huntley is a she," she said, "and very experienced and competent. But because she's a woman, her ability doesn't seem to matter to some people."

Gordon blushed. "I'm sorry. I heard 'Chris' and assumed. You shouldn't assume."

"I was just filling Gordon in on Jennifer and Michelle," Bob said.

"And I was leading up to a question," Gordon said. "They were last seen on the community college campus. Would somebody really have abducted them in broad daylight?"

"You didn't explain?" Elizabeth said.

"I was just getting there," Bob replied. He turned to Gordon. "The college is about two miles outside town. That's where the land was cheap when they built it. Not all the kids have a car, so it's pretty common for the ones who don't to hitch a ride into town. That's been going on for years and never been a problem."

"Until now," Sandy said. "Although nobody saw for sure, it's pretty likely the last thing the missing women did on campus was put out their thumbs and get into somebody's car."

"It's a scandal," Elizabeth said. "There should be a shuttle service to town. Some of us have been pushing for that since before this happened."

"Is money the problem?" Sam asked.

"It's the excuse, anyway. County thinks the college should pay, and the college wants the county to do it."

"But surely," Gordon said, looking at Bob, "that's something a couple of reasonably competent bureaucrats could hash out."

"You'd think so, wouldn't you," Elizabeth said. "But you don't know Dean Breeze."

"College president," Bob said. "A nice man, but…."

"Too much education for his intelligence," Elizabeth said. "He doesn't really get that it's a problem, and even if he did, I don't know that he'd push too hard for a solution."

Gordon turned to Bob again. "You teach a class at the college, don't you?"

"Broadcast radio. Michelle, the second girl who disappeared, took it last spring."

"Woman," Elizabeth said. "She was 20 years old." She paused and caught herself. "Still is, I hope."

"Anyway," Bob continued, "Elizabeth and I have been trying to press people on this."

"Are you talking about it on your show?" Sam said.

"Not yet. I don't want to be scaring people if they did just run away."

"What do you mean?" Sandy interjected. "Every woman in town is terrified. The missing women have friends who're saying something's wrong, and it's spreading like wildfire. If there's one more disappearance, it'll be impossible to keep a lid on it."

"Let's hope there isn't – another disappearance," Bob said. "Until then, we keep our eyes open and push for the shuttle."

Elizabeth took a sip of her white wine.

"How about the other thing, Bob?"

"Nothing yet. I'll explain later, Gordon. But I *may* have a lead. I'll let you know."

The food arrived, and despite the invitation to stay, Sandy and Elizabeth rose.

"We'll leave you to your dinner," Elizabeth said. "Good to meet you, Gordon, Sam." She began to turn, then looked back at Gordon.

"And thank you for buying 'Reflection Lake.' That painting means a lot to me."

THE FOOD WAS EXCELLENT, and they ate silently for several minutes. Sam spoke first.

"She seems like a real feminist."

Bob laughed. "She's a feminist, all right. They both are. That was the first thing I noticed. But I've worked with her at the college for over a year now, and she's all right." He chewed a piece of tri-tip slowly and swallowed. "Anyway, I got two daughters, so maybe I should be a feminist, too."

"Does she teach art?" Gordon asked.

"No, that's a sideline. You'll find a lot of people here have one. She teaches English and one Women's Studies class. Talked the college into that one, but when they offered it this semester, it filled right up.

"Seems like a strange place for someone like her to end up," Sam said.

"Oh, it's not her choice. She'd rather be closer to San Francisco or LA, but teaching jobs are hard to come by. She's started warming up to this place, though. Like moss, it kind of grows on you." He laughed.

After a brief spell of silence and chewing, Gordon asked:

"So what was that about a second case?"

"Picked up on that, did you?"

"It was pretty blatant, Bob. What could compare with the other one?"

Bob finished chewing a piece of meat with exaggerated slowness.

"We still fishing tomorrow afternoon?"

Gordon nodded.

"I'll tell you then. But first I need you to give me a hand."

"Sure, Bob. Anything."

"Great. I knew I could count on you. Can you come by the radio station at 10:45?"

"I thought you finished at noon."

"I do, but I always have a live interview at 11:05. Tomorrow was supposed to be the executive director of the water reclamation district, but he checked into the hospital last night, and when he checks out in a couple of days, he'll be without the appendix he went in with. I was sort of hoping you could take his place."

"Now wait just a minute, Bob. I don't know the first thing about water reclamation."

"No, no, no! I wouldn't put you on the spot like that. We can talk about the high school basketball team and the prospects for the coming season. Sports interviews go over better than public affairs, anyway."

Gordon put his face in his hands and shook his head.

"Bob, I'd love to help, but think about it for a second. I just got into town last night. I've never seen the team play. I don't know any of the players or what the competition is like in your league. There's no way I could possibly have anything intelligent to say."

Bob nodded placidly.

"That's true for a lot of my guests, actually. But you know something, Flyboy? If you go to the Buckhorn Café for breakfast or lunch between December and March, the high school basketball team is one of two things they're talking about – the other being the weather. And you know what? Not one of them knows any more about it than you. So don't start pleading qualifications with me."

Gordon realized he was holding a losing hand.

"Well, I suppose I could…."

"That's the spirit. And don't worry about it. I'll just feed you open-ended questions and you just say what you're comfortable saying. It'll be over before you know it. And I appreciate your bailing me out here. Lighten up, and we'll have a little fun together."

Bob looked in the direction of the bar and waved.

"Hey, Howard!" he called.

Sam leaned over to Gordon and whispered:

"This is like being with Walter Winchell at the Stork Club."

Gordon nodded, and they looked up to see a man heading for their table. He was tall, with a once-thin build showing a bit of belly. He wore dress slacks, legs pulled over dark brown cowboy boots, a navy blazer, and a blue button-down shirt open at the collar, with a loosened navy and gold-striped tie. His dark hair, flecked with gray, was short, curly, and tightly coiled, and his thin-lipped mouth was tightly set. In his left hand was a tall glass with a bubbly, light amber liquid, and from the way his eyes darted around, taking in everything, Gordon pegged him for a lawman.

"Howard, I'd like you to meet a couple of friends of mine, up here for a bit of fishing. Quill Gordon and Sam Akers. Gentlemen, this is Howard Honig, Chief Deputy Sheriff of Plateau County.

As they shook hands all around, Howard fixed his glare on Gordon.

"Quill Gordon, eh? Like the trout fly?"

"I'm afraid so. You can call me Gordon. My friends do."

"Have a seat," Bob said, and Howard did. "How do you see tomorrow's game shaping up?" He turned to Gordon and Sam. "Howard's the PA announcer for the high school football games, and I call 'em for the radio station. We've spent a lot time together in that press box over the years."

"A lot of time," Howard said. "This late in the season, we know our boys pretty well. And we've heard a bit about the other teams. We're playing Black Mesa tomorrow night, at our place. Alta Mira's 8-1, and Black Mesa is 4-5. We should win, probably by three touchdowns."

"And if we do," Bob said, "Alta Mira's in the playoffs with home-field advantage next Friday. We got a good team this year."

"Best since '84, I'd say. You boys coming to the game?"

"I'm inviting 'em to join us in the press box. There should be room. Gordon was a football star in high school."

"Actually, I played a year of JV, then decided to concentrate on basketball."

"You look like a basketball player," Howard said.

"That's got me thinking, though, Gordon…," Bob said.

"Forget it, Bob. I'm not doing color commentary on the football game. You got me on the morning show. Leave it at that."

"How about you, Akers and Pains? You got more of a football player build. Or look like you used to. You know much about the game?"

"About as much as the average drunk in the stands."

"Perfect! We don't want some pointy-headed intellectual on the air. You'll do just fine."

"He's leading you on, Sam," said Gordon. "Don't pay any attention to him."

Everyone laughed, and there was a moment of silence afterward.

"Where you been fishing?" Howard asked.

"Just started today," Gordon said. "We worked Powder Creek this afternoon, and they kept us pretty busy there."

"Catch and release?"

"About all I do any more," Gordon said.

"I'm catch and eat myself," Howard said. "But I'm also live and let live. You should try some of the higher lakes. They're usually pretty good late in the season."

"We're giving Storm Lake a look tomorrow afternoon," Bob said.

"Good call."

"Can I ask a question?" said Sam. "As we were leaving the creek this afternoon, I thought I heard a shot. Is it still hunting season?"

"Not for anything up there," Howard said. "But people are always shooting in the woods. It's what we do around here. I wouldn't worry about it. That time of day, this time of year, you two were probably the only ones around who could have been hit. And going by appearances, I'd say you're still alive."

OUR ROOM AT THE DANUBE was clean, comfortable and dated. It had two standard double beds, a bathroom sink with ancient fixtures and a bit of an iron stain, and old-fashioned windows that could be pushed up to let in a breeze. Not now, though. It was surprisingly chilly when we left the restaurant, and the first thing we did when we got in was turn on the standing radiator. It hissed and rattled, but put out quite a bit of heat pretty quickly. The painting, all wrapped up, was leaning against one of the walls. Gordon carefully opened the wrapping and set the painting on his bed for a good look.

This was not a good sign. I moved over for a closer look myself. The light in the room wasn't the best, but even so, I could see, better than in the gallery, that the colors and texture seemed to work, though I couldn't say more than that.

"It goes with the artist," I finally said.

Gordon nodded, and began to re-wrap it.

"Are we going to the football game tomorrow?" I asked.

"We have to. Bob would be hurt if we didn't."

"I haven't seen a high school football game since high school. They take it pretty seriously here, don't they?"

"It's a big deal. The smaller the town, the more the school team's part of its identity. That has its good and bad points, I suppose."

I yawned. It had been a long day, and it was beginning to hit me.

"We can sleep in, anyway," Gordon said. "Fishing with Bob tomorrow afternoon, then the game. It's going to be a late day."

"You'd better get your rest," I said. "You need to be clear-headed when you're on the air."

"You didn't have to remind me," he said.

Friday November 7

"WHAT ARE WE DOING HERE?" Sam asked. "I would have bet money you'd be having sausage and eggs at a diner."

Gordon sat up straight and looked around the room, as if searching for an answer. Kemper's Bakery, just off Chaparral Boulevard a couple of blocks from the hotel, was an Alta Mira icon. Family owned since 1934 (Why, he wondered, are there so many businesses still around that started in the heart of the Great Depression?), it occupied the ground floor of another of the town's turn-of-the-century commercial buildings. The outside temperature had been 39 degrees when they walked in at 9:30 to be greeted by an overpowering aroma of sugar, baked flour, butter and coffee. A large glass counter, holding pies and cakes baked earlier in the morning, faced the front door, and, perpendicular to it on the left, with a space in between for a cash register and order station, was another glass counter holding breads and pastries. About 20 plain restaurant-supply tables for two or four filled the floor space framed by the glass counters. The chairs at the tables were in a wide variety of styles, as if they had been pulled in from yard sales one or two at a time. The wall to the right had windows from waist-level to the 11-foot ceiling, showing a room beyond where long tables were set up in a rectangle. It was the overflow room, where people were put on particularly busy days, and also the room where the Rotary Club of Alta Mira had met every Wednesday (except holidays) since 1947, when old man Emil Kemper stole the Rotary business from the Danube Hotel. The place was nearly full, but Sam and Gordon had commandeered a table for two in the middle of the room, loud with local news and gossip. Barely audible over the hum was Kenny Rogers singing "The Gambler," most likely on Bob's morning radio show.

Gordon methodically cut his cinnamon roll in half, took a bite, and washed it down with a swallow of coffee while Sam nibbled on a bear claw.

"First of all," Gordon said, "I eat other things for breakfast besides sausage and eggs. Second, I don't want a heavy breakfast if I'm going to be on live radio. That's nerve-wracking enough as it is. And third, we're having lunch with Bob before we go fishing when his show ends. I expect to have a better appetite by then and want to reserve the right to have a late breakfast, rather than lunch, if the spirit so moves me."

After a sip of coffee, Sam said:

"This place is good. You know how to pick 'em."

Gordon chewed his cinnamon roll contemplatively, saying nothing.

"Looks like we got a nice day, though," Sam continued.

"It should start warming up pretty soon."

"I'm surprised by how nice it is up here."

"It could change like that," Gordon snapped his fingers. "Let's enjoy it while it lasts."

Two or three more minutes of silence ensued, before Sam tried again.

"Gordon, you're not thinking of getting involved are you?"

Gordon gave Sam a quizzical look.

"I mean whatever it is that Bob's looking into. The missing students."

"I've had enough of that, Sam. From now on, I'm leaving investigations to the properly constituted authorities."

"Easy to say, but you have a way of being sucked into things."

"I'm here for the fishing." Gordon finished his coffee. "Besides, I'm not the one who claimed to hear a gunshot in the middle of nowhere last night."

IN ALL MY 39 YEARS, I've never been inside a radio station before. KNEP is probably pretty humble compared to some of the big Bay Area stations, but small as it is, you get a feeling it's a part of the community. You can just imagine what goes out from here beaming straight into one of those ranch homes we drove by on the way out, and the people listening to it knowing just what Bob looks like and seeing him in their minds as they do their chores with the radio going.

KNEP is located about a mile and a half outside town on the state highway, heading west. There's a one-story stucco building that could use a coat of paint, part of which is sunk into a marsh on pilings, and two towers, also built on the marsh. You couldn't do that today, what with the environmental laws and all, but I'm guessing this went up 50 years ago when anybody could do anything they wanted with their land. The building could have been designed with a view of the marshes behind, but whoever built it put the windows in front, facing the highway and a mini-storage complex across it.

It's eleven o'clock and Gordon and I are waiting in the front reception area. There's a desk where a switchboard operator seems to be waiting for calls that never come, and four chairs that, judging by the number of coffee stains, are about 30 years old. A corridor leads back to a few small offices on one side and a studio on the other.

Mountain Bob is reading the news, and Gordon is fidgeting. I don't get this. Here's a guy who could stand in front of 20,000 screaming fans at a hostile arena and make two free throws with the game on the line, and his heartbeat wouldn't even go up. But ask him to talk in front of an audience, even an audience that's in his head, like for this radio show, and he turns into a blithering wuss. Funny how we're all afraid of something.

A singing commercial just came on for Burnett's Farm Supply, and Bob poked his head out the studio door.

"All right, Gordon. You're on."

Gordon rose and moved toward the studio, like a prisoner heading for his execution.

"IT'S FIVE MINUTES PAST ELEVEN, beginning to wind down the last hour of Morning Coffee with Mountain Bob. That means it's time for Heart to Heart, our daily interview on local issues, brought to you by DeShayne's Plumbing, the full-service solution for all your plumbing needs, big or small, anywhere in Plateau County.

DeShayne's wants to remind you that a flush is better than a full house.

"Today we have a very special guest. Now I know that everybody's excited about the Alta Mira football team right now, and with good reason. Our Eagles are at home tonight against Black Mesa, and with a win, they should be in the playoffs. We'll be bringing that game to you live, right here on KNEP, starting with the pre-game show at 6:45. But let's not forget that basketball season is less than a month away, with the first game just four weeks from today. So I've brought in an old friend of mine, former Cal basketball star Quill Gordon, to help us understand our team's prospects for the 97-98 season. Gordon, thank you for joining us today."

"My pleasure," Gordon lied. "Glad to be here."

"Now some of you might not be familiar with Gordon, but let me tell you he was one of the best and smartest basketball players I've ever seen. He was all Pac-Ten and averaged 20 points a game, if I remember right."

"Actually it was 18.6."

"A rounding error. Anyway, folks, the point is, he was good and he knows the game, so I want to see what he has to say about our team this year. Now the first thing we have going for us is that four out of five starters are coming back from last year. What do you say, Gordon? Is that cause for optimism?"

Gordon started to say that it would depend on how good they were, but realized before the words got out that it might be too candid an assessment.

"Well, Bob," he said slowly as he tried to regroup, "experience rarely hurts a team and usually helps it. When you have a bunch of players who've played together a lot, they get to know each others' tendencies and can anticipate the moves they'll make. Teamwork and chemistry matter a lot, so that can be a definite plus."

"That's what we're hoping, too. But tell me, Gordon, if you were putting together a basketball team from scratch, what would you want from the first three players you picked? Height? Speed? Shooting ability?"

"If I'm picking three players to be the nucleus of a team, my number one choice would be a point guard. Someone who can handle the ball, pass it around, direct the offense. Ideally play tough defense, too, and be at least a decent outside shooter.

"Then I'd want size. A center or power forward who can take up space near the basket, grab rebounds, score from underneath, and make the other team think twice about driving to the basket.

"And for the third choice, I'd go with an outside shooter — somebody capable of hitting a few three-point shots in a row and loosening up the other team's defense. With an inside-outside threat and a point guard who can get the ball to the right players at the right time, a team has a good chance of scoring on every possession. If you take three players like that and surround them with five or six others who work hard and can be coached, you'll have a team that can compete with anybody and maybe go a ways into the postseason."

"I'm glad to hear you say that, Gordon, because that sounds something like the team we got coming back. There's a senior point guard, Kara DeShayne, who started the last two years. We've got a six-four center, Renee Morgan, who also started last year, and plays a real aggressive game. And then our shooting guard/small forward is junior Brandy Brock. She made an average of four and a half three-point shots a game last year, and we're looking for her to do even better this season."

"In that case, I'd have to say, without having seen the players, that you have some room for optimism, and I'd wish the team the best."

"Now you were quite a three-point shooter back in the day, weren't you, Gordon?"

"Actually, no."

"No? I remember you putting up a lot of shots from 25 feet and hitting nothing but net."

"Yeah, but they were only worth two points. The three-point shot came along a few years later, when I was working in an office."

"Well, if they had it when you were playing, you *would* have averaged 20 points a game. Now let me ask you one more question, and then we have to go to some music. If we're going to win the league, we're going to have to beat Forestville. They're the defending champs and have a six-eight center coming back who was second team all state last year. She averaged 30 points a game, but our Renee held her to 23 and 24 in the two games. We still lost 'em both. Any thoughts on how to handle that challenge?"

"Without knowing the players involved, I can only tell you what coaching experience suggests. If man defense or a standard zone don't do the job, you could try something like a box-and-one to keep a double-team on at all times. In a clutch situation, you could even triple-team the star and make somebody else on the team beat you — the way Jim Valvano and North Carolina State did against Ralph Sampson and Virginia in the 1983 regional finals."

"Did it work?"

"They were defending a one-point lead in the last seconds, and Virginia couldn't get it to Sampson, so somebody else took an open shot and missed. State went on to win it all. So yeah, it can work."

"Amazing. Well, this has been really interesting, and I thank you for coming today. Heart to Heart has been sponsored by DeShayne Plumbing, serving Alta Mira and all of Plateau County since 1948. Whatever your plumbing needs, be they great or small, DeShayne Plumbing can handle them all. And now we have a little Conway Twitty for you — one of his big hits from a while ago, 'Tight Fittin' Jeans.' You're listening to Morning Coffee with Mountain Bob on Radio KNEP, Alta Mira, the voice of the high desert."

The coyote howl came on full-throat, fading into the opening line of the song. Gordon exhaled deeply, removed his headset, and slumped in his chair.

"Thanks, good buddy," Bob said. "You saved my bacon today, and I appreciate it."

"OK, Bob. That was for old time's sake, but please don't ask me again."

IT WAS A SUNNY DAY, but with a few more clouds than Thursday. The clock on the bank showed a temperature of 66 degrees as the three men drove by in Gordon's Cherokee after lunch at the Buckhorn Café.

"Head out toward Big Piney," Bob said. "As we're going over the mountains, we'll turn left and go three miles to Storm Lake."

Gordon nodded. At Alta Mira's lone traffic light, he turned right on the east-west state highway, heading toward Big Piney, and, after that, Nevada. Several miles past the college, the road forked; heading toward Big Piney, it climbed rapidly through fields with cattle at first, then brush and rocks, then some pine and cedar trees signaling the beginning of a higher elevation. As they passed over Dead Mule Summit (elevation 6,195 feet), Bob, in the front passenger seat, touched Gordon's right arm.

"Slow down, Flyboy. We'll be turning left pretty quick."

Half a mile down from the summit, they turned onto a paved road that went a quarter of a mile to an 11-space campground next to a creek, now a trickle awaiting refreshment from winter snows. Past the campground, the road turned to dirt, and they made the three miles to the lake without undue jostling or seeing another vehicle.

Glacially carved during the last Ice Age, Storm Lake was a mile long and three-quarters of a mile wide. It was ringed by pine trees and jagged mountains, the upper parts of which were denuded of any vegetation. At the end of the road, they pulled into a gravel parking area, big enough for a dozen cars, with a boat-launch just beyond. There was one Chevy pickup in the lot, and one boat with two anglers halfway out on the lake.

The three men got out of the Cherokee simultaneously. The high mountain air was clean and bracing, with a slight aroma of pine needles. The lake was deep, blue, and clear, falling off sharply from the shore. For the moment, there was no wind, and its surface was placid, reflecting the surrounding mountains.

"Not bad," Gordon finally said.

"How do we fish it?" Sam asked.

"Just follow me," Bob said. He pointed to the left shore. "See that cove there? There's a bit less dropoff than most of the lake and some weed beds with a lot of insects." He looked at his watch. "One-thirty now. We might be a bit early, but as the sun starts going down, the fish move in there to feed. Work a nymph under an indicator or run a Woolly Bugger through there, and you're sure to catch something."

They set up their rods and walked a quarter-mile down a narrow path to the cove. As they did, Gordon asked about the lake's name. Bob responded by pointing to a cleft in the mountains on the opposite side.

"See that notch there? When a storm moves in from the west or northwest, the wind picks up speed as it comes through there. It actually howls, and the lake gets really choppy. Two summers ago, we lost two people — father and his ten-year-old son — when their boat capsized in a thunderstorm in late July. Never did find the boy's body. They were from Sacramento. The locals would have known to get off the water."

The cove, about 150 feet across, had a small gravel beach and a slight promontory on the side farthest from the parking lot. After some discussion, Gordon moved to the promontory, while Sam and Bob stood 50 feet apart on the beach. For an hour they repeatedly cast into the waters and got no response. Finally, Gordon came back to the beach.

"It might still be too early," he said. "Let's break for something to drink, then hit it again in a bit." He opened a small ice chest he'd brought along and looked up at Bob. "Beer or 7-Up?"

"I'm calling the game tonight. Better make it a 7-Up." The other two followed suit. They moved back from the beach to a shaded area, where they could sit or lean on rocks. Out of the sun, at 6,000 feet, it was cool, almost chilly. A breeze with no warmth to it came up, adding to the chill.

"So, Bob," Gordon said after a few minutes, "You said last night that there's something else going on that you'd tell us about later. Is it later yet?"

Bob took a sip of his soda and looked toward the notch. "Might as well be, I suppose, but don't tell anybody. I'm still hoping it's not true."

Sam and Gordon looked at him expectantly, and finally he continued.

"It supposedly happened last Saturday night. The football game was on Friday, and some of the team members, girlfriends and followers, got together at a house where the parents were out of town for the weekend. One of the kids' older brothers bought some alcohol, and though it didn't get to a point where the law was called, it looks like things got out of hand." He took a deep breath and a pull of 7-Up. "It's not the sort of thing I want to believe would happen in our town, but one of the cheerleaders was drinking alcohol for the first time, didn't know when to quit, and went over her limit. She passed out, and they took her into one of the bedrooms. She hardly remembers anything after that, but when she got home and her mother saw her underwear, she flipped out. The girl said she vaguely remembers waking up and finding a boy on top of her. She knew him, she says, but under the circumstances, it's a less than ideal ID."

The wind had stopped and the three of them sat in silence for a minute. Gordon finally said, "That *is* awful. But if they have the underwear, they could run a DNA test, couldn't they?"

Bob shook his head. "The parents are religious and conservative. The mother was so overwhelmed by what she saw that she took the underwear out to the incinerator and threw it in the fire. The evidence is gone. They waited until Monday, then went to the sheriff's office after school to make a complaint. A medical exam showed she'd been treated a bit rough down there, but so long after the fact, there was no evidence of who did it."

"Can't the sheriff talk to the people who were at the party?" Sam asked.

"Not as easy as that. For starters, the party was at the DeShayne residence … "

"The plumber with the daughter on the basketball team," Gordon said.

Bob nodded. "The locals call it the House that Shit Built. It's too bad Kara wasn't there. She's a good kid with a level head and probably could have kept things from getting out of hand."

"Why wasn't she there?" said Gordon.

"Last Saturday was November First. That's when the girls' basketball team holds its first practice, and they always do it after dinner, with half the town out. Kara was there with her team. The ringleader behind the party was her younger sister Caitlin."

"Not as good and level-headed?" Sam said.

"Let me put it this way. She's boy crazy, she wants to be a cheerleader next year, and if common sense was dynamite, she wouldn't have enough to blow her nose."

"How about the parents?"

"Sheriff's already talked to Norv DeShayne, and he's in complete denial. Says he talked to Caitlin and she claims there were just a few people over and that nothing stronger than Coca-Cola passed their lips and that she's not talking to the sheriff without an attorney present. And if having the party at the home of one of our leading citizens wasn't sensitive enough, there's another hot potato."

Gordon and Sam looked at him.

"The boy she's fairly sure she remembers being on top of her. It was our football team's all-league quarterback."

THEY FINISHED THEIR DRINKS and resumed fishing. The trout had moved into the cove, and all of them caught several fish in the next hour. But Bob's story had cast a shadow over the collective mood. By 4:15 the sun had gone behind the mountains, and they started back.

When they dropped Bob off in front of his house, he reminded them they were invited to dinner the following evening. "I'd have asked you for tonight," he said, "but I have to eat and run, and Brenda wants to catch up with you, Gordon. See you in the press box. Kickoff's at seven. Buy your tickets at the gate and walk up there. If anybody asks where you're going, just mention my name."

The light was all but gone from the sky, and there was a chill in the air when they drove into Elizalde's parking lot at 5:15. It was nearly full, and so was the interior — most likely, they assumed, from people like them trying to eat and get to the game. As Ruby led them into the dining area, they saw Elizabeth Macondray and

Sandy Steadman at a table for four against the right wall. The women waved them over, and they went, with Ruby shuffling behind.

"We just sat down," Elizabeth said. "Why don't you join us? Anyway, I'd like to buy you a drink to thank you for buying my painting."

Ruby looked at Elizabeth, looked at Gordon, set two more menus on the table, and walked away.

"I'd be honored," Gordon said. Sam took the seat against the wall, facing Sandy, while Gordon sat on the outside, opposite Elizabeth. "It's a terrific painting, but then, I guess you know that."

Elizabeth ran her index finger over the condensation on her water glass. "I know it's one of the best things I've done, but what I don't know is where that puts it in today's art world. Which is hard to stay in touch with when you're this far away."

"So why are you here?"

"I needed a job now, and this was where they had one. I'd rather be in San Francisco or LA, but they weren't hiring."

"You've obviously developed some sort of affinity with this place. When you painted that lake, you had a feeling for it that was real. It isn't something an artist can fake."

"The plateau and the mountains do grow on you, but I think I'd like to enjoy it as a visitor, preferably in the summer, rather than as a permanent resident."

A younger waitress, probably in her late fifties, arrived to take drink orders. Elizabeth ordered a red wine, and Gordon looked at Sandy.

"Will I be arrested if I have just one beer?"

"If you stop at just one, probably not, and certainly not by me. Not tonight. I'm off, then tomorrow I start a stint on day shift."

Gordon and Sam ordered beers; Sandy asked for an iced tea. When the waitress departed, Sam asked:

"So if you're becoming part of this town, are you going to the high school football game tonight? That seems to be where the action is."

"Good God, no," Elizabeth said. "I'd rather be scourged with hot coals. I *hate* football."

SO FAR, SO GOOD. I did my best to make the next line as nonchalant and helpful-sounding as I possibly could.

"That's too bad. Gordon here is a real sports fan. In fact he was a star basketball player in college."

"I know," she said. "I heard the interview on Bob's show this morning."

I forgot about that.

"You did a pretty good job of sounding authoritative about something you knew nothing about," she continued.

"It comes with practice," Gordon said. "I worked as a stockbroker for a number of years."

Elizabeth laughed. "Anyway, I make an exception for the women's basketball team at the high school. I'm rooting for them to get out of this place any way they can, and it's been a good escape route for a few of them."

The drinks arrived, and Gordon raised his bottle in a toast.

"To escape," he said.

A FEW MINUTES LATER, Gordon said, "We were fishing with Bob this afternoon, and he told us about the situation with the party and the cheerleader."

"Please don't call her the cheerleader," Elizabeth said. "Her name is Alicia, and I'm going to do everything I can to see she gets whatever justice she can. It'll never be enough."

"So you have no doubt about her story?"

"None whatsoever. She said she was raped, and I have no reason to doubt her."

Sandy leaned forward. "I sometimes have to remind my friend here that what you know in your gut isn't the same as evidence that will hold up in front of a jury."

"It sounds like a tough case to prove in court," Gordon said.

"Hard, but not impossible," Elizabeth replied. "And made harder by the fact that the sheriff is walking on eggshells."

"High profile family, politically sensitive?"

"That, certainly, but there's also the whole question of how the sheriff came to be sheriff."

Gordon raised his eyebrows.

"Why don't you tell the story, Sandy," Elizabeth said. "You were there when it happened."

Sandy shook her head and took a sip of tea.

"No one expected it," she said. "That's for sure. We had a sheriff named Bill McNutt — everybody called him Wild Bill. He was elected five times, and nobody even bothered running against him anymore. He was telling everybody he was going to die with his boots on, and that's exactly what happened. One day this past January, he had an appointment to meet with the Highway Patrol commander. His secretary went into the office to let Wild Bill know his three o'clock appointment was here and found him asleep in his chair, with his boots up on the desk. Only when she went to wake him up, it didn't happen, on account of he was dead. Heart attack while taking a nap. He was only 61.

"Well, the County Board of Stupidvisors, as we like to call them, was too cheap to pay for a special election, so they decided to pick the successor themselves and asked for applications. Most people figured Howard Honig would get it; he's been around for years and knows everyone in the community, which seemed to be the main standard. Plus, he has some cop smarts, but isn't smart enough overall to be too threatening. Just right for the job, a lot of people would say.

"Now there are nine of us in local law enforcement — women, that is — and we decided it was about time a woman got considered for the job. Problem is, most of us have been doing it less than five years. The only plausible candidate was Chris Huntley. She's been a detective in Sacramento and had training at the FBI Academy in Quantico, which probably made her more qualified on paper than Howard. But she just moved here two years ago, which meant that politically she had no chance.

"Even so, we wanted to make the gesture. We talked her into running, and we leaned on the two women on the Board of Supervisors to support her. By the time it came up for a vote the first week of March, an elaborate little charade had been worked out. Doris Smythe, one of the female supervisors, was going to nominate Chris, and Irene Paxton, the other woman supervisor, would second the nomination. The board would vote 3-2 against her, but the women could at least say they tried. Then one of the men would nominate Howard and they'd make him sheriff on a unanimous vote.

"Well, they outsmarted themselves. Doris and Irene felt compelled to give big speeches about how qualified Chris was for the job, and one of the other supervisors, who's a good friend of Howard's, Wesley Morgan, felt he had to speak up on Howard's behalf. He talked about how great Howard was for so long that Boyd Winnett, one of the other supervisors got confused. Boyd's 84 and probably has early-stage Alzheimer's. Wesley's speech had Boyd probably thinking they'd already rejected Chris and were about to vote for Howard. When they call the roll, they do it in alphabetical order, so Boyd came last, breaking a 2-2 tie on the motion to make Chris the sheriff. He voted yes, thinking he was voting for Howard, and it was total bedlam. The clerk announced that Chris was the sheriff and it was too late to change the vote.

"And that, my friends, is how our little backwoods cow county ended up with the first female sheriff in California."

Gordon set his beer on the table, shaking his head.

"And I thought San Francisco politics was crazy," he said.

LATER, AS THEY WERE EATING, Gordon asked why he hadn't seen anything in this week's local newspaper about either of the crimes. Elizabeth answered.

"The *Plateau Courier* is a very conservative little paper, and I don't mean that only in terms of politics. It's afraid of offending anyone and afraid of ruffling feathers. One of the other English instructors teaches a journalism class, and he says he uses the *Courier* as an example of what *not* to do.

"Because the two missing women are legally adults, they've been handled as standing missing-persons stories. Reported briefly in the crime log, which runs on page 7. As far as the paper's concerned, it's no big deal, even though everybody in town's talking about it. The parents of one of the students even put up flyers around town, though they're almost all gone now."

"Would that do any good?" Gordon asked.

"Probably not. I mean, if you live here, you can't go anywhere without running into ten people you know. But if you're a worried and desperate parent, I suppose you'll try anything. I hope that never happens to me. But back to the *Courier*: They're not going to stick their necks out and make it a big story until a body turns up or a whole lot more women go missing.

"The rape, on the other hand, hasn't been officially reported. Alicia went to the sheriff after school on Tuesday, and Chris interviewed her personally. She has a lot of notes, but is calling it an investigation in progress. She hasn't yet written a report that will go into the stack where the press can see it. When the report does get out, it'll be very interesting to see how the *Courier* reports it. The case is a hot potato.

"Because it involves the football team?"

"Not just the team. The one rapist she identified is Kyle Burnett. Name ring a bell?"

"There's a Burnett's Farm Supply on the south side of town," Sam said.

"Bingo. Full-page ad every week, and, so I'm told, they pay on time. Some weeks that ad is the difference between the paper's making and losing money. And old man Burnett is big in the Chamber of Commerce and gives to political campaigns. He isn't someone most people in town would want to cross."

"So a lot of people around here would be happy if the rape story just went away?"

"That isn't how they put it, but yeah."

"One thing I don't understand," Sam said, "is how you know about all this if the sheriff is keeping it under wraps."

"I can answer that one," Sandy said. "One of the things about having a woman sheriff is that she understands some things that the men in this county just didn't get before. For instance, Plateau County had never had a rape-victim support program, which is pretty much standard in any place that calls itself civilized. One of the first things Chris did was set one up. There was no budget for it, so it had to be done with volunteers. Elizabeth and I are the co-chairs of the committee."

"And Alicia," Elizabeth said, "was our first case. When she came in and told her story on Tuesday, Chris called us right away. We talked to Alicia for an hour that night, and we talked to her parents the next night. They're good people, Gordon. They've raised three good kids, and they've both worked five times harder than the Burnetts and DeShaynes of this town, who make their money off other people's labor and bloviate about how the problem with this country is that people don't want to work any more."

"You're getting excited," Gordon murmured.

"I can't help it. Alicia's a wonderful young woman, utterly without guile. She can't believe what happened to her; she can't believe that her friends would let it happen; and she's starting to believe that the people who did it aren't going to suffer any consequences."

"I hate to say it, but she might be right about the last part," Gordon said. "My father is a judge, and he always says that the toughest criminal case to prove is a rape charge where the rapist and victim know each other. It's hard for a jury not to have some doubt."

"Well," Sandy said, "I know Chris is going to do everything she can to get to the bottom of it, which is more than Howard Honig would have done. But, as I keep telling Elizabeth, it's an uphill fight."

"Is there any chance," Gordon said, "that the rape and the missing women are connected in some way?"

Elizabeth and Sandy looked at each other. Elizabeth spoke first.

"I never thought of it, but there could be. It does almost seem like it's open season on women in this town."

Sandy shook her head. "Anything's possible, but I don't think so. Two completely different MO's. If I were heading the investigation, I wouldn't even try to connect the two without some more evidence."

The check arrived 12 minutes before kickoff. Gordon offered to get the meal since Elizabeth had picked up the drinks, but she declined on feminist grounds. From four different wallets, the party put enough cash on the tray to cover the dinner and a generous tip.

"One other question," said Sam, as they were rising to leave. "If the rape report hasn't gone public, how did Bob know about it?"

"Bob knows everything that's happening in this town," Sandy said. "Don't ask me how, but if somebody has a secret on Monday, Bob knows about it by Tuesday. Ask when you get him alone. I'd like to know the answer myself."

"And while you're watching the game," Elizabeth added, "Keep an eye on Number 12, Kyle Burnett. When he throws a beautiful touchdown pass and the crowd is on its feet, cheering for him, try not to think too hard about what he did to Alicia. It might spoil the game for you."

ALTA MIRA HIGH SCHOOL sits at the southeastern corner of town, a few blocks off Chaparral Boulevard. Edgar Hammond Field, where the Eagles play football, is on the southern part of the campus, where the school boundary and the city limit are the same. The home bleachers, which can accommodate up to 1,500 people for a big game, sit on the west side of the field, and the visiting team's bleachers — half as high and a third as wide — face west, looking into the setting sun early in the season. Beyond the southern goalpost and the track, a six-foot chain-link fence with a windscreen of trees separates the football field from a cattle pasture.

It was exactly seven o'clock when Gordon decided the parking was getting worse and grabbed a spot in on the street two blocks away. At 7:05, he handed a ten-dollar bill to two female students in parkas and wool caps, sitting at a table with a cash box by the entrance gate. He received three dollars change and two tickets, and followed Sam through the gate. The Indian Summer warmth of the day was gone, and Gordon and Sam could see their breath when they exhaled. As they stepped through, they heard a roar from the stadium, and when it subsided, the voice of Howard Honig over the public address system:

"That was Danny Jacobs returning the opening kickoff for Alta Mira, from the eight yard line to the —

call it the 34. Number 55 (*pause*) Ronnie Smathers, made the tackle for Black Mesa. First and ten, Eagles."

The football field was encircled by a track, a quarter-mile long, with running lanes. They passed along a heavily traveled area between the track and the bleachers, and when Gordon saw they were just on the far side of the press box, he started up the nearest flight of stairs to the press box door. Several plays had elapsed, but the home crowd was quiet, indicating that the team wasn't up to much. As they stepped into the press box, they could see Howard sitting at a long counter that spanned the open window, bisected by a post. He was directly to the left of the post, holding a wireless microphone against his chest and talking to the two spotters to his left. At his right were the two scoreboard operators, and to their right was Bob, leaning into a microphone, keeping up a running commentary. At Bob's right was a young man, possibly a community college student, covering the game for the *Plateau Courier*.

Howard brought the microphone to his mouth, pushing a button to turn it on. "Raul Tavarez back to punt for Alta Mira. Deep to return for Black Mesa is number 25 …" he leaned toward the spotters, one of whom said something, "… Matthew Dixon. Tavarez' kick is up, and it's a low line drive angling toward the right sideline. Dixon can't get it, and it goes out of bounds at, let's see, looks like the Black Mesa 31, and the Scorpions will start from there."

He switched off the mic, turned, and extended a hand to Gordon and Sam.

"Glad you could make it tonight. Hope you weren't counting on much company from Bob, though. He has to keep going all night." Indeed, Bob was squeezing in a 30-second commercial for a local burger shack as the new offense and defense trotted onto the field. When he finished, he turned, waved to Gordon and Sam, then swiveled back to his microphone and resumed speaking.

It was slightly warmer in the press box than in the bleachers, but Gordon was glad he was wearing a good parka. The interior of the press box was unfinished wood, with the wiring for the lights, sound system, and scoreboard encased in piping attached to the walls. There was no restroom facility; that need was met for the entire stadium by a half-dozen porta-potties situated well behind the north goalpost. A table with chips, dips, and nuts lined the back wall of the press box, and one of the scoreboard operators and one of the spotters were finishing off burgers purchased from the snack shack by the gate.

For most of the first quarter, Gordon paid little attention to the game and soaked in the atmosphere, instead. There were scarcely 200 people in the visitors' bleachers — apparently the team wasn't good enough to justify a 120-mile round trip. The home bleachers were 80 percent full, and for many of the adults, the game was clearly a social occasion. On the visitors' side of the field, to the left of the bleachers, were two soccer nets, with a gaggle of kids, mostly under ten, kicking a ball around. Some day in the future, Gordon thought, soccer, not football, will be the main attraction on this field. He turned his attention to the cheerleaders, telling himself he was just trying to understand Alicia's situation. They wore green and gold dresses, hems 15 inches above the knee, and on their arms were strapped coverings, designed to mimic eagles' wings. When the cheerleaders flapped their arms, the imagery was impressive. They stood in two rows, front and back; those in the back row were positioned exactly between the two in front of them so that they were all visible to the crowd at all times.

The scene didn't look right to Gordon, and it took him a minute to figure it out. He began counting the cheerleaders and confirmed his impression.

"Something's out of kilter," he said to Sam in a low voice. "There should be 16 cheerleaders — eight in each row — but there are only 15, eight in front and seven in the back."

After a moment, Sam replied, "You think Alicia's missing?"

"Could you blame her if she is?"

BY THE END OF THE FIRST QUARTER, Gordon was focusing more intently on the game and less on the surroundings. Black Mesa scored first, temporarily quieting the home crowd, but at the end of the quarter,

Alta Mira scored on a short slant pass, where the receiver outran the defenders 40 yards for a touchdown, and the score stood at 7-7. Aside from that play, Alta Mira seemed tentative and inconsistent. Burnett, the quarterback, was throwing tight, precise passes, but a throw that should have gone for a touchdown was dropped, and a 20-yard toss was called back for an illegal formation. Alta Mira also had a running back, Harry Hooper, who was gaining yards consistently, and who always seemed to fall forward when tackled. Gordon found himself taking a liking to Hooper, based solely on his grit and determination.

The home team remained erratic in the second quarter. Burnett threw a beautiful 40-yard spiral to a receiver running down the right sideline, a step and a half ahead of a defender, for one score. But on another possession, a throw to receiver Cody Jarrett bounced off Jarrett's hands, going straight to a defender, who ran it back for a Black Mesa touchdown. Another drive stalled when a Burnett touchdown pass to Jarrett was called back because of a holding penalty. It was 14-14 at the half.

Bob, after doing a quick recap of the game so far, got a ten-minute break as an announcer at the station read a newscast and a large number of commercials. Howard turned the microphone over to Principal Duane Raymond, who called the halftime show.

"Team's sluggish tonight," Bob said, after turning the broadcast over to the station. "Should be ahead by two touchdowns now. We're better than this."

"Maybe they're rattled about something," Gordon said softly.

Bob blinked, then shrugged. "Have you met everybody else here?"

"I think so," Sam said.

"But you probably didn't get their real names. On the scoreboard, we have Rudy 'Red Nose' Hoffman, and 'Bogart.' Bogart's real name is Paul Humphrey." They nodded and smiled. "Our spotters tonight are Joe 'Apple,' real name McIntosh, and 'Jed Clampett.' His real name is Buddy Hepson. Get it? Buddy Hepson – Buddy Ebsen? Played Jed Clampett on *The Beverly Hillbillies*."

Gordon smiled in spite of himself, as Bob introduced him as Flyboy and Sam as Akers and Pains.

"So do you have a nickname for Howard Honig?"

Sam looked around to be sure Honig was still gone.

"I call him Sergeant Friday," he said, "when he can't hear. Otherwise I call him Howard. You don't mess with Howard."

In the second half, Alta Mira pulled away. Burnett got into a groove, completing nearly every pass he threw. Two of them went to Jarrett for touchdowns, and another put Alta Mira on the two-yard line, from which Hooper dragged two defenders into the end zone.

Midway through the third quarter, Jed Clampett realized he should have visited the porta-potties at halftime. Gordon agreed to sub for him while he was gone, which, with the long walk, turned out to be 15 minutes. Gordon sat next to Honig, with a visiting team roster in front of him, and began identifying the key players on each play. With his keen eyes and athletic sense he was good at it, and Honig appreciated being told, for instance, that not only had Jordan made the tackle for Black Mesa, but had done so with one arm. In the short time, the two men developed a slight rapport, and when 'Clampett' returned, Gordon gave up the seat reluctantly.

As the game ended just before 9:30, the crowd was on its feet cheering the team, and Bob was passionately wrapping up the game.

"The final 20 seconds are ticking down. No need to run another play. Alta Mira wins the game, 35-14, to finish the regular season at 9-1. Next week, we'll be hosting a playoff game right here at Edgar Hammond Field, and if you can't make it in person, we'll be broadcasting live on Radio KNEP. We now send you back to our studios for Music Til Midnight with Rick Patterson. For Alta Mira football, I'm Mountain Bob, and thank you for listening tonight."

He switched off the microphone, leaned back in his chair, and exhaled a long blast of air before turning to Gordon and Sam.

"Another game, another 30 bucks," he said. "You up for some pie and coffee before turning in? My treat, since I get paid for an extra game next week."

DANNY'S DINER was the only eating establishment still open after ten o'clock. It wasn't the best place in town, as Bob freely admitted, but the pies came from Kemper's Bakery and the place had a buzz from the after-game crowd, which took up three quarters of the tables.

"You only get 30 dollars for calling a full game?" Gordon asked as they sat down.

"Extra money," Bob said. "If we had to make it on just my salary and what Brenda gets working two-thirds time at the bank, it'd be pretty tight. Teaching two classes a year on radio broadcasting at Homestead and calling the high school games brings in just enough to give us a couple of extras and a bit of a cushion."

"Still doesn't seem like much to me," said Sam.

"This isn't San Francisco, Akers and Pains. KNEP has to fight the *Plateau Courier,* in a civilized way of course, for every advertising dollar in town. Jud Diamond, who owns the station, may have a nicer house than I do and drive a nicer car, but he's not a wealthy man, and in a year when the economy's sour, things get a bit tight. I do a little extra for him, get a little goodwill for myself. I'm not complaining."

The waitress arrived with their order. Bob and Sam were having apple pie; Gordon cherry. Sam and Gordon were drinking cocoa, and Bob was having a cup of coffee. Gordon figured that after years of drinking coffee throughout a six-hour morning radio show, Bob was immune to its effects; it neither picked him up or tired him out, but was simply a comforting presence.

"Fishing tomorrow?" Gordon asked.

"I said I had a real treat lined up for you, Flyboy. You know where Jackson Valley is?"

"I've seen it on the maps. Southwest of town, if I recall."

"You remembered right. I've gotten us admitted to Blue Moon Ranch. A mile of the headwaters of Big Hole River run through it — beautiful meadow stream with some good fish. And there's a pond with a lot of good fish, too. We could have a banner day."

"How did you swing that?" Sam asked.

"I know the owners. The Brinkley family. The daughter, Diane, is chief deputy district attorney."

"Is there anybody in town you don't know?" Gordon said.

Bob paused as if seriously considering the question.

"Probably not," he finally said.

"Must be nice. Knowing everyone, I mean."

"I always thought so, but lately I'm not so sure."

Gordon said nothing. Bob took another bite of pie and continued:

"That's the good thing about a small town like this. It's comfortable feeling you know everybody and can trust 'em. Or at least know how far to trust 'em. But in the last few weeks, I'm beginning to wonder how much I really know about the people here. We got two girls missing from the community college, and it's hard to believe they just ran off. I have to feel if they were all right, they would have reached out to somebody by now. If something happened to them …"

"It would have to be somebody here," Gordon said.

Bob nodded and took another swallow of coffee.

"Couldn't it have been someone passing through?" Sam asked.

"Nice try, Akers and Pains. Much as I'd like to believe that, I can't. Not too likely a stranger would go up to the college and get a local student to get in the car. It'd have to be somebody who knows the layout of the place, knows the students hitchhike, and would seem like a safe person to be with. In short, one of us."

"And then there's Alicia," Gordon said.

"You must have been talking to Elizabeth," Bob said. "Yeah, that one's got me down, too. Calling the game tonight was harder than usual. When Kyle Burnett threw a nice pass, I couldn't just enjoy it like I usually do, and say good for him. I was thinking about what he was accused of, and how I'd feel if something like that happened to one of my daughters. I've lived here most of my life, and I never thought it *could* happen, but now I'm not so sure anymore. It's a bad thing to feel that the place you call home may have a rattlesnake on the porch."

"Rattlesnakes," Gordon said. "The plural would seem more appropriate."

WHEN WE GOT BACK TO THE ROOM, Gordon unwrapped the painting and looked at it for several minutes. I've seen that look on his face before. It's hard to describe, but it's as if he's trying to coax a solution out of something by focusing on it.

I imagined his 17th floor condo — two bedrooms, 1,100 square feet on Russian Hill — and tried to think of where I'd hang it. He uses one of the bedrooms as an office, and I decided he'd put it there so he could look at it while he's working, though I'm not sure how much actual work he needs to do these days.

"A penny for your thoughts," I finally said.

He broke out of his trance. "Sorry, Sam."

"It's OK. I'm just trying to think where you're going to hang that painting. My guess is your office."

"I suppose I could," he said, "but I'd want anyone who came over to be able to see it. Hard to say until I get back and can look at it in place, but I was thinking of the wall to the right of the fireplace."

"Where the Chinese tapestry is now?"

He nodded. "Between the fireplace and the window. It could be a visual bridge to the view of the world outside."

"What would you do with the tapestry, then?"

"I'm thinking it would work pretty well in the master bedroom. Certainly enough wall space there. But again, I'd have to see things in place before making a decision."

I can see it in my mind's eye, and I think he's right. But then, it's his place. He ought to know what should go where. He set the painting on the floor and leaned it against the wall.

"I'd like to leave it here overnight, if that's OK with you, Sam. I want to see what it looks like first thing in the morning."

"Fine by me. Can I ask a question? Change the subject?"

"Sure."

"How did you get to know Mountain Bob, anyway? On the surface, it wouldn't seem as if you'd run in the same circles."

Gordon smiled. "Bob got to Cal the same year I did, and, unsurprisingly, got involved with the campus radio station. Sophomore year, he covered the basketball team, and as he was hanging around during practices, we found out we both like fishing. He invited me to Alta Mira that summer, and when I came here that July, I learned that he'd been offered a job at KNEP, was going to marry Brenda and quit school. But we stayed in touch, after a fashion."

He stood and stretched. "I'm going to take a quick shower and turn in. Sounds as if we have a long and pleasant day ahead of us."

Alone, and listening to the running water, I looked hard at the painting again for several minutes, trying to find a flaw in it. I couldn't. I don't much care for Miss Macondray, but there's no question she can paint. I'll give her that, if nothing else.

Saturday November 8

WHEN GORDON FIRST MET Sheriff Chris Huntley, she was working the room at the 4-H breakfast, held the second Saturday of each month at the Grange Hall. Bob had insisted it was the only place that someone who supports the community would eat on the second Saturday of each month, so Gordon and Sam had met him there shortly before sunrise.

"No need to rush breakfast," Bob said when they arrived. "This time of year the fish won't be doing much before nine o'clock anyway."

The Grange Hall sat near the end of Third Street on the west side of town, four blocks off Chaparral Boulevard. It was a Quonset-style building, put up after the end of the War and kept in serviceable condition by countless hours of community elbow grease ever since. For three decades it had stood at the edge of town, but in 1978 the new Plateau Middle School had been built just past it, and now it was the school that looked out on the alfalfa fields stretching from just north of the airport to the mountains four miles away.

Inside, it was a rectangular space, with long rows of folding tables, flanked by folding chairs. The building smelled of bacon, coffee, maple syrup, and burning dust, the latter owing to its being the first time this fall the heaters had been turned on. They hadn't yet taken the chill out of the room when Gordon, Sam and Bob entered through the long side of the building, facing the parking lot. After they paid their $3.50 each and stepped inside, they could see the sheriff leaning over a table in the far right corner.

When Bob pointed out the sheriff, Gordon realized he had seen her making the rounds at the game last night. She was in her forties, five-eight and whippet-thin, wearing a sharply pressed khaki uniform with the sheriff's star prominent over her left breast. Her hair was short, the type of light brown that might have been blond at some point in the past, and her face was angular with a large Roman nose. Even at a distance, it had the slightly mournful look of a face that had seen too many things no one should have to see. When she waved to Bob and began walking in their direction, her bearing was erect in a way that owed more to the military than the catwalk. As she drew closer to them, she flashed a quick smile, and for an instant, her face lit up before retreating into melancholy.

Bob introduced them, and said, unnecessarily, that she might know Gordon's father, the judge.

"Judge Gordon from San Francisco?" she said. "He subbed for a local judge on a stolen-property case I was working in Sacramento back in '88. Threw out the search, and the perps walked, even though we caught them red-handed with the goods."

Gordon had been in situations like this often enough that he knew how to respond.

"Was it a legal search?" he asked.

She laughed, and again her face lit up for a second. "Sorry. But I'm sure that's exactly what your father would say. And the answer's no. I was working with another detective who liked to cut corners, and he tried to claim exigent circumstances when he should have gotten a warrant. It worked with a couple of our local judges, but after Judge Gordon spanked him on it, he never did it again. Far as I know, anyway."

"And the defendants," Gordon continued. "Did they see the error of their way, join a church and become model citizens thanks to their good fortune?"

"Of course not. They almost never do. We busted them again three months later, and that time it stuck."

"So in the end, justice was delayed, not denied?"

"Tell that to the people whose houses they ripped off in the meantime. But if we'd done our job right, it wouldn't have happened. No hard feelings."

She declined Bob's offer to join them for breakfast, saying she had to "network," and resumed going around the tables. As set up, the hall would seat about 250 people; it was already half full and lively with conversation, much of it about last night's game.

"I guess the campaign never ends," Gordon said, after she was out of earshot.

"She'll have an uphill battle next June," Bob said. "The bad news is that she's new to the area and still doesn't know everybody. She's smart to be here shaking hands."

"Is there any good news?" Sam asked.

"The good news is that she'll be running against Howard, and she hasn't pissed off as many people as he has."

"I'M GUESSING THIS IS your guest from Friday."

They had just taken a seat — plates heaped with eggs, bacon and pancakes — when a tall, balding man in his mid- to late forties, round face, booming voice, and the beginning of a gut, showed up next to them.

"Howdy, Rooter," said Bob. He turned to Gordon and Sam. "This is Norv DeShayne of DeShayne Plumbing, one of my fine sponsors."

"Plumbing," Sam said. "Hence the 'Rooter.' "

DeShayne laughed, a deep laugh that seemed to explode from his larynx and fly halfway across the room.

"Actually," Bob grimaced, "he's the head of the Alta Mira High School Boosters Club and one of the school's big rooters."

"I think I like your friend's explanation better," DeShayne said. "Maybe we could work that into a jingle for one of my ads. What do you think, Bob?"

"I think anything's possible in radio."

"That's the spirit. We'll talk about it next week." He turned to Gordon. "You're the tall guy here, so you must be the basketball star."

Gordon nodded without saying anything. DeShayne continued:

"I liked what you said about our team on the show yesterday, and I'm guessing you've never seen them play."

"Not yet, but basketball is basketball."

"Sure, but some people know it better than others. My daughter's on the team, you know. The point guard, actually, so you'd probably pick her first. I'd pick her first myself, but then, I'm kind of prejudiced."

"Bob says she's really good," Gordon said.

"And she is. The whole team is. But we've got to get past Forestville and their big center to win the league championship. That's where I like what you had to say about how to play a team with a really big player. I'm going to see that your thoughts on that get passed along to the coach."

"I'm sure she'll be very appreciative," Gordon murmured.

"It's a he. Nick Ballard. And he should be," DeShayne said. "Had no idea how to play them last year. Anyway, it's worth a try."

"When what you're doing isn't working," Bob said, "anything's worth a try. Right, Gordon?"

He shrugged. "That's how I see it."

"That's the spirit," DeShayne said "Keep on trying. It's what makes America great." He looked up and saw the sheriff talking to a small group on the other side of the room. "Oh," he said, making it sound like an expletive. They followed his gaze.

After an awkward silence, Bob said, "Maybe you should go over and shake her hand, Rooter."

"I will not," he spat out. "The bitch is trying to frame my daughter."

WELL, WE GOT THROUGH that one, somehow, but it took us awhile to eat breakfast. It seemed as though everybody in town was there, and since everybody in town knows Bob, most of them stopped by to chat. Even the highway patrolman who pulled Gordon over on Thursday came by to shake hands and say he hoped there were no hard feelings. Why should there be? I'm sure Gordon was guilty.

Most of the people who came along had apparently heard Gordon on Bob's show yesterday morning and wanted to comment on it. Gordon took it in good stride, and people seemed to accept him pretty quickly. Of course, it helped that we were with Bob.

While everybody was talking to Bob and Gordon, I got to thinking about how Gordon seems to fit in when he comes to these small towns where we go fishing. Some of it's his quiet demeanor, and some of it's that trustworthy face of his, but it has to be allowed at the end of the day that the man is something of a chameleon. You see him here in jeans and a flannel shirt, and he fits right in. But you see him looking sharp and confident in a suit in one of San Francisco's best hotels or restaurants and you wouldn't credit it's the same man.

Funny, though. With all the people coming by, the one we haven't seen is our painter-teacher friend. She's out there somewhere. I wonder if she understands what she's stalking. Several years ago, when Gordon was still working at the brokerage, he invited me to lunch with his squeeze at the time. She was attractive, vivacious, well dressed and smart — and not necessarily in that order. At one point, he had to step out and take a call from a client, and she started pumping me about him. It was kind of awkward, and after a couple of minutes, she sighed and said:

"I don't know, Sam. He reminds me of the Charles Aznavour character in *Shoot the Piano Player*. Have you seen it? There's a scene where his girlfriend says of him, 'Even when he's with someone else, he walks alone.' "

When she said that, I thought maybe she's the one. Maybe he's finally found someone who understands him. Two weeks later she must have gotten tired of walking alone with him and dumped him. It shows you what I know.

What with all the social activity, our breakfast dragged on until eight o'clock. People kept coming by and filling Bob's coffee cup. And Gordon's. And mine. It was my first five-cup breakfast in a long time. When we stepped out of the Grange Hall, the sun was shining right down on us, and the chill was just beginning to leave the air.

"We're in good shape, Flyboy," Bob said. "We don't want to be working too much ahead of the fish."

Gordon has a distaste for crowded parking lots, so he'd parked the Cherokee on the street across from the school, pointing toward town. That way we could start and go. The school has a large grass field, and a group of girls in shorts and T-shirts were running drills on it. The coach looked familiar.

Gordon pulled up short. "Is that ...?"

"Yep. It's Armstrong," Bob said.

"So this is what he does when he isn't pulling over speeders."

"It's not the only thing. If you ever catch a fish you don't want to release, bring it to John Armstrong and he'll stuff it for you. He does a bit of taxidermy on the side, and his rates are very reasonable."

"A man of many talents," I said.

"A lot of us are, Akers and Pains. I teach a class at the community college. Elizabeth paints pictures and even sells one when a sophisticated buyer comes to town. John does taxidermy. Almost everyone has a little sideline around here. It's the mountains."

THEY TOOK THE STATE HIGHWAY south from Alta Mira about ten miles and turned west on Jackson Valley Road. After a couple of straight miles through fields (with and without cattle) it met up with the west fork of the Big Hole River and followed it into the mountains. The river at this point was more like a creek, but a fishy looking one, and one or two cars pulled into turnouts suggested anglers trying their luck.

After rising for a little over three miles, the road entered a lush valley, shaped like an oval, and came to a fork. Bob gestured left, and Gordon, driving, proceeded. The road, paved, but with no center line, skirted the perimeter of the valley, with pine forest on the left and lush grassy meadows behind barbed wire fences on the right. A mile up the left fork, the pavement ended at the entrance to a ranch, while the road continued as a dirt track.

A wooden archway with a sign reading "Blue Moon Ranch" sat over an electrically operated gate. Bob jumped out of the Cherokee, moved to a keypad on the right-side post and punched in four numbers. The gate swung open inward, and they proceeded along a well-maintained gravel road that took them through a meadow, over a one-lane wooden bridge traversing the river, and to a large gravel parking area at one side of a splendid ranch house, built log-cabin style with a large covered veranda facing the meadow and wood smoke wafting from its large river-rock chimney. It was still a bit chilly and there was a coating of frost on the meadow, but in the sunlight, it was beginning to feel comfortable.

They were immediately approached by a middle-aged man, heavy but not soft, wearing jeans, boots, flannel shirt, and a white straw cowboy hat creased in the crown and sharply curled upward at the sides.

"Mister Bob," he said, extending his hand. "They said you were coming today."

"I never turn down an invitation to the ranch, Jesus. How's everything going?"

He paused. "A bit better. You need anything?"

"We're good thanks. Jesus, these are my friends, Gordon and Sam." They shook hands all around, and Bob asked if any of the Brinkleys were in. Jesus nodded toward the house.

A woman was standing on the veranda now, drinking a cup of coffee and watching them. She wore a tasteful gray plaid skirt, black stockings, sensible flats, and a wool sweater with a hint of white blouse peeking over the top of the crew neck. Her legs were long, her hair was jet black and cascaded down over her shoulders in a tumble of curls, and her body language suggested confidence and self-possession. The men walked over, and as they got closer, Gordon realized that she was younger (mid-thirties) than he had guessed at a distance, had immaculately done crimson nails and was wearing no ring.

"Glad you could make it, Bob," she said.

"Thanks for having us. Diane, I'd like you to meet Gordon and Sam. Gentlemen, this is Diane Brinkley. Chief Deputy District Attorney Diane Brinkley."

She shook hands with both of them, holding Gordon's a bit longer than Sam's, and looking up at him.

"You're tall," she said in a husky voice. "I'll bet you played basketball."

Bob guffawed. "Come off it, Diane. I'll bet you were listening to the show yesterday. And if you weren't, somebody at the office told you about it."

The corners of her mouth moved slightly upward in a mysterious, Mona Lisa smile, and she shrugged her left shoulder almost imperceptibly.

"I make a point of knowing things, Bob. Just like you. Does it matter how I know?" He had no answer, and she continued. "Anyway, it's a bit chilly so I'm going back in, but I'll be here if you need anything. Have a good time, guys."

Back at the car, as they were getting their rods ready, Sam, glancing sideways at Gordon, said, "The rancher's daughter seems to be a friendly sort."

"She can be," Bob said after a pause, "but she's not someone you want to cross. Diane Brinkley is the odds-on favorite to be the next District Attorney of Plateau County."

THERE ARE DAYS when the fishing gods smile upon an angler, and this was one of them. On those rare days there is generally a combination of decent weather (though it's not essential) and a good place to fish. The weather came in the form of an autumn day that featured bright sunshine and an intermittent cool breeze that never became severe enough to put the fish down or make casting difficult.

The stream ran clear and slow through the meadow, with undercut banks and enough weeds to provide insect food for the trout. Above the ranch house, as it came into the meadow from the mountains, the Big Hole had a number of pools and riffles. Downstream, water was diverted into a pond, about 300 by 400 feet, with productive weed beds and large cruising trout visible in the clear water. At Bob's suggestion, they walked to the pond and started there. Fish were rising intermittently when they arrived, and Sam and Bob decided to work dry flies. Gordon decided to stick with a small nymph under an indicator. He took up a position by where the water flowed into the pond and cast a few feet into the current, letting out line so the fly could drift with the flow into the pond. Twenty-five feet from shore, the indicator went under water as a fish mouthed the fly, and Gordon raised his rod to set the hook. For a second, he felt something solid, as though the submerged fly had hooked a log.

It was no log. The fish that had taken the fly raced toward the other side of the pond as Gordon's reel screeched and all the fly line went out, leaving only the backing on the reel. He tried to turn the fish, but something snapped, and the line went limp. He reeled it in and saw that his fly had been broken off. Bob had been watching from the bank to Gordon's right.

"I hear there are a couple of fish in here that are almost ten pounds," he said. "I think you just got one, Flyboy. Next time, bring him in."

They each caught and released several good fish in the pond, and after an hour and a half moved down to the stream, where the fish continued to be obliging. All day long, the three men worked the stream (with a mid-afternoon detour back to the pond). Wherever they went and however they fished, none of them went more than 15 minutes without a bite, and many of the fish were Rainbows and Browns in the 14-to-20-inch range. It was a day of fishing they would remember the rest of their lives.

At 4:30, the sun was behind the mountains and the breeze had gone from cool to cold. They decided to call it a day and trudged contentedly back to the ranch house. As they got there, they saw a sheriff's car parked not far from Gordon's Cherokee. Bob came to attention like a bird dog on a scent.

"I guess some deputy's on official business," Gordon said.

"Not just a deputy," Bob replied. "That's Car 17 — the one the sheriff herself drives. That tells me something big is going on."

He leaned his fly rod against the Cherokee.

"Follow me, gentlemen. We're going to exercise the public's right to know."

BOB RAPPED ON THE DOOR three times, and a moment later, Diane Brinkley opened it, the sheriff behind her, both of them looking a bit sheepish. For several seconds, no one said anything, then Chris spoke first.

"I should have known you'd see my car, Bob. I'm still not used to the fact you can't go anywhere in this county without being seen." She turned to Diane. "Should we invite them in?"

Diane looked briefly at Bob, at Gordon for several seconds, and gave Sam a quick glance. Without saying a word, she gestured toward the inside of the house with her head and turned around. They followed her in.

To the right of the spacious entrance area was a large living room, with hardwood floors, high-beamed ceilings and a river-rock fireplace with a cheerful blaze. A couch wide enough to seat four people faced the fire, with two chairs flanking it on either side. The couch and chairs were in a Western style, with gnarled wood framing above the cushioned areas. It's a hard look to achieve without being kitschy, but the furniture hit the right notes. In front of the couch was a long glass coffee table with two glasses of wine on it, one of them with a smudge of lipstick on the rim, corresponding to the color of Diane's lips. Above the fireplace was a large landscape painting, showing what looked like one of the local mountain ranges at twilight, with a vast expanse of sagebrush in the foreground shadows. Gordon looked at it intently.

"A Macondray?" he asked.

Diane nodded. "I think it's the only thing she's sold in this county."

"Actually," Sam said, "she sold another one two days ago. I saw it go down."

Diane looked at Gordon again, and the corners of her mouth turned up in a slight smile.

"I respect your taste. Can I offer you something to drink? We just uncorked a nice Merlot."

"Thanks," Gordon said, "but it's a long drive back to town. I'll pass."

Bob and Sam looked at each other and shook their heads. Bob leaned forward.

"Now, ladies, I don't want to interfere with official business, but it seems to me a couple of questions are in order. First and foremost, what the heck is going on?"

Diane turned to Chris and shrugged.

"Your call," she said.

Chris took a sip of her wine to buy time, and leaned back in her chair, looking up at the ceiling. Finally, she sat up straight.

"All right, Bob. I'll give it to you straight, but before I do, I need to explain it's a touchy situation. Will you sit on it for 24 hours and give us a chance to sort it out?"

Bob leaned forward and brought his hands, fingers together in a prayer position, to his mouth. After half a minute, he exhaled loudly.

"I don't like holding back the news, but I'll give you the 24 hours, but with the understanding that if anything else happens to push the story out in the open, I'm going on the air with it."

"Fair enough," Chris said, looking everyone in the room in the eye before continuing.

"Another student's gone missing from Homestead College."

IT SEEMED AS IF THE TEMPERATURE in the room dropped by 20 degrees. Bob tried not to show it, but it wasn't what he was expecting. I glanced over at Gordon and saw him lean forward slightly, his body tensing the way it does when he suddenly gets interested in something. It's about his only "tell," and I don't think anyone but me notices it.

Bob spoke first. "Who? When?"

The sheriff picked up a steno pad at the side of her chair and opened it.

"The name's Jessica Milland. She was doing some tutoring at the writing lab Thursday afternoon and left about 3:45. She has a dorm room on campus, a boyfriend with an apartment in town, and a mother who lives in Big Piney, so it's not unusual for her to be away for a night. Which is why her roommate wasn't worried when she didn't come home on Thursday"

"Wait a minute," Gordon said. "Dorm room? At a community college?"

Chris set down her pad. "Not something you see in the Bay Area, but our college serves three counties, and a lot of the students come from a long way off. And some of our college athletes come from all over the state for a chance to play. Plus, some days in the winter it's tough sledding getting the two miles from town to the college. Hence the dorms. Anyway, if I can continue, what Jessica doesn't have is a car. When she has to get anywhere, she bums a ride with a friend or hitchhikes. Like the other two who disappeared."

I noticed that Bob had buried his face in his hands and was shaking his head.

"You OK?" I asked.

"Shoot, shoot, shoot," he said. "I had Jessica in my radio class last spring. Really sweet kid. Tell me this isn't happening." He sat up and put his hands on his thighs. "But I'll tell you something. Of all the students I've ever had, she was the least afraid to challenge the teacher. If anyone tried to abduct her, she'd have fought and fought hard."

"Good to know," Chris said, "but this is the first time a missing student has been reported in less than 48 hours. Jessica's roommate worried when she was away for two nights in a row without calling. This morning she checked with the mother and the boyfriend, and when neither of them had seen her, sat on it for a couple of hours before letting us know this afternoon."

"What are you going to do?" Bob said.

"I've got Howard checking into people at the college, and I was thinking of calling out the posse for a search tomorrow. I don't know where to start looking, but we should at least try."

There was a pause in the conversation, and I decided to put in my two cents' worth.

"You say the student disappeared Thursday afternoon? Gordon and I were fishing on Powder Creek then, and just before sunset, I heard a gunshot."

Diane fixed me with a cool look that said she wasn't impressed. After several seconds of dramatic silence, she said:

"So?"

"Well," I stammered, "an hour after the student disappears, there's a gunshot in the mountains not all that far from where she was last seen. It might be worth looking into."

Chris smiled. "If we were back in Sacramento, Sam, I'd agree with you. But around here, gunfire is as much a natural sound as the wind or the birds singing. Probably just somebody taking target practice."

"I'm afraid she's right, Akers and Pains," Bob said. "But it does raise an interesting point. There's a lot of country around here. Where do you start looking with the posse, and what are you looking for?"

"Aside from the body? If I knew that, Bob, I'd be looking now. What we really should do is an aerial search, but ..."

"But Crawford's out of town," Bob said.

"Exactly." Chris turned to Gordon and me. "Dick Crawford is a private pilot who holds the contract to do aerial searches for the county. We budget for three a year, and he has one left on budget, but he's visiting his sister in Arizona. Won't be back until Wednesday."

I was still smarting from the women's dismissal. I mean, target practice? Who takes target practice and only fires one shot? But this was too good a chance to pass up.

"I have a plane," I said. "I flew it up here. I'd be happy to be pilot for the search."

I could see the wheels turning in the sheriff's head, but I knew I had her at the first four words. Finally she said:

"You're not an approved vendor, and it could take a while to get you paid back ..."

I looked at Gordon.

"We're good for it," he said. "Pay us back if and when you can. The important thing is to do the search as soon as possible."

"Thank you," she said. "That's very generous."

"The only condition," I said, "is that Gordon comes along."

"I don't know," she said. "The other person in the plane should be a trained law enforcement officer."

"My plane's a four-seater. You can send *two* trained officers if you want."

"Then we have a deal. Can you take us up in the morning? What I'll do is assemble the posse, but have them hold off on going anywhere until we've looked around."

"Great!" I said. "So we fly at dawn?"

"Let's not get carried away. Make it nine o'clock. That way the eastern slopes won't be in such deep shadow."

"Who are you sending up?" asked Bob.

"I have to send Howard, since he's done more aerial searches than anyone else on the force. If there's room for one more, I'm coming, too."

"To keep an eye on him?" murmured Diane.

"You said that, not me." She turned to Gordon and me. "Let's meet at the airport at 8:30. I'll talk to some people tonight and get an idea where we should look, and we can go over the flight plan before we take off."

"Fine by me," I said.

Glances were exchanged all around, then Bob slapped his thighs and stood up.

"Unless you find something or call me off sooner, this goes on the air at five o'clock tomorrow afternoon. Thanks for leveling with us, and we'd better get going now. Brenda's expecting us for dinner in 15 minutes, so can I use your phone to call and tell her we'll be a bit late?"

Chris was grinning.

"What?" said Bob.

"I should have known you'd come up with a pilot."

"Mountain Bob gets the job done," he said. "Don't ever try to put something past me."

He made the call, and a couple of minutes later, we were outside. It was completely dark by now and colder than I expected. I pulled my jacket around me, but it didn't help much. I was glad it was dark, though, because Bob and Gordon couldn't see me smile. The sheriff can come up with any flight plan she wants, but the airplane goes where the pilot flies it. And we're not going back to the airport tomorrow until I've flown over the area where Gordon and I were fishing Thursday.

I know what I heard that night.

BRENDA HASTINGS handled the late arrival of Bob and his friends with a mixture of stoicism and calm efficiency. It was hardly the first time, after all. She had already fed the daughters and sent them to watch TV, but they were called in again for introductions.

Gordon was immediately struck by the change in Eileen. When he last saw her four years ago, she was ten years old, less than five feet tall, and very much a little girl. Now she was a coltish five-seven and very much a young woman with reddish-brown hair pulled up in a bun and a bit of attitude. After shaking hands with Gordon, she looked him in the eye and said:

"Dad says you used to be a pretty good basketball player."

"I think he still is," Bob said.

"Want to play some one-on-one tomorrow?"

"I don't know about that," Gordon said. "When I play basketball, I tend to throw elbows."

"So do I."

"Well, let's wait and see. I have to be somewhere tomorrow morning. Maybe in the afternoon."

"You live in San Francisco," said Sarah, the younger daughter, shaking her blond curls. "It must be fun to live in San Francisco."

"I like it. But it's nice being up here, too."

"Can I stay with you the next time I'm in San Francisco?"

"Sarah!" Brenda said. "That's quite enough."

"I have an extra room in my place," Gordon said. "You're welcome to stay there as long as your mom or dad comes with you. Maybe you could get down this summer."

"Hard for me to get away, Gordon," Bob said. "But thanks."

Eileen and Sarah retreated to the TV room, and Brenda began putting dinner out. After offering to help and being shooed away, Gordon watched from a distance. She was five-six, a year or two younger than Bob, with short, light brown hair and glasses. She wore jeans, a long-sleeved pale-blue blouse, and a necklace with a sapphire charm around her neck. Her movements were economical and effortless, conveying a pleasantly domestic sense of a woman in control of her kitchen. Presently the food was on the table.

"Bob," she said, as they sat down, "will you say the blessing?"

Impromptu speech being second nature, Bob tossed off a few sentences of heartfelt and appropriate thanks for the meal and their gathering together. Brenda had fixed pork chops, lightly seared, then slow-cooked in a crock pot with apple slices, dried apricots and Gallo Tawny Port, served with boiled and buttered red potatoes and green beans from the backyard garden. Everything was delicious.

"Too late in the season for fresh beans, but we had a bumper crop this summer," Brenda said. "We put up enough to get us through the winter. Bi-Rite Grocery's loss."

After assuring her the fishing had been wonderful, Bob began to outline what they had learned about Jessica Milland from the sheriff and deputy district attorney. Once he'd made his tight and accurate presentation of the information, Brenda frowned.

"Bob, that's awful. I can't wrap my head around this. What's going on in our town?"

"I don't know, but you're hardly the only one asking."

The phone rang in the kitchen. Bob rose to get it, but Brenda put a hand on his arm.

"I told the girls to answer it. It makes them feel important."

A minute later, Sarah came in.

"Dad, it's for you?"

"Who is it?"

"Didn't say."

"All right." He rose, walked into the kitchen, and picked up the extension. "You can hang up now, Sarah," and with that he pulled the door shut, allowing only muffled and incoherent sounds from his end of the conversation to reach the dinner table.

Brenda turned to Gordon, clasped fingers together with elbows on the table, and rested her chin on them.

"Would you boys like to come to church with us tomorrow morning?"

Gordon looked at Sam, then back at Brenda.

"I'm afraid we'll have to pass. Sam and I are involved in the aerial search tomorrow."

She gazed at him for a moment.

"I see. And would you come if you didn't have to do that?"

He took a sip of iced tea and replied, "Probably not."

"Fair enough. It's just an offer and it's up to you. It just seems to me, well, that you're a good man, but there's room for some spiritual growth there. Maybe one of these days, we'll get you to renounce your heathen ways." She smiled. He did, too.

"I certainly hope so, but I'm afraid it won't be tomorrow."

Bob opened the door and came in, looking preoccupied. He sat down, looked around at everyone at the table, and leaned forward conspiratorially.

"I may have a lead on the case."

"Who were you talking to?" asked Sam.

"Don't want to say just yet, but I think it could really be something."

Brenda shook her head slightly.

"It's great that you care, Bob, but we have a sheriff to look into this."

"I know that, honey, but it's my town, too. If I can help in any way, move things forward, well, I've got to do it, don't I?"

"It'll always be your town, Bob. But that doesn't mean you have to do everything."

He put a hand on her arm. "Just helping out," he said. "Stand by your man."

Dessert was pumpkin pie (Brenda's recipe) with vanilla ice cream (store-bought). As she brought the plates, Eileen walked in.

"Mom, Jennifer just called. Can we go over to her place for a bit?" Bob and Brenda looked at each other. "Dad'll probably be wanting to take his friends to the TV room to watch football anyway."

"Well, aren't you considerate," Brenda said without a touch of irony. "Are her parents home?"

"Both of 'em. Her dad'll bring us back if you take us over. Please, Mom."

Bob nodded slightly. "All right," Brenda said, "but you have to be back by ten."

"Oh, Mom, that's less than two hours, and it's Saturday night. Can't we make it 11?"

"Ten-thirty."

Eileen appeared to be giving the offer serious consideration.

"All right. Ten-thirty. Deal."

Brenda ate dessert quickly (not difficult, as she'd taken only a small piece of pie) and left with the girls. The men heard the car's engine start outside.

"Her friend lives just six blocks away," Bob said. "A few months ago, we'd have told them to walk over, but now — we don't want 'em out alone at night."

They finished their pie and coffee.

"You didn't tell me Eileen was a basketball player," Gordon said.

Bob perked up. "A good one, too. I expect her to be starting as a sophomore. Play her at your own risk, Gordon. She just might kick your butt." He instinctively turned and looked at the chair Brenda had vacated. "If you'll pardon my French."

BOB TOOK THEM DOWN to the TV room. Down, literally. His house was three bedrooms, two baths, on a 10,000-square-foot lot on East Fourth Street, two blocks off Chaparral Boulevard and a four-block walk to the high school. It was built in the early 1960s and reflected the style of the period. The bedrooms, baths, kitchen, dining room, living room and appliance area used up 1,500 square feet. Underneath, however, was a large, windowless basement area. It had been made into a TV room/party room, with two folding tables in one corner, waiting to be brought out to hold refreshments at the next gathering.

"This is really nice," Sam said. "Is this sort of basement common around here?"

"Not really," Bob said. "Some of the older houses have basements you can get into from the outside, but this is what we call a Pinelli. Benny Pinelli was a contractor who bought up some lots around here and built houses on them from the late fifties to late seventies. This sort of basement was his trademark, and because most of the newer homes don't have one, the Pinellis sell at a premium. We got lucky when this one came on the market ten years ago." Bob turned to Gordon. "You're the money man, Flyboy. You could probably tell me what this would cost in the Bay Area, but what would you guess I paid for it ten years ago?"

Gordon looked around the room, and squinted, trying to remember the layout of the main floor.

"Sixty?" he finally said.

Bob snorted. "Ten years ago, 60 would almost have bought The House That Shit Built. They were asking $44,900 and took our offer of $43,900."

"A sweet deal. Looks to me like you're set for life, Bob."

"We feel pretty good about it." He looked at the TV. "The late game isn't exactly a must-see. Want to just have a beer and talk?"

"Works for me."

Bob brought Budweisers for himself and Gordon; Sam, because he was flying the next morning, took a soft drink. Gordon and Sam sat on the couch facing the TV set, and Bob plunked himself down in one of the recliners flanking it. From the way he did so, it was clear that it was his chair. They drank silently for a few moments, basking in the afterglow of a good day fishing followed by an excellent dinner.

"That call you took during dinner," Gordon said. "Want to tell us about it?"

"What makes you think it's worth telling?

"When you came back to the table, you had that look — like you were thinking about something. You wouldn't have reacted like that if it were a routine call."

Bob laughed. "Remind me not to play poker with you. It may be something or it may be nothing. I don't know, so I'd rather not say right now."

"About the local crime wave, I'm guessing."

"You're getting warm. It could be a lead, but I don't know. We're meeting tomorrow after church."

"Could I ask you something, Bob?" Sam interjected. "Just how jittery do you think the town is right now? You mentioned your daughters would have walked to their friend's place a few months ago, but now Brenda's driving them. And Sandy Steadman, the Highway Patrol officer, told us that every woman in town is terrified. So how bad do you think it is?"

Bob took a pull on his beer and looked at the ceiling for several seconds.

"Maybe not as bad as she says, but there's no question people are getting edgy. With two young women gone missing, you can at least hope they just ran away and they'll call home any day, unlikely as that is. But when the word gets out about Jessica, it's probably going to be one coincidence too many. I was talking to Ken Burbage, who owns the sporting goods store, and he told me he's been selling a lot of handguns in the last two weeks. Most people here own shotguns or rifles, but the bump in handgun sales is a new development."

"And probably more business on Monday," Gordon said.

"Exactly. Now how about you, Gordon? What kind of gun do you keep for protection?"

Gordon clearly hadn't expected the question, and it took him several seconds to reply.

"I don't own a gun, Bob. Never have."

"You're kidding. You live in a big, dangerous city and you don't have a gun to protect yourself. Mind if I ask why not?"

Gordon took a long sip of his beer.

"I guess I've never felt I needed one. When you lead as blameless a life as I do ... " Sam stifled a snort.

"Come on, Flyboy. Anybody can be a victim."

"That's true. Anybody can. But I just don't think I need one. There's an element of self-selection in crime victims. A pretty large element, really. I avoid the company of people who traffic in illicit substances; I don't fool around with women who have husbands or serious boyfriends; and when I'm out at night, I stick to crowded, well-lit neighborhoods. Right there, I figure I've eliminated about 95 percent of the reason for needing a gun to protect myself."

"All right. But what about the other five percent?"

"Still a remote possibility. I'd rather play the odds and take my chances."

Bob shook his head. "I guess we disagree. I'd still want the chance to defend myself."

"How about you?" Sam said. "I see you have a rack of rifles on that wall ..."

"Two of 'em are shotguns."

"Whatever. But do you have a handgun, too?"

"I have two. One's upstairs in the bedroom closet, where I can get at it right away to protect the house. The other one's in my locker at work, and when I go on the air, I put it in the desk drawer right under the mic."

"And have you ever had to use either of them?" Gordon asked.

"Not yet. But let me tell you a little story. Three years ago, my morning guest, same slot you were in Friday, was the Highway Patrol commander, talking about tougher enforcement of the weight laws on commercial trucks. Not basketball, but in a small market you get the guests you can. Anyway, some trucker driving through the county was listening and didn't like what the officer said. He showed up at the studio door five minutes after the commander left. He was as tall as you are and about 30 pounds heavier, and mad as I've ever seen anybody. I was able to talk him down, but you know what? If I hadn't, he could have snapped me in two. That happened on a Thursday morning, and on Saturday afternoon, I went to Ken Burbage and bought a nine-millimeter for the office."

GORDON LET IT GO, and I was glad he did. I'm not really comfortable with heavy discussions, especially when I don't know one of the participants all that well.

Besides, there was something I'd been wanting to bring up. This seemed like a good time to do it and change the subject.

"Bob," I said, "I've got a question or two about this afternoon."

He and Gordon looked at me. I got the sense they were grateful for the interruption.

"I've never been here before, and maybe they do things different in this county, but I'm curious as to why the sheriff went to the home of the deputy district attorney. I mean if there was something big going on, wouldn't she go to the district attorney himself instead of a deputy?"

Bob smiled. "Good point, Akers and Pains. But there's a simple explanation. Carson Hawley, who's been our DA for almost 20 years, suffered a massive stroke in the spring. He hasn't come back to work yet, and just between us, I don't think he ever will. He turns 65 next July, and since he can collect a full pension then, I expect him to resign the next day."

"So Diane's running the show?" Gordon said.

"Exactly. And to take it to the next step, I figure — and I'm not the only one — that since Carson won't go for another term, she'll run for the job next June."

"Can she win?" I asked. "She doesn't seem like much of a politician from what little I saw of her today."

"Allowing for the fact that you never know what the voters are going to do until they do it, I think so. Not everybody likes her — and she's probably OK with that — but almost everybody respects her. Plus, she was born and raised in this county, she'll probably have Carson's endorsement, and there aren't a whole lot of hungry lawyers who'd want to run for district attorney and have to face the winner later in court if they lost."

"Well put, Bob," Gordon said. "Sounds like an argument my father would make."

"Then my second question," I said, looking at Bob, "is even if the sheriff was visiting the right prosecutor, why would she be there to discuss a missing person when there's no case to prosecute at this point?"

"Hadn't thought about that." He nervously slapped his thigh several times with the palm of his hand. "Unless — yeah, that has to be it. She was there for another reason."

"Am I right in guessing you think that reason is the football rape case?" Gordon asked.

Bob nodded. "I know for a fact Diane is really interested in it."

"And it stands to reason," Gordon said, "that the sheriff would have some questions early on. What kind of evidence would you want before you could prosecute? What would be probable cause for getting a warrant from the judge we'd have to deal with? That sort of thing."

"With our judge, I don't think a warrant would be a problem," Bob said, "but yeah, you're on the right track."

"So," I continued, "you said Diane is really interested in the case. Any reason for that beside the obvious?"

"You mean, enforcing the law? Good question, Akers and Pains. Yeah. That case, if it ever becomes a case, is a bit personal for Diane."

"How so?" I asked.

Bob finished his beer, shook the bottle, and set it on the end table next to his chair.

"You remember when we got to the ranch this morning, there was a fellow named Jesus who greeted us?"

Gordon and I nodded.

"His full name is Jesus Rios. He's Alicia's father."

Sunday November 9

SAM SAW HER FIRST, as they were walking through the main entrance to the Vienna Café. He gave Gordon a light jab in the ribs with an elbow and gestured with his head.

"Trouble," he whispered.

Gordon looked up to see Elizabeth Macondray sitting in a booth near the back, with a clear view of the entry. She waved at them and followed the wave with a "come over" gesture.

He waved back, and they strolled through the dining area, sparsely populated at 7:30 a.m., to her booth.

"Quite a coincidence running into you here, and so early, Miss Macondray," Gordon said.

"Nothing coincidental about it," she said, " and please call me Elizabeth. I was waiting for you. Have a seat."

Gordon gestured for Sam to get into the booth. They sat side by side, facing her. A young waitress — a brunette who might have been pretty if she weren't so obviously bored — appeared with a coffee pot. Two well-worn porcelain cups, upside down on paper coasters sat in front of Gordon and Sam. They turned the cups face up, and she filled them.

"Can I top yours off, Miss Macondray?"

"No thanks, Jenna. I'm fine. But check back in a few minutes. I think the gentlemen are in a bit of a hurry this morning."

The waitress nodded and walked off. When she was presumably out of earshot, Elizabeth leaned forward.

"One of my students. I run into them everywhere."

"But you were looking for us," said Sam. "Or at least Gordon."

"Do you want to see the menu?" she asked.

"No need," Sam said. "Gordon's having what he's always having. Sausage and eggs. I'll have the same, just to speed things up."

She smiled and looked at Gordon. "Bob did say you were a man of regular habits. Not necessarily a bad thing.

In any case, it was Bob who told me you'd be here around this time."

"Bob sees all, knows all," Gordon said.

"In this town, anyway."

"But I just mentioned it to him on the way out the door, and it was after ten. You called him that late?"

She shook her head. "He called me. He told me about your running into the sheriff and the DA yesterday afternoon, and about Jessica Milland being missing." She stopped for a sip of coffee. "Jessica was in my first women's studies class last year. Really nice, and very much someone who would stand up for herself."

"That's what Bob said, yesterday at the ranch."

"I can hardly believe it, but, of course, it's already happened before. Bob said Sam was going to lend his plane to an aerial search effort."

Gordon nodded.

"What do you expect to find?"

"I don't know. I've never done this before."

"The sheriff said Howard Honig would know what to do," Sam said.

"I doubt that," she said. "But I suppose he has to be deferred to. Anyway, that's not what I'm here for. Bob said something else."

She paused for effect, and Gordon nodded at her to continue.

"He said he may be onto something; that someone called him last night ..."

"I remember the call," Sam said.

"And that he's meeting with that person today. He seemed pretty excited about it."

"Bob's continually excited about life," Gordon said.

"In any event, maybe things are starting to break in our crime wave here. And it got me to thinking that maybe there's a role for you to play in all this, Gordon."

"Um, I don't think so. I'm just here on a fishing trip, and I'd rather not get involved in a criminal investigation."

"Oh, but Bob said you've already done that, and you have a flair for it. Isn't that right, Sam?"

"Almost got me killed once," Sam nodded.

"Besides, I think there may be something special that only you can contribute to the effort."

"And what would that be?"

"I want to talk to Bob after his meeting today. Can we get together for a cup of coffee tonight? I'll fill you in then."

Gordon took a long swallow of his coffee, looked up at the ceiling, took a deep breath, and exhaled.

"You're very persuasive, ... Elizabeth."

She beamed. "Thank you. Thank you. I knew you would. Let's exchange cell phone numbers, and I'll call you this afternoon to set things up."

He took out his phone, and as they were entering each others' numbers, Jenna came up to the table.

"Ready to order?"

"I'm just going to finish this coffee and go, Jenna. Can you ring it up at the register for me?"

"Sure." She looked at Sam. "How about you?"

"Sausage and eggs," he said.

"How do you want the eggs done?"

"Over easy, please."

"Link or patty?"

"Links."

"How about toast?"

"What are my choices?"

"White, whole wheat, sourdough, rye, or English muffin."

"English muffin."

She turned to Gordon. "And you, sir?"

"Same as him," Gordon said, looking up from his phone and folding down the flip cover. "Only with the eggs scrambled, patties, and rye."

Elizabeth closed her phone and looked up at him.

"Rye, Gordon? Really? I'd have guessed sourdough."

After she left, Gordon moved to the side of the booth where Elizabeth had been sitting. He drank his coffee pensively for several minutes before Sam finally asked what he was thinking about

"I've been thinking about the latest disappearance," Gordon said. "Did you notice there was something different about it?"

"No."

"The first two times one of the students went missing, it was on a Friday afternoon. This time, it was on a Thursday. Why do you suppose that was?"

"I have no idea."

"Neither do I at this point. But I suspect it means something, and if we knew what, it might move things along."

THE THERMOMETER outside the airport administrative building read 34 degrees as Gordon and Sam pulled up at 8:30, but the sun was just beginning to provide a hint of warmth where it shone. Chris and Howard were there, waiting. The sheriff was wearing a blue down parka, jeans, and a wool watch cap pulled down over her ears. Even so, she was standing with arms crossed in front of her, pressing against her torso, and was stamping the ground to warm up her feet. Howard was wearing a heavy suede jacket with a sheepskin collar over his uniform, along with a white Stetson. He looked as if he were auditioning to be a Marlboro model. In his leather-gloved hand, he held a clipboard.

"A great day for flying," he said, as they came toward him.

"It's always a great day for flying," Sam said. "Let me do the pre-flight check, then we'll be good to go." Sam started toward his plane, but Chris stopped him.

"First, I have to make you both members of the sheriff's posse. Howard."

He handed over the clipboard.

"You're on top, Gordon. Sign here." He did. "Now you, Sam."

"Where did you get my home address?" Gordon asked.

"I called Bob last night." Gordon shook his head

The other three stood and fidgeted as Sam looked over his plane. As they waited, Gordon took a closer look at the airport, such as it was. The administration building was a modular unit, 20-by-30 feet, flanked on one side by a flagpole and on the other by a pole with a wind sock at the top. It fluttered occasionally as a breeze came along. A short distance away was an area with 14 planes tied down and room for 16 more (Gordon had time, so he counted) plus Sam's on the ground. The paved runway looked as if it could use a new seal, and the fuel pump near where the planes were tied down looked as if it had been installed a half-century ago. The sun sat low in a blue sky dotted with white clouds.

It was clear that Chris and Howard were uncomfortable in the presence of each other, and the sense of that tension, along with the cold and the wait, was getting on Gordon's nerves. Finally, he turned to Chris and said:

"So what, exactly, are we looking for anyway?"

"Short answer," Howard said, before Chris could speak, "is something different or suspicious. If the victim was abducted ..."

"Her name is Jessica," snapped Chris.

" ... chances are, she was taken somewhere remote, at least at first. It'd be pretty risky bringing a kidnap victim, even a dead one, into town where people might notice something suspicious. Our perp — if there is one, and she's not a runaway — might have taken her to a place where he'd be less likely to be noticed. So maybe we see a summer cabin with smoke in the fireplace when it shouldn't be in use, or an outbuilding on a large lot that looks like it's just been put to use. You're not likely to see those things from ground level and public roads, but maybe we see something that calls for ground follow-up. And maybe we get lucky."

"Thank you for speaking up, Howard," said Chris. "Saved me the trouble of asking for your opinion."

"No problem."

"But it sounds as if you're looking for a needle in a haystack," Gordon said. "Realistically, what's the chance of finding something?"

"Realistically?" said Chris. "Not very good. But as long as there's a chance, it's worth a try."

Howard nodded. "That's about right."

They lapsed into silence until Sam returned several minutes later.

"Good to go," he said.

"All right," Chris said. She turned to Howard. "Who's putting together the posse?"

"Joe Dawson. They'll be ready to roll the minute we need 'em."

He turned to Sam, and continued.

"I've never flown with you before, Akers, so let me lay down a couple of ground rules. I like cautious pilots. The more cautious the better. Just do what I tell you, and concentrate on making it a safe flight. If you're flying alongside a mountain, give it plenty of room. And don't feel like you have to get too close to the ground for us to see anything."

"That's right," Chris said. "I have binoculars."

"And I," Howard said, "have eyes like a hawk."

THERE'S A MOMENT, shortly after takeoff, when you can hear the passengers — if there are any — collectively draw in their breaths. It happens a few seconds after the plane's off the ground. Although the plane is going up and forward, to the uninitiated, it seems as if it might not have the oomph to keep doing so. The pilot, if he's any good, knows better. I'd checked everything before takeoff and knew we were all right. The only question even close was weight, and we made it with a bit to spare, no thanks to Gordon. He's the biggest of us, and while he's hardly fat, it's true that some of his belts show a sign of being buckled one notch further out than before. He probably thinks no one notices, but I do.

Anyway, when the plane kept going up and forward for a few more seconds, I could hear everyone exhale, and we settled down to the task at hand. It wasn't made any easier by the tension between the sheriff and Howard, who were like an old married couple that can't stand each other anymore. Whenever they bickered, Gordon kept quiet and tried to ignore it, which is his way of dealing with unpleasantness.

Using my outdoor voice to be heard above the engine, I bellowed, "When I gain a bit more altitude, I'm going to loop back over Homestead College and fly over as if we're about to leave, just like Jessica was when she was last seen. Tell me what to do next."

Howard, unsurprisingly, got in the first word. "The logical thing would have been for her abductor to turn right toward town. If she was hitching a ride, it's what she'd be expecting, and he wouldn't want her to get the game up right away."

Chris was sitting behind him in the right rear passenger seat, and out of the corner of my eye, I could see her shaking her head.

"I disagree. If you're abducting someone, the last thing you want to do is drive *toward* a populated area. Plus, she's from Big Piney, and may have been asking for a ride there."

"How many people would be going to Big Piney that time of day?" Howard asked. "Not many. She'd be suspicious if someone was willing to drive her there."

"If she was picked up by a serial killer, he'd have said yes to taking her to Boise, if that's what it took to get her in the car." We were over the campus now. "Turn left, Sam, and follow the state highway north."

Howard audibly sucked in his breath, and I did what she said. It was a clear direction, anyway.

I held it at 1,500 feet above the ground, 100 yards to the right of the highway, between the road and the mountain range. There wasn't much there but ranches and some isolated homes. I wouldn't even have known where to look. Chris kept her binoculars trained on the ground.

"Down there!" she said at one point. "There's a little cottage about a hundred yards from the main house, with smoke coming from the chimney. Is that unusual?"

Howard yawned, a bit theatrically, I thought.

"That's the Driscoll place. His mother in law is arriving early for Thanksgiving." He paused for effect. "Everybody who was at Elizalde's Wednesday night knows he's not too happy about it."

She set her binoculars on her lap.

"I guess that's what he gets for giving her grandchildren," she said.

Not long afterward, we came to the road that headed east toward Big Piney. I angled the plane to the right and began climbing so we'd clear the mountains by plenty. The sun was far enough to the south that it wasn't directly in my eyes. It was utterly clear, and the air was bracing — the kind of day where I could fly for hours. It occurred to me that we might do just that without ever finding anything.

"Can I make a suggestion?" Howard asked.

"Do you need my permission?" Chris said.

"On the other side of the summit, there's a tract of about 20 summer cabins. It's late enough in the season that if anyone's there now, it might be a good idea to have a deputy pay them a call."

"Worth a look, I suppose," Chris said.

I followed his direction and flew over the cabins. One of them had smoke coming from the chimney and a fairly late-model SUV parked outside. Howard radioed the information and was told that a deputy was near Big Piney and would check it out promptly.

On the other side of the mountain was Serendipity Valley, and I was surprised by how big it was, with cattle grazing in fields dotted with rolled up hay, ready to get them through the winter. The fields sloped down to a large, dry lake bed, then to another range of mountains in the distance. Big Piney, which can't have more than three hundred people, was about in the center of it, and there didn't appear to be much of interest there.

"We may as well fly up and down the valley and give it a look," Chris said. I immediately turned right, with a definite purpose. By flying south first, we'd end up at the north end after doubling back. When we headed west, then, back over the mountains, I'd be able to get us over the area where Gordon and I were fishing on Thursday.

Serendipity Valley was as boring as it was beautiful. Outside of Big Piney, there weren't many dwellings, and the ones we saw didn't look suspicious at all, though I'm not even sure what suspicious would look like. The only excitement came as we were nearing the north end of the valley, and the deputy who had been sent to check on the cabin called in.

"Unit Four to Honig."

"Honig here."

"I called at the cabin. It appears to be a gentleman from Sacramento, mid-forties, who was up here for some deer hunting."

"Doesn't he know the season ended last weekend?"

"I think he does, sir, but that's probably just what he told his wife. It looks to me like this buck brought his doe with him, and she was quite a bit younger, if you catch my drift."

The deputy and Howard both laughed heartily. Chris leaned forward and shouted toward the radio.

"Deputy!" she snapped.

"Sheriff?"

"Can we show some professionalism? Please."

A slight pause, followed by a chastened, "Yes, ma'am."

"Did you check the young woman's ID to make sure she wasn't Jessica?"

"Different name on her driver's license, and a Sacramento address, ma'am."

She leaned back in her seat and shook her head. I took advantage of the diversion to angle west and start back over the mountain range. As we crossed the summit, Chris said:

"My way didn't turn up anything, so let's try yours, Howard. Head south along the highway when you get there, Sam."

"Right," I said. But instead, I kept going about three miles west after crossing the highway before turning south on a path that would take us right over Powder Creek. It was a few minutes before anyone noticed, and Howard spoke first.

"Aren't you a bit off the highway, Akers?"

"As long as we're doubling back," I said, "I figured we might as well fly over some country we haven't seen before. Humor me."

As if they had a choice.

GORDON SAW THE BUZZARDS FIRST. He was looking ahead to find the campground where they had parked while fishing, when he spotted the four birds circling lazily ahead and slightly to the left of the plane.

"Could be a dead cow," Howard said, when Gordon pointed to the birds.

"We might as well look," Chris said. "Not much else to see here."

Sam was keeping the plane 1,500 feet above the ground, but dropped to 1,000 feet as they approached the area the birds were circling. A minute or two later, Gordon saw the campground where they had parked Thursday night. A lone pickup truck was parked at the entrance, but its occupants were nowhere in sight.

"We're awful close to the mountainside," Sam said. "I'd like to go south a bit and loop back from the other side. I could get a bit lower, then." Hearing no objection, he set about to do so. As he began to climb and turn east, Gordon, looking down to the left of the plane, saw something in the tree branches below, then it was gone as Sam pulled away. It could have been a human form or an optical illusion. He decided to wait for a second look.

Gordon noted the location as being near a rocky slope with a dirt road carved into it, and as the plane looped back several minutes later, he told the sheriff and Howard.

"I see something!" Howard said a few seconds later. "Can't tell what it is. Can you get us a bit lower, Akers?"

"How many lives have you got?" asked Sam.

"No need," Chris said, looking through the binoculars. "I can see it. It's a partially nude body, probably female. We may have found Jessica."

Several seconds of silence ensued as the reality sunk in. Howard finally radioed the information to the posse and told Sam to head back to the airport. As they were passing over the scene on the way back, Honig looked down again and shook his head.

"How the hell did she end up halfway up a tree?" he said.

IT WAS JUST PAST NOON when the four of them rolled up to the crime scene in one of the Sheriff's Department's 1992 Blazers. Howard was driving. Yellow tape had been strung across the road, and three dozen people were milling about behind it. Five were uniformed sheriff's deputies, three were highway patrol officers (including Sandy Steadman and John Armstrong), and the rest were citizen members of the posse, excited about having finally been called out on a case.

"Find Dawson and see how badly the scene's been compromised," Chris said to Howard. He nodded and left the car. She shook her head.

"Something wrong?" Gordon asked.

"I'd have wanted this sealed off farther back, but it's too late now. Let's hope everybody at least stayed behind the tape." She sighed. "One more lesson for the posse training course."

"How often do they have something like this?" Sam said.

"Not very often, which is why they don't know what to do. The last murder in this county was in 1990. Two guys in a bar got into an argument, and a dozen witnesses in various stages of inebriation were willing to testify that the guy standing over the body with the knife in his hand was the killer. In that case, the state of the crime scene didn't affect the outcome. Here, it's going to matter more that the protocols are followed."

They got out of the vehicle. The temperature was in the low 50s, but it was pleasant in the sun. Just behind the tape, Howard was talking with a silver-haired deputy with a thick, drooping mustache. They nodded at each other, and Howard returned.

"Not too bad," he said. "One of the volunteers got about ten feet past where the tape is before Dawson called him back. Otherwise, it's clean from the tape onward."

"As much as you could hope for, I guess," Chris said. "Do we have a photographer?"

"Bob Lovejoy."

"Probably our best. Tell Dawson we're coming through in a minute."

Howard started back toward the tape. Chris turned to Gordon and Sam.

"I need two witnesses who can swear we're doing this right, and I don't know who I can trust in the posse. So you're it. Stay ten feet behind me, watch where you're going, and don't speak unless spoken to. And try to remember everything you see. Can you do that?"

They nodded.

"Let's go."

At the tape, they met Lovejoy, who turned out to be a civilian in his late thirties with a medium build and sandy hair. Gordon later learned that he kept a photo studio behind his bookkeeping office, and remembered Bob's remark that everyone in town had a sideline.

"The road's barely 20 feet wide," Chris said to Howard. "Can you cover half of it?"

"Sure."

"You take the left side; I'll take the right. We take a step forward, look carefully around, and don't move forward until we're satisfied there's nothing to be seen." She turned to Gordon, Sam and Lovejoy. "When we've gone in ten to 15 feet, slip in behind us and match us step for step. If you see something you think we missed, holler."

She took a pair of latex gloves from a pants pocket and pulled them on. Howard did the same, and they ducked under the tape.

Slowly and meticulously, they made their way up the road. No one saw anything out of the ordinary for 20 minutes, before Chris exclaimed, "Hold it!" She was standing near a slight pothole.

"The road surface is too hard for any kind of tracks, but in this pothole, there's some loose gravel and what looks like a tire track. Shoot it, Lovejoy."

The photographer obediently came forward, looked at the pothole, and moved to one side, where he knelt, took one photo, and rose, taking a step backward.

"From four sides," Chris said.

"But, ma'am, that's going to use up a lot of film."

She glared daggers at him for several seconds.

"Yes, ma'am," he finally said, and shot it from the other three sides.

It was the only "clue" they found before reaching the stretch of road parallel to where the body was below. All five of them looked over the side. The female body, topless but for a bra, lay cradled in branches 20 feet below the roadway. A large red stain in the middle of the torso was visible from where they stood. Howard spoke first.

"Looks like the buzzards got one of her eyes."

Chris raised her binoculars and looked.

"Both of them, actually. Howard, is there any way in hell we can get someone besides her mother to do the ID?"

Gordon stepped back from the edge, feeling faint. For some reason, one of his father's sayings popped into his head. Judge Gordon had been talking about evidence given at a trial, but the sentiment held in this instance as well:

"That which has been seen cannot be unseen."

"It can probably be arranged," Howard said, bringing them back to the moment.

"Everybody stand back," Chris said. They did as told.

"If what I'm thinking is right, he told her to undress, she fought back, and was shot, with the recoil knocking her over the edge. Damn! I wish I'd known about that wound before we came up here. There may be blood spatters on the ground we just walked all over." She got on her hands and knees and began looking closely at the ground. With an exclamation, she picked up a small rock with her gloved hand and put it into a plastic bag. She found several more potential spatters over the next few minutes.

"We'll see what the lab says," she said, "but I'm pretty sure."

"What I don't get," Howard said, "is why he'd bring her up here and have her start undressing at twilight — that is, if Akers was right about the shot. It's kinda … kinky."

"For some serial killers, Howard, it's not just about the killing. It's about having power over the victim. Making her take off her clothes in the cold, in the middle of nowhere, would have been a form of torture, a way of showing he owned her."

Howard looked skeptical, but held his counsel.

They worked up the road a bit, finding nothing else of interest, and returned to where the body was.

"All right," Chris said. "Let's start working on getting her out of here."

"How would you do that?" Sam asked.

"I've never seen a situation like this before," Howard drawled.

"For crying out loud," she said. "Can we get a utility truck with a cherry picker? That would be a start."

"I'll put Dawson on it." Howard started for the tape.

He returned a few minutes later, with a thoughtful look on his face.

"I just thought of something," he said.

Chris eyed him warily.

"A mile and a half ahead, the road dead-ends at an old logging camp. It's been empty since mid-August, but the company uses it to park machinery. If someone was looking for a place to hide a kidnap victim or a body ..."

"We have to check it out," Chris said. "Let's get the civilian posse on it. I want them away from the crime scene."

"I HOPE I'M RIGHT ABOUT THIS," Chris said, as she, Gordon and I led the convoy up the road toward the abandoned logging camp. "It's a question of where these well-meaning amateurs will do the least amount of harm."

"Aren't we amateurs?" I asked.

"I suppose so, but you know enough to wait for instructions and do as you're told. Half the people in this posse want to be helpful, but they have no impulse control."

I took that as a modest compliment and noted that Gordon showed the slightest of smiles. He was in the front seat, of course, so I could see them both. Turning around, I could see the three vehicles following us. It was three o'clock now, and the autumn sun was getting lower. After several minutes, the road moved away from the edge of the mountain and into a natural flat, or shelf, in the side of the mountain. There it ended in a large clearing. Actually, it ended at a locked gate, a large log blocking the road, and chained to a metal fence post. Behind it was an open area and, back by the trees, three wooden buildings. One had an almost squarish front and was two stories high. On either side of it were long, one-story buildings, extending about 60 feet in either direction.

Howard and six members of the posse jumped out of the van behind us. Behind them, Sandy Steadman,

John Armstrong, and two other posse members clambered out of a Highway Patrol SUV. Behind that, another four posse members got out of another SUV, the last in the line. I recognized Norv DeShayne and Lovejoy in Honig's bunch, and a couple of the others looked somewhat familiar from around town.

Quite a few amateurs underfoot, if you ask me.

Chris vaulted the log gate, and others followed with varying degrees of athleticism. Gordon, with his long legs, simply stepped over it. She motioned them to follow her and led the way to the large building in the middle.

"This is the dining hall and offices," Honig said. "Or it used to be. The two buildings on the right were bunkhouses."

"I should have thought of this sooner," she said, "but I don't suppose anyone has a key to these buildings."

DeShayne stepped forward. "Not a problem," he said. "I know the regional manager. He told me this place is so remote they don't bother locking it."

He grabbed the doorknob with an ungloved hand, turned it, and opened the door inward.

"See?"

I looked over at Chris, and if the situation hadn't been so serious, I would have stifled a laugh. She was doing a slow burn worthy of Yosemite Sam, and it was all she could do to hold her anger in.

"Honorary Deputy DeShayne," she said after several seconds, the strain of not screaming coming through in her voice, "I sincerely hope that hand of yours did not wipe out any fingerprints on that doorknob."

"Aw, shit," he said. "How was I supposed to know that?"

She motioned him aside and stood with her back to the building, facing the group. In the shade now, we could feel a bit of chill in the air.

"All right, listen up. We're going to break into three groups. Howard, you take half the posse and go over every square inch of the bunkhouse on the right. "John, Sandy, you take the other half of the posse and do the same with the bunkhouse on the left. Posse members!" She barked the two words, and the civilians clearly took notice. "You will put on latex gloves before entering these buildings, and even so, you will not touch anything with your gloved hands unless you have explicit approval from one of the law enforcement professionals. Does everybody understand?"

It took a few minutes for everybody to get ready, and only when she was satisfied that they were did she give the order to go into the buildings. Gordon and I followed her into the dining hall.

It was dark, cold and musty, smelling of mold, dust and disuse. The floor was concrete, which added to the chill. The roof was a good 20 to 25 feet above us, which also did nothing to add warmth. People had presumably been here as recently as the past summer, but it sure seemed a lot longer ago than that. Along the walls on either side were overhanging balconies, each with several doors presumably leading to office or storage rooms. It was so still that when a gust of wind came up and falling pine needles hit the roof, it seemed as if we could hear each one land.

"It's a good place to be lonely," Gordon finally said. "How come you took this building instead of one of the others?"

"Because Howard said there were offices in here. Better place to hide or hold someone than a large open bunk area." She sighed. "I really hope there's nothing here, and even more than that, I hope there's nothing in the other two buildings."

"You don't trust the posse?" I asked.

"I don't trust Howard. He came up through the cowboy school of detective work. Sandy and Armstrong I feel better about. Unlike our department, the highway patrol actually trains people. But you saw what we're up against with the civilians."

"What do you want us to do?" Gordon asked.

"There's nothing in this main area. We need to check out the balconies and the kitchen." She pointed to separate sets of stairs on the other side of the room, climbing to the balconies on either side and gestured to the right. "You take that side, Gordon, and I'll take the other one. Sam, the kitchen and pantry are through the doors on either side of the stairs. Check 'em out. And remember. No touching anything unless I say so."

As we walked across the empty floor, I tried to imagine what it would have been like full of tables, with a hundred lumberjacks eating a hearty breakfast or dinner. It hardly seemed possible. When we got to the other side, Gordon started up the stairs on the right and Chris went up the ones on the left.

I pushed through the swinging doors to the kitchen, touching wood, not the metal part, which might have prints. I came in on the skeleton of a kitchen. Counters, stove tops and freezer doors were still there, but all utensils and signs of food were absent. On the right, a window with six panes was missing one of them. On the left was a door partially open, leading to what looked like a pantry. I grabbed the wood frame of the door and pulled it open. It seemed to go a ways back and was dark toward the rear. I saw a light switch just inside and flipped it up. Nothing happened.

Wishing I had a flashlight, I left the door wide open to provide as much illumination as possible and started toward the back. There appeared to be a few boxes and bundles back there, and I moved deliberately toward them. My eyes were just adjusting to the gloom when I heard another gust of wind outside.

The door to the pantry blew shut and I was in total darkness.

Every man has his irrational fears, and my two biggest are snakes and the dark. Actually, it's not that irrational to be afraid of snakes, especially in the tropics. Being trapped in this pantry, literally unable to see my hand in front of my face, put the other fear into overdrive. Very slowly, I turned around, then put out my left hand. It touched nothing but air. I stepped slightly to the left and it contacted what I assumed was one of the pantry shelves.

Moving forward one tentative step at a time, I tried to get back to the door. It was probably 15 feet away, but it seemed like a thousand. It must have been nearly a minute before I got to it, but it seemed like an eternity. I fumbled for the doorknob, and as I did remembered Chris's directive not to touch anything. Never mind that.

As cold as it was, I could feel sweat running down the back of my neck, and a panic attack was not far away.

I found the doorknob, grabbed it with my gloved hand, and turned it to the right.

It wouldn't move.

I took a deep breath. Eventually, I knew, they would find me, but it was a cold comfort to know that. I thought about trying to kick the door down, and about the chewing out I'd get from Chris if I did that. But it wasn't getting any lighter in there, and I decided to risk it. But before I did, it occurred to me to try one more thing.

I turned the doorknob to the left. It moved, and I pushed the door out. As I stepped out, I could hear Gordon shouting in the main room, and a clatter of running feet, presumably Chris on the stairs. I pushed open the swinging kitchen doors and smacked her dead on as she was running toward the stairs on Gordon's side. She cried out in pain and grabbed the left side of her face.

"Sorry," I said, for lack of a more original response.

"Keep going!" she snapped, and ran up the stairs ahead of me.

Gordon was standing in front of one of the doors. As we drew nearer, I could smell a foul and overwhelming odor of putrid decay. He didn't need to say why he'd called us over.

"What do you want to do?" he asked Chris.

"Don't touch the doorknob," she said. "Do you think you can kick it in?"

"I'll try."

The door was flimsy, and he only needed two tries. When it flew open, the stench was almost unbearable. Chris pulled a handkerchief out of her pants pocket, put it over her nose, and stepped across the threshold. Gordon and I moved behind her.

Then I saw the body, or what was left of it, and it was all I could do not to throw up.

At one time it had no doubt been a fine specimen of a raccoon, but it had been dead long enough that it was bloated with gas and set upon by maggots, which were crawling over the corpse in unimaginable numbers. Acting as one, the three of us moved out of the room and down the balcony toward the stairs, trying to get as far away from the smell as possible.

At the top of the stairs, Chris lowered her handkerchief, and I could see a bruise forming under her left eye. I'd given her what, by tomorrow morning, would probably be a shiner that would be the talk of the town.

She started laughing, and so did Gordon and I. After a minute, gasping for breath, she pointed toward the room we'd just departed.

"Well, we found a body anyway. Good call, Howard."

NONE OF THE OTHERS FOUND ANYTHING, and everyone headed back but one deputy and one posse volunteer, who were watching the crime scene until the state crime lab professionals could get there in the morning.

Shortly before seven o'clock, Gordon was stalling the waitress at Danny's Diner about dessert when Bob walked in. Gordon had asked for a small booth at the back, and when Bob joined him, they had as much privacy as possible in a public restaurant. It helped that the Sunday dinner rush was generally from four to six, and the place was only a third full.

"Cherry pie," Bob said, when the waitress came again. "And coffee."

"Apple for me," Gordon said, "with a scoop of vanilla ice cream. And you can top off my coffee when you bring his."

"You're not worried about getting out of shape?" Bob said as she left.

"The process is already under way. And I'm feeling old and tired now, though not hungry, thanks to Danny."

"Danny died 15 years ago."

"His heirs and successors, then. I haven't eaten since breakfast." Gordon swallowed the last of his coffee. "It's been a busy day, as I'm sure you're aware."

"We just did a special report on it. Awful business, but in one sense I'm relieved. At least we know what's going on now."

"But not much more."

"That's always true at the beginning. I have faith in our new sheriff. She isn't going to let this go."

"She's wound up tighter than a violin string right now."

"Can you blame her? She not only has to deal with the pressure of solving the case, but also the political consequences. Either one would be a dead weight, and she's carrying two."

Pie arrived, and they ate and sipped coffee for several minutes.

"So where were you this afternoon?" Gordon finally said. "I'd have expected you to beat us to the crime scene."

"Dropped the ball on that one," Bob admitted. "But I had my reasons." He shoveled a piece of pie into his mouth.

"Care to tell me about it? For old times' sake."

"Sorry, Flyboy, but I can't just yet. Let's say I've been doing a bit of detective work and leave it at that."

"And this detective work of yours, is it turning up any results?"

"Maybe. I just might be on to something really big."

"Shouldn't you tell the sheriff?"

"Oh, I intend to. I fully intend to. When I get a definite answer from a certain someone."

"And how close to definite are you?"

Bob shrugged, and Gordon pressed on.

"Are you 20 percent of the way there? 40? 75 or more?"

"You know something, I'd forgotten how bothersome you can be when you want to know something. Let's say more than half at this point. You'll know when it's time."

"Have it your way." Gordon finished his pie, washed it down with the last of the coffee. "Are we on for some fishing tomorrow afternoon?"

"Possibly, but I hope not. Tomorrow afternoon may be when I have something definite."

"That soon?"

"No promises, just a hope. By the way, what happened to Akers and Pains?"

"He's been summoned to a private meeting with the sheriff. She wants to talk to him more about the shot he heard. Pretty routine, I suppose."

I GOT TO THE COURTHOUSE promptly at seven. It's a pretty impressive building for such a small town. I'm no expert on architecture, but I'd call it a classical style, with a wide row of limestone steps across the front, Grecian columns, and a dome at the top that lights up at night. The front door is at the top of the steps, but I'd been told to go around back, enter through the basement, take the stairs to the first floor and proceed to Room 101. I was a bit surprised to find that it was the District Attorney's office.

I went in and was immediately stopped short by a counter running the length of the room. A light was on in a large office in the back, and I heard the sheriff call my name. She came out and brought me back. I was placed in a chair directly facing Diane Brinkley across her desk, and Chris took a seat on a small couch to my right. Brinkley looked, if anything, even frostier than she had the day before, and when I turned to look at Chris, she avoided my gaze.

Don't ask me why, but I suddenly felt like a piece of raw meat between two hungry pit bulls. And it didn't get any better when Diane started to speak.

"Mr. Akers, we'd like to ask you a few questions, but before we do, just as a matter of form, I want to remind you that you have the right to remain silent; you have the right to an attorney ..."

"Whoa, whoa, whoa," I said. "What's this all about? I've been helping the sheriff's office in this investigation."

The two women exchanged what, to me, seemed like a meaningful glance.

"I'm aware of that, Mr. Akers, and I'm not accusing you of anything. At the same time, by your own admission, you were present very near the scene of a capital crime in a remote area that could reasonably be expected to be deserted at the time. Until we have more conclusive information, we wouldn't be doing our jobs if we didn't at least regard you as a possible suspect."

"I can't believe this. I volunteered my plane and paid for the gas ..."

"We'll reimburse you for the gas," Chris said.

" ... to do an aerial search when you wanted to and didn't have a plane."

"And the county appreciates that," Diane said. "But bear in mind that you also took the initiative in leading investigators to the body."

"I led them to where I heard the shot."

"Let me finish, please, Mr. Akers. Unfortunately — and the sheriff can correct me if I'm wrong — it's not uncommon for persons who commit a crime to try to divert suspicion from themselves by offering to help the authorities." She looked at the sheriff.

"I've seen it happen," said Chris.

"And so, until you've been absolutely ruled out as a suspect, we need to be sure you've been properly warned."

"You don't have to read me my rights," I said. "I have nothing to hide. What do you want to know?" I crossed my arms over my chest, leaned back in the chair, and gave the prosecutor the most intimidating glare I could.

She didn't seem to be impressed.

"Have it your way," she said. "I know you've already done this, but could you please go over your movements on Thursday the sixth between the hours of two and seven p.m."

I told her in as much detail as possible.

"So by your account," she continued, "you were fishing Powder Creek for about three hours, with your friend, Mr. Gordon."

I nodded.

"And did you see anyone during that time — aside from Mr. Gordon?"

"No."

"Might anyone have seen you?"

"Maybe, but it's hard to imagine."

"Assuming, for the moment, that the killer was someone else, wouldn't he have had to have driven past Mr. Gordon's Cherokee, parked in plain view of the road, in order to get to where the body was found?"

"I suppose so. I hadn't thought of that."

"But you didn't see another vehicle pass?"

"No. We were out of sight of the road almost the whole time."

"And if the shot you heard from up the road ..."

"I just heard a shot. I couldn't tell where it came from."

"Let me follow the hypothesis, Mr. Akers. If the shot came from the crime scene, and it was the shot that killed Jessica, the person who fired it would have had to come back right past you, is that correct?"

"I don't know the back roads that well, but ..."

"Come on, Diane. It's the only way out," Chris said.

"So," Diane continued, "Did you see or hear anything after the shot?"

"Nothing."

"You didn't hear a car engine? See any lights behind you as you were driving back."

"Nothing, sorry."

"Hmm."

"Look," I said, my irritation boiling over. "I flew into the airport a little before noon. You can confirm that through my flight log and airport records. That's the first time I've ever been in this county in my life. How many serial killers fly into a strange town, where they stand out as strangers, and abduct someone before they've been around even a few hours. Does that seem likely to you? And bear in mind that I was in the Bay Area when the other women disappeared."

She didn't say anything for just long enough to get my skin crawling a bit.

"I didn't say you were a *likely* suspect, Mr. Akers. I said you were a *possible* suspect. And I'm just doing my job in Mirandizing you. Is there anything at all you can tell us? The slightest detail or sensation from that night? Anything?"

"Just that I heard the shot and Gordon didn't, and that I was hungry and wanted to get to dinner. We left within a minute of the shot."

"All right. I guess that'll do it for now. How long are you going to be in the area?"

"Through Saturday night."

"And you're staying at the Danube?"

"The whole time."

"Then we know where to find you. Thank you for your time, Mr. Akers. You can go now."

I got up and walked to the door, but before leaving, decided to get in the last word.

"Call me any time," I said. "I'll do anything I can to help, even if you think I'm a person of interest."

BONE WEARY AND BRAIN WEARY, Gordon slouched through the front door of the Danube. Walking across the lobby, he looked into the bar, where Elizabeth had said she'd be. She was sitting by herself on a barstool, halfway down the bar. He watched her as she lifted a clear, carbonated beverage to her lips and turned her head toward the door. Their eyes met, and he nodded as he walked in.

The only other customer was a man in his fifties with long gray hair under a Vietnam Veteran cap and an unkempt salt and pepper beard. He and the bartender were at one end of the bar, watching the Sunday Night Football game, leaving Gordon and Elizabeth essentially alone.

"Good to have you here," she said. "There's something depressing about a single woman sitting alone at a deserted bar on a Sunday night in a small town. It seems so desperate, don't you think?"

"You don't look desperate to me."

She nodded. "Rough day?"

"I've had worse, but, yeah, it was a rough day."

"Where's your amigo?"

"Sam? He was off to the sheriff to go over what he heard the other night. He's probably tired of talking about it by now."

"The horror is still sinking in. It's real now. I mean, it was always real in that we were pretty sure they'd been abducted. Now there isn't even that sliver of hope that we were wrong and they might be OK."

"Doesn't look like it."

There was a commercial timeout in the football game, and the bartender walked over with a slight limp.

"What can I get you?"

"Just a beer," Gordon said.

"Budweiser or Coors?"

"Bud."

The bartender turned to a small refrigerator behind him, took out two bottles of beer, twisted off the tops, and pushed one toward Gordon.

"Glass?"

"Why?"

The bartender shrugged and looked at Elizabeth. "Anything for the lady?"

"I'm fine," she said.

"You can pay later," he said, and walked back to the end of the bar.

"Shall we move to a table?" Gordon asked.

She nodded, and they moved to a circular table as far from the bartender and the other customer as possible. The tables and chairs had been bought more than four decades ago but were serviceable despite their wear and tear. The carpet was worn, but not yet dangerous.

"You must admit," she said, as they sat down, "the place has character."

"Of a certain kind," Gordon said. He took a long pull on his beer, set it on the table, and closed his eyes.

"Bob called me this afternoon," she said

"I was just talking to him myself."

"Did he tell you he was doing a little investigating?"

"It's about all he told me."

"He said he thinks he's onto something that he got from a babe."

"You let him use language like that?"

"It's just Bob being Bob. Anyway, he wanted to talk to me about it tomorrow, right after his show ends at noon."

"I guess I wasn't invited."

"It got me thinking that maybe there's something you can contribute, Gordon. Can you meet me at my office at the college later in the afternoon to talk about it."

"Can you give me a hint about this?"

"I'd rather not until I talk to Bob. It may be all three of us will be there. Sam can come, too, if he likes."

Gordon took another swallow of beer and rubbed his eyes.

"Desperate woman in dive bar issues mysterious invitation. How can I refuse?"

"You'll be doing it for Bob, too."

"All right. I'll ask Sam when he gets back."

"I think he just did."

She was looking over Gordon's shoulder toward the bar entrance, and Gordon turned to see Sam heading in their direction. The grim purposefulness of his stride, in contrast to his usual casual amble, told Gordon his friend was agitated. Sam looked at both of them when he reached the table.

"Am I interrupting something?" he said.

"Not yet," she said.

"You look like you could use one of these," Gordon said, holding up his beer. He saw the bartender heading toward the refrigerator and pointed to his bottle and Sam. "Go get it, and tell him to put it on my tab. How about you, Elizabeth?"

She shook her head. "I'm just having soda with a twist. I have a long drive home."

"You don't live in town?"

"The apartments are too small to give me a place to paint. I found an outbuilding on a ranch a few miles north where I can have a little studio. You should come take a look some time."

"Maybe I will."

Sam returned with his drink.

"I can't believe it," he said. "They read me my rights and they're treating me as a suspect."

"Was it Diane Brinkley who did that?" Elizabeth said. Sam nodded. "Maybe you should cut her some slack. She has a brilliant legal mind, but her diplomatic skills aren't exactly suited to the Foreign Service."

"And you have to admit," Gordon said, "that being so close to the crime scene, we probably look a bit suspicious. Don't worry about it, Sam. I'm sure it'll all work out. And we have an invitation to join Bob and Elizabeth for a discussion about some mysterious matter tomorrow afternoon."

"I thought we were going fishing."

"We can fish all morning. It'll be fine."

They lapsed into a silence that lasted half a minute. Elizabeth finally spoke.

"You know, Sam, I was thinking about what happened to you. It's just the beginning of what's going to be going on in this town now that we know for sure there's a killer on the loose. And it has to be someone in this town or the general area. Someone we all know, someone who seems like a normal member of the community for all intents and purposes. When the shock over the discovery of Jessica's body fades away, all of us in this community are going to be looking sideways at each other, wondering who it is. It's going to be awful."

"I hadn't thought of that," Gordon said, "but you're right. In a big city, even a suburban town, you can always tell yourself it must be some loner you don't even know. Hard to do that here."

She finished her drink and stood up. "And on that note, I'm going to drive seven miles home down a dark, deserted highway so I can get some sleep before my eight o'clock class tomorrow."

"Sweet dreams," Gordon said.

Monday November 10

THEY AWAKENED to the voice of Mountain Bob on the radio; they ate breakfast with the voice of Mountain Bob playing in the background of the Buckhorn Café; and Mountain Bob was giving full throat to the morning news when Gordon and Sam started up the Cherokee to go fishing.

"What's the plan?" asked Sam.

"The Big Hole River flows through another valley about ten miles west," Gordon said. "A dirt road leads to a campground and a long stretch of public access. Sound all right to you?"

"It sounds just fine to me. It'll be good to be fishing again."

The sun had risen but not many people were out and about as they drove through town. Mountain Bob was wrapping up the news with a weather report.

"And we had a beautiful sunrise this morning, but if the weatherman is right, clouds will be moving in later in the day, and we'll have a chance of a shower late afternoon and evening. In fact, our weather friends say that spell of Indian Summer we've been having is over and we're moving into more typical fall weather. Today's high is expected to be 58, and we're looking at steadily cooling temperatures the rest of the week with a serious chance of rain on Thursday and maybe even the first snow of the season on Saturday. So if you get caught without your cold-weather outfit, don't go around saying Mountain Bob didn't tell you.

"And that's the news at seven, brought to you by Nate's Towing and Body Shop. If you run off the road, Nate'll get you back in business. And remember: Nate has thousands of friends, and he met them all by accident."

"Where does he come up with that stuff?" asked Sam.

"He can probably do it in his sleep," Gordon replied. "We're almost at the radio station. Let's wave to him as we go by."

They did, knowing Bob couldn't see them anyway. His patter continued.

"It's 7:06 a.m., just past the top of hour two of Morning Coffee with Mountain Bob. You're listening to Radio KNEP, the voice of the high desert." Again, the coyote howl. "Don't go away, folks. We've got a lot of good music coming up between now and noon, and at eleven, our guest interview will be with Sheriff Chris Huntley, who will tell us in her own words what's going on in the investigation into the murder of Jessica Milland, whose body was found yesterday off a logging road above Powder Creek.

"Just to remind you, Mountain Bob and Radio KNEP are committed to reporting the events that have shattered and horrified our community, and we will continue to do so until the person or persons involved are brought to justice. Along those lines, just between you and me, Mountain Bob has been doing some investigating on his own, involving someone with a famous name, and I'm hoping that later on, I can give the sheriff information that could lead to an arrest. So this could be an eventful day, and you'll hear it all first on Radio KNEP.

"And now for some music. We're going to start things off with Patsy Cline's classic rendition of 'I Fall to Pieces,' and then go to Porter Wagoner, before he teamed up with Dolly Parton, singing 'Green, Green Grass of Home,' a song that, if my investigation is right, someone in this town may be singing before long."

Gordon slammed on the brakes and skidded to a stop in a turnout. He slapped the top of the steering wheel with both hands.

"What's wrong?" Sam asked.

"I'm half tempted to turn around, go back to the radio station, and box Bob's ears," Gordon said. "Last night at dinner he was being cute about it, but he definitely thought he was onto something, though he wouldn't say what. He's putting himself in danger talking like that."

Sam nodded gently, once. "He probably isn't in much danger now, and you'll be seeing him this afternoon. Maybe you can say a word then." They sat for a minute listening to Patsy. "She has a big voice."

"And a great voice. Too bad she died so young. Plane crash."

"Like Buddy Holly."

"You're probably right about Bob. I'll talk to him later. I love the guy, but he can be exasperating."

Gordon pulled back onto the highway as the Wagoner song — about a prison inmate remembering his hometown shortly before his execution — came on. As it wound down to its final notes, Gordon unconsciously leaned slightly toward the radio to hear what Bob would say when he came back on.

Bob said nothing. When the song ended, there was dead silence. At first, Gordon thought Bob may have been momentarily distracted, but as the silence dragged on, second after agonizing second, it became more sinister. Half a minute passed, but it felt like two hours.

"Something's not right," Gordon said.

Another turnout materialized ahead, and Gordon pulled into it. Looking both ways down the deserted highway, he turned the Cherokee around and started back toward the radio station.

I THOUGHT OF TELLING GORDON he was driving too fast, but he was clearly in no mood for the message, and he's never listened to it anyway. At least not when it comes from me. Instead, he got the message from another source when a set of police lights began blinking at us a couple of minutes later.

"Not again," he said. "I won't be able to afford insurance."

Actually, he would, but he caught a break. When he pulled on to the shoulder, the Highway Patrol sedan blew past us.

"You dodged a bullet," I said. "There must be an accident ahead."

"He can't pull me over if I'm behind him," Gordon said, getting back on the highway and obliterating the speed limit again. He doesn't learn.

We were only a few minutes from town, and the CHP vehicle remained in sight most of the way on the straight highway. Near the edge of town, it made a left turn.

"Did he turn into the radio station?" Gordon said.

Apparently so. As we got there, we saw Sandy Steadman getting out of the car. She looked up as Gordon skidded into the parking lot.

"You," she said, as he and I got out, "drive too fast. Next time I'm ticketing your ass."

"Something's not right," Gordon said. The radio had been silent all the way back.

"A couple of other people thought so, too, but they called 911 instead of driving here like lunatics. There's probably a harmless explanation, so follow me in, but don't touch anything."

She opened the front door with a gloved hand and went in. It was nearly 7:20, and apparently no one else was there yet. Aside from our cars and Bob's pickup, the parking lot was deserted. The smell of coffee wafted from a room down the hall.

"Bob!" she shouted.

No answer.

"Bob, are you all right?"

Again, no response.

We followed her down the hallway to the studio door.

"Bob!"

Nothing. She turned the door handle, and it was locked. This wasn't looking good. She turned to Gordon.

"I hear you're good at kicking in doors." She pointed to it.

This door was flimsier than the one at the logging camp, and it gave way on Gordon's first kick. As it flew open, we saw Bob sitting in his seat by the microphone, earphones pulled down so they were around his neck and resting on his shoulders. His eyes were open, and the look on his face was one of bewilderment, or at least that's how I read it. We never got a chance to ask, because the two bullet holes in his torso, right around his heart, had done what they were intended to do. We were looking at a dead man, who just minutes ago had been alive and talking to an audience over an area of hundreds of square miles.

Sandy immediately took charge. "Out," she said crisply, without raising her voice. "Get out in the parking lot and don't go anywhere until I tell you to. This is a crime scene now." She opened the door for us with her gloved hand, in case there were any prints on the knob, but I'm pretty sure she didn't expect the killer to have been so sloppy.

Once we were outside, I could see that Gordon's face was drained of color. He was as shaken as I've ever seen him, and I probably wasn't much better myself. Up until a couple of years ago, I'd lived a quiet, upper-middle class life where violence just didn't figure in. I reacted to this with my stomach. I didn't throw up, but my insides were in a knot. Bob made the third murder victim I've encountered on a fishing trip with Gordon, and that's a habit I'd like to break.

Within minutes, the radio station parking lot was full of law enforcement vehicles, plus a fire department paramedic truck and an ambulance, not that there was anything to be done medically. The sheriff was one of the first ones there, beating Howard to the scene by a couple of minutes. She immediately took charge, and no one questioned her, though there were one or two times when it looked as if Howard wanted to.

It wasn't yet eight o'clock, and the temperature was in the 30s. Even with our heavy jackets, Gordon and I were cold. We stood by his Cherokee, watching the action unfold and staying out of the way like good citizens. Eventually Gordon pulled himself together enough to talk.

"There are two things about this that bother me," he said.

I nodded, and he kept going.

"The first one is Bob's gun. Remember how he told us Saturday night that he keeps a gun in his drawer just in case. I wonder if it's still there?"

"Maybe he knew his killer and didn't feel threatened."

Gordon thought about that for a moment.

"That makes sense, Sam. The only problem is it doesn't help much. If he knew his killer, that pretty much includes the entire population of Plateau County."

"Maybe he was surprised."

"Maybe, but I don't think so. Bob spent as much time in that studio as he did in his house. I don't think it would be easy to sneak up on him. And in the few seconds we were there, I noticed something I didn't see when I was on his show last Friday."

I nodded.

"Let me show you," he said. We walked across the parking lot and turned to look at the building. "See that window there?" he pointed.

"Yeah."

"Now turn around."

I did, and right away I got his point. Behind us was the entry to the parking lot, in a direct line with the window.

"The window was behind me when I was on his show, but he had a clear view out of it. He could see anyone pulling up to the station."

"If he was looking."

"Bob was always looking. He didn't miss much. And that leads to another question. He'd just been on the air talking about how he might have information that could lead to an arrest. It was reckless of him to say that, but he wouldn't have said it unless he knew who was going to be arrested. And therefore who might want to stop him. And yet, there's a pretty good chance he saw his killer in the parking lot and no red flag went up. What's with that?"

I didn't have an answer, so I didn't say anything. It was almost a minute later before he spoke again.

"The second thing is that he kept a pen and writing pad on the desk next to him. That I did see last Friday. He was writing down notes to himself in some sort of shorthand that made sense to him, but not necessarily anyone else. Don't ask me why, but I noticed the pad was there when we were shooed out. If Bob was working on leads, there just might be something on that pad. And the killer had to be acting super fast and might not have realized it was important."

"We can hope so," I said.

AN HOUR LATER, with the crime scene properly photographed, and a physician having pronounced Bob officially dead, the body was wheeled out to the ambulance and driven to the morgue. The entire parking lot was surrounded by tape, and two uniformed deputies were stationed at the door. The sheriff came out not long after the gurney carrying Bob, looked around the parking lot, and went straight for Gordon and Sam.

"Interesting, isn't it," she said, "how you two always seem to be in the vicinity when somebody gets shot."

Gordon started to say something, but realized there was no good answer and stopped himself.

"Officer Steadman said she followed you part of the way here. If Bob was shot during Porter Wagoner, you probably have an alibi, but if it happened early in Patsy Cline, you could still be a suspect. Do you own a gun, Gordon?"

"No. I don't like 'em."

"I wouldn't cop to that around here if I were you. What about you, Akers?"

"Me neither."

"I believe you, for whatever it's worth, but I need to verify. Do I have your permission to search the vehicle, Gordon, or are you going to make me wait around for a warrant."

"Go right ahead," he said.

"Akers, you all right if we check any of your possessions in there?"

"I've got nothing to hide," he said.

"Is that a yes?"

"It's a yes."

She brought over one of the deputies from the front door and had them repeat their consent in front of him. He looked like he was barely 21, with carrot-colored hair no more than three-eighths of an inch long. He gave the Cherokee a thorough going-over, even looking under the hood, and found no gun, or anything else of interest.

"All right," she said, after the deputy had left. "I need to have a word with you in my office, Gordon. Be there at one o'clock."

"Me, too?" Sam asked.

"Just Gordon. We raked you over the coals yesterday. Now it's his turn. One o'clock."

"I'll be there," Gordon said. She turned to walk away, and he called after her.

"What?"

"Has Brenda been notified yet?"

Chris nodded. "I was going to do it myself, but Officer Steadman pointed out, correctly, that people were already calling in about the dead air on the radio and that time was of the essence. She offered to do it, and I let her."

Gordon nodded, and as she walked off, he turned to Sam.

"Then I have a social obligation. It's ten thirty, so there's enough time for me to pay a call at Bob's house and do what I can to comfort the widow. Though I don't see how. Want to join me?"

"Count me in," said Sam.

SO MANY CARS WERE PARKED near Bob's house that Gordon and Sam had to park a block away. Brenda had come straight home after being told, and even though the radio station was off the air, the small-town grapevine had spread the news. The front door was open, and two dozen people, mostly women, were in the living room, where Brenda was sitting in the middle of the couch. Coffee was being made by the gallon in the kitchen, and plates of cookies and pastries, brought by the visitors, were set out.

Brenda was surrounded by a half-dozen people offering condolences and support, but, edging toward her patiently, Gordon and Sam finally got near the couch. When she saw Gordon, she stood up, opening her arms for a hug, which he delivered awkwardly.

"I'm sorry," he said, murmuring in her ear. "I wish I knew what to say."

"You're saying something by being here, Gordon. That's enough. There aren't any right words for something like this."

A gray-haired woman materialized next to Gordon with a mug of coffee, and Brenda sat down on the couch, patting the cushion to her left.

"Sit with me for a minute, Gordon." She looked up. "And thanks for coming, Sam."

Gordon took a seat and made a slight head gesture to Sam to leave them alone. Sam took the hint. Brenda picked up a half-full cup of coffee and took a swallow.

"I haven't cried yet," she said softly. "I guess that'll come later, but right now, I think I'm still in denial."

"I'm pretty stunned myself."

"The Highway Patrol officer said you were with her when Bob was found." He nodded. "I'm sorry you had to see that, but can you tell me what he looked like?" Gordon flinched. "Not the wounds and the blood, I mean, but how did his face look? Peaceful? Angry?"

Gordon thought for a minute, feeling there had never been such a need to get the words right.

"My impression," he finally said, "is that he looked surprised. Almost as if he was expecting a friend and suddenly found himself staring down the wrong end of a gun."

"That has to be what happened, don't you think?"

"I don't know, but it makes sense. He was shot while two songs were playing on the air, and just before they started, he said he had some information about the crime."

"Oh, Bob," she said softly.

"He hinted at that when I had coffee with him last night. Did he say anything to you?"

"He didn't, but he was in one of his moods. I've seen it before. It's like, I know something you don't, and I can hardly wait to surprise you with maximum impact."

"But he didn't say what it was?"

"He never does in that situation. He likes — liked — knowing something that wasn't supposed to get out. He was like a little boy about that. It was one of the things I loved about him."

"I'm sure the sheriff will be asking you."

"And I wish I had more to tell her."

For a minute or two they sat quietly. The initial crush of visitors was dwindling, though others would no doubt be coming throughout the day. For better or worse, Brenda would not be alone with her thoughts for several hours, but at some point later in the day, she would be left to confront the new darkness in her life.

"Brenda," he finally said, "I'm not just saying this. I really mean it. But is there anything I can do? Anything at all?"

"I'll tell you what," she said, after a long pause. "You can go fishing tomorrow. It's what Bob would have wanted, and I think there's a chance he just might be there with you in spirit. Yes, go fishing and think of Bob. That's the best thing. Promise me you'll do that?"

"I promise."

They drank more coffee, and then Brenda sat down her cup and let out a choked, one-syllable laugh, in which the "ha" sounded more like a "huh."

"What?" said Gordon.

"I just thought of something, and when I did, I thought about how Bob would have enjoyed the irony.

"Here we are in the middle of the biggest story to hit this town in ages, and the only man who could tell it right isn't around to cover it."

And, finally, the tears came.

IT WAS CLOUDING OVER, and there was a damp chill in the air as Gordon walked up the courthouse steps. He paused at the top to look at the clouds, and his cell phone rang. It was a number in the local area code, and he answered.

"It's Elizabeth," the caller said. "I take it you heard about Bob."

"Worse than that. I was there when he was found."

"Oh my God. That's awful." She said no more for a minute. "I was calling to remind you that we were going to get together this afternoon, but if you'd rather not, under the circumstances ..."

"Actually, I think I would. Right now I want to stay as busy as possible. I'm trying to put off the moment when I'm left alone to think about it."

"I don't blame you. Can you meet me at the college?"

"Sure."

"My office is on the second floor of the English building, Room 247. I have office hours until 3:30, but we can meet then."

"Sam and I will be there."

"Oh, no. Was he with you when …"

"Yep."

"At times like this, I wish I kept a bottle of scotch in my desk drawer, but the school authorities frown on it. We'll have to settle for coffee, but I'll see that it's fresh."

"Whatever. I have an appointment with the sheriff in three minutes."

"Go, then. See you at 3:30." She rang off.

At the sheriff's office, Gordon was taken straight to Chris's corner sanctum. She and Diane Brinkley were seated at a round table in one corner, and she motioned for Gordon to take one of the two remaining seats at it. The sheriff was wearing her khaki uniform with crisply pleated trousers. The district attorney was wearing a maroon blouse and a blue-green pleated skirt that looked as if it might be part of a parochial school uniform. Gordon took the seat closer to Chris.

"For starters," the sheriff said, "you're in the clear on Jessica Milland's murder. You can tell your friend when you see him."

"To what do we owe the pleasure?"

"Dumb luck. It turns out a Forest Service ranger was doing an end-of-season check on all their campgrounds last Thursday. She was at Powder Creek at 3:45 p.m., which is about the time Jessica disappeared, and after looking it over, she wrote down the license number of your car. In case they found the campground vandalized later."

"Sam will be glad to hear that."

"Came in this morning while I was at the radio station. But moving along, I wanted to have a word with you about Bob. He's an old friend, I know, and you've spent a lot of time with him the past few days. Is there anything he said that might put us on a line of questioning?"

"I don't know. Could you be a bit more specific?"

Diane leaned forward. "We're looking for two things, Mr. Gordon. First of all, leads that might result in an arrest, but also information that will provide evidence in court. I have an investigator who can help the sheriff, who is, obviously, stretched pretty thin right now. We have two separate murder investigations, which may or may not be connected, and a serious rape allegation that probably isn't going to get the attention it deserves because of the murders. At the moment, there are no leads, so the sheriff will be going through time-consuming routine investigations that may serve only to rule out possibilities. Any information that might get us forward a bit faster would be welcome."

"I'll tell you what I know, but it's not much," Gordon said. "Bob was really upset about the rape case, I think because of his daughters. He was helping a couple of people look into it ..."

"Their names wouldn't be Steadman and Macondray, by any chance?" asked Chris.

Gordon nodded. "But I didn't get the sense they really had anything."

Diane shook her head. "I don't see how that case would have gotten Bob killed. The people involved would slug it out with lawyers, not bullets, and that's assuming we had something, which we don't."

"I agree," Chris said. "Bob's murder was a bold act by a cool customer. The profile's a better fit with our serial killer than the families of some kids who might be in trouble."

"If you don't mind my asking," Gordon said, "did anyone see anything? The killer must have been parked at the radio station for at least a few minutes."

"So far, we've had three calls from people who claim they saw a car parked at the radio station that time this morning. The problem is one saw a red pickup, which would probably be Bob's car, one saw a white sedan, and one saw a black SUV. No plates, no driver ID — nothing. It's looking like a dead end."

"All right," Gordon said. "One other thing that I know is that Bob met with somebody yesterday afternoon at the college. He didn't say who and he was putting on like he might really have something. And, frankly, after all we went through yesterday, I was in no mood to play along with him."

"Do you have any idea," Diane said, "even a guess, as to whom he might have met with?"

"None whatsoever. Sorry. I wish I could help more."

Chris and Diane looked at each other as if it were time to end the interview. Gordon pressed on.

"Could I ask a question or two?"

"Sure," said Chris. "The jackals from the Sacramento TV stations are calling for interviews this afternoon. I thought I was done with them for good, but a little practice wouldn't hurt."

"What, exactly, are you looking into?"

"Well, from all accounts Jessica was a smart and sensible young woman, and she certainly knew about the other two students who disappeared. She wouldn't have taken a ride from just anyone. So we're looking at people at the college she might have trusted, and particularly faculty."

"Why faculty and not staff?"

"Because staff work until five o'clock, but faculty often leave early."

"Makes sense. Then my second question is, when I was on Bob's show last Friday, he had a note pad in front of him that he wrote things down on. I thought I saw one on his desk when we looked in today, but it happened pretty fast. Did you find one?"

"I'd like to see it, too," said Brinkley.

"All right." Chris left the room for a moment and returned with a baggie holding a five-by-eight note pad. She set it face up on the desk between the prosecutor and Gordon. There was a drop of blood in the upper right corner and a list of five items that read:

SBYM - TW
Time - :30
Geiser - Wed
DS - Gurgle
Wheaties

"Looks like messages in his own shorthand and the beginning of a grocery list," Diane finally said. "I don't see that it gets us anywhere."

"Isn't the football coach named Geiser?" Gordon asked.

"Lloyd Geiser," Chris said.

"Then that probably means he was going to ask Geiser to be a guest on his show on Wednesday."

"Good deduction, Sherlock," Diane said, "but I still don't see that it gets us anywhere. Anything else make sense to you?"

Gordon squinted at the paper. "No," he finally said, "but would it be all right if I copied this down so I could think about it later?"

The women looked at each other. Diane nodded ever so slightly.

"All right," Chris said, "but only on the condition that you don't share it with anyone else and if you have a brain flash about it, you'll call me directly."

"Understood." He took a small notebook from his shirt pocket and copied the list on to it. As soon as he had finished, Chris pulled the baggie toward her and turned it over.

"One last question, then, and I'll go," Gordon said. "Bob told me Saturday night that he kept a gun in his desk drawer for self-defense. Is that what he was shot with?"

"So that's what it was for," said Chris. "No, it was in the drawer untouched and unfired."

"So having it there didn't do him any good."

"It almost never does. Don't get me started on guns for self defense. Yeah, occasionally someone gets lucky and uses one that way, but there's a good reason it hardly ever happens."

"You're not going to say that in your campaign," Diane said.

"I'm not stupid, Diane. Look, people have the right to buy a gun for self-defense, and if they do, God bless 'em and good luck to 'em. Good luck because it almost never helps. The critical problem with having a gun for self defense is that it does you no good unless the criminal is dumb enough to let you get to it. Now criminals are dumb, God bless 'em. If they weren't we wouldn't catch 'em. But not many are *that* dumb. Bob's killer sure wasn't, and it looks like Bob never had a chance."

IT WAS STARTING TO RAIN as we drove onto the campus of Homestead Community College. It was a slow drizzle of a rain — the kind that, when you're fishing, you figure you can work through. That is, until the steady accumulation of all those small drops begins to form bigger drops that roll off the back of your hat brim and trickle down the back of your shirt. It was cold, too. The clock on the bank as we left town said 50 degrees, but when we found the English building and got out of the car, it felt ten degrees colder.

Gordon decided to make a run for it without a hat, but I was more circumspect, putting a cap over my thinning hair before jogging across the parking lot to the building. There was a staircase just inside the door when we entered, and we took it to the second floor, where we quickly found Room 247. My watch said 3:35, which made us five minutes fashionably late.

Not that it mattered. Elizabeth Macondray's door was open, and she was inside with a female student, working the kid through the problems with the paper she'd turned in. Gordon and I sat down on a bench near the door, out of sight.

There wasn't much to do but eavesdrop on the discussion, so of course I did. Within a few minutes, it became obvious that, even though office hours had ended, the student wasn't going away any time soon. I started to get irritated about having my time wasted, but as the minutes dragged on like hours, with nothing to do but keep eavesdropping, I found myself having a change of heart.

As I listened to the conversation between Elizabeth and Karen (the student), it became obvious that I was hearing something special. Some real teaching and learning was going on in that tiny office. I'm no writer — anything more than a simple business memo is a challenge for me — but even so, I could tell, as Elizabeth dissected Karen's paper sentence by sentence, that she had an eye for the problems and was communicating them effectively. And since I'm pretty sure she wasn't getting paid overtime, she was showing a professional dedication and competence that had to be respected.

Gordon, meanwhile, was sitting silently with his hands folded over his stomach, head back and eyes closed. I call it his meditating Buddha look, and it seems to drive women wild. They think it's mysterious and profound, when most of the time he's just taking a catnap.

Finally at 4:25, Karen left the office, and I wondered if she appreciated the value of the attention she just got. Elizabeth looked tired as she invited us in.

"Sorry," she said. "I lost track of the time. It happens sometimes when a student really needs help."

"That's all right," Gordon said.

She looked at us cautiously.

"Do they have any leads on who shot Bob?" she finally said.

"It sounds as if they have nothing," Gordon said.

"Did you hear what he said before he went off the air?"

"On the car radio as we were heading out of town."

"I heard it driving to the college. What was your take on it?"

"I was upset. I thought he was being a show-off and maybe putting himself in danger."

"No, what was your take on what it *meant?*"

Gordon looked puzzled. "Well, I figured he had a lead on Jessica's killer, of course."

She said nothing for a moment, then very softly, "I don't think so."

"What do you mean?" I asked. "What else could it be?"

"You're forgetting, Sam, that there are two crimes being investigated here: the disappearing students and the rape of Alicia. I think Bob had something in the rape case."

What makes you say so?"

"You've known Bob longer than I have, so let me run this by you. I don't think Bob would know where to begin in the serial killer case. The mentality of that sort of crime isn't something he could wrap his head around. It's too foreign to him. To almost anybody, really. Plus he'd arranged to meet with somebody before the body was found.

"Alicia's rape, on the other hand, really bothered him in a personal way. He has daughters and he could imagine something like that happening to them. And he and I were working on it together. Plus there was his remark about getting information from a babe. My guess is that he got one of the girls at the party to talk, or to think about talking. I'll bet that's who he was meeting on campus yesterday, when almost no one is around. It would be a discreet place for a delicate meeting."

"But who would it be? Everybody in town knew him, and even in a small town, that's a big pool of possibilities."

"I know. I'm stumped. I was hoping he might have said something to you. That's why I asked you here."

Several minutes of silence ensued, during which a thought crossed my mind. I wasn't sure whether or not it was a good idea, but the quiet was getting to me, and I finally blurted it out.

"He taught a class here, didn"t he? Maybe he was talking to one of the students in his class."

"That's an inspired idea, Sam," she said, and I have to admit I blushed. "A lot of high school students take an extra class at the college, and Bob's was in the afternoon, when they can easily get out of school to get here."

"It's a good beginning, anyway," Gordon said. "Is there any way to get a list of who's in his class?"

"I can get it from the registrar, but the office is almost closed. We may have to wait until tomorrow."

"It's not closed tomorrow?"

"What? Oh, Veterans Day. I forgot. Shit." She opened a desk drawer and took out a spiral-bound campus directory, flipped quickly through the pages, picked up the phone and dialed a four-digit extension. It seemed like the phone was ringing a long time on the other end, and I was resigning myself to waiting until Wednesday to see if my idea would come to anything.

"Zoe?" she said. "Elizabeth Macondray in English. I need to get a class list today. Is there any way you can do that for me? (Pause) Of course I know who's in my class. It's another one I need. Pretty please? (Pause) Thank you so much, Zoe. I owe you one. It's Bob Hastings' Fundamentals of Radio class for this quarter. I know you close in ten minutes. I can be there in seven. Bye."

She hung up. "Let's go," she said. "There's not much time." She grabbed her purse and a pile of student papers and headed out the door. We followed her out and down the stairs, where she stopped by the entrance to the building. The rain was falling even harder, and with the cloud cover, it was almost dark. The lights were on in the parking lot.

"We may be onto something. Shall we keep it going? I've got three-quarters of a pan of leftover lasagna at home that's even better the second day. Would you guys like to come over for dinner and go over the class list afterward?"

"Sure," Gordon said, without hesitation.

"I don't know," I said after a brief pause. "We're going fishing tomorrow and I need to tie some flies before then. I think I'll pass and get the report from Gordon."

"All right," she said. "My margin's two minutes now. See you later."

"But I don't know where you live," Gordon said.

"I'll call with directions."

And with that, she took off, running gracefully across the parking lot. Gordon watched her until she rounded the corner of another building and was out of sight. He turned and gave me a funny look without saying anything.

I'm guessing the funny look was because he knows I've never tied a trout fly in my life and always buy them at the shop.

BEFORE HEADING OUT to Elizabeth's place, Gordon stopped at Al's Wine and Spirits on Chaparral Boulevard and selected a serviceable Napa Valley Cabernet to go with the lasagna. Judging from the layer of dust on the bottle, Al did a better trade in spirits than in wine, but he cheerfully wiped the bottle clean before bagging it.

Once Gordon was out of town, the darkness and solitude of the highway became absolute. Her place, she had said, was on the Nuñes Ranch, a few miles past

Homestead College. In that stretch of road, he counted three cars coming the other direction and had no one in front of or behind him the entire way. The rain took the form of sporadic light showers, and the roadway was wet, glistening in the bright headlights.

Fortunately the ranch was marked with a large sign. Gordon turned right into a driveway and followed a gravel road flanked by white fences on either side for a quarter mile. He drove over a cattle guard, and shortly afterward the road forked. He could see the main ranch house to the right and a smaller outbuilding to the left. He took the left fork as directed and was soon at a wood building, painted white, with a Subaru Legacy station wagon, dark green, parked in front. He parked next to it and got out.

The rain had stopped for a moment, and it was cold enough that he could see his breath. He smelled smoke from a wood fire and heard the sound of frogs croaking from wherever they were nearby. She welcomed him into the house, which was bright, warm and cheerful. A wood stove with a glass front burned in one corner, with two chairs and a small couch facing it. There was a full kitchen, with a round table that seated four. On the walls were several paintings and photographs in an eclectic range of styles. The photographs included black and white cityscapes, portraits, and full-color landscapes with the colors muted and subtle. The paintings ranged from abstract color jumbles to landscapes and portraits. All in all, the assemblage of art on the walls reflected a broad, open-minded aesthetic sense.

"Nice place," Gordon said.

"It was a find."

He looked around, slightly puzzled.

"Anything wrong?" she asked.

"No, just that it looked bigger from the outside."

"That's because you're not seeing the studio. Over here."

She motioned him to the door on the wall to the left of the front entrance, and they went through it into a 15-by-20-foot space with a skylight. Several easels stood against one of the long walls, each with a canvas on it, covered by cloth.

"My works in progress," she said.

"Can I get a sneak preview?"

"No deal, Gordon. Asking an artist to show her work before it's done is like asking a woman to drop her panties when you've known her only five minutes. You need to wait."

"Sorry."

"Well, I didn't say never. I just said not now. Let's open that bottle of wine you brought. Dinner should be ready in 15 minutes."

She served the lasagna with a salad and store-bought French bread, and it was a satisfying meal. They talked easily before and during it. She inquired gently about his family and work history, and he learned how she had ended up at Homestead College but really wanted to get back to Los Angeles or San Francisco. If she taught elementary or high school, she could have landed a job anywhere, but tenure-track community college positions were hard to find. When they had finished eating and cleaning the few dishes, she suggested they move over by the wood stove.

"Would you like another glass of wine?"

He shook his head. "I have to drive back."

"If you say so."

Elizabeth sat in one of the chairs, and he sat at the edge of the couch next to it. She was holding a manila file folder.

"I barely got there in time to get the class list," she said, "but I'm not sure if it was worth the soaking. Only a third of Bob's class was female, and I don't see any likely candidates for 'the babe.' You want to see?"

"Of course."

He looked it over, running his forefinger down the list of names. Halfway through, he paused and tapped the paper, then kept going. When he finished, he moved his finger back to where it had previously stopped and stared at the page for several seconds before turning the sheet over on his lap.

"Let me ask you a question," he said. "When you first told me about this, you said Bob had been talking to '*a* babe.' Just now, you said, '*the* babe.' Are you sure Bob didn't say '*the* babe,' too?"

"He might have, but why would it matter?"

"We know Bob had a fondness for assigning silly names to people, right? Like Flyboy because I'm a fly fisherman. Well, there's a name here that might go with *the* babe, but I'm not sure, and I'd have to look something up." He got up and began pacing. "How could I find out at this time of night?" He paced for another half-minute. "My sister. It's worth a try."

He took out his Nokia cell phone, scrolled to a number on the directory and dialed it.

"Come on, Donna. Be there."

A woman's voice answered after the third ring.

"Donna, it's me."

"What do you want, Gordon?"

"What makes you think I want something?"

"You never call unless you do."

"Come on, now. That's not fair." A long pause. "But I *was* wondering if you could look something up for me."

"Aha! All right, but tit for tat."

"What's the tat?"

"I'll tell you later. What do you want me to look up?"

"Remember that baseball encyclopedia you gave Steve a few years ago? The one that lists everybody who ever played in the Major Leagues? Can you look up a name for me?"

"Are you sure he's in there?"

"He's in the Hall of Fame, so he'd better be."

"All right, hold on while I go fetch the book. I thought you were on a fishing trip now."

"I am."

"How's the fishing?"

"I haven't been doing much the last couple of days."

"I see."

"It's not what you think."

"All right, here's the book."

"The players are listed in alphabetical order, so it should be easy. Go to Harry Hooper."

"Just a minute." He could hear the sound of pages turning. "Got it. What do you need?"

"Just tell me which teams he played for and when?"

"OK. It looks like he played for the Boston Red Sox from 1909 to 1921 — no, wait. 1920."

"That's it. Thank you."

"Not so fast, Gordon. We haven't got to tat yet."

"Whatever it is. I owe you one."

"Steve and I are trying to do a weekend getaway before Christmas, December fifth and sixth, and Aaron and Claudia need to be taken care of. I assume you're free then. Or could arrange to be."

"As far as I know."

"Consider it done. We'll make the reservations and I'll let you know when you get back."

Gordon turned to Elizabeth after ending the call. "I might just have it."

"Harry Hooper," she said. 'That sounds familiar."

"He was a Hall of Fame shortstop for the Boston Red Sox, and more importantly, he played with them when they had another famous player on the roster. Babe Ruth. 'The Babe.' It's the kind of quirky nickname Bob would have come up with, and given that a certain Harry Hooper of Alta Mira was both in Bob's radio class and on the football team, I'd say he moves to the head of the list of people we might want to talk to."

THERE WAS A PHONE NUMBER for Hooper, and all the other students, on the class list. After some discussion, they decided that Elizabeth would call him in the morning and try to get him to campus for an interview Tuesday afternoon, when, owing to the holiday, few people would be around.

They talked for another hour, touching on several subjects in a relaxed fashion. Gordon was enjoying the warmth and coziness of the place, especially when a squall hit from time to time, and they could hear the rain hitting the roof. Shortly after nine, he decided it was time to go. They walked to the door together, and just as he opened it, the rain began to fall again, heavily. They stood in the doorway together, feeling the warmth of the woodstove behind them and the moist coolness of the wind and the rain in front of them. The porch light was just bright enough for them to see the large drops falling, and they watched for a moment.

Gordon turned to Elizabeth.

"It's pretty lonely out here," he said. "Do you ever worry about your safety?"

"Are you offering to stay here and protect me tonight?"

"That wasn't what I was thinking, but ..."

"Because I don't need to be protected. Let me show you something."

She closed the door and walked back to a small desk against a wall. It had three drawers down the right side; she opened one and removed a 9mm pistol, checking it to make sure the safety was set. She carried it to the table on which they'd eaten dinner and set it down.

"The single woman's best friend," she said. "I bought it not long after I came here."

"How's your aim?"

"Pretty damn good, since you ask. I take it to the range and practice almost every weekend. Actually, I was pleasantly surprised by how much I enjoy shooting it."

"I was talking to the sheriff this morning," Gordon said. "She's of the opinion that having a gun for self-defense doesn't help much because the bad guys rarely give you a chance to use it."

"I don't know about that. What I do know is that I want *some* protection. All it has to do is help me once, you know."

Gordon shrugged. She took the gun back to the desk drawer, and they walked to the front door again.

The rain had eased up considerably, and Gordon was about to make a sprint for the Cherokee, when she said his name.

"Yes," he said.

"I've shared one of my secrets with you. The gun. Now you need to tell me one of yours."

"I don't know. I'm pretty close with my secrets."

"Well, I'll ask anyway, because I'm dying to know."

There was a moment of expectant silence.

"How did you get your name?" she asked.

"My father's last name was Gordon."

"Get serious. Your first name."

"Oh, that. Pretty straightforward, I'm afraid. My mother's maiden name was Quillan, and she wanted to give her son the family name. But my father pointed out that Quillan Gordon would be too many 'un' sounds in one name, so they made it Quill."

"And he didn't know about the Quill Gordon trout fly?"

"Not until later, and by then the damage was done."

"I wish I hadn't asked. I'd much rather believe you were named for the trout fly. It's more exotic somehow."

"Sorry to disappoint."

"If it makes you feel any better, that's not even in the top ten disappointments I've suffered at the hands of men.

He said nothing.

"The rain's stopped, if you want to go."

Gordon made it to the Cherokee without getting wet.

Tuesday November 11

THE WEATHER FRONT passed through the area overnight, favoring the people of Alta Mira with a brilliant sunrise in a sky washed clean by the rains. Gordon and Sam watched it from the Rodeo Café, two miles south of town near a grandstand where, unsurprisingly, spectators could view the Sheriff's Posse Rodeo every August.

The parking area in front of the café was a large open area where several pickup trucks and big rigs parked higgledy-piggledy. Faded paintings of rodeo scenes decorated the wormwood walls inside, and faded red-checked plastic-covered tablecloths covered the tables. The coffee was terrible, but the food was decent.

Gordon and Sam ate in silence, eavesdropping on the conversation at a nearby table. A group of men, apparently locals, were talking about the Jessica Milland murder and what they would like to do to the person responsible if they ever caught him. That blood-curdling discussion eventually wore itself out, and the subject changed to the football game coming up Friday night.

"Gotta like our chances."

"You seen the other team play?"

"Nah, but I hear they can't defend the pass, and we've got the quarterback."

Everyone nodded at this.

"Too bad Mountain Bob won't be there to call the game. Won't be the same without him."

That drew another round of nods and turned the conversation to a blood-curdling description of what they'd do to whoever killed Bob, if they got their hands on him. Gordon thought, as he chewed his food, that if indeed one killer committed both crimes, he should be grateful that he could only die once.

Gordon and Sam emerged into the parking area after breakfast, feeling both well-fed and uneasy. They'd had a reasonably good meal and were going fishing, but would it be enough to take their minds off what they'd seen the last two days?

"It'll be quieter at the lake," Gordon said, giving voice to the sentiment. "I hope there aren't too many people there."

They drove south several miles, turned left on a narrow paved road (which turned to dirt four miles from the highway) and followed it seven miles to Reflection Lake. The rain had wet down the dirt road and filled its depressions with water, but it had been dry enough in preceding weeks that the road was firm and easily passable. The parking area was deserted as they arrived, and when they got out of the Cherokee, the surrounding pines, heavily watered by the rain, practically blasted their scent into the air. It was still and cool, with an occasional breeze adding even more coolness.

A boat ramp went down to the lake from the parking area, and on either side of the ramp were piers extending about 30 feet into the water.

"We're in luck," Gordon said, as they began assembling their gear. "Those piers get you far enough out that you can cast over some nice weed beds. If the fish are feeding, they'll be there."

"Think it's worth trying dry flies?"

Gordon shook his head. "I've seen one fish rise in the last three minutes. They aren't feeding on the surface in any numbers. I'd go with a nymph or streamer, but you could try a dry. Maybe they'd come up if it's there."

"What the heck. I'll try. Easy enough to switch to something else if it isn't working."

Gordon took the pier to the right of the boat ramp and Sam moved toward the one on the left. As Sam walked across the grated steel toward the end of the pier, he hit an icy spot and lost his footing. But he was able to break the fall with his free hand and land on the pier, rather than falling into the icy water.

"Sorry," Gordon shouted across the boat ramp. "I should have warned you. It can be slippery first thing in the morning."

The piers ended with the walkway opening onto an 8-by-8 foot square surface covered with tarpaper and hence less slippery. It was 8:15, and the sun had not completely come over the mountains to the east, leaving half the lake, including the piers, still in shadow. As

Gordon reached the square, he noticed a large rock — the one in Elizabeth's painting — about 200 feet out in the lake. It occurred to him that she must have painted the picture from the pier. He gazed at the rock for several minutes before making his first cast.

He was fishing a Hare's Ear nymph seven feet under an indicator — a painted cork ball three-eighths of an inch thick — floating on the surface of the water. He cast it out about 40 feet and concentrated on the indicator as it slowly drifted back toward the pier. If a fish grabbed the fly below it, the indicator should go down, indicating a strike, but nothing happened on his first two casts. On the third cast, he tried something different.

He cast to a spot about 20 degrees to the right of where the first two casts had been. After allowing 15 to 20 seconds for the fly to sink, he raised his rod and gave it a couple of quick, short twitches, making the fly jerk upward toward the surface, like an emerging insect rising. Almost immediately, he felt the rod jerk back as a fish grabbed the fly. It was a 12-inch Lahontan Cutthroat, brilliant in its fall spawning colors, and he briefly took it out of the water to admire it before letting it go.

For the next hour and a half, using the same technique, he caught and released a dozen fish, ranging in size from six to 14 inches. Most were Rainbows, including the largest, but four of the dozen were Cutthroats, and he appreciated them all the more for their rarity. Sam, having no success with the dry fly, switched to the nymph like Gordon and caught several decent fish himself.

By ten o'clock they were in the sun — not that it was providing much warmth — and Gordon had had enough. Ordinarily, fishing allowed Gordon to leave his cares behind, but after what he'd seen the past two days, no lake was beautiful enough and no fish satisfying enough to have that result. After missing several strikes because his mind was elsewhere, he reeled in his line, walked back to shore, leaned against a pine tree, and looked at Sam and the lake.

When the breeze wasn't blowing, the lake was utterly calm and showed the provenance of its name in the way it reflected the surrounding mountains. The rock in the lake was bright white in the sun, but without much cloud cover to darken the rest of the scenery, it didn't stand out the way it did in Elizabeth's painting. Gordon was looking at it and considering that circumstance when he realized Sam had walked up to him without being noticed.

"You all right?" Sam said.

"Not all right, but OK. I can't get my mind entirely on the fishing. Would you mind if we packed it up early?"

"Sure," said Sam after a slight hesitation. Then he laughed.

"What's so funny?"

"I was just thinking. In all the years we've been fishing together, this is the first time you've wanted to quit before I did."

IT WAS PRETTY CLEAR that the equilibrium of our trip has been upset, that Gordon is badly rattled by Bob's murder and is still trying to figure out how to handle it. Ordinarily, when he's bothered or agitated, he tries to work his way through it by keeping himself really busy or doing something to take his mind off it. He doesn't want to confront his feelings about it. The fact that he walked away from good fishing after only an hour and a half is a sign that his usual approach isn't getting the job done, and I suppose he's going to deal with it by trying to help catch Bob's killer.

And then there's the issue of our teacher-painter friend. I figured yesterday that keeping her away from him had become a lost cause, which is why I stepped aside so they could have a cozy dinner together. I must admit I was surprised when Gordon got back to the hotel before ten o'clock. I can only conclude she wasn't really trying.

As soon as we got back to town, Gordon pulled over at the first place he could and took out his phone. There had been no reception at the lake, and now he saw that he had missed a call from Miss M. He listened to the message and turned to me.

"She got hold of Hooper, and he's coming to her office at 1:30. She wants us to be there. You in?"

I nodded. He'd filled me in on his hunch last night, and following up on it seemed more interesting than killing time in Alta Mira on a holiday, when half the businesses were closed.

As we drove into the heart of town, we saw a cluster of people gathered on Third Street, where it met Chaparral Boulevard. There were a lot of American flags, and several people were in military uniform.

"The Veterans Day parade," Gordon said. "Bob mentioned it to me Sunday night, but I'd forgotten all about it." He looked at his watch. "It's 10:53. They'll be starting at 11 o'clock, the time of the Armistice in World War I. What do you say we check it out?"

"Sure," I said.

Gordon turned right onto Fourth Street, drove down half a block, and parked at the curb in front of a house. We hopped out, walked to the next street over, and cut down to Third Street.

I was surprised by what I saw when we got there. There must have been at least a thousand people lining the street on both sides for the two blocks between Chaparral Boulevard and the courthouse. A lot of them were waving small American flags, and several cars along the way were decorated in red-white-and-blue bunting.

At exactly eleven o'clock, a lone bugle began playing "Taps" down by Chaparral Boulevard, and when it finished, the American Legion Marching band, eight members strong, broke into John Philip Sousa's "Washington Post March" and began marching up Third Street toward the courthouse. Behind them walked the veterans of Plateau County. A couple of them could still fit into their service uniforms, but most just wore their military hats and tried to stand as tall as they could. There were 60 to 75 of them all told. The Vietnam veteran from the bar Sunday night was in the parade, and so was the bartender, walking with his limp. Korea, I guessed, going by how old he looked. There were several veterans who must have been from World War II, some of them walking with canes. As they passed by, the crowd cheered lustily, and when the last veteran had passed, the people lining the street moved onto it and followed the veterans to the courthouse. The band switched to "The Battle Hymn of the Republic" halfway through, and that took them to the courthouse steps.

A lectern with a microphone had been set up at the top of the stairs. On either side of it were several men in coats and ties, and on the far side, to the left from where we stood, was an ancient man in a wheelchair, wearing large eyeglasses and a doughboy hat. He was later introduced as the county's lone surviving veteran of World War I, and as he waved to the applause, I couldn't help feeling that he knew this was the last time he'd be hearing it.

Three people gave brief speeches thanking the veterans for what they had done: someone from the American Legion, the chairman of the Board of Supervisors, and a State Senator whose name sounded like Sturges. Then one of the World War II veterans from the parade walked up the courthouse steps with the help of a cane and read a list of names of men (and two women) from Plateau County who had gone off to serve and never returned. A minister from the Baptist Church said a brief prayer, the band played "The Star-Spangled Banner," and it was over. I looked at my watch for the first time since it started, and it said 11:38.

I'd never seen anything like this. I grew up in a suburb across the Bay from San Francisco, a town that hardly existed when World War II ended. Unlike Alta Mira, the town had no serious history of sending its own off to fight. I had to admit I was impressed by the parade and rally, and glad Gordon suggested taking it in. When we get together in San Francisco, we tend to eat lunch or dinner at the same tried and true restaurants or do the same sorts of activities — ball games, concerts. But when he goes on the road, he gets more adventurous. One of the good things about traveling with him is that he has a nose for local activities in the places we go fishing. If not for him, I'd have missed this parade; I'd never have watched the high school football game from the press box last Friday; and I'd never have taken in the Roundup Barbecue at the McHenry Ranch four years ago. Has it really been that long?

As people milled around afterward, I saw Chris Huntley working her way through the crowd in our direction. I was standing next to Gordon when she reached him.

"Glad I found you here," she said. "Can we talk in my office?"

Gordon nodded.

"You, too, Akers," she said.

And with that, she started to walk around toward the back of the building with the two of us following. What the hell, I thought. Maybe this is what Gordon needs. Maybe we both need it.

THE COURTHOUSE WAS LOCKED, of course, for the holiday, but the service entrance at the rear was open. With two murder investigations in the works, sheriff's deputies were coming and going on a steady basis, and a pair left the building as Chris, Gordon and Sam reached the door. They stepped aside to let her through, and she greeted them by name.

Once in her office, she sat at her desk, motioned them to chairs, leaned back to look at the tiles on the ceiling, took a deep breath and exhaled loudly.

"Rough day?" Gordon said.

"Going from bad to worse, but at least there's a direction to it."

He nodded almost imperceptibly.

"I wanted to ask if you'd been able to make head or tail of those notes on Bob's desk."

"Hardly had time to think about it. There's still something that bothers me, though I don't know what it is."

"All right. Well, let me know if you figure anything out."

"How's the investigation going?"

"Which one?"

"Bob's shooting was what I meant, but I'd be interested in what you have on any of the others, too."

"Howard, Diane and I had a meeting this morning. It wasn't terribly collegial, but we finally got a couple of things decided, though I had to pull rank.

"We concluded that Bob's murder is probably tied into Jessica Milland's murder and the disappearance of the other students. Everybody agreed that Bob has no enemies, so the killer of the students must have misunderstood what Bob was saying on the air and thought Bob was getting too close to him. We also all agreed that the killer was likely to be someone known on campus, so the female students wouldn't be afraid to take a ride from him."

"Makes sense," Sam said.

"That's where the agreement ended. Howard wants us to start looking at some of the athletes who play on the football and basketball teams. He feels that no one who's known in town could be the killer, but that the young men who came here from somewhere else — sometimes having darker skin and coming from troubled backgrounds — are a good pool of suspects.

"Diane and I think it's an inside job, though. Someone would have to know the area pretty well to go to that logging road where Jessica was killed. So I made the call that we're focusing on faculty and staff at Homestead College at first. If we need to, we'll look at the athletes later. Howard didn't take it too well, but one thing you can say for him is that he's been in the Army and understands chain of command. So he's spent the entire morning on campus, interviewing top administrators and every teacher Jessica ever took a class from."

"Any leads?" Gordon asked.

"He called just before the parade to tell me he's still going, but he said he's already talked to three teachers who should be arrested for perversion. I told him to refer it to the vice squad."

"You have a vice squad in a county this size?" Sam said.

"Of course not. That was my point. But the problem is, I don't know how much of that is Howard and how much there might actually be to it, meaning someone is worth a harder look. I'll have to spend a lot of time with him at the end of the day trying to figure that out. I don't have the time or the energy for that, but there it is."

"Anything from the crime scene experts?"

"Where Jessica was killed — not a thing beyond what we found on Sunday. If the killer had lost a couple of hairs on Thursday, the wind would have blown them away by now. And our killer didn't oblige us by dropping a button or a cigarette butt. Bob's studio, on the other hand, had so much interesting stuff they didn't know where to start. Fingerprints all over the place, and God knows how old they were and how many people they might have belonged to. A lot of seemingly insignificant litter on the floor. I gather that studio was cleaned every Wednesday, and it was coming on five days. Even if we strike gold in all that stuff, we might not know which piece of it is the nugget. In conclusion, we have too much and too little."

"And two dead bodies and two missing persons," Gordon said.

Chris's expression changed, and she said nothing for several seconds, while Gordon and Sam waited expectantly.

"Actually, that's not right."

"There's another body?" Gordon asked.

"There's another missing person, and she fits the profile. But she's not from here."

Gordon and Sam looked at each other.

"On the second Monday of each month," she continued, "there's a meeting of the sheriffs of four counties in this corner of the state. We talk about what's going on in crime, training issues, political concerns, whatever. The meeting was at 3:30 yesterday, and for obvious reasons, I didn't make it. But Leon Kinninger, the sheriff of Ponderosa County, just south, called me this morning.

"It seems that on Friday October 17, a female student named Tiffany Reese disappeared after leaving an afternoon class at Ponderosa Community College. Nobody saw anything, and when they started asking questions after a few days, a couple of her friends said she'd been hinting at a secret boyfriend, though they were skeptical. Because of that, they didn't pursue it too far. But she hasn't turned up, and now, with Jessica's body being found, they're ramping up their investigation.

"So if Tiffany didn't run off with some young man, we may have a serial killer operating on a much larger scale than we suspected."

There was a long silence, before Gordon replied:

"And it might not be someone from this county?"

"Possible, but not likely. Three of four student victims from here, plus Bob, tells me it's a local, though I'd love to have it turn out otherwise. Anyway," she sighed, "I'm going to try to keep it quiet for as long as possible. What are you smiling about, Gordon?"

"If Bob were around, it would be on the air tomorrow."

"Don't I know it. But keep it to yourself. I don't want it getting out because of you. Now, if there's nothing else, I have work to do."

They rose to leave, but as Gordon turned toward the door, Sam spoke up:

"How about the rape case? What's happening with that?"

"God forgive me," Chris finally said, "but it's barely on the radar. We're stretched so thin on these murders and disappearances that there simply isn't anyone to work on it. I'm afraid Alicia Rios is going to be a victim again, but unless somebody brings us something on a silver platter, I don't see that case going anywhere soon."

HOMESTEAD COMMUNITY COLLEGE on the holiday looked like a ghost town. As Gordon and Sam drove to the parking lot near Elizabeth's office, they passed no other cars and only two people — a pair of student joggers. In the near-empty parking lot they had their choice of spaces adjacent to the faculty offices.

Elizabeth had asked them to arrive a few minutes before Hooper so they could prepare. She had a chair set out facing her desk and another to her right, in which she seated Gordon. Sam was seated in a corner chair, where he would be behind and out of sight of Hooper.

"You were right," she said, as Gordon and Sam sat down. "It was Harry Hooper that Bob met here on Sunday."

"How did you get him to come out and see you?" Sam asked from the corner.

"I bluffed. I told him Bob had told me about meeting with him, and that Bob and I had been working together on this, and that I'd like to continue where Bob left off. He sounded a bit reluctant, but after a minute or so of gentle persuasion, he agreed to come out."

"So he doesn't know that you know nothing," Gordon said.

"No, he does not. And part of your job, Gordon, is to help me make sure he doesn't find out how little we know."

"And the other part?"

"I figured that as an athlete yourself, you might be able to bond with him. Plus, I need a man for this. I barely know what an adult male is thinking, aside from the obvious, and I have no idea at all what's going on in an adolescent's mind."

Gordon thought about it for a minute, then said:

"Well, if you go with the obvious, you'd probably be right about three-quarters of the time."

She exhaled a quick laugh and shook her head.

"I grew up with two brothers in the house. I should have remembered."

A few minutes later there was a knock on the door, and Elizabeth told the knocker to come in. The door opened, and Hooper took a step inside. He was six feet tall and a muscular 190 pounds. His light brown hair was cut close to his scalp, with no strand of it more than a half-inch long, and he looked as if he hadn't shaved for a couple of days, though the resulting growth was uneven. He was handsome in a callowness-of-youth sort of way, and when he registered Gordon and Sam's presence in the room, he stiffened slightly and a look of apprehension crossed his face.

Gordon stood up, extending his long arm and right hand.

"I'm Quill Gordon, Harry. Bob and I go back a long time, to when we were in college together. I'm pleased to meet you."

Hooper shook his hand. "Pleased to meet you, Mr. Gordon."

"You can drop the 'mister' and just call me Gordon. Everyone else does."

Sam shook Hooper's hand and introduced himself as well. Hooper relaxed slightly and sat in the offered chair.

Elizabeth looked at Gordon, who remained impassive, and decided to start it off herself.

"Thank you for coming out here today, Harry. It means a lot to me, and I know it would have meant a lot to Bob." Hooper nodded. "I asked Gordon to be here because he's an old friend of Bob's who's been following what's been going on in town. Also, he used to be a star basketball player at Cal."

Hooper turned and looked at Gordon suspiciously.

"A long time ago," Gordon said.

Elizabeth continued, "I know Bob would have wanted us to carry on, and that's why we asked you here. We were hoping we might be able to pick up where you left off with Bob yesterday."

"And anything you say," Gordon interjected, speaking softly, "stays in this room until you tell us otherwise."

Hooper, clearly trying to decide what to do, looked back and forth at Gordon and Elizabeth. Gordon, as if stalking a particularly wary trout, remained utterly immobile.

"I guess you know we were talking about the party at DeShayne's," Hooper finally said.

Elizabeth nodded, as if she'd known it all along.

"Mr. Hastings was pressing me for details. Not in any kind of obnoxious way; he was pretty gentle. But he kept at it. I told him I had two problems with reporting what I knew. The first was chemistry. Our football team's in the playoffs now, and I don't want to do anything to upset the team chemistry and put us against each other."

"Chemistry," Gordon said, "is vital to a team. I understand that, and I've seen what happens when it goes south. But it works in a lot of different ways. A sensational revelation can damage a team's chemistry, but so can a cover-up. When everybody's trying to keep the lid on something, it's hard to stay focused on the game. Sometimes, it's better to get it out in the open and move on so you can concentrate on playing your best."

Hooper nodded. "That's sort of what Mr. Hastings said, too, and I finally told him I'd sleep on it."

"You said there were two problems," Sam said from the back corner. "What was the other one?"

"Well, that I really wasn't there very long. I got to the party thinking the DeShaynes would be there, but it was just us, and the booze was already out. I don't want you to think I'm a prude or anything; I mean, I drink some in the spring and summer. But all the football players signed a contract saying we'd lay off alcohol and tobacco from the beginning of practice through the end of the season. Not everybody takes it seriously, but my dad says when you sign a contract, you have to live up to it. So I have. When I saw all the alcohol out, and almost everybody drinking, well ..."

"You were a bit uncomfortable," Gordon said. Hooper nodded. "I know how it is. When I was at Cal, cocaine was becoming a big deal. Anytime it came out at a party, I started looking for the exit."

"Maybe it's easier when you're older," Hooper said. "But, yeah. It took me 20 minutes or so to finally slip out of there, I did notice that Kyle brought Alicia a drink, and Cody brought her another one not ten minutes later."

"Just to clarify," Gordon said, "We're talking about Kyle Burnett, the quarterback, and Cody Jarrett the wide receiver?"

"That's right. And though I wasn't there long, I could tell that she was getting looser and louder faster than the other girls. I'm not sure she has much of a head for alcohol."

"Some people don't," Elizabeth said. "Would you say that when you left, she was still in control?"

"Last time I saw her was about five minutes before I split. She was standing and laughing, and talking. Her voice was a bit slurred and she obviously had a buzz on, but for whatever it's worth, I'd say she was still at least somewhat in control."

Gordon and Elizabeth looked at each other.

"So then you left," Gordon said. "Unless you saw something else, that doesn't seem to give us much to work with. How come Bob was suggesting that you report what you knew?"

Hooper looked surprised.

"So Mr. Hastings didn't tell you?"

"Tell us what, Harry?" Elizabeth asked. Hooper looked at her, then at Gordon, realization finally dawning.

"He didn't tell you about the video?"

AT MOMENTS LIKE THIS, I remember why I no longer play poker with Gordon. Elizabeth did a pretty respectable job of stifling her surprise, but there was a definite "tell" if you were looking at her, which Hooper wasn't. Gordon, on the other hand, didn't move a single muscle in his face or body. If you didn't know better, you'd have thought he'd just been handed a grocery receipt, instead of a critical clue in a major crime case.

After a few seconds, Gordon sat up a bit straighter and took a breath.

"No, he didn't, Harry. But I think he was about to when he was killed."

"Wait a minute. They don't think he was killed over that, do they? I can't believe it."

"The sheriff's department doesn't know what to think at this point. But from what he was talking about on the air, it sure sounded like it was a follow-up to his talk with you on Sunday."

"Whoever killed him might not have known that," Elizabeth said, "but that's one of the questions that still has to be answered."

"Listen, Harry," Gordon said, "let's set the video aside for a minute and talk about Bob's murder. You want to see whoever did that get caught, don't you?"

Hooper nodded.

"Then there may be something you can help with. You were in Bob's radio class, right? Did you enjoy it?"

"Yeah. It was real interesting to hear from somebody who does it for a living how it's done."

"That's exactly where you might be able to help. You'd know more about Bob's radio techniques than we do."

"I guess."

"I'm going to show you something." Gordon reached into his shirt pocket, took out the notebook and set it on the desk in front of Hooper. As Hooper leaned forward to read it, I stood up behind him to take a look. It was open to the page of Bob's notes at the time he was shot:

SBYM - TW
Time - :30
Geiser - Wed
DS - Gurgle
Wheaties

"Does any of this mean anything to you?" Gordon asked. As Hooper leaned forward, he continued, "It's just my handwritten copy of the original, so go ahead and pick it up if that helps you."

Hooper did and looked at it for several seconds.

"Geiser probably means he wanted the coach on his show Wednesday or he was reminding himself to announce that coach was going to be on the show. I'm not sure which."

"That's good," Elizabeth said. "Anything else?"

"The thing about time. He told us in class that you're supposed to give the time at least once every half hour, and that even people who have been doing radio for years sometimes forget. I'm guessing he was reminding himself."

"Now we're getting somewhere," Gordon said.

"I don't see how," replied Hooper. "That seems like pretty ordinary stuff."

"But now we can eliminate it and concentrate on the other three. A lot of a criminal investigation is eliminating unimportant things so you can get to the important ones. Do any of the other three things mean anything to you?"

Hooper picked up the list, looked at it again, then set it down with a shake of his head.

"Sorry."

"That's all right. What you gave us was a big help." He paused. "Now I don't want to push you, but we want to finish what Bob started. If you can tell us about the video, that would help, too. But it's up to you."

Hooper shifted in his chair. "That's what Mr. Hastings said on Sunday. That it's up to me." He sighed. "If I tell you, will you promise not to let it go any further unless I say it's OK?"

Gordon looked at Elizabeth, who nodded.

"That's a deal, Harry. And if there's anything you want to ask us, we'll try to answer the best we can."

"Well, like I said, when the drinking started, I was getting uncomfortable at the party. About ten minutes before I left, Caitlin DeShayne went into her room and got out a video camera she'd been given for her birthday earlier in the month and started filming the party."

I sat there thinking, as the father of a daughter, this is what I have to be worried about.

"That freaked me out," he continued, "because I didn't want to be seen in a video of a drinking party, even if I wasn't drinking."

"I get the sense," Gordon said, "that you take your obligations seriously. Your parents must have taught you to keep your word."

"Well, they taught me that the rules are the rules anyway. I don't know if you relate to that."

"My father is a judge, so I understand the rule of law. And I understand that a contract, which is what you signed with the coach, is a contract."

"I know. Anyway, between the drinking and the filming, I wanted to get out of there as soon as possible."

"Did you see what she was filming?" Elizabeth asked.

"She was kind of moving around the room, trying to get pictures of everybody, which was one of the things that creeped me out. I do remember that she got a shot of either Kyle or Cody — I don't remember which — giving Alicia a glass of something. I left just a few minutes after that, and I don't know how long she kept filming or what she shot. That's what I told Mr. Hastings."

"And what did he say?" Gordon asked.

"He said I should tell the sheriff and the district attorney. I told him I wanted to think about it overnight. What do you think I should do?"

"Before I answer, let me ask you a question. Why did you want to think about it?"

"A couple of reasons, I guess. The big one is that I don't want to let the team down, and these guys are my friends. I don't really want to snitch on them. And also I'm not sure how important the video is, since I don't really know what happened after I left. Do I really want to mess up the team's chemistry and lose a couple of friends by going to the sheriff with something that may not even be important?"

"That's a good case you just made, but can I ask just one more question, Harry? Do you believe it?"

"I don't know. I wish I could. What would you have done if something like this happened when you played for Cal?"

"I don't know what I would have done, either, since it never happened. But I can tell you one thing. I know now what I should have done in a situation like that and what I'd wish I'd have done if it happened. I'd be sleeping a lot easier today if I'd reported it and let the chips fall where they may."

"And you wouldn't have worried about team chemistry?"

"Of course I would have. But what I know now and didn't know then is that nothing hurts team chemistry more than having a cloud hanging over the team. If something bad happens, like losing a couple of key players, it's easier to move on from that than it is to deal with a lot of uncertainty about what might happen next."

"And you wouldn't have worried about snitching on your friends?"

"Sure. But it's one thing if you're protecting them from a prank and another thing altogether when they may have committed a felony."

"A felony? But she was drunk and flirting with them. If they fooled around later, how would that be a felony?"

Gordon turned to Elizabeth, and it seemed as if the room stopped moving. She finally took a deep breath and leaned forward slightly.

"Let me ask you a question, Harry. Do you have a sister?"

"No. Just a little brother."

"If you had a sister, would it have bothered you to see her acting the way Alicia was acting that night — drinking and flirting?

"Yeah. I guess so. I don't know."

"You're a decent guy, Harry, so I'm pretty sure it would have. You'd have understood that she was maybe getting herself into a situation she wouldn't be able to control. Too many women have to learn that lesson the hard way, and when they do, they have to live with the horror of it for the rest of their lives. Alicia will. Just because a woman is drinking and flirting with someone doesn't mean she's agreeing to what happens next — or if she's had too much to drink, that she even has the ability to deal with it. And too often, the men who take advantage of women in those circumstances get away with it because no one is willing to step forward."

"Do you really think it would help to report the video? When I don't even know what's on it?"

"Let me answer that," Gordon said. "Granted that we don't know what the video will show, telling the sheriff about it breaks the investigation open. Maybe the video doesn't show anything conclusive, but it can still provide background information, raise questions. And there's even a chance it could exonerate your friends. Until it's looked at by the proper authorities, nothing happens and everyone is under a cloud of rumor and suspicion.

"That's why it matters, so I'm going to stop talking and just repeat what Bob said on Sunday. It's up to you now."

It seemed to me that the silence that followed those words lasted five minutes, though it was probably more like 15 seconds. When Hooper finally spoke, he sounded utterly drained.

"All right. I'll tell the sheriff."

The rest of us exhaled.

"When should I do it?"

"No time like now," Gordon said. "Do you really want to be worrying it any longer?" Hooper shook his head. "Did you drive over here?"

"I got a lift from a friend."

"Then I'll drive us back to town."

"Is that your Cherokee parked outside?"

"It sure is."

"Well, at least I'll get a good ride."

That broke the ice a bit, and as we stood to go, Elizabeth picked up the paper with Bob's list on it.

"Gordon," she said. "I think I know what one of the other items on this means."

"Spill."

"DS – Gurgle. DeShayne Plumbing is one of Bob's big advertisers, and Bob was always trying to find new plumbing noises for the commercials. It was part of his gross-out sense of humor. I think he was just reminding himself to find a flushing noise or something for DeShayne's next ad. Do you think that could be right?"

"Yes, and no comment," Gordon said as he turned toward the door.

THREE AND A HALF HOURS LATER, Gordon and Elizabeth were with the sheriff in her office. Sam had borrowed the Cherokee to drive Hooper home, and Diane Brinkley, having called in a secretary on overtime to take down what Hooper said, was en route to Judge Jackson's house with the deposition and a search warrant for the judge's signature.

"It shouldn't be a problem, should it?" asked Elizabeth.

"I hope not," Chris said. "All we're asking for is permission to search for the video camera and videotape. The judge is pretty supportive of law enforcement, but judges have to stand for election, and the DeShaynes are a prominent family. So we'll wait to hear."

"Assuming you get the warrant," Gordon said, "when would you serve it?"

"Nine o'clock tomorrow morning."

"Why not tonight?"

"No sense upsetting the DeShaynes any more than we have to. Tomorrow morning, the girls'll be in school, and Norv will be off to work. With any luck, we just have to search Caitlin's room, and we're done in ten to 15 minutes."

"How big an operation will it be?" Elizabeth said.

"Just Howard and me, and I'm not telling Howard about it until he comes in tomorrow morning."

"What do you expect to find?" Gordon asked.

"I'm not expecting anything. Expectations are disappointments waiting to happen. We'll find what we find and move on from there."

"Let me put it another way. What do you think is the likelihood that this could be a breakthrough in the case?"

"A breakthrough? Pretty small. It would be too much to hope for indisputable evidence of a crime."

"But we're talking about teenagers," Elizabeth said. "Anything can happen."

"Granted. But it's a long way from *can* to *will*. There's a fair chance that any video that was shot that night has been erased or discarded. And even if it's not, what it does show is likely to be blurry and inconclusive."

"So you're saying this might be a wild goose chase?" Gordon asked.

"Not at all. It could tell us who was there; it could open up lines of questioning that might lead somewhere; it might suggest an approach we hadn't considered. And if it does nothing else, this sends a message."

Elizabeth and Gordon waited for her to continue. The phone rang, and Chris picked it up.

"Sheriff Huntley."

She listened to the voice on the other end for several seconds, then said one word:

"Good." And she hung up. Gordon and Elizabeth were leaning forward in their chairs.

"Relax," she said. "That was Howard. He said he hasn't arrested any of the faculty, though some of them richly deserve it, and he'll be here with a full report in half an hour."

Gordon and Elizabeth leaned back in their chairs.

"You were talking about sending a message," Gordon said after several seconds.

"Right. What I mean by that is that when the top two officers in the sheriff's department show up at the home of a prominent family to serve a search warrant, the word's going to get out pretty fast. It'll show that we're taking this seriously and no one's above suspicion. That might cause a parent or student to come to Jesus and step forward. We can hope, anyway."

They sat silently for a minute and a half. The phone rang, and in the silence, it sounded like the bell announcing the end of school. The sheriff answered, then listened, nodding, for a quarter of a minute.

"Good," she said, and hung up. She turned to Gordon and Elizabeth, who were leaning forward again.

"That was Diane. No problem with Judge Jackson. She signed the warrant."

ELIZABETH AND GORDON met Sam for dinner at Elizalde's. It seemed as if half the town was there, and they had to be careful about being overheard. But the air at their table was charged with a barely suppressed excitement.

The waitress arrived with drinks — red wine for Elizabeth and Gordon and a beer for Sam — and Elizabeth lifted her glass in a toast.

"To our investigation. May justice be done."

They touched glasses and bottle.

"That's a lot to ask for," Gordon said. "But at least this is a beginning."

"I'm glad you were there this afternoon, Gordon." She looked around and lowered her voice slightly. "I don't know if I could have gotten him to go to the sheriff."

"I think he's basically a good kid," Gordon answered. "Once he was led to where he could see the right thing to do, and could take ownership of the decision, he went ahead and did it."

"But the right thing was easier to see when the direction was coming from someone who spoke his language."

"Maybe. I still believe he'd have come around eventually."

Sam raised his beer bottle.

"I think we should have a toast to Bob. If he hadn't talked to Harry in the first place, we wouldn't have had anything to go on.

Gordon and Elizabeth lifted their glasses and said simultaneously, "To Bob."

They fell silent for a minute, remembering. Gordon finally spoke.

"That reminds me," he said. "I was going to stop by to see Brenda this afternoon, but this whole business took so long, I clean forgot."

Soup arrived, a hearty blend of ham, beans and noodles, and they dug in. After a couple of swallows, Gordon set his spoon down and opened his notebook to Bob's list.

"I'll be sure to see her tomorrow," he said. "And one thing I want to ask her about is this list." He looked at Elizabeth. "What you said about 'DS – Gurgle' being a sound effect for a DeShayne ad rings true, and if it is, we've accounted for three of the five things on this list. That still leaves us scratching our heads over 'SBYM – TW' and 'Wheaties.' And there's still something about this list that bothers me, though I can't put my finger on it."

"Let me see that," she said, taking the list from Gordon. "I'm wondering if the first item isn't the important one. "If Bob had something on his mind, wouldn't it be the first thing he wrote down in the morning that was important."

"That makes sense," Gordon said, taking the list back. "So does the idea that the last thing he wrote was the most important. I don't know."

They finished their soup, and the salad arrived. As they were eating, Elizabeth sat bolt upright.

"I almost forgot. Tomorrow morning. What are you guys doing tomorrow morning?"

"What did you have in mind?" Gordon said.

"Monday night I got hold of Jessica Milland's mother in Big Piney. I set up an interview for nine o'clock tomorrow morning."

"Don't you have to be at work then?" Sam asked.

"On what grounds?" Gordon asked.

"To answer Sam first, on Mondays and Wednesdays, I only teach the Women's Studies class at one o'clock. I asked to meet with her as a representative of the campus safety committee ..."

"Is there actually such a thing?" said Sam.

"Yes, and I'm actually on it. But I'm also hoping that I might be able to get some piece of information out of her that the sheriff's department didn't get. They sent a male detective to talk to her. Would you guys like to come along?"

"But we're male, too," Sam said.

"That's all right as long as you don't talk. It'll look more impressive if a couple of people from the committee are there, which is how I'll introduce you. And I'll ask all the questions."

"We'd have to leave by eight to be at Big Piney by nine," Gordon said.

"You'd get up that early to go fishing, wouldn't you?"

"I suppose. What do you say, Sam?"

"Sure. Why not?" he replied after a pause.

"Great. Shall we meet at Kemper's at 7:15 for breakfast and go from there?"

Gordon and Sam nodded.

"I'll drive," Gordon said.

"Not so fast, Flyboy. You need to learn how to let the woman do some things. I'll do the driving and you can sit in the passenger seat and not comment on it."

"Whatever you say," he said after a pause. They finished their salads without further conversation. When Gordon was done, he stood up.

"If we're going to be out all of tomorrow morning, I'm going to excuse myself and give Brenda a call right now. I need to let her know I haven't forgotten about her. If dinner comes while I'm out, go ahead and start without me."

He headed for the front door.

AS SOON AS GORDON was out of earshot, Elizabeth turned toward me and flashed a smile that might even have been sincere.

"Now that we're alone," she said in a confidential tone, "can I ask you a question, Sam?"

No way to get out of that, so I told her to go ahead.

"I've been wondering, and Bob wasn't much help on this point, but I'm curious." She took a deep breath. "What, exactly, does Gordon do for a living?"

"You know, my wife asks that question all the time."

"That's all right," she purred. "You don't have to give me the same answer you give her."

There was nothing left to do but play it straight, so I did the best I could.

"I don't know all the details, but he worked for a dozen years at Howell, Burns & Bledsoe, an old-line San Francisco brokerage. He brought in some clients who were pro athletes, and I gather generally did pretty well for them. In addition to that, he began investing his own money and did really well at it. Well enough that he quit the brokerage a few years back."

"And what's he been doing since?"

"I think he's still managing a few portfolios for clients he knows pretty well. And of course he's managing his own investments, which I expect takes some time. And he occasionally does some consulting for nonprofit groups about managing their finances, though I don't think he makes much money off that."

"In other words, he's essentially at loose ends."

"Well, I don't know about that. But he certainly seems to be able to go fishing whenever he wants."

"What you're saying is very interesting, Sam, because in the short time I've known him, I've gotten the impression of a very sharp but also restless man who's searching for himself in some way. And maybe trying to come to terms with a void in his life. Tell me, Sam, was there a tragic love affair in his past?"

I squirmed. This was getting a bit uncomfortable.

"What makes you ask that?"

"He's almost 40 years old, and he let it drop when we were having dinner the other night that he's never been married. I kind of think that any man who wants to be married is going to be by that point in his life. Unless there's something that's blocking him emotionally. That's why I suspect a tragic love affair. What about it?"

"It wasn't really tragic," I said, trying to choose my words carefully. "I mean, nobody died. Well, actually, some people did, but it wasn't Gordon or her. Anyway, I think he thought she was The One, and so did I for a while. They were together for about six months, and then all of a sudden, it was over."

I stopped and took a pull of my beer. She had me off balance, and I wanted to right things.

"Did he ever say why?"

"Why what?"

"Why they broke up?"

"No, he didn't, and whenever I asked, he just said, 'I'd rather not talk about it, Sam.' And when Gordon says that, you don't argue with him."

"Maybe you need to take the circular route."

"You can try if you want. Good luck."

"And so do you know what happened to The One?"

"As a matter of fact, yes. It turns out she's now engaged to be married. To an undertaker."

"An undertaker. How interesting. That's not exactly where I'd start looking for Mr. Right, but then you never know."

"You never know," I said. "I just found out about it last week. In fact, I had to break the news to Gordon when I got here."

"And how did he take it?"

"You can't always tell with him, but I think he was a bit disturbed."

"You think he wants her back?"

"I think some small part of him does, but he knows it's not going to happen."

"So why do you think he was disturbed?"

"My best guess? I think he wanted to hold on to that little bit of hope. And now he can't."

"On the other hand, maybe that finally frees him."

That's what you're hoping, I thought. What's taking Gordon so long, anyway?

"Could I ask one more thing, Sam?"

"We've gone this far."

"How did he meet The One?"

I realized the answer was dynamite, but I couldn't come up with any other way of putting it, so I finally said:

"He met her on a fishing trip."

"Oh. So he has a history of this." She took another sip of her wine. "I suppose I shouldn't be surprised. I mean, let's be real, Sam. He does come across as a man who knows his way around a woman."

I'd just taken another swallow of beer when she said that, and I aspirated, sending carbonated alcoholic liquid simultaneously down my throat and up my nose. As I sat there, helplessly gasping, coughing and wheezing, dinner and Gordon arrived at the table simultaneously. He gave me a queer look but was either too smart or too much of a gentleman to say anything.

Wednesday November 12

SHE MET US AT KEMPER'S Bakery shortly after 7 a.m. The place was about three-quarters full and noisy, but we grabbed the only remaining table for four. She had a croissant, Gordon had a bear claw and I got a lemon Danish. They sent me to get the pastries and coffee while they talked. Not that it matters. We head home on Sunday, and after that, she will gradually begin to fade from memory.

When I got back with the goodies, she was filling him in on the investigation at the college. She paused long enough to thank me and kept going.

"After I got back last night, the phone was ringing pretty much nonstop until I finally unplugged it at 10 so I could get some sleep. No one can remember having a detective on campus interviewing people all day, so it was quite the deal."

"How did people react?" Gordon asked.

"From what I'm hearing, Howard picked up a lot of votes for when he runs for sheriff in June. Unfortunately for him, he picked them up for Chris. People didn't care much for his old-school lawman approach, and the faculty in particular were aware of the fact that he didn't seem to like them."

"Did anyone think he got anywhere?" I asked.

"They seemed to feel he was spinning his wheels and wasting a lot of time looking in the wrong places. For instance, he seemed to really get his back up when he talked to Arthur Melton. Arthur's been in the English Department since before dirt, and he has tenure, so getting rid of him is out of the question. Everyone in the office seemed to think it was funny that Howard thought Arthur was guilty."

"You think he isn't?" Gordon said.

"Oh, he's plenty guilty all right. Just not of kidnapping and murdering Jessica or any of the other women. He simply hasn't got the temperament. Arthur is a — oh, what's the Yiddish word I'm looking for?"

"Schmuck?" Gordon suggested.

"Yes. Thank you. He's thoroughly disreputable, but he has no mean streak and no nerve. Over the years, he's hit on any number of female students. But the thing is, he always backs off when they say no. I think he's secretly grateful that they do. He's kind of like the dog that chases the car but wouldn't know what to do with it if he caught it."

"I'm surprised that, as a feminist, you're taking his behavior so lightly."

"I don't take it lightly. It's inappropriate and unacceptable. But I don't see it changing, and, unfortunately, I don't see the college doing anything about it. The administration is as uninterested in pursuing sexual harassment claims as it is in getting a shuttle bus running to town so the female students don't have to hitch rides from serial killers. But at least there's hope for getting the shuttle bus some day, so that's where I'm going to spend my energy."

"Maybe you could use Arthur as a teaching lesson," I said.

"Actually, I do. Not by name, of course — that would be bad form. But when I do the lesson on sexual harassment, I do try to drive home the lesson that a woman can't count on help from the institution where the harassment is taking place. So I tell the women in my class that they have to be ready to stand up for themselves, and that if they do, a lot of the time the men will back down. They're bullies, after all, and bullies rarely keep going when they're called on it."

"So do you tell your students how to get a man to back off?" said Gordon.

"Do I ever. I've been compiling a notebook of rebukes and put-downs for over ten years now. Would you like to hear some of them?"

I swallowed fast, to get the words out quickly.

"Maybe some other time."

Gordon jumped in.

"Do you talk about drugs and alcohol at parties?"

"Absolutely. It's a fact of life these days. And even if you're ready to stand up for yourself, you can't do it if you're impaired."

She took the last bite of her croissant, chewed it slowly, and washed it down with coffee before continuing.

"And I'll never be able to do that lesson again without thinking of Alicia. In the last couple of weeks, I've talked to her enough to form an opinion, and I think she's got a good enough head on her shoulders that Kyle Burnett or Cody Jarrett never would have gotten anywhere with her if she was sober. No, let me put it another way. Maybe they could have if they'd been willing to put out a real effort to show her that they were the kind of man a woman could get serious about. But they weren't serious about her and never would have made the effort."

She drained the last of her coffee.

"And Alicia, as we're all aware, never got the chance to say no."

THE SHERIFF AND HOWARD knocked on the door of the DeShayne residence at exactly 9:01 a.m. A flustered Mildred DeShayne — her wet hair and bathrobe suggested she'd just gotten out of the shower — opened the door. Having brought up to respect the law, she admitted them to the house when they presented the warrant. And having learned to fear and obey her husband, she immediately picked up the phone and called him. He was several miles away, and by the time he got to his house, it was all over.

They went straight into Caitlin DeShayne's bedroom, which, being occupied by a 15-year-old girl, would not have passed an Army inspection. There were several posters on the walls of rock stars Chris and Howard had never heard of. He looked at the posters with disgust; she with a certain wistfulness. The clutter in the room was impressive, but seemed navigable.

"Where do we start?" he asked.

"When I was her age," Chris said after surveying the room carefully, "I had a diary I didn't want anybody to see, and I do mean *anybody*. I kept it in a box under the bed." She dropped to her knees and looked under the bed.

"Bingo!" she said, pulling out a shoebox.

She set it on the bed and took off the lid. Inside, they found a brand-name camcorder, three film cassettes, and two boxes of condoms — one with the seal broken. Lifting the camera out, she set it on its side and opened it. Another cassette was inside. She closed the camera, handed it and the three cassettes to Howard, replaced the shoebox lid, and put the box back under the bed, where it had been.

"Shouldn't we take the condoms, too?" Howard asked.

"The search warrant specifies only video and photographic cameras and film. We've invaded her privacy enough as it is, and if the video in this camera," she tapped it, "shows what we think it's going to show, the condom stash is the least of her problems."

A DENSE CLOUD COVER had moved into the area overnight, offering a foretaste of the winter to come. The clouds were in various gradations of gray, and nothing about them signaled that they were bringing rain or snow; rather, they blocked out the sunlight, muted the colors of the autumn landscape, and imparted a dampness to the morning cold that hadn't been there before.

Under these conditions, it was a generally quiet group that Elizabeth drove from Alta Mira to Big Piney, some 30 miles away. The route led north from Alta Mira, then east over the Wikiup Mountain Range to Serendipity Valley. At the foot of the east slope of the mountains sat Big Piney, overlooking the valley and its two dry lake beds. The town had attained a population of a thousand around 1900, and the number had been slowly declining since.

They turned right off the highway onto the main street, driving three blocks past a grocery store, a gas station, a coffee shop, a real estate office, and a hardware and feed store, as well as a number of houses. Many of the buildings were at least a half-century old, but were still well maintained. Elizabeth turned left onto C Street and drove two blocks to where it ended at the top of a short dropoff, overlooking the dry lake beds and the York Mountains on its east side, just across the Nevada border. She stopped in front of a house that looked to have been built in the 1920s or 30s, with a large porch, small front yard, and two tall oak trees providing shade. With no sunlight breaking through the clouds, the house looked dark and gloomy, as if it knew there had been a death in the family.

"Let me do all the talking for the first five minutes," Elizabeth said after she turned off the engine. "Then, if you have a question, you can jump in. But try to wait until they're at ease."

The door was answered quickly by a young, clean-cut man with brown eyes and brown, short-cropped hair, who looked as if he might be on leave from the military.

"I'm Michael," he said, extending his hand, "Jessica's brother. Come on in."

"Elizabeth Macondray, Jessica's English teacher this semester," she said. "And this is Professor Gordon and Mr. Akers, the deputy dean of admissions."

They stepped into a living room that was well lit, with furniture that was old but comfortable, rather than threadbare. A pungent bouquet of cooked bacon, lavender air freshener, and something sweet, baking or freshly baked, permeated the room.

"Mom's making cinnamon rolls," he said. "She'll be right in. And coffee's almost ready."

They took a seat on a large couch, Elizabeth sitting between the two men. Michael looked at them in a way that was intent and a bit unsettling, then lowered his voice to keep his mother from hearing.

"So, is the college sending you over to talk us out of suing?"

Elizabeth was stunned by the question and showed it, but she recovered quickly.

"Not at all. I'm sorry if you think that, but we have nothing to do with the college's legal issues. I've been deeply involved with a faculty/administration committee looking at women's safety issues on campus, and that's why I asked if your mother could talk to us." She paused and took a deep breath. "If you don't think that's a good idea, we can try another time or forget about it, whichever the family thinks is better."

"I guess I believe you," he said after a long pause. "Being a county employee, I'm used to being around people who think about lawsuits all the time."

"This county?" Gordon asked.

"No. Yolo County Sheriff's Department. I just got through my probationary period."

"Congratulations."

"Thank you."

They sat silently for a minute.

"Mom's been spending a lot of time in the kitchen," he finally said. "Keeping herself busy in there takes her mind off what happened. At least for a little bit. It never goes away for long."

"Michael! Coffee's ready," came a voice from the kitchen.

He excused himself and returned a minute later with a coffee pot, four cups, milk and sugar on a tray. By the time coffee was poured, mixed and sampled, Anita Milland had come in with a large plate of cinnamon rolls. Short and stout, she had a spring in her step that was at odds with the look of defeat and confusion on her face.

After Kemper's, the cinnamon rolls were wretched excess, but the three visitors each took one and ate it all. They made small talk for several minutes before Elizabeth turned the conversation to the matter at hand. Luckily for them, Anita Milland was one of those people who work through a difficult time by talking.

"I'm wondering," Elizabeth said, "if Jessica ever said anything to you about anyone or anything suspicious on campus."

"Well, like I told the detective the other day, she was aware of the fact that two other girls had gone missing. She didn't seem to be particularly worried about herself, though. I asked about it, and she said she usually got a ride to town with someone, and that if she had to hitchhike, she only took rides from women or men she knew really well."

"Jessica was a mature and poised young woman, more so than most of the women in my classes," Elizabeth said. "It's hard to believe she'd just get into a car with a total stranger."

"I'm certain she wouldn't have," Michael said. "When I was in training, we had a case of a hitchhiker who was raped. Jessica and I had a couple of long conversations about that. She had a whole protocol about who she'd ride with, and it even extended to who she'd let drive her home from a party. That's why I think whoever killed her had to be someone she knew. Do you know if the sheriff's office is investigating that angle?"

Gordon looked at Elizabeth and she nodded.

"I can't speak for the sheriff's department, of course," Gordon said, "but they've had a detective on campus interviewing people, and especially faculty members. From what the people being interviewed are saying, that seems to be the thrust of the questioning." He paused. "Is there any question you'd be asking?"

"I don't know. It's not my case and not my job. I came here as soon as mom got the news, but mostly to be with her."

Anita put her hand on his arm. "He's such a good son. But I don't think he's been eating right. I'm making sure he gets a good breakfast."

Gordon took another breath, inhaling the mixed scents of bacon and lavender.

"Did Jessica say anything," Elizabeth asked, "about things that were going on at the college in the last few weeks? Did she have any complaints?"

"She didn't talk about that very much," Anita said. "Mostly she said school was going well, and I think things were all right with her boyfriend. She seemed to be in good spirits."

"Nothing at all that indicated she was worried or suspicious about anything?" Elizabeth pressed.

Anita shook her head. "I'm sorry," she said. "The detective went over all that, and I couldn't help him much."

Gordon looked at Michael.

"Did she say anything to you?"

"Not like that. The last time we talked, she was in a good mood. A bit exasperated by her boyfriend for going out with his buddies instead of her, but not like she was going to break up with him or anything. We talked a bit about the missing students, and she promised me she wouldn't take a ride from someone she didn't know. That was about it."

"And when did you have that conversation?"

"Saturday night, five days before she disappeared."

They continued talking until 9:45, which got them through a cinnamon roll and coffee, but came up with nothing of any substance. Taking their leave, they stepped outside into the overcast day. It felt as if the temperature had dropped a degree or two since they went into the house."

"Well," said Sam, as they settled into the Subaru, "that didn't get us very far."

"Mmm," Elizabeth said.

"I'm not so sure about that," Gordon said. "If nothing else it cleared up one point for me. Not about Jessica, but about Bob and his list."

Elizabeth turned toward him in the front passenger seat, and Sam leaned forward in the back seat.

"I've been thinking all along," Gordon continued, "that there was something off about Bob's list, but I couldn't put my finger on it. That family dynamic in there," he head-gestured toward the house, " not to mention the smell of bacon and lavender, helped me see it.

"One of Bob's little quirks, for as long as I've known him, is that he couldn't stand cold cereal. His mother always cooked him a hot breakfast, he told me in college, and that's what he was used to. That's why Wheaties on his list didn't seem right. I'm almost certain now that we should be looking at Wheaties not as food, but as something else."

Elizabeth started the engine.

"And there was something else, too," he continued. "An idea that was starting to come to me, but then I had to pay attention to the conversation and it slipped away. No, we didn't get any concrete leads on Jessica, but the trip out here is turning my thinking a bit. It may lead to something yet."

MOST OF THE DRIVE over the mountains took place in silence. On the way back down to the north-south state highway, they came around a curve to a relatively straight stretch of road with a dirt turnout on either side. On the side heading toward Big Piney was a Nissan of 1980s vintage with its hood up, and behind it a Highway Patrol car.

"Oh, look. That's Sandy," Elizabeth said, skidding across the deserted highway and coming to a stop behind the patrol car. They got out and walked toward the Nissan, where Sandy was talking to a woman of about 20.

"Radiator warning light came on going up the hill," Sandy said. "Her phone can't get a signal, so I've radioed for a tow truck from Alta Mira. They're saying 45 minutes."

"Is there anything we can do?" Elizabeth asked. "We can give you a ride back to the college or Alta Mira," she said to the young woman.

"No, thanks. I need to go home to Big Piney. The tow truck will take it to the garage there. They've fixed it before. And they said I could ride with them."

"All right then," Elizabeth said. Then, looking at Sandy, "Are you ... ?"

Sandy took a couple of steps forward and pulled Elizabeth aside. Gordon, jacketless and shivering in the cold, could barely hear her saying:

"Don't worry. I'm staying with her until the tow truck arrives. I think, given what's going on around here, that's more important than patrolling the road and seeing if I can write another speeding ticket."

Elizabeth nodded. They returned to the car and got back on the road.

"This is how our community has been poisoned," Elizabeth said. "That young woman had to be terrified when her car broke down around here. She fits the demographic for our serial killer, and what's to say he wouldn't be above scooping up another victim this way?"

"Uh huh," Gordon said. He'd taken her point, but another idea was forming inside his head, and he was wondering whether it was well enough developed to take to the sheriff.

GORDON HAD LEFT THE CHEROKEE at the college, in the event that Elizabeth might be in a hurry to get back for her class. It was 11:35 when she stopped behind it and Gordon's phone rang simultaneously.

"I think it's the sheriff," he said, and answered.

"I wanted to give you an update," Chris said. "Howard and I served the warrant this morning and struck pay dirt. Her video from the party was still in the camera."

"What was in it?"

"No definitive proof, but enough to make the horses nervous and maybe shake some more information out of someone. Anyway, we're going to have a select screening by invitation only at 1:30, and I wanted to be sure you, Elizabeth and Sam were invited. If it wasn't for you, we wouldn't have gotten our hands on this."

Gordon checked quickly with the others.

"Sam and I will be there, but Elizabeth has to be in class."

"All right, and I should warn you. It's pretty disgusting, so I wouldn't eat a heavy lunch beforehand, if I were you."

"I hear you."

"What I don't understand," she continued, "is why she held on to the video at all. People knew we were looking into that party. Why wouldn't she have destroyed or erased the tape?"

Gordon laughed.

"What's so funny, Gordon?"

"I was just thinking about what Bob said when he told us about this last week."

"Spit it out. I don't have a lot of time today."

"He said, 'If brains were dynamite, Caitlin DeShayne wouldn't be able to blow her nose.' "

She laughed as well. "Maybe not, but going from the other videos in her possession, she seems to be a young lady of advanced talents her parents probably don't recognize. However, as those videos are not germane to the case at hand, no one will ever see them. See you at 1:30."

GORDON AND SAM ARRIVED a few minutes early, and Chris escorted them to a conference room where Howard Honig and Diane Brinkley were waiting. The blinds to the room's windows were drawn, and a 28-inch television set and video player stood in front of a wall at one end.

At 1:05, two men entered together. One was Duane Raymond, the high school principal, with a tired, stooped look about him; the other was in his late thirties with thinning hair and a muscular, athletic build. Chris introduced him as Lloyd Geiser, the football coach.

"Pleased to make your acquaintance, Gordon," Geiser said as they shook hands. "I'm certainly familiar with the name. I was playing football at Santa Clara while you were a basketball star at Cal."

Raymond offered Gordon a limp handshake and a standard greeting, then turned to the sheriff.

"I hope this is important," he said. "I had to put the vice principal in charge of Lloyd's one o'clock class, and I'd like to have him back for the two o'clock."

Chris looked at Diane, who was sitting at the head of the table, near the TV. Diane stood and spoke forcefully and calmly.

"I'm afraid that isn't happening, Mr. Raymond. We called you and Coach Geiser here as a courtesy so you won't be blindsided by this. Once we've made our presentation, I'm hoping you'll see how serious this is and won't resent the time you spent here."

She gave them a piercing look, and the two men shifted uneasily in their chairs.

"Good. Then let's get going so this doesn't take any longer than it has to. As I'm sure you're aware, there was a party at the DeShayne residence Saturday night two weeks ago from which a complaint of rape was lodged with the sheriff's office. The initial investigation stalled, in large part owing to lack of cooperation from people at that party. We've now come into new evidence that is causing the investigation to be more aggressively pursued. We invited you here for a briefing because this is a matter that affects both the high school and its football team."

She looked around the room. Raymond and Geiser had drawn their faces tighter, but said nothing.

"Early this morning, based on a sworn affidavit, the sheriff's department served a search warrant at the DeShayne residence and confiscated a video camera and four videotapes from the room of Caitlin DeShayne. Most of the videotapes are of no interest to this investigation, but one of them contained approximately 40 minutes of footage of the party in question. That's what we'd like to show you now. Howard."

He moved to the TV, flipped it on, and popped the video into the player.

For several seconds, nothing appeared on the screen. The first image showed about two dozen students in an unevenly lit recreation room. Most of them had their backs to the camera and were standing in a semicircle around a young man, clearly identifiable as the quarterback, Kyle Burnett.

"Go, Kyle," said a woman's voice from near the camera.

Kyle raised his right hand, which was holding a beer can.

"What are we gonna do tonight?" he shouted.

"Paaarty!" chorused the crowd.

"And who's gonna get wasted tonight?"

"Everybody!" the group shouted back, followed by a round of applause.

On the left side of the semicircle, visible even in the dim light, stood Hooper, looking uneasy. He didn't join the group in shouting back the answers to Kyle's questions.

For the remainder of the video, the camera went off and on, offering a series of vignettes. It appeared that Caitlin was doing most of the photography, though occasionally someone else took over the camera so she could be filmed briefly. In between vignettes, the camera was turned off, except for a couple of times when Caitlin forgot and recorded a couple of minutes of footage of the camera moving through the room, pointing at the floor. The first scene of interest occurred when Caitlin stood before the camera and announced:

"Now we're going to photograph the good girls. They're boring, so we'll get them out of the way early, but maybe after a few drinks, they'll be more interesting."

The backup cinematographer handed the camera to Caitlin without turning it off, and the audience followed its wobbles through the crowd to a group of three young women standing near a wall.

"These are three of Alta Mira's top cheerleaders: Julie Billings, Alicia Rios, and Emma Thornton. Wave for the camera, girls."

They giggled and waved. Watching the video, Gordon realized this was the first time he had seen Alicia, even in an image. She was beautiful, with long black hair falling below her shoulders, classical features, and large bright eyes that seemed to be trying to make sense of a social situation that appeared to be new to her.

"Good evening, ladies," said a male voice, and the camera pulled back to show Kyle and Cody Jarrett joining the group. Each was holding an open beer in one hand and two capped bottles in the other.

"Are we having fun yet?" Kyle asked, and they smiled. "Can we offer you a beer?"

Julie, Alicia, and Emma looked at each other for support.

"I'll try one," Emma said, and Cody handed her a bottle.

"I don't know," Julie said. "I might have to drive home."

"Then just take one and sip it all night. You'll be fine," Kyle said.

"OK," she said, taking a bottle from him with an eagerness that suggested her resistance had been perfunctory.

"How about you, Alicia?"

"I don't know," she said, looking slightly uncomfortable. "I tried a beer once and didn't like it."

"That's all right," Kyle said. "Not everybody does. Hey, I've got an idea. How about if I bring you a glass of orange juice with just a little bit" — he held up a hand with the thumb and index finger a fraction of an inch apart — "of vodka in it."

Alicia looked at Julie and Emma holding their beers.

"Well, all right," she said.

"That's the way to party," he said, turning to the camera and winking at it.

The camera switched off, and subsequently photographed several groups of people drinking and speaking in voices growing louder and more unsteady. Eventually, it returned to the "good girls" group. Alicia was holding a 12-ounce glass with a bit of orange liquid at the bottom and speaking in a louder and more uninhibited manner than earlier. Gordon thought that a glass that size could easily have been half filled with vodka without a novice drinker realizing it, and he felt slightly sick.

"Alicia," Kyle said, approaching from her right. "I saw that you were almost out, so I made you another one." He handed her another 12-ounce glass and took the one in her hand.

"Thank you," she said, slowly and with a bit of effort. "This is really nice, but it seems to be making me a bit dizzy."

"Nah. There's not enough alcohol in there to do that. Probably too many people in this room, and it's a bit stuffy. That's all."

"OK," Alicia said, taking another sip.

The camera made another round of the party, and it seemed as if the volume was being steadily turned up, though it was really the partiers becoming more inebriated. At one point, the camera turned a corner and went into a dimly lit hallway, and there was enough light to see a male and female body in a tight clinch, with the female's back against the wall.

"Hey, Sarah," came Caitlin's voice. "Smile for the camera."

Sarah responded by raising her left hand with the middle finger extended. Caitlin held the shot for several seconds before switching off the camera.

A few more brief party scenes followed before there was a shot of Alicia asleep, or perhaps more accurately, unconscious on a couch. The camera was back at a distance, but zoomed in to focus on her face, unflattering with its mouth open.

"Aww, man, she couldn't handle it," said Cody's voice off camera.

"What did you put in that drink, anyway?" Julie asked.

"Just a little vodka, that's all," Kyle said. "I guess she's never had a drink before."

"We need to get her somewhere where she can lie down," Cody said.

"Yeah, we need to get her horizontal," Kyle said, then laughed.

"There's a spare bedroom down the hall," came Caitlin's voice from behind the camera.

Cody stepped into the frame, slid his right arm under Alicia's back and his left under her knees. She hung limply as he lifted her from the couch.

With Kyle leading the way, Cody carried her down the hall, the camera following them.

"Next door on the left," called Caitlin.

Kyle held it open as Cody carried Alicia into the room. He closed the door, and the camera remained on it for what seemed like hours, but was only 45 seconds before Kyle and Cody came out.

"You know she wants me," Kyle said. "So I'm gonna give her what she wants. But I'm sure she'd be happy to have you after that."

Cody said nothing.

"Or if that's not your flavor," Kyle continued, "I'll bet you can get head from Emma if you score a touchdown next Friday." He clapped Cody on the shoulder. "Don't worry, man. I'll get you the ball."

And with that, he went back in the room, closing the door behind him.

Several seconds later the camera turned off, then came on again with another general party scene. The crowd seemed to have diminished some.

"All right, Howard," Diane said, standing up. "You can stop it there."

CHRIS TURNED ON THE LIGHTS as Howard stopped the video. The room was still. The four men who were seeing the video for the first time looked shaken and disoriented. Without giving them a chance to recover, Diane began talking.

"The rest of this video isn't relevant to the case, but as you can see, it gives the investigation a direction it hasn't had up to now. And we're taking it very seriously. That's why when Alta Mira High School lets out at 3:10 (she looked at her watch), about an hour from now, all three sheriff's patrol cars on duty will be waiting outside. They will be bringing Kyle Burnett, Cody Jarrett, and Caitlin DeShayne separately to my office for a formal reading of their Miranda rights and further questioning — that is, if they don't lawyer up.

"Sheriff Huntley and I conferred this morning and agreed that because of the two unsolved murder cases before the sheriff's office, the rape investigation will be handled by the district attorney's office. Deputy District Attorney Goodwin and I will be conducting it, and, if the evidence is convincing, we will file criminal charges. The sheriff's office will, of course, cooperate fully with us and will be apprised of developments as they occur."

She stopped and looked around the room, not moving on from any of its occupants until her eyes and theirs had met.

"Are there any questions?"

The room was silent for half a minute, then:

"I have a question," Geiser said.

"Yes?"

"Before the deputies bring Burnett and Jarrett down here, can I have a word with them?"

She arched an eyebrow. "Why? So you can tip them off?"

"No," the coach said. "So I can kick their sorry asses off the football team."

Raymond, suddenly animated, whipped around.

"Lloyd, are you sure you want to do that? This video doesn't prove they committed any crime, and don't you think you should give them the benefit of the doubt? Especially with a playoff game Friday night."

"How much doubt is there, Duane? You saw what I saw. Before the season began, they signed a contract agreeing they could be dismissed from the team for a variety of offenses, including drinking during the season and conduct detrimental to the team. And I'm the sole judge of that. Sorry, but they're gone."

"But can't you wait until after Friday's game?"

"Use your head, Duane. Once the whole school sees them driven off in patrol cars, they're a dead weight on the rest of the team. No, we have 35 players on varsity, and with Jarrett and Burnett gone, we still have 33. I'll see that those 33 give Aspen Valley a game to remember."

He turned to Diane.

"So can I talk to them when school's out?"

She nodded. "Go ahead. You may be able to punish them more than the law can."

Geiser rose and turned to the principal.

"Then I'm heading back to campus to make sure they get the message to see me as soon as school's out." He looked back at Chris. "You might want to tell your deputies to wait by my office for those two."

And, clearly on a mission, he stormed out of the room. Raymond stayed for another half minute, then rose and left without so much as a farewell to anyone.

A few seconds later, the five people remaining in the room exhaled simultaneously.

"Well, what do you think?" Diane asked.

"I wish I could get that video out of my mind," Gordon said. "But you didn't leave any doubt about where you're going."

"Yeah. The problem is, Duane was right. This video certainly shows conduct detrimental to the team, whatever that is, but there's no solid proof of a crime here. Kyle can say anything he wants about what happened in that room, and Alicia doesn't remember enough to contradict him effectively. Maybe, though, it'll loosen someone's tongue. We can hope, anyway. How about you, Sam?"

"I think if I'd seen that video when I got married, I wouldn't have any children today."

"Makes you think, doesn't it, but don't give up hope altogether. Howard, what are you thinking now?"

"I don't know if they're guilty of a crime or not, but I do know the football team is screwed on Friday night. Still, you've got to hand it to Coach. He has a pair."

"Your highest compliment," Chris murmured.

"All right then," Diane said, moving toward the door. "I've got to prepare. I have a long night of interviews ahead."

Howard, Gordon and Sam also stood. Gordon turned to the sheriff.

"Chris, could I have a couple of minutes alone with you now?"

She nodded wearily, and Gordon turned to Sam.

"I'll meet you at the hotel in less than an hour. If you want to drive … "

Sam waved him off.

"I'll walk. I need some exercise, and I'm not going to get it fishing today."

"WHAT'S ON YOUR MIND, GORDON?" she said after the others had left.

He shifted in his chair.

"First of all," he said, "I want you to understand this is just an unformed idea at this point. But a couple of things I noticed this morning put that idea in my head."

"Is this about our killer?" He nodded. "Well," she continued, "an unformed idea is better than no idea, which is what we have now. Let's hear it."

"All right. This morning, Sam and I accompanied Elizabeth Macondray to the home of Jessica Milland's mother in Big Piney. Elizabeth's on the campus safety committee …"

"You don't have to rationalize. Keep going."

" … Anyway, her brother was there — Jessica's brother, I mean — and that got me to thinking." He paused momentarily, took a deep breath, and kept going. "Her brother is a sheriff's deputy in Yolo County, and he was very emphatic on the point that she wouldn't have accepted a ride from someone she didn't know. And you've been interviewing people on campus with the same idea in mind, right?"

She nodded.

"Something was starting to come to me then, and I lost the thread," he continued. "Then, a while later, as we were driving back to Alta Mira, we saw Sandy Steadman on the side of the road, calling for help for a Homestead student whose car had broken down on the road to Big

Piney. That's when the penny dropped. We've been assuming Jessica knew the person who picked her up, but there's one class of stranger who could have offered her a ride without attracting suspicion."

"Oh, shit," she said.

"A uniformed law enforcement officer in an official car would have seemed like a safe bet, especially to a woman whose brother is a sheriff's deputy. It's just a hunch, Chris, but I'm putting it out there for whatever it's worth."

They sat silently for more than a minute. The blinds over the conference room windows were still drawn, and they were entirely isolated in that silence.

"For whatever it's worth, I hope you're wrong," she finally said. "But I can't deny it's a possibility."

"Please don't think I'm anti-law enforcement or anything ... "

She waved her arm to dismiss the idea.

"Don't worry about it, Gordon. I've been in the business 20 years and I've yet to meet the law enforcement officer who would qualify as an angel. And I've known several — and thankfully it was only several — who were downright unfit." She let out a harsh, guttural laugh. "In fact, I married one."

Gordon said nothing, and after a while, she continued.

"He was an investigator for the district attorney's office and a former policeman. There wasn't a clue all the time we were dating, then once we said, 'I do,' the trouble started. He got steadily more abusive, and I put up with it for three years, thinking it would get better. In spite of everything I've seen on the job. I finally moved out and filed for divorce, but he kept on harassing me."

"Did you get a restraining order?"

"I was spending too much on legal fees already, so I handled it informally."

"Informally?"

She nodded. "That's right. I told him if he showed up at my door again, I'd shoot his jewels off. That got his attention, at least for a while, and it bought me enough time to apply for jobs away from Sacramento and get hired here. Now you know the whole sordid story."

Gordon couldn't think of much to say, so he remained silent. She shifted in her chair and continued.

"But about that idea of yours. I need to figure out where would I start looking, and how to do it without anybody getting the wind up."

"I did have a thought along those lines. Or maybe more like a question, actually. Does the college have a campus police force?"

She shook her head. "Good point. No, they contract with the sheriff's department for law enforcement services. They pay salaries and benefits for three deputies, and we ensure that at least one of them is on patrol at the campus between 6 a.m. and 10 p.m. daily."

"Maybe a starting point would be to see if any of those deputies was off duty the day the student disappeared in Ponderosa County. Would it be possible for any of them to have access to a patrol car when off duty?"

"Under certain circumstances, but we're not too strict about it. Maybe we should be. In any event, this is prodding me to be more virtuous. Last month's personnel records have been sitting on my desk since Monday, waiting for sign-off. I'll look at them after dinner, paying attention to the dates our first two students went missing and the date Tiffany Reese disappeared in Ponderosa County. I'm not expecting a hallelujah moment, but who knows? I might see something that bears a second look."

"You've got to start somewhere. And thanks for not laughing me out of the room when I threw out that idea."

"It's an idea. We'll see if it goes anywhere."

Gordon rose to leave, but she asked another question.

"By the way, I'm curious about what you, as a former athlete, make of the coach's decision. I have to say it surprised me a bit. I thought he might try to cover for them."

"I don't know," he finally said. "He *is* a Santa Clara man, so maybe that Jesuit education left him with a bit of a conscience."

"Or there could be a simpler answer. I understand he has a daughter."

I WAITED IN THE HOTEL ROOM for nearly an hour, before Gordon came back. For most of that time, I was feeling that I should take a shower, but I knew it would take more than hot, running water to wash away the slime from that video. Something like that, you don't forget very easily.

Gordon was a bit grumpy when he got back. It was nothing I haven't seen before, and I waited for it to pass, which it finally did. He announced that Brenda Hastings and Elizabeth would be joining us for dinner at Elizalde's. At the rate we've been going there, they should put a plaque on one of the tables in our honor.

We picked Brenda up at five. She'd made herself up a bit and looked better than on Monday, and the black dress became her. But the strain was still evident. I was thinking that some man will probably ask her to marry him in a few years, but I wonder if she could ever do that. When you've been married 15 years to someone like Mountain Bob, who is, let's face it, *sui generis*, would it ever be possible for anyone else to take his place?

On the way to the restaurant, she told Gordon the funeral would be Monday morning, and I wondered if any church in town would be big enough. She also asked Gordon if he would say a few words, and he said yes without hesitation, even though he hates public speaking.

Elizabeth was waiting at the restaurant, and we were quickly seated. The place was just starting to fill up, but a couple of the other customers clearly took note of Brenda and knew who she was.

"I hope nobody thinks I'm being wicked for going to a restaurant," she said after drink orders were taken. "But if they do — well, tough! I haven't been out of the house in two days, and I need to get away a bit. Thanks for asking, Gordon."

The drinks came. She had a cherry Coke, and I noticed Gordon ordered a 7-Up. We made small talk for a few minutes before Elizabeth turned to Brenda.

"You may have heard this already," she said, "but two football players have been brought in for questioning in connection with the rape at that party two weeks ago. What you might not know is that it wouldn't have happened without Bob."

"But … how?"

"He was onto something on Sunday, and he left enough of a clue as to what it was that Gordon figured it out. That enabled us to run down a student who was a witness and get a break that the sheriff could follow."

"Elizabeth is being far too modest," Gordon said. "She had a lot to do with it."

"No, Gordon. You cracked Bob's code and you talked the kid into going to the sheriff. Bob would have been proud."

"I'm glad to hear that," Brenda finally said. "Bob was really upset about that. Do you think they'll make an arrest?"

"Too soon to say," Gordon replied. "But it opens up the investigation. And it was Bob who did most of the digging. We just had to figure out where the bone was."

Brenda smiled. "When Bob was onto something, he *was* like a dog with a bone."

The waitress came, and we ordered dinner. After she left, Gordon leaned toward Brenda just a bit and lowered his voice.

"Brenda, I don't know if you're up to it, and if not, just say so. But I wanted to ask if you could help with something."

"Tell me more. I'll help if I can."

Gordon reached into his shirt pocket and took out the notebook.

"The morning Bob was killed, he had some notes on a notepad by his side. It seemed to be a list of five things in his own peculiar shorthand, and the sheriff let me copy it down. Do you think you might be able to make sense of any of it?"

He placed the open paper in front of her.

"Let's take this from the bottom up," Gordon said. "The last thing he wrote was 'Wheaties.' Does that mean anything to you?"

She shook her head. "He hated cold cereal, and they didn't advertise. Sorry. I have no idea."

"All right, then. 'DS – Gurgle,' we thought might be a note about a sound effect for DeShayne Plumbing."

"It has to be," she said. "Bob loved coming up with weird sounds for those ads. It appealed to his inner eight-year-old."

"How about 'Geiser – Wed?' We think …"

"He told me Sunday night he wanted to get the coach on his show this week."

"Good. And 'Time - :30' we think is a memo to himself to remember to give the time."

She nodded. "He'd get so carried away with his routines he'd forget to do that sometimes, so he often wrote a note to himself."

"Great. We're making some progress. Now, does this first one, 'SBYM – TW' mean anything to you?"

Her jaw dropped and she sat open-mouthed for a second. Then her eyes teared up, and big drops began running down her cheeks.

"Brenda! Are you all right?"

She shook her head and waved him off.

"You couldn't have known, Gordon. It's not your fault. That was our special song."

"Song?" he echoed.

"It was even a little inside joke with us. Whenever he'd get off on a high horse about something and I tried to calm him down, he'd go, 'SBYM, Brenda. SBYM.' It means Stand By Your Man. He'd play the song every week and always called to tell me when it was going to be on."

She began sobbing violently. Elizabeth quickly talked her into going to the ladies' room. They went off, leaving us men to our discomfort.

"That didn't go too well," Gordon said, when they were out of earshot.

"Yeah," I said. "But how could you have known? Between this and Jessica's mother this morning, all I can say is I'm glad I'm not a police officer. I wouldn't want to do this more than once every lifetime."

"Same here," he said, putting the notebook back in his pocket.

"By the way, what does TW mean?"

"Tammy Wynette," he said. "It's her signature song."

BRENDA RECOVERED ENOUGH to get through the dinner and even reasonably enjoy it, but said afterward she needed to go straight home. Elizabeth invited Gordon and Sam to her place to hear about the video, but Sam pleaded fatigue. So after dropping Brenda at her home and Sam at the hotel, Gordon started for the Nuñes Ranch, where Elizabeth lived.

The dull overcast had lingered over the area all day and into the night. The moonless, starless sky provided no light at all, and Gordon felt as if he were driving through a tank of oil. Just outside town, he became aware of a pair of headlights behind him, perhaps a bit closer than necessary. In the complete darkness, he couldn't see what kind of vehicle it was. After several miles of being closely tailed, Gordon slowed down on a long straightaway. Instead of passing, the car stayed behind him, and he began to get nervous. There was no one else on the road, and he'd seen only a couple of vehicles coming the other direction. Just as he was beginning to worry seriously, he heard a loud engine noise, and his follower pulled out to pass. It was a smaller pickup and was quickly far ahead of him. He exhaled with relief.

"Thanks for coming," Elizabeth said, as she let him in. "I really want to hear about the video, but it didn't seem like appropriate dinner conversation."

"Maybe at Caligula's table," Gordon said. "Part of me wishes I hadn't seen it."

"Steel yourself with a small glass of wine," she said, pouring a few ounces of Russian River Cabernet into a glass. "But first I want to show you something." She led him to the door at the edge of the living area and grasped the knob.

"I've changed my mind," she said.

She turned the knob and flipped a light switch in the room. As Gordon stepped in, he saw that the half-dozen easels that had been covered Monday night were now unveiled, their paintings open for inspection. Without saying a word, he started at the one farthest to his left and made the rounds clockwise, stopping before each painting — longer at some than others. Between the paintings and her physical presence, Elizabeth seemed to have enveloped the room, and he was aware of her with every step and every breath he took.

When he had looked at all six, he stepped back to take a second look at the painting fourth from the left. It was a scene of Alta Mira, viewed from the mountains to the west, at twilight, after a thunderstorm. The town was an indistinct mélange of light points, the light contrasting with the dark sky above. It looked safe and inviting, and Gordon wondered when she had painted it.

"If you want my opinion," he finally said, "I think this is the best one."

"Damn! I thought you'd go for the one with the fisherman."

"That's a good picture, and it'll probably sell faster than this one. But it doesn't have the boldness of light and color and the dramatic composition. Just my opinion, for whatever it's worth."

"For whatever it's worth, that's pretty much what I think, too."

They stepped back into the living area. She sat on the couch, and Gordon began to take a seat in a facing chair, but she patted the couch next to her with her left hand and he sat there, a discreet distance from her.

Elizabeth asked him to describe the video, and he did, in considerable detail. She listened intently, interrupting once or twice to ask a question.

"That is so awful," she said when he finished. "I've been to some wild parties, but I don't recall anything like that ever happening."

"Same here. Watching that, I couldn't help thinking that there don't seem to be any rules anymore."

"It doesn't sound like it. What you've told me is enough to make me a believer in the Antioch Rules."

"I'm sorry," Gordon said.

"You've never heard of the Antioch Rules?"

Gordon shook his head.

"I thought everybody had," she continued. "Anyway, Antioch is a liberal-arts college in Ohio, and because of cases like this one, they established a code of sexual conduct for their students a few years ago. What it basically comes down to is that if you want to have sex with someone, you have to ask permission for every action you take along the way. You look skeptical."

"I am. So let's say, hypothetically, of course, that a normally healthy pair of college students has been sitting together as we are, baring their innermost souls to each other, and the guy decides he wants to take matters to a less spiritual plane … "

"Spirituality can be expressed in many ways, Gordon."

" … He would have to say something like, 'I'd like to put my arms around you.' "

"You have to frame it as a question."

"May I put my arms around you?"

"Yes, you may." He sat still for a second. "That wasn't a hypothetical answer."

He slid his arms around her and drew her toward him.

"Then I'd follow it up with something like, 'May I kiss you?' "

"Yes, you may."

He leaned forward and kissed her. She returned it warmly, and the kiss, growing steadily more intense, lasted over a minute before she broke it off.

"You're getting ahead of yourself, Gordon. You have to ask before your hands do that."

"Sorry. Instinctive reflex. May I slide my hands up your body."

"Sure."

They kissed again, and he slid a hand up either side of her torso, stopping with his thumbs just under her breasts.

"No more until you ask," she said.

"May I lick your ear?"

She jerked her head back several inches.

"Whoa! That was *not* what I was expecting."

"Well, if you need a minute to think about it …"

"No, go ahead."

"I'm confused. Was that no, or go ahead?"

"It was go ahead."

He began licking her left earlobe. She squirmed at first, then began giggling and finally pushed him back.

"I'm sorry," she said. "That's a real turn-on, but it tickles like hell."

"Then let's go back to where we were. May I touch your breasts?"

"Yes, you may."

He slid his hands under her blouse, and when they reached breast level, they moved to the back to undo her bra.

"I just said yes to touching the breasts. If you want to take the bra off, you need to ask."

"May I remove that stifling contraption you're wearing?"

"Which one?"

"Your bra."

"Yes."

He began to slide his hands around her back, but at that moment his cell phone went off. She immediately jumped to her feet, and his hands came out from under her blouse.

"You'd better answer that," she said. "It might be your mother."

"At moments like this, I miss my pager," he said, taking the phone out of his pocket, "It looks like the sheriff." He put it to his ear. "Gordon."

"Gordon! Thank God you picked up." Chris's voice sounded strained and worried. "I need to talk to you right now. Where are you?"

He looked up at Elizabeth, who appeared only slightly disheveled.

"Isn't that kind of a personal question?"

"Don't be a smartass, Gordon. This is big."

"I'm at Elizabeth Macondray's place. It's ..."

"I know where it is. I'll be there in 10 minutes."

She rang off. Gordon looked at the phone for several seconds, then put it back in his pocket.

"The sheriff will be here in 10 minutes," he said.

"Funny. I don't recall inviting her."

"She's the law, Elizabeth. When you're the law, you don't have to play by Antioch Rules. You don't have to ask permission."

CHRIS CAME IN ON SCHEDULE, looking haggard and worried. Something had obviously shaken her. She declined a glass of wine, took a glass of water, and sat in a chair. Gordon and Elizabeth sat on the couch facing her, leaving a couple of feet of discreet space between them.

After drinking half a glass, the sheriff took a deep breath and began.

"I'll take it from the beginning. It may help compose me. Back on the 17th of August there was a high-speed vehicle chase that started south of Ponderosa, blew through that town, and kept heading north. A 19-year-old kid got hopped up on meth, stole a car, and hit the accelerator instead of the brake when the red lights started flashing behind him. This was all in broad daylight, by the way.

"Anyway, when the chase left Ponderosa and was headed toward our county, we got a call and quickly set up a little welcoming committee a couple of miles into Plateau County. Several law enforcement vehicles established a roadblock at a point where the guy who stole the car could see them up ahead, but couldn't get around because the road was a bit elevated at that point. If he made it that far, he wasn't going to get any farther.

"Or so we thought. When the kid saw the roadblock, he sped up, swerved off the road and went airborne. He cleared a barbed-wire fence at the bottom of the embankment and landed in the meadow below. He could have killed himself, but the impaired are sometimes lucky. The car was disabled, but he got out and made a run for it before he was finally tackled and handcuffed.

"That was our biggest excitement for the month, but because the chase began in Ponderosa County, they were handling the prosecution, so it kind of faded from my mind. Then, a couple of hours ago, Gordon, I started looking at our personnel logs for last month, like you suggested, and ..."

She shook her head, took a big gulp of water, followed by a deep breath, and plunged forward.

"On Friday October 17, they had a preliminary hearing for the kid, who was facing a bazillion charges. It was held from 9:30 a.m. to noon at the Ponderosa County Courthouse, and just before noon the judge ruled there was enough evidence to bind the defendant over for trial in superior court. But because the chase ended here, one of our people was subpoenaed as a witness to testify about it.

"So, in short, a Plateau County sheriff's officer was in Ponderosa, in court, until noon that day. And at 1:30 p.m. that same day, Tiffany Reese was last seen heading toward the entrance to Ponderosa Community College. She hasn't been seen since. I still can't believe it."

She leaned back in her chair and looked up at the ceiling.

"Was it one of your campus police officers?" Gordon asked.

"No. It was worse than that."

She picked up the glass of water, drank what was left of it, and set it down.

"It was Howard Honig."

Gordon whistled, and Elizabeth's eyes grew wider.

"And it gets worse. Reviewing the personnel records, I saw that Howard had the day off and put in for overtime for the testimony. But he was off all afternoon, and didn't return the department vehicle he drove down there until Saturday morning. If nothing else, he had the means and opportunity to commit the crime.

"And I don't know what to do next. I've never had to handle a case where a major crime investigation swept up one of ours. And for obvious reasons, I can't talk about it to anyone in the department — or even to Diane, at this point. But I needed to talk to somebody, and since it was your idea in the first place to look at law enforcement, Gordon, I'm dumping it in your lap.

"Any thoughts or questions?"

They sat in stunned silence for nearly a minute before Elizabeth spoke.

"Wouldn't the patrol car from this county look different enough to arouse suspicion?"

"I thought of that, too. But they're both a green-and-white motif, though the designs are a bit different. Your average person is probably going to see the colors, the lines of the car, the lights on top, and the guy in uniform driving it and not think twice."

For the next hour and a quarter, they discussed the situation. With someone to bounce her thoughts off, Chris began to develop an outline of what she needed to do. It included:

Say nothing to Howard and look into what she could without arousing suspicion from him or anyone else in the department.

Identify the vehicle he drove to Ponderosa for the court hearing and search it herself.

Review Howard's personnel records to see where he was when the three women disappeared from Homestead College.

Review the records of the campus police officers for those dates as well.

By the end of that discussion, she had calmed down considerably and thanked Gordon and Elizabeth for listening and for promising to say nothing to anyone else. Gordon then brought up the rape investigation and asked whether Diane Brinkley had been able to get anything from the students.

Chris snorted.

"A lot of attitude, mostly. They all lawyered up, but she thinks Cody Jarrett may understand he has a problem and be amenable to reason down the line. Oh, and you'll love this. The attorney retained by Kyle Burnett's father has filed for a temporary restraining order tomorrow. He's going to argue that the coach shouldn't be allowed to throw Kyle off the team without giving him a hearing and due process. Since the district attorney represents the school district, Diane's going to have to drop everything else for a couple of hours and argue that case."

Elizabeth shook her head. "When the parents send that kind of message, well, the apple doesn't fall far from the tree."

"I hope Diane doesn't spend too much time on the restraining order," Gordon said. "It really doesn't matter, you know."

"What do you mean?" Chris asked.

"I guess you've never played for a school team before. Even if the judge rules in Burnett's favor, it's still the coach's decision who plays — even who gets in uniform for the game. If Kyle Burnett wins tomorrow morning, it just means that he might get to watch the game from the sidelines in civilian clothes. He won't even be able to hold a football. I'd bet money on that."

IT WAS AFTER TEN O'CLOCK, and rain had begun falling outside when Chris finally left. Elizabeth closed the door behind her and returned, with Gordon, to the couch. For five minutes, they stared at the ceiling, listening to the rain fall.

"What a night," Gordon finally said. "I suppose the seminar on Antioch Rules will have to wait for another time."

"I don't know. Is that what *you* want?"

"Well, I suppose we could try to pick up where we left off."

She smiled just enough to embolden the idea.

"But look here," he said. "This is all really confusing. I mean, am I supposed to assume that after all this time, prior consent is still valid? Or do I have to go back and start at the beginning? How does this sort of thing work in real life?"

She gave the impression of thinking it over for a minute.

"Tell you what, Gordon. It's getting late, and I have to be in the classroom at 8:30 tomorrow morning. So what if we just cut to the chase, and I say yes to everything."

"Works for me," he said.

Thursday November 13

THE FIRST THING I DID when I woke up was to roll over and see if Gordon had come in during the night when I was asleep. His bed was still crisply made and unoccupied. Less work for the maid. The clock on the nightstand said 7:10, and I sat up. Could it really be so late?

I'd been thinking that maybe I'd take the plane up today. When I talked to Nancy last night, and vented about Gordon (not for the first time), she suggested it might take my mind off things. With no fishing on the horizon, and being something of a fifth wheel around Gordon and Elizabeth, I could use a little something to free my spirits. Ever since I did my first takeoff in flight school, I've experienced a feeling of sheer joy when I leave the ground in a small plane and can see the earth growing smaller beneath me. I don't get that on a commercial flight because I can't see so well, and I'm not the pilot. I got out of bed, walked to the window, and drew the curtains.

They opened to a vista of unabated gray, seen through steady rain. A red car passed below on the street, and as it moved up Chaparral Boulevard, it got darker and darker, finally fading almost to gray, except for the brake lights. Although I was in one of the highest places in Alta Mira, I couldn't see to the edge of town, less than half a mile away. The dark gray clouds hung so low they obscured the mountains. Flying was out of the question. There are old pilots and there are bold pilots, but there are no old, bold pilots. I am not bold enough to go up in weather like this.

Gordon called at 7:30 to suggest meeting at Danny's Diner in half an hour. Fifteen minutes later, I stood at the front door of the Danube, put on a cap I'd gotten from a riverfront resort Gordon and I stayed at two years earlier, pulled the hood of my parka over it, and stepped outside. It was cold — damp, East Coast cold, with a breeze that whipped you with icy lashes and sent the rain sideways into your face. The time and temperature sign on the bank said it was 43 degrees, but it felt like 23. It was a long three blocks to the diner, and my jeans were more than damp when I arrived.

I snagged one of the few remaining tables and sat down to wait for him. With nothing else to do, I eavesdropped on the conversations around me. Most of them had to do with the football game coming up tomorrow night, and the suspension of the quarterback and star receiver. From the snatches of conversation I picked up, there seemed to be a division of opinion about whether the players should have been suspended. On another point, however, there was a strong consensus: Without Burnett and Jarrett in the game, Alta Mira would face an uphill battle against Aspen Valley.

Five minutes after I arrived, Gordon came in. He'd pulled into the parking lot just as someone parked near the front door was leaving. He was barely wet and sat down after removing his jacket and hanging it over the back of his chair.

"Nice weather for ducks," I said conversationally.

He grunted. It was going to be that kind of morning. He improved slightly after a cup of coffee, but for someone who presumably had a good time last night, he was awfully taciturn. At least I've known him long enough not to take offense.

Just as the waitress was setting down his plate of sausage and eggs, Gordon's phone rang.

"It's the sheriff," he said. "Hello."

A pause and a change of expression. Pretty dramatic for Gordon.

"No, I wasn't expecting it to be you, but no problem. What can I do?"

Pause.

"Oh, I'm sorry to hear that. Will he be OK?"

Pause.

"Well, I don't know. I've never done that before."

Pause.

"Well, I suppose I could. I'm flattered that you thought of me."

Pause.

"All right. I'll give it a try. What time?"

Pause.

"OK. See you then. Thanks for asking."

Pause.

"No problem. Bye."

He turned the phone off, set it on the table and stared at it. After a minute passed without his saying anything or starting to eat, I decided to take matters into my own hands.

"What was that all about, Gordon? You look like a felon who just got a call from his parole officer."

He jerked his head slightly and his thoughts returned to the table. "No. It was just — that was Howard. It turns out Jed Clampett, one of his spotters, fell down his back stairs last night and broke a leg. No way he can get up to the press box tomorrow. Howard wanted to know if I could fill in as a spotter at the big game."

"And that shook you up this badly? I sense something's going on, Gordon. Why aren't you telling me about it?"

He looked around the café. "Not here," he finally mumbled. "Too crowded."

He dug into his sausage and eggs and ate for three minutes without saying a word. He finished his coffee, the waitress materialized out of nowhere to refill his cup, and he held it up but stopped before taking a sip.

"Save some room for a piece of pie, Sam. We're going for a drive after breakfast."

AT 9:15 A.M. — AFTER ARRAIGNING two drunk drivers, a shoplifter, and a litterbug — the Honorable Susan Jackson heard the petition for a temporary restraining order allowing Kyle Burnett and Cody Jarrett to be reinstated to the football team pending a formal hearing. A jury trial in a domestic violence case was resuming at 10 a.m., and the judge wanted the restraining order to be decided one way or another by then.

By agreement of all parties, only the attorneys were present. Deputy District Attorney Diane Brinkley represented the school district. Owen Waterman, partner in one of the largest law firms in Redding, nearly 150 miles away, represented both students, with the stipulation that he did so only on the matter of the restraining order; Jarrett had separate counsel for the investigation against him. The judge glumly calculated that Waterman was probably charging his clients more for the drive to Alta Mira than she earned in two days.

Waterman argued that the district was required to provide a formal hearing for the students before taking them off the team. Brinkley argued that playing for the football team was a voluntary, elective activity that was governed by a contract between the players and coach, giving the coach sole discretion in disciplinary matters. Both attorneys cited sections of the state's voluminous education code to support their positions, and after 35 minutes of argument, Judge Jackson told them to make their final summaries in three minutes or less.

They did, and finished at 9:58. Two minutes until the jury trial was to resume. The judge, who had to stand for election in June, realized she was in a no-win situation. Both sides had constituencies, and however she ruled, one side would be angry with her. With 30 seconds left, she remembered the advice of her favorite law professor: When in doubt, simplify. The judge lowered her eyes from the ceiling, at which she had been staring, and looked at the two attorneys.

"A contract is a contract. Motion for the restraining order is denied."

GORDON AND SAM DROVE WEST out of town. As the miles added up, the scenery changed — encompassing meadow, forest, riverside, and the occasional small town, desolate in the rain — but the skyline remained the same: a monotonous mélange of grays. The rain never achieved downpour status, but it never let up, either, falling steadily at light to moderate levels. In the 40-mile drive to the town of Piper Creek, Gordon's windshield wipers and headlights were never off.

Once Alta Mira was well behind them, Gordon began to relax and open up. He enjoyed driving, and even in the rain, an open road with almost no traffic was a tonic to his soul.

"I wanted to drive for two reasons," he said, as much to himself as to Sam. "I want to put that town behind me for a while, and I wanted to tell you a couple of things I couldn't in the restaurant."

Sam, looking out the window, nodded. Gordon continued:

"An idea occurred to me yesterday. I've been trying to think who a student at the college would trust enough to ride with, and it flashed into my brain that a law enforcement officer would be high on the list. When I was alone with Chris yesterday, after we were watching the video, I suggested the idea to her."

"And how did *that* go over?"

"Actually, she was pretty responsive. I guess she learned from her ex-husband that not every law enforcement officer is a wonderful human being. She was going to check her staffing records to see if any of the deputies who work on campus were off the day the student went missing in Ponderosa last month. She found more than she bargained for.

"It seems that Howard was in Ponderosa that day, testifying at a hearing on a high-speed chase that began there and ended up in this county. He was in court that morning, and would have been starting back to Plateau County about the time the student was last seen."

Sam whistled. "Does she think he's a suspect?"

"She was pretty agitated about it. She came over to Elizabeth's last night ..."

"Sorry to hear that."

"Came over to tell us about it. It's a tough position for her. The guy who's been in the sheriff's department longer than just about everybody, and who's going to run for her job in June, is suddenly in a place where there's a suspicion against him, but no real evidence that he's the guy who's been making off with the students. She has to go *real* slow with that one."

They drove on for a minute without saying anything.

"Well," Sam said, "that explains your reaction when Howard asked you to help with the football game."

"If you have to be with a serial killer, that press box during a game is probably as safe a place as any. But his call shook me up, knowing what I know."

"Can I ask a question, Gordon? You said the *guy* who was making off with the students. Is there any way they know for sure it was a man, and not a woman?"

"Good question. Did you have a suspect in mind?"

"No, just asking. I mean if a female student would feel safe getting into a car with a male police officer, wouldn't she feel safer, if anything, getting into a car with another female student?" He paused for effect. "Or a female faculty member?"

Gordon shot him a dirty look.

"The part about getting into the car makes sense," Gordon said, "but the abductions and the taking a woman out to that lonely logging road — just doesn't feel like a woman's work to me."

"Maybe you need to examine your cultural assumptions."

"Maybe."

They drove in silence for another two minutes before Gordon continued:

"Speaking of things that don't feel right, I don't entirely like Howard as a suspect. I'm no FBI profiler, but from everything I've read and heard, serial killing is a young man's work — or, to keep your theory in play, Sam, a young *person's* work. Howard has to be, what, 55? That's pretty old to be running around, disposing of bodies."

"That's the problem with this case, Gordon. There's something wrong with every theory, but one of them is probably right. We just don't know which one."

It was a bit after ten when they rolled into Piper Creek, a depressed town of 500 souls that looked even more depressed on this rainy day. The lumber mill had closed in 1981, and when they drove over the railroad track that used to serve it, weeds several feet high were growing between the rails. In the center of the town's commercial area, such as it was, stood a long, one-story building with four storefronts. Three of them had "For Rent" signs in the windows, and the fourth housed the Piper Creek Café and Bakery, which had four pickups parked in front and a neon "Open" sign glowing in the window.

"Still here," Gordon said as he parked. "The last time I drove back from visiting Bob, I stopped here during an afternoon thunderstorm. A good place to have pie and coffee when it's raining."

The first thing they saw, coming through the door, was the counter, with a long refrigerated rack of pies behind it. Three men in jeans and Stetsons were sitting at a corner table on the left, and a fourth man was slowly chewing a solitary breakfast at the counter. Gordon and Sam took the table in the far right corner, as far from the other customers as possible. They were quickly approached by a very young, red-headed waitress, who flirted with them a bit for want of anything better to do. Sam ordered apple pie and coffee; Gordon coconut cream and coffee. Before getting their order, the waitress took the coffee pot to the table of three and flirted with the men there as she refilled their cups. Gordon and Sam's table was next to a large window, and they stared out at the rain falling on the parking lot as they waited for pie.

The pies were excellent, and their moods improved as they ate and drank coffee. It was comforting to be in a warm, clean place, eating dessert in the middle of the morning with the rain falling outside. Sam was down to his last bite of pie when his cell phone rang. As he fumbled for it, Gordon's phone rang as well. They answered, and carried on overlapping, parallel conversations.

"Sam Akers."

"This is Gordon."

"Oh, hi. I wasn't expecting it to be you."

"Good morning, sheriff. What's up?"

"Oh, no. I'm sorry to hear that. Yes, I knew it was coming, but ..."

"You don't say. I guess that rules out one possibility."

"No, no. Thanks for letting me know."

"You'd like to what?"

"Yes, I'll be sure to tell him."

"I suppose we could do that. It's not exactly like we had other plans."

"I'll definitely give him your regards and ask."

"All right. See you then."

"Bye now."

They ended their calls and set their phones on the table in an almost synchronous motion. Then they looked at each other.

"You first," Sam said.

"It was the sheriff. Two things. She was being a bit vague — probably because she's afraid of being overheard — but it sounds as if Howard is off the hook."

"Now you can enjoy the game tomorrow."

"And she wants to meet us in our hotel room this afternoon. I said yes." He looked at his watch. "We agreed on two o'clock, which is in about three hours, so we can have another cup of coffee and enjoy the scenery before we head back. Now what was your call about?"

"It was Sheriff Mike in Summit County. Kitty died this morning."

Gordon closed his eyes and said nothing for a full minute.

"Too bad," he finally replied, taking a sip of coffee. "She was a hell of a woman and ran a great café. Kind of appropriate, isn't it, that we were in a café when we got the news."

"I hadn't thought of that," Sam said. "Gordon, does this change anything with ..."

"No, Sam, it doesn't. It's over. I've made my peace with that."

BY THE TIME THE SHERIFF ARRIVED, Gordon and Sam had got the hotel room looking as good as a room occupied by two men on a fishing trip could be expected to look. They heard three raps on the door and opened it to find Chris and Diane Brinkley in the hall. The women sat at the two chairs by the round table in the room; Sam pulled up the room's third chair, and Gordon sat on the edge of his bed.

"It looks like Howard's out," Chris said.

"I gathered as much from your call," Gordon said.

"Jessica Milland was last seen alive a little after 3:30 last Thursday. You guys — well, Sam, anyway — heard the shot at five o'clock. Howard was at a meeting of supervising officers from 3:30 to about 5:15 that day. Some of my best people can back up his alibi."

"That seems pretty solid."

"I did ask him about Ponderosa, though. I framed it as a case of the sheriff there looking into a disappearance similar to ours, and I was wondering if he'd seen or heard anything while he was down there."

"And?"

"He said he was in court all morning, then had a two-hour lunch with a Ponderosa detective who used to work in this county. And he volunteered that the community college was on the far side of town from here and that he never passed it. Nor saw or heard anything unusual."

"The more I thought about it," Gordon said, "the less Howard seemed to fit the part. But you have to admit even the wariest hitchhiker would probably be comfortable taking a ride from a peace officer."

"Nothing jumped out about our three officers on campus, either. It was a good idea, Gordon, but it doesn't look like the answer here."

"Have you thought about the possibility the killer could be a woman?" Sam asked.

"Actually, I have," Chris said. "But only briefly. It doesn't fit too well, either. Diane, you want to tell them about the other case?"

She nodded.

"We won on the restraining order this morning, though I think it was all a waste of time. I had a one-on-one meeting afterwards with Owen Waterman. He's the attorney for Kyle Burnett. It was, shall we say, interesting."

"Did he say anything about the video?" Sam asked.

"Oh, he had quite a bit to say about it. Youthful high spirits and gross-out humor that his client now regrets, but it doesn't *prove* anything. And, of course, his client, while acting like a clod, perhaps, was the soul of respect toward Alicia Rios after she passed out. He came back out the door five seconds after the video stopped and never laid a hand on her, consensually or otherwise."

"Do you believe that?" Gordon said.

"Of course not. But I'm 99 percent sure that one out of 12 jurors would, unless we have more evidence than we do now."

"So what's next?"

"We keep investigating. Talk to every kid we see in that video. Hope something breaks our way. The problem is that it'll take days, which gives them all a chance to get their stories straight."

"So you think Burnett and Jarrett will get away with it?"

"Plenty of men have. Unfortunately, rape and perjury are the two toughest crimes to prove. But I won't give up until I've pursued every last lead there is. That's all I can do."

The four of them spent a minute in reflective silence, before Diane continued.

"I did pull off one neat trick yesterday, though. I got Burnett to have a glass of water while we were talking and saved the paper cup with his saliva on it. It's on its way to the state lab for testing as we speak. Our budget for this fiscal year, from July 1 until June 30 allows for two DNA tests, and I made the call to spend one of them on Burnett."

"That *was* a neat trick," Gordon said. "Where did you get the idea?"

"Actually, I saw it on *Law & Order*."

Chris laughed. "Our budgets are so tight, we're using *Law & Order* episodes as training videos."

They all laughed, and the women rose to leave. As they reached the door, Chris turned back.

"Oh, Gordon! I almost forgot the other big thing I was going to tell you. The ballistics tests came back this morning, and the bullet that killed Bob was fired from the same gun as the bullet that killed Jessica. That leaves no doubt at all that the killer is local. He's one of us."

AFTER CHRIS AND DIANE LEFT, Gordon got up from the bed and went to the window. It was only 2:45, but with the rain still falling, it was dark as twilight. Nearly every car driving down Chaparral Boulevard had its lights on. For the first time since they'd arrived, the lights in the hotel room seemed inadequate.

Gordon unwrapped Elizabeth's painting and carried it to the window, where the light was less awful than in the rest of the room. He looked at it for several minutes before taking it back to his bed and rewrapping it.

"Tell me, Sam, do you think it's possible to see into a painter's soul by looking at her paintings?"

"It's all I can do to look at a painting and decide if it's good. I think that one is."

Gordon grunted.

"So what are we doing the rest of the afternoon?" Sam asked.

"I'm open to suggestions."

"We haven't had lunch, and I'm a bit hungry, but dinner will be in a couple of hours. What about going to Kemper's Bakery for coffee and a snack?"

"Sure. Why not?"

They decided to walk the two blocks, and arrived mostly dry under their rain gear. The lunch crowd was long gone, and not many people felt like braving the rain for an afternoon coffee and treat. Most of the customers while they were there consisted of people coming in to get a pie or cake for the evening's dessert. Gordon and Sam each ordered a cinnamon roll and coffee, and they repaired to a corner booth that afforded privacy from the eight or nine other customers scattered throughout the facility.

"Is it too early to ask what the three of us are doing for dinner tonight?" Sam said as an opener. "Elizalde's again?"

Gordon took a sip of coffee to let the implied rebuke slide.

"There's an Italian restaurant in town, Castagnola's. It's only open Thursday to Sunday in the winter, but Elizabeth says it's pretty good. You all right with that?"

"I'm all right with a change of pace."

"And it may be a party of four. Sandy Steadman is off today, and Elizabeth was going to ask her to join us."

Sam nodded. "A good hostess wants gender balance at the table."

"Tell me about it. I could write a book about my life as the balancing man at dinner parties in San Francisco."

"Ever take a tumble for the woman you were balancing?"

"They're usually old enough to be my mother, but quite a few are excellent conversationalists. That can make the evening fun, with no pressure."

"It must be good to be you."

"Sometimes."

They ate and drank coffee for a couple of minutes before Sam tried again.

"How serious are you about Elizabeth, Gordon?

"Too soon to say."

"Are you starting to think it might be serious?"

"Ask me when we get back to San Francisco."

"Aren't you a bit nervous that she's such a strong feminist?"

"Every woman's a feminist. Most of them just don't say so."

"How do you think your mother would like her?"

"Ask me when it gets that far."

"Can I ask you a question, Gordon? As a friend who's known you a long time?"

"You can always ask."

"I *knew* you were going to say that. My question is, doesn't it bother you to get involved with a woman in a situation like this, where you know you're going to be going home on Sunday?"

"Monday, actually. Remember, I have to say a few words at Bob's funeral Monday morning."

"The point's the same. You know it's going to be over in a few days, so why start in the first place?"

"I don't know any such thing. And when two people are attracted to each other, it makes sense to follow the attraction as far as it goes. You never know what'll happen, and you might be surprised."

"Come on, Gordon. How are you going to carry on with someone who lives more than 300 miles away? On roads that can be shut down by snow in the winter?"

"I could always get a pilot's license."

"Get real."

"And you seem to be forgetting that there was another long-distance relationship a few years ago that went on for quite a while."

"I'm still dying to hear the whole story. But all that affair did was drive her into the arms of an undertaker."

"You give me too much power, Sam. Knowing the lady in question, I'd say she weighed all the options carefully and made the best decision she could. I wish her nothing but love. Now can we change the subject?"

"To what?"

Gordon rose and went to refill his coffee cup. When he returned, he reached into his shirt pocket and took out Mountain Bob's list.

"I'm not going to be satisfied until I get to the bottom of Wheaties," he said. "That was probably the last word Bob ever wrote, and my gut tells me it means something."

He closed it and put it back into his pocket.

"But what? Do you have any ideas, Sam?"

Sam shook his head.

WHENEVER GORDON GETS SLIPPERY AND EVASIVE, like he did about Elizabeth, I know the subject's bothering him, and he hasn't worked out his feelings. The fact that he dressed for dinner in crisply pressed khakis, a dark blue Brooks Brothers shirt with a bold white stripe (I have the same shirt, but it doesn't seem to do as much for me as it does for him) and his Navy blazer was an indication that he wanted to build on the good impression he thinks he made last night.

Elizabeth apparently had a similar idea. She showed up at the restaurant with a burgundy dress that suited her well, nicely cut (as far as I can tell, which isn't saying much) with a neckline low enough to suggest the possibility of cleavage below. We'd gotten there first, and when she walked to the table, she did it with confidence, and, I must say, a bit of grace and elegance.

"You look great," Gordon said, holding the chair for her.

Sandy arrived a minute later, and the contrast was unavoidable. She was wearing slacks and a light blue blouse that were functional, but no more; when she entered the restaurant, she stood rigidly by the door and cased the room like a cop; when she walked to the table, she was all business.

"Hi, Sandy," Gordon said. He held the chair for her, too.

The place was pretty nice. There were photographs of Italy on the wall and burgundy tablecloths on the tables and the background music was eclectic and low enough that it didn't drown the room. We hunkered down at a table for four against the wall to the right as you came in.

"I've been working overtime," Sandy said, after the drinks were ordered. "I'm out of the loop. Fill me in."

Gordon and Elizabeth brought her up to speed on the rape case, and also about the missing students and the investigation into Bob's murder. She listened intently and asked no questions until they'd finished.

"Sounds like things are bogging down on both fronts," she said. "But at least in Alicia's case there's something to go on. If they keep after it, something might come out of the video. That was good work you did to find out about it."

"Bob was onto it first," Gordon said. "We just did the follow-up. What really bothers me is that it looks like whoever abducted Jessica shot Bob, too, and it was probably a mistake. Bob's killer must have been on the road, listening to the radio, and he heard Bob talk about a break in the case. The killer must have panicked and not realized it was the wrong case. We'll never know for sure, but I don't think Bob had any leads at all on the disappearing students."

"The killer may have panicked about what Bob said, but he was a pretty cool customer when he committed the crime. He drove up to the radio station in broad daylight, parked outside, went in and shot Bob, then came right back out and drove off without being seen. That took balls."

"Let me throw something out," I said. "Are you sure the killer was a man? Is it possible the killer is a she?"

Sandy and Elizabeth looked at each other.

"Anything's possible," Sandy finally said, "but not everything's likely. I'd put that theory in the unlikely category. You don't see very many lesbian serial killers, period, and I'd say the odds are even less around here. Just my take, though."

At that point, Howard came through the front door with a middle-aged woman I presumed to be Mrs. Honig.

He waved at our table and took a seat on the opposite side of the restaurant. The place wasn't all that big, but it was big enough that neither of our tables could hear the conversation at the other. And the restaurant was beginning to fill up and get noisier. We chatted aimlessly for a while, and when the salad plates had been cleared, Gordon excused himself for a few minutes to check in with Howard about spotting at the game tomorrow night.

As soon as he was out of earshot, Elizabeth pounced.

"I've been thinking about what you said yesterday, Sam. Is the undertaker still in the picture?"

"Undertaker?" Sandy said.

"I'll explain later."

And I was sitting there thinking that among the other indignities Gordon has subjected me to, I'm now taking on the role of a go-between in a French bedroom farce.

"The undertaker's definitely still in, and Gordon's come to terms with that." I looked across the room, where Gordon and Howard were in a spirited discussion. "But I'd caution you against falling for him too hard. It hasn't worked for anybody yet."

"You're so sweet, Sam, but don't worry about me." She took a sip of wine. "When I was growing up, my father always told me, 'Lizzie, don't wait around for some man to pick you. Pick the man *you* want.' Good advice for a daughter, don't you think? And I am so much my father's daughter. When I saw Gordon talking to Harry two days ago, leading him to his own decision about doing the right thing, I realized that this was a man I could be serious about. Even if it's a long shot, I'm ready to bet some emotional currency on it. How about you, Sandy? Your father ever give you any advice about men?"

"My father was a cop. The only thing he said was, 'If some guy asks you out, give me his name and I'll run his records.' But I went into law enforcement, so I guess I'm my father's daughter, too."

"You know, I've been thinking about what's going on around here," Elizabeth said. "We have students going missing from Homestead College; we have a high school student getting raped when she was unconscious. It's as if the daughters of Alta Mira are under siege and nobody wants to come out and say it. The other fathers don't seem to realize that if it's happening to those young women, it could happen to their daughters, too. There's more denial than outrage. Why do you think that is, Sam?"

"I don't know. I'm not a sociologist. All I know is that what I've seen here is making me very fearful for my own daughter — especially for what may be coming up in the next few years. And seeing what's happened here makes me realize there's no such thing as a safe place anymore. Here comes Gordon."

He stopped as he reached the table and looked at the three of us, sitting silently.

"I won't ask what you were talking about," he said.

"You, of course," Elizabeth said. "Do you want to know what we were saying?"

He sat down without answering. Wise man.

THREE QUARTERS OF AN HOUR LATER, as they were finishing dinner, Gordon reached into his shirt pocket and took out Mountain Bob's list. He pushed his plate aside and smoothed it out on the paper placemat.

"I'm still hung up on Bob's list," he announced. "Sam and I had another go at it this afternoon and got nowhere." He looked at Elizabeth on his right and Sandy sitting next to me. "I was wondering if four heads might not be better than two. The puzzler here is 'Wheaties.' What does that mean? It just might tell us something."

"Are you sure it's not just the start of a grocery list?" Sandy asked.

"Positive. Bob didn't eat cold cereal."

"Something to do with advertising?" Elizabeth said.

"National food brands generally don't advertise on small radio stations like KNEP," Gordon said.

It was a little after seven o'clock, and the restaurant was beginning to thin out. The early diners, and those who were eating with more purpose than the foursome, had left, or were about to leave. Howard and his wife waved goodbye on the way out.

"This is a bit weird, but then so was Bob," Sandy said. "In that way, anyway. What if 'Wheaties' was one of his nicknames for somebody?"

Gordon slapped the table so hard everyone started.

"Why didn't I think of that?" he said. "It's been right in front of us all along. Wheaties is probably his name for somebody. And it's possible that he looked out into the parking lot, saw his killer driving up — though he didn't know it was going to be his killer — and jotted down a nickname that just occurred to him for that person."

"Well …" Elizabeth said doubtfully.

"Still, Gordon said, it's probably the last word Bob wrote in his life. We owe it to him to take it seriously. So, if Wheaties is a person, who would it be?"

In the quarter-hour between when Gordon asked the question and when he signed the credit card statement for the bill, no one was able to come up with so much as an even remotely plausible idea.

BY THE TIME GORDON ARRIVED at Elizabeth's place, the rain had stopped. The air was moist and fresh when he stepped out of his Cherokee, and the frogs that lived in a nearby ditch had come out and were harmonizing full-throat. Elizabeth's heater had begun to warm up her place, and it was bright and inviting when Gordon came in and kissed her. After they finally broke off the kiss, they sat on the couch, shoulder to shoulder.

"We're meeting with Alicia tomorrow," Elizabeth said.

"We?"

"Sandy and I."

"To what purpose?"

"I don't know. To remind her that someone cares. To let her know there are people seeking justice for her. Isn't that enough?"

"It's a lot, actually."

"And maybe, if we're lucky, she'll remember something else."

"Maybe. Good luck."

"We'll need it. *She'll* need it."

Gordon nodded. After a moment of silence, he took Bob's list out of his pocket and stared at it again. Elizabeth finally gave him a light jab in the ribs.

"You really know how to make a woman feel like the center of attention, Gordon."

"Sorry." He set the list on his lap. "I keep thinking that if I look at it long enough, and in context, maybe it'll come to me — who Wheaties is."

She took the list off his lap and looked at it intently.

"The only thing that strikes me is that everything else on the list had to do with his show. A song to play, a sound effect for a commercial, a reminder to give the time, a guest for later in the week. Maybe we should be asking how Wheaties has anything to do with Morning Coffee with Mountain Bob."

"You may have something there, but what?"

They considered the idea for five silent minutes and came up empty.

"Or maybe," she said, "it has something to do with Wheaties and radio in general."

Gordon stirred.

"That makes sense, too," he said. "Bob was a great student of radio. He knew all about the old-time radio shows and personalities. He very easily could have drawn on that for one of his nicknames."

"Too bad there isn't another radio expert in this county."

Gordon stood up and began pacing around the room.

"No, but that gives me an idea. My college roommate works for the *San Francisco Chronicle,* and a couple of months ago, at a party, he introduced me to one of their columnists, Gerald Nachman, who's working on a book about old-time radio. We talked for a while and exchanged phone numbers after I told him my father knew the whereabouts of an old radio actor." He took out his phone and began scrolling. "He's still here."

"Would he talk to you? Does he even remember you?"

"Only one way to find out." He dialed the number. Nachman answered on the third ring, and Gordon introduced himself.

"Ah, Gordon," Nachman said. "I was just thinking about you the other day, and that I should get around to following up with you about that actor … his name is in my notes here somewhere."

"I'd be delighted to help when I get back to San Francisco next week. Would you like me to give you a call then?"

"That would be wonderful."

"But in the meantime, I was wondering if I could pick your brain about something having to do with radio history."

"I'm always happy to talk about radio. What did you have in mind?"

"Well, it's kind of an open-ended question, but anything you can do would be appreciated. What can you tell me about Wheaties and radio?"

"That *is* a big subject. How much time have you got."

"All night, if that's what it takes."

"Let's try not to go that long. Why don't I throw out a few major points and if one of them is close to what you're looking for, we can keep going in that direction."

"Fair enough."

"To begin with, Wheaties — in fact, General Mills, the parent company — was one of the early big advertisers on radio. They pretty much had a strategy, which they still use today, of associating the product with sports and athletes. In the early 1930s, they signed on as the sponsor for radio broadcasts of the Minneapolis minor league baseball team …"

"The Minneapolis Millers."

"Not surprising you'd know that, being an athlete and all. Anyway, for sponsoring the radio broadcasts, they got a billboard on the outfield wall of the ballpark. So they decided they needed to come up with a slogan for that space. Care to guess what it was?"

"Breakfast of Champions?"

"That was too easy. In any event, they made a point of sponsoring radio broadcasts of athletic events, associating with athletes, in fact, putting athletes on the front of the cereal box. I'll bet you didn't know that at the

1939 baseball All-Star game, almost every ball player there did an endorsement for Wheaties."

"I did not know that."

"There you go. You've learned something already. And along those lines, they developed a radio drama program that had quite a run, with the express purpose of selling Wheaties. It was about a clean-cut young hero who ate Wheaties and vanquished all sorts of bad guys. They figured that if their hero ate Wheaties, other young men would want to as well."

"Interesting."

"You may have heard of the title of the show. It was called *Jack Armstrong, the All-American Boy.*"

"*What?!*" Gordon sat straight up, and Elizabeth shot him a sideways look.

"No need to shout, Gordon. I can hear you perfectly well. Jack Armstrong was actually a college buddy of the man who created the show — it's in my notes somewhere — and he took a lot of ribbing about it. But it sounds as if the name registers with you."

"Well, without boring you with details, we've been trying to figure out who around here could be connected with Wheaties. One person we hadn't thought of, but who's been hanging around the periphery of the discussion is a man named John Armstrong."

"This sounds very mysterious, Gordon, kind of like one of those 1940s spy shows with secret codes and everything."

"You could certainly say there's a lot of drama going on."

"In any event, I was just getting started on Wheaties. Would you like me to go on, or do you think you have your answer."

"No, I think this is it. Thank you so much."

"I hope it helps some."

"It's a great clue. The only trouble is, I don't know if anybody is going to believe it. But that's my problem, not yours. So, about that phone number I promised you: I'll be getting back to the City late Monday night. I'll get the number from my dad and call you Tuesday or Wednesday, if you're going to be around."

"I will, and I'll be looking forward to your call. Perhaps you can tell me more about your little mystery then."

"I hope so. We'll talk next week, and thanks again."

Gordon turned off the phone and leaned back on the couch, staring at the ceiling. He said nothing for a full minute, and Elizabeth finally jabbed him in the ribs.

"So are you going to tell me, or do I have to beg?"

Gordon shook his head.

"Sorry. This is so big I'm having a hard time wrapping my head around it. I think we have an answer to the meaning of Wheaties, and if it means what I think, it's both huge and terrifying."

"Well."

"Wheaties created and sponsored a radio show called *Jack Armstrong, the All-American Boy."*

"Oh my God. My father used to listen to it when he was a kid back in the forties. I remember him mentioning it. But I don't see ..."

"John Armstrong. The Highway Patrolman who wrote up my speeding ticket a week ago. Who was at the crime scene when Jessica Milland was found. Who *looks* like an All-American boy."

"Oh, Gordon, no."

"If I'm guessing right, Bob saw him drive up to the radio station Monday morning, and the nickname popped into his head. He wrote it down to keep it in his mind, and it was about the last thing he did."

"This certainly goes with your theory about someone in law enforcement being trusted by a hitchhiker."

"I'd say Armstrong is more trustworthy, based on appearances, than Howard Honig — wouldn't you?"

"No contest."

"It fits, Elizabeth. It absolutely fits. But it's only a vapor of a clue, with nothing solid to go on. And after leading the sheriff down a path with Howard, I'm almost afraid to mention this. I mean, I have to, but how do I do it without being laughed out of her office — laughed out of town?"

"You know, Gordon, you don't have to make a decision right now."

She leaned into him, hooked a finger under his shirt collar, pulled it out slightly and began nuzzling the back of his neck.

"Maybe we should sleep on it," she said.

Friday November 14

I DIDN'T SLEEP ALL THAT WELL, and at around four in the morning pretty much gave up trying. There was too much going on now, and I found myself trying to sort it out, even though the county has a sheriff who's being paid to do that. Gordon was off conjugating verbs with the English teacher, and I had a hotel room, which suddenly seemed very large, all to myself. I listened to the hisses and rattles of the radiator and the sound of the occasional truck rumbling down Chaparral Boulevard below. A little after five, I decided there was no point maintaining the fiction that I could get back to sleep. I got up, threw on some clothes, made sure I had my phone with me, and set off to brave the elements for a cup of coffee at Danny's Diner, open 24 hours.

It had stopped raining, which was good, and the clouds had parted enough to show patches of stars in between. The sidewalks were still wet, and the streetlights were reflected in pools of water on the road. It was cold, that damp cold that started a couple of days ago, and I was glad to get into the warmth of the diner.

Four or five tables were occupied when I got there a little after 5:30. I didn't know how long I'd be there and didn't want to tie up a table by myself when the rush started, so I sat on a stool at the edge of the counter, where no one could sit on my right side. The waitress was a perky blonde of about 19 who didn't go easy on the makeup. She'd have been fawning all over Gordon, but it took me a while to get noticed and get a cup of coffee and a cinnamon roll (from Kemper's, if I'm not mistaken). I knew I'd hate myself later in the morning for having all that caffeine and sugar, but it was what I needed at the time.

As the coffee began to take hold, my mind flitted about from this to that. I have a friend who likes to say that expectations are resentments waiting to happen, and my expectations for this fishing trip certainly hadn't materialized. It turned into another opera altogether, and I am but a spear-carrier in the background. As such, however, I have had the opportunity to watch the principals in action and perhaps learn a bit more about them than they might know themselves.

Somewhat against my better instincts, I am beginning to warm to Elizabeth. Just a bit, but still … I now feel that she's more solid than I gave her credit for at first, and that, in some ways, she might be a good fit for Gordon. But therein lies the rub. For reasons unclear to me, even after knowing the man nearly two decades, Gordon seems to get involved with really good women only when they're unattainable. He can talk a good talk about learning to fly and getting a pilot's license, but he and I both know it isn't going to happen.

As for the criminal drama going on around here, I simply have no idea. After seeing that party video, I'm hoping that smug, entitled quarterback gets his comeuppance, yet I have no expectation that he will. I'm no lawyer, but I've seen enough about how important football is in this town to conclude that at least one juror would probably buy his story, however far-fetched and inconsistent it might be. And his parents can afford a good lawyer, so there you are.

When it comes to the missing students, I am similarly baffled. Some psycho in this town has been cleverly disguising himself as a responsible adult, and until he gets caught with a body in the trunk of his car, well, odds are he'll keep getting away with it. It's hardly the sort of thing that makes you feel good about the state of the world, and, sitting alone in a small-town diner, with sunrise more than half an hour away, that's not a thought you want to linger on.

At 6:45, I had finished the cinnamon roll and my fourth cup of coffee and was seeing the beginning of a good case of the shakes. I was about to leave, when my phone rang. Gordon — who else?

"Sam," he said. "Big news. I'll pick you up at the front door of the hotel in half an hour, all right?"

"Sure," I said, and that was the extent of the conversation. Gordon is apt to forget the niceties when he gets excited, but on the other hand, what else am I going to do, stuck here without a car? And maybe he's made some headway on the meaning of Wheaties.

I paid the bill, leaving a generous percent tip, and trudged back to the Danube. I could see my breath in the pre-dawn light, which meant that with the cloud cover breaking up, it was getting colder. I should have brought a scarf.

GORDON'S CHEROKEE ROLLED UP to the main entrance of the Danube at 7:17 a.m., and Sam was out the door before the vehicle had come to a complete stop. He headed for the front passenger door, but stopped when he saw Elizabeth there, next to Gordon. He jumped in the back, and they took off.

"We're heading to the Rodeo Café," Gordon said.

"Why the Rodeo?" Sam asked.

"Because we can talk on the drive out there. What I have to tell you isn't something I can say where we might be overheard."

"Good morning, Sam," Elizabeth said.

"Good morning, Elizabeth," Sam said.

Once they were out of town, Gordon told Sam about the conversation with Nachman and the conclusion drawn from it.

Sam nodded.

"Speaking as Akers and Pains to Flyboy, that sounds exactly like something Bob would have come up with. Now what?"

"We're going to get something to eat," Elizabeth said, "and then we're coming straight back to town. Gordon is going to the sheriff with this … "

"You're welcome to join me, Sam,"

" … and Sandy and I are meeting with Alicia. She has study hall from 10:27 to 11:19, and we're talking to her in the nurse's office. Her lunch break's after that, if we need to keep going."

"Are you going to come along, Sam?" Gordon asked.

"Of course I'm coming. For two reasons. One, I don't have anything else to do, and second, I wouldn't miss the chance to see the sheriff's reaction to *that* theory."

CHRIS AND DIANE STARED AT GORDON without saying a word for a full 30 seconds. They were in the

DA's conference room, where Caitlin DeShayne's video had been played on Wednesday, and the blinds were drawn. Gordon finally squirmed in his chair, and said:

"Is it really that dumb?"

"I don't suppose I'd exactly call it *dumb,*" Diane finally said. "I'm just trying to imagine what a jury would say if I tried to put that in front of them as evidence."

"Not a fair comment," Gordon said. "It isn't *evidence*. I know that. But it could be a *lead*, and if you followed the lead, it might generate some evidence."

Chris and Diane looked at each other.

"You have to admit he has a point," Chris finally said. "We can make discreet inquiries into Officer Armstrong and see if anything turns up. But I'll tell you right now, Gordon, looking into someone in my own department was bad enough. Approaching another law enforcement agency with the suggestion that one of their officers might be a serial killer … well, let's just say that isn't something they spend a lot of time on when we get our training."

"And what Chris didn't mention," Diane said, "is that she's not exactly popular with the Highway Patrol right now. The area commander's an old friend of Howard's and thinks he should have been appointed sheriff."

"Never mind that. It's been four days since Bob was killed, and the trail's going cold. This is all we've got, and I'll have to figure out how to follow it. And fast."

After another period of silence, Sam spoke up.

"I don't know how these things work, but could I ask a question?"

Chris nodded distractedly.

"I'm wondering what you've done to find out if anyone saw something at the radio station the morning Bob was killed. When Gordon and I were driving on that highway, there were cars on the road just about the whole time. I mean, it wasn't the Bayshore Freeway at rush hour, but still. You'd think somebody must have seen something."

"Funny you should say that, Sam," Chris said. "Howard made the same point yesterday afternoon. But it doesn't work that way. Sometimes a criminal gets lucky, and sometimes he gets unlucky. It reminds me of a case in Santa Cruz County back in the seventies."

She saw she had the room's attention and continued.

"There was a serial killer at work there — two of them, in fact, as it later turned out — but the one I'm talking about was killing people at random and with various weapons. The victims had nothing in common, unlike here, where they're all female college students. He killed over a dozen people, and the police had no leads whatsoever.

"Then one morning, the killer did a drive-by. He drove down a quiet residential street, saw a man in front of his house, and shot him to death. Only this time, there happened to be a neighbor watching. The neighbor got a license number, called the police, and minutes later they'd pulled the perp over and arrested him without incident. He now has a life tenancy in one of our fine correctional institutions.

"Which brings me to the moral of the story, if you can call it that. A serial killer, even with the edge of having no connection with the victims, has to be lucky. He can't be accidentally seen by anyone; he can't leave something at the crime scene, and so forth. And here's the thing: The killer has to be lucky every time. The police only have to be lucky once."

"That's true, of course," Diane finally said. "But people around here are getting angry. They want to know what the sheriff is doing *now* to find Bob's killer and Jessica's killer. How long can you wait for luck, and how many more women are going to die before it shows up?"

"I'm not waiting for luck," Chris snapped. "I'm doing my best to speed it along. And I'm a great believer in the notion that the more you tie up your loose ends, the more you create your own luck. So I guess I'd better get back to my office and resume tying up loose ends."

Gordon and Sam took the hint and rose to leave. They closed the door behind them, then Gordon quickly opened it again and ducked his head in.

"One last thought," he said. "I wouldn't want to tell you how to do your job, but if the Highway Patrol commander's a good friend of Howard's, maybe it's time to bring Howard into the loop. Just saying."

"Oh, God," Chris said. "Is this what it's come to?"

GORDON AND SAM whiled away the morning driving around town for an hour before lunch. A banner announcing the football game that night had appeared over Chaparral Boulevard, and several storefronts had signs urging the Eagles on to victory. The football reminders gave a disquieting sense of normalcy to a town that was anything but.

After lunch, Gordon dropped Sam off at the hotel for a nap and paid a call on Brenda. She was with a friend when Gordon arrived, and the friend quickly scampered into the kitchen to make coffee, leaving Gordon and Brenda to talk.

"How are you doing?" Gordon opened.

"Horrible. I mean, let's be honest about it. But not as bad as it could be. I've been amazed by how kind and helpful people have been. I'd kind of known that happens in a small town, but this is the first time I've been on the receiving end."

Gordon nodded, and she continued.

"The sheriff's been by every day since Bob was shot. That means a lot. It would mean more if she could tell me she's close to catching his killer, but I'm sure she's trying."

"Very hard," Gordon said.

"Are you picking up on anything? Are there any leads at all?"

He chose his words carefully. "They have some ideas, but it's hard to say how they'll pan out. And Bob left a couple of clues behind, but they're tantalizingly vague."

"Like Wheaties. Ever since you told me about it, I've been racking my brain trying to think what he might have meant. I still have no idea. Does anybody?"

"The sheriff's looking into one possibility that I know of, but it's still early days. It's probably best not to hope for too much just yet."

The friend returned with two cups of coffee. "I'm heating up some cinnamon rolls," she said. "Back with those in a couple of minutes."

She ducked back into the kitchen, and Gordon leaned forward.

"How are Eileen and Sarah doing?"

"I don't know. They're in shock and trying not to show it — each in her own way. They're holding together on the outside, but I really don't know what's going on inside. And I'm not in the best shape myself, so I haven't been pressing."

"Understandable."

"But now that I mention it, could I ask you something?"

He nodded.

"When you were here last Saturday, Sarah asked if she could stay at your place in San Francisco. Good heavens. Saturday seems like five years ago now. Anyway, we didn't take it too seriously at the time, but now ... Do you think I could bring the girls down next summer?"

"Absolutely. Or if you'd like, come down for Christmas or spring break. I'd love to have them, and you, around, and I've got a spare bedroom. I'd do everything I could to make it a trip to remember for them."

"You're too sweet. But it could be good for them. Bob didn't like big cities, so we've never been to San Francisco as a family. Reno once or twice a year is about the most we've done."

"It might not just be good for them; it could be good for you, too. When you're ready. But take what I said as an absolute yes."

The friend returned with cinnamon rolls on three small plates, handed a plate to Brenda and Gordon, and sat on the couch next to Gordon. He could hear the radio going in the kitchen and was grateful that it had added an extra measure of privacy to his conversation with Brenda.

She looked at the cinnamon roll on her plate.

"I really shouldn't." she said. "I'm going to get so fat."

"I don't see how," the friend said. "You've hardly touched any food in five days. Now eat."

Brenda took a small bite of the roll and set the plate on a table at her side.

"They're talking about the big game on the radio," the friend said. "I don't follow it as much as the men do around here, but I guess the coach took our star player out of the game. Why would he do such a thing?"

"I think he had his reasons," Gordon said.

"Hardly matters anyway. It won't be the same without Bob announcing it on the radio. I always used to clean the kitchen Friday nights with the game on the radio. Not so much to follow the game as to listen to Bob and to feel that most of the town was gathered in one place to support our sons. It made me feel like part of the community."

Brenda picked up the coffee cup, her hand visibly shaking.

"Tonight's going to be hard," she said. "I always listened to the games, too, and I'd pretend that Bob was just talking to me. It made me feel closer to him. Jud Diamond, who owns the radio station, was by yesterday, and he let it drop that he'd be announcing the game on KNEP tonight. He did it for years before he hired Bob.

"So I have a decision to make in a few hours. Do I turn on the radio at seven o'clock and listen to the game, being aware every second that in a fair world, Bob would be calling it? Or do I leave the radio off and sit here in silence for two hours, thinking about how I would have been listening to Bob calling the game and having a great time tonight? What do you say, Gordon? What do you think I should do?"

This time, Gordon had no answer. When he left, a few minutes later, Brenda's plate was still sitting on the table next to her, the cinnamon roll still with just one small bite taken from it.

THE PHONE RANG as Gordon was climbing into the Cherokee and a light shower was beginning to fall. It was the sheriff.

"You may have put us onto something," she said. "Can you meet me in my office at three o'clock?"

He looked at his watch and saw that he had 20 minutes to make the three-minute drive to the courthouse.

"Sure," he said.

"Good," she said, and rang off.

All business, he thought. The phone rang again when he reached the next stop sign.

"It's your little passion flower," Elizabeth said. "How did it go with the sheriff?"

"She didn't laugh out loud, if that's what you mean. I'm meeting her again in a few minutes for a briefing."

"Do you have any plans for dinner?"

"I was hoping you'd be available."

"I suppose I could make time for you. Can I bring Sandy along?"

"Can I bring Sam?"

"Table for four at Elizalde's at six?"

"Better make it five o'clock. I have to make it to the stadium by six thirty to be a spotter at the game, remember?"

"I don't know. Five o'clock is when old people eat. But if you have to work ..."

"I have to work. But I really want to have dinner with you."

"And Sandy and Sam. We'll be well chaperoned. Five o'clock, then, and I'll have some news, too."

"We both will. I can hardly wait to hear yours."

"I DON'T KNOW HOW YOU DID IT," Chris said, "but the lead on Armstrong is starting to hold out a glimmer of hope. Much as I didn't want to, I talked to Howard."

"Yes," Gordon said.

"So I started out by asking him if anyone else from law enforcement in this county went down to Ponderosa last month for that preliminary hearing. Would you care to hazard a guess as to who chased the suspect across the field, wrestled with him, and was needed in court to testify that the suspect resisted arrest and assaulted a peace officer?"

"Armstrong?"

"Armstrong, all right. Howard said they went down separately and he didn't recall whether Armstrong took an official car or not. But he said he could find out if it was important. And you could tell that he was beginning to figure it was. So I made an executive decision to bring him up to speed on your theory of Wheaties."

"He probably got a big belly laugh out of that."

"That's what I would have expected, too. But the man surprises me sometimes. He did a little bit of a double take and said, 'You know what: that sounds just like Bob. He's been calling me Joe Friday behind my back for years, but I haven't let on that I know.' So the upshot of all this was that he went over and had a private cup of coffee with the CHP area commander."

She looked at Gordon.

"The commander said he'd check the vehicle records for that day. He called Howard back right before I called you. Armstrong took a patrol car to Ponderosa."

Gordon whistled. "Now what?"

"One of the officers has it out today, but it's due back at four o'clock. It'll be taken out of commission, then, and when the coast is clear, brought over to the fleet area behind the courthouse, where our forensic officer will give it an extremely close examination."

"But do you think he'll find anything? I mean, a month has passed, right?"

"Here's what we're up against, at least the way Howard tells it," Chris said. "The cars all get washed at least once a week, and that includes a vacuuming of the interior. On some occasions, more than once a week."

"Like what occasions?" Gordon asked.

"Like if a drunk throws up all over the upholstery and they have to give it a really thorough cleaning."

"Sorry I asked."

"That's the glory and prestige of law enforcement. But there are a few ways something could still be there. The interior cleaning's done pretty fast, and there's always a chance a hair could remain in the car through a few cleanings. And they don't generally look at everything in the car, so a really thorough search could turn something up that wasn't found in routine cleaning. Plus, Howard says they don't always get around to doing the trunk, though I wouldn't dwell on that image too much if I were you."

"So now we're waiting for the car."

"Waiting, waiting. 'A policeman's lot is not a happy one.' "

"I didn't know you were a Gilbert and Sullivan fan."

"I'm not, but I've picked up a lot of cop quotes along the way."

They sat with their thoughts for a minute before Gordon turned to Diane.

"And the rape case? How's that going?"

"Slow and frustrating. The guys are hanging together like the French Resistance, and the young women are hesitant to step forward. Diane's been leaning on them about how what happened to Alicia could happen to them. I think a couple of them are going to crack eventually, but I can't tell you when, and I don't know what they'll be able to give her when they do."

"Do you think he might get away with it?"

"He might. The standard of evidence for conviction is high, and rightfully so. I hate to say it, but there's always a chance this could be one of those cases where we know what happened but can't prove it. At least, not in court."

Gordon shook his head. "So one case is stalled for now, and the other case is waiting for the surreptitious arrival of a vehicle and a forensic inspection. At least you'll know the results of that tonight."

Chris laughed.

"No such luck, I'm afraid. Our forensic expert's son is the starting middle linebacker for Alta Mira High, so he has to be at the game tonight. He'll be coming in at 7:30 tomorrow morning to check the car. There are priorities that have to be weighed. On the one hand, there's catching a serial killer. On the other hand, there's football. Tonight, football wins.

"Welcome to Alta Mira."

IN AN ODD WAY, I'm looking forward to the game tonight. Going to a high school football game wasn't what I figured I was signing up for on this fishing trip with Gordon. If he and I had come here in the ordinary way — put in a few hours of fishing every day, done a little driving around, socialized with Bob — it would have been a very pleasant little end-of-season holiday in the mountains, and we would have innocently enjoyed all the charms Alta Mira has to offer.

Instead, we got a serial killer, Gordon's friend being murdered, and a teenage girl getting raped at a party. If this town were an apple, we've certainly come across every worm in it. So a high school football game is looking like good, clean fun — even if it can't help reminding us of the rape.

There's no getting away from that feeling anywhere around here. Take Elizalde's, where Gordon and I are now waiting for the ladies. If this were a normal fishing trip, I'd be singing its praises to everyone who would listen, telling them if they ever got up to these parts, they should check it out — that it's a great Basque restaurant. And maybe I will, and maybe they'll see it that way. For me, however, it will always be associated with discussions of vicious felonies, and watching a woman try — with a bit of result, if I'm not mistaken — to steal my buddy's heart.

Speaking of which, here come the ladies now. Gordon and I rise to greet them. Elizabeth comes up to him and gives him a nice warm hug that goes on long enough to tell anyone who's watching that they're more than just friends. I, on the other hand, get a brisk, professional handshake from Sandy, who sits next to me as Elizabeth sits next to Gordon.

"I have some news," Elizabeth said.

"So do we," Gordon said. "But you go first."

"Let's start with the meeting with Alicia," Elizabeth said. "Sandy, why don't you tell them."

Sandy nodded.

"She's wobbling. It happens in rape cases sometimes. As the crime fades into the past and it begins to look as if no one will be caught and prosecuted, it's not unusual to see a woman want to just forget it and move on. Elizabeth and I were trying to give her the courage to hang in there."

"It's hardly over yet, though," I said. "Chris and Diane are going after it pretty hard, and they both seem pretty competent."

"They are," Sandy said. "But rape is *so* hard to prove. There are a lot of cases where you know it was rape and you know who did it, and you still can't make it stand up in court."

"What's breaking my heart," Elizabeth said, "is that Alicia is starting to blame herself. This morning she was saying she shouldn't have gone to the party; she shouldn't have had a drink, and, unbelievably, she feels sorry that she was responsible for Kyle not playing in the game tonight."

"Sorry," Gordon said, "but Kyle's responsible for the fact he isn't playing. It's not on anyone else."

"That's what I told her, and I think it helped her buck up a bit. But it's hard for her. She feels most of the kids are blaming her. And she even said that Kyle may have suffered enough, just from missing tonight's game."

"Rape is different from almost every other crime," Sandy said. "If someone sticks a gun in your ribs and takes your wallet, you don't generally waste a lot of time wondering what you could have done different. You're pissed off at the bandit. But in a rape, the woman often wonders if she could have dressed differently, shouldn't have been drinking, whatever."

"Our job right now," Elizabeth said, "is to keep Alicia focused on the fact that whatever she might wish she had done differently, she did nothing to deserve what happened to her. Kyle Burnett, and maybe Cody Jarrett, too, crossed a line, and she needs to stand up for herself and see that they're held accountable for it. Sandy was really persuasive on that point."

"I had my reasons," Sandy said. "I went through that myself."

The table fell silent, and so, it seemed to me, did the entire room, but it was probably a figment of my imagination.

She continued, "It was at a dorm party my freshman year in college. I drank more than I should have, and if I had it to do over again, I wouldn't have worn my shortest skirt. But, by God, I did not consent, though that's what the bastard told the police." She looked around the table. "I've never told anyone in Alta Mira about this, but listening to Alicia this morning brought it back, and I decided I needed to talk about it. I hope you all don't mind."

After a brief silence, Gordon said, "What happened to the rapist?"

"He was real smooth, and the police and the DA could never see it as more of a he-said-she-said story. After a three-week investigation, they decided not to prosecute, even though I was sober enough to remember it pretty well and testify against him if it came to that."

"How do you feel about it now?" Gordon said quietly.

"Well, I'm over blaming myself anyway. And I know the great spiritual leaders would tell me I should forgive him and move on, but I can't do that yet. I don't know if I'll ever be able to. But over the years, I've developed a nice little fantasy that keeps me going some dark winter nights. It's that I pull a car over on one of our lonely roads, and it's him — driving all alone. And he doesn't recognize me, with the uniform and all. Then when I ask him for his ID, it looks to me like he's reaching for a gun, and I let him have it."

She looked around the table and saw that we were all listening raptly.

"I'd never actually do it," she said, "but it's the least he deserves."

THEY ORDERED DINNER, and after the waitress left, Gordon, speaking in a low voice, filled them in on the Armstrong investigation.

"That's very interesting," Sandy said, after he had explained about the patrol car being brought in for a forensic examination. "It's not likely they'll turn up anything after all this time, but it's fascinating for two reasons.

"The first is that I've always thought Johnny Armstrong was a bit of a queer duck. I mean, in some ways, he's too good to be true. Young, handsome, self-effacing, coaches youth sports, always goes by the book at work. Actually, if you ask me, he's a little too gung-ho about the job, which put me off him a bit. But I can't get over the feeling that there's some backstory there that's more than a little bit interesting."

"And the second reason?"

"When you mentioned the patrol car, I had a flashback to that morning. I remember I was coming in from the graveyard shift, and there he was, pleading for a patrol car to drive to the court hearing. And he seemed really agitated about it. I mean, I remember thinking, 'Dude, what's the big deal? If you have to take your own car, you get mileage, and even though your trip's official business, you're not patrolling and there's no reason you *need* the patrol car.' But I just wrote it off to his gung-ho-ness. On the other hand, if your theory's right, Gordon, that would be another little thing to back it up."

"Bob left us a clue in the rape case," Gordon said. "Let's hope he left us one to his own killer, too."

Dinner arrived, and Gordon looked at his watch.

"I'll have to run as soon as we finish eating if I'm going to get to the stadium on time, but meanwhile," he lifted his glass of 7-Up, "Here's to us."

They lifted their glasses and touched them all around. When they were finished, Elizabeth spoke up.

"If everyone else is done, can I give my news now?"

"You have something else?" Sandy said.

"That's right, and it's big."

They set down their forks to listen.

"As you know, I've been trying to get a teaching job somewhere else. I've come to love Alta Mira, but it isn't where I want to spend the rest of my life. Last summer, I was a finalist for three jobs at community colleges in the Bay Area, so I decided this afternoon to give them a call and see if there were any openings looming in the future.

"The first two places I called, there was no answer and I left a message. Then I called the English Department chair at City College of San Francisco. He was in his office, digging out the applications from last summer. It seems a tenured instructor, a 46-year-old male, eloped with a 19-year-old student — just took off, abandoned all his classes and everything. What do you think of that?"

There was a brief silence, before Gordon ventured a comment.

"I think he's old enough to know better, and I think he'll come to regret it very much."

"It figures that you'd take the man's point of view," she said. "But he's been suspended without pay while they start the tedious process of firing him, and they need someone to teach his classes next semester. Because there's no time to go through the formal hiring process, and because it's an interim appointment, the department chair has the authority to offer the position to anyone with an application on file. I think he was planning on spending the weekend with all the applications, but then I called and he saw a way out. After we talked for ten minutes, he offered it to me on the spot."

"Wow," Sam said. "That's really something. Congratulations."

"Elizabeth, that's wonderful," Sandy said. "But we're going to miss you here so much."

"I'll come back from time to time. I'll have to for the painting, and I'll stay in touch. I promise I will."

She turned to Gordon.

"That means I'll be moving to San Francisco next month, Gordon." She threw her arms around his neck and kissed him on the cheek. "Isn't it exciting?"

"That's wonderful," he said calmly.

BEFORE WE EVEN REACHED Edgar Hammond Field, I could tell there was a different vibe for this game than for the one last week. Back then — it seems like ages ago now — Alta Mira was grinding out a win against a team that was playing out the string of a losing season. As Gordon and I walked up to the stadium, our exhaled breaths preceding us on a cold autumn night, we could hear not only more noise, but more buzz. You got a sense of excitement and anticipation as you approached the gates, a feeling that the game really mattered.

Once Gordon and I made the trek up that long flight of stairs to the press box, I had a chance to get a better look at the picture. The home bleachers were rapidly filling up, with ten minutes to go to kickoff, and some people were already taking standing-room places along the sideline. Across the way, it was different, too. Aspen Valley had sent five busloads of students to the game (you could see the buses behind the puny visitors' bleachers) and a number of parents had driven up, as well, from the looks of things. There must have been four or five times more people on the other side than last week, and they were making noise. That inspired the Alta Mira side to respond in kind, with the cheerleaders urging them on.

Alta Mira still had only 15 cheerleaders. Alicia was missing.

The Eagles of Alta Mira were wearing green jerseys with gold pants and gold helmets as they warmed up. One kid, wearing Number 8, was throwing the ball to a couple of others. The throws tended to flutter, and a number of them were wide of the mark.

"Billy Simmons, Number 8, is going to be the quarterback tonight," Howard said to Gordon. "He hasn't played but a dozen snaps all season, and those were in games where we were winning big at the end."

"What's his completion percentage," Gordon asked.

"He's never had to throw a pass in a game. When he went in, his job was to hand the ball off until the clock ran out."

"Who's replacing Jarrett?"

"Dalton Brown. Only a sophomore, but he caught a few this year."

Gordon grunted.

Over where Bob had been sitting last week was a middle-aged, bald man, wearing glasses with heavy, dark frames. I guessed he was Jud Diamond, owner of the radio station, and I thought of introducing myself to him, but he was deeply immersed in reading a commercial for a local bookkeeper, so I held back. When he finished it, he heaved a sigh, took a wool cap from his parka pocket, and placed it over his bald head. Considering the direction in which the weather seemed to be going, it seemed like a wise move.

Finally, the teams lined up for the opening kickoff. Aspen Valley was dressed in red pants and white jerseys with red lettering, and white helmets with a red stripe down the center. Their cheerleaders, I noticed, were wearing red skirts and white sweaters.

"Raul Tavarez to kick off for Alta Mira," Howard said, and leaned toward Gordon. "Josh Gardner and

Frank Trump deep to receive for Aspen Valley ... and the kick is up!"

A roar went through the crowd on both sides. The ball sailed through the air end over end, and I realized I could see moisture on the grass from the showers that had fallen intermittently before the game. Things could get sloppy.

"Trump takes the kickoff on the 15, runs right," Howard announced. "A wall of blockers forming on that side ... Look out!" An Alta Mira player knifed between the blockers and hit Trump, who was running sideways, full force, knocking him backward and to the ground. The home side roared. "Great special teams play by Harry Hooper, number 24, breaking the wedge to make the tackle."

It *was* a pretty good play, and it was about the only excitement in the first quarter. In the cold and slop, neither team was able to do much offensively. Both teams would get the ball, make at best a first down or two, and punt. The Aspen Valley quarterback threw two passes that hit nothing but turf. Simmons, starting his first game for Alta Mira, didn't throw a pass, but rather handed off to Hooper, and occasionally another back, Rick Garcia.

It was still a scoreless game halfway through the second quarter, when Alta Mira got a break. Punting into the wind. Tavarez got off a high kick that went only about 25 yards. The Aspen Valley returner called for a fair catch, but a gust of wind caught the ball on the way down, blowing it away from him. He moved forward to catch it, but it was farther in front of him than he thought, and it skidded off his fingertips. Brown, the receiver filling in for Jarrett, fell on it at the Aspen Valley 32.

It was the first time either team had the ball in opposition territory, and the Alta Mira bleachers got louder and more vocal. Simmons handed the ball to Hooper, who went off tackle and gained five yards, falling forward with two defenders on top of him. Garcia took the ball on a sweep to the right and gained three more yards, bringing up third-and-two on the Aspen Valley 24.

The Eagles lined up with Simmons under center. He took the snap, turned and handed the ball to Hooper, who glided to the right, as if looking for an opening.

Suddenly, he stopped, spun around, and lateraled back to Simmons, who caught the ball, and in a continuous motion, heaved a wounded duck toward the right corner of the end zone.

No one was there but Brown. Aspen Valley had been completely faked out.

The entire stadium was on its feet screaming, as the wobbling ball descended through the air toward Brown. It had started raining again, but no one noticed. The ball hit Brown square on the chest and squirted upward. He snagged it with his right hand, drew it back against his chest, covered it with his left hand, and fell backwards on the end zone turf, never losing control of the ball.

It wasn't pretty, but it was a touchdown. The Alta Mira players mobbed Brown, and it took a minute or two to get them off the field for the extra point attempt, which was good. Nothing much happened the rest of the half, and Alta Mira went into the locker room with a 7-0 lead.

ALMOST EVERYONE CLEARED OUT of the press box at halftime, leaving Gordon and Howard alone. The principal was on the sidelines with a mic, calling the halftime show, and the press box felt strangely calm and quiet.

Howard set his microphone down on the counter and put his face in his hands for a minute. Finally, he turned to Gordon.

"So you want to be a detective, eh?"

"Nothing I ever aspired to. It just seems to happen."

"You may have a flair for it, Gordon. That was a good hunch about Wheaties, and I sure as hell wouldn't have known a radio expert to ask about it."

"I've known Bob for a long time."

"So have I, and I see him more often than you do. Maybe that's why I missed the obvious thing about his name games. That, or I'm getting too old to do the job anymore."

"Do you mind if I ask a question?"

"If it's whether I'm running for sheriff next June, the answer is yes. What the hell? I should have gotten it after Wild Bill died, so let the voters decide now."

"You should have an advantage. You've been here longer than Chris. You know everybody in the county."

Howard laughed. "That cuts both ways. I've pissed some people off, too. But we'll see. You know, I have nothing to lose. If I win, I'll cap my career by being sheriff for a term or two, and I wouldn't mind that at all. If not — well, I qualify for full retirement already, so I'll probably take it. Just another old law-enforcement dinosaur, waiting for that meteor to hit, so we'll all be extinct."

"You sell yourself short."

"Not really. The dinosaurs ruled in their time. I don't doubt that I could rule awhile longer. But Chris, difficult as she is to get along with, is the wave of the future. I don't like her personally, but I respect her professionalism. I just wish she had a little more respect for my understanding of small-town law enforcement."

"You think you're going to win?"

"I hope so. We'll all know the answer in seven months."

The halftime show was winding down, and the players were running back on the field.

"Back to work," Howard said. "We're giving them a better game than I thought we would without Burnett and Jarrett. But I think we're going to have to make that touchdown stand up if we're going to win."

"I think you're right," Gordon said. "If Alta Mira's going to win, they'll have to do it on heart."

THE THIRD QUARTER started out following the pattern of the first two. Alta Mira received the kickoff, returned it to the 30, made a first down, and punted. Aspen Valley racked up two first downs to get near midfield, then punted, pinning Alta Mira back on its own 20. For the first time all night, the Eagles went three-and-out and had to punt from their own 27-yard-line.

It began to rain as they lined up for the punt, and the wet ball rolled off Tavarez' foot, angling for the sideline as it sailed downfield. The official said it went out of bounds at the Alta Mira 48, giving Aspen Valley the ball in Alta Mira territory for the first time in the game.

On the first play, Aspen Valley's quarterback handed the ball to one of the running backs for what looked like a sweep to the left side. But the running back made a quick lateral to Bennett, a fleet receiver, coming behind him. Alta Mira's defense had committed to following the running back and was caught flat-footed by the reverse. Bennett curled around the right side and streaked to the end zone untouched. The home side of the stadium went deathly silent, while the visitor side went wild.

On the extra point attempt, the Aspen Valley kicker drilled the ball into the gluteus maximus of the right guard, and the score stood 7-6 in favor of Alta Mira. The scoreboard clock showed 5:48 remaining in the third quarter.

As the teams prepared for the ensuing kickoff, one of the Alta Mira players jumped up and began exhorting his teammates, waving his arms and shouting at them. It was Hooper, and 20 seconds later, the kickoff return team ran onto the field full speed.

The kickoff was returned to the 28-yard-line, and Alta Mira began its longest drive of the night. Aspen Valley was treated to a steady diet of Hooper carrying the ball, with Garcia getting a chance every few plays. Simmons still had thrown only one pass in the game, the trick-play touchdown in the second quarter. The Eagles ground out three first downs and were at the Aspen Valley 37-yard-line when the quarter ended.

Three plays later, on a sweep to the right, Hooper dragged an Aspen Valley defender over the 30-yard-line and fell forward for a first down at the 27. Three grinding runs later, it was fourth-and-five at the 22-yard-line. A field goal was out of the kicker's range, and the offense was too close to the end zone for a punt, so the coach called a timeout to settle on a play.

He called the team's second pass play of the night, but Simmons threw the ball over the head of a covered receiver, and Aspen Valley took over on downs.

Howard switched off his microphone and shook his head. "We had a man open on the other side," he said. "Burnett would have made that play."

Aspen Valley ran two running plays that gained 12 yards for a first down, then had to punt on fourth-and-four. Alta Mira got the ball on its 23-yard-line with 5:09 left in the game.

"I'm guessing we'll see a lot of Hooper," Gordon said.

"I'm guessing you're right," Howard said.

That turned out to be the case. Hooper carried the ball three times for 12 yards, took a breather while Garcia got three on a sweep, then ran twice more for eight yards, giving Alta Mira a first down on its 47-yard-line with 1:48 remaining. After Hooper ran for three on first down, Aspen Valley called a timeout. A carry by Garcia got two yards, and Hooper gained two more. It was fourth-and-three at the Aspen Valley 47 when the visitors took their final timeout with 57 seconds left in the game.

The punt team began forming on the sideline to get directions from the assistant coach. Gordon shook his head sharply.

"No, no. Don't punt," he said.

"What do you mean?" Howard asked. "It's fourth down. You've got to punt."

"Not now. You have to think of the situation. Aspen Valley has less than a minute left, no timeouts, a quarterback who hasn't completed a pass, and a kicker who can't even make an extra point. And that's if we don't make it. I don't think Hooper can be stopped. Look at him. He's yelling at the coach. I'll bet he's saying, 'Give me the ball!' "

"That's what every player says. But every point you make is even more valid if Aspen Valley's 30 yards farther away after a punt."

"Too much can go wrong with a punt — especially at this level," Gordon said. "They should go for it. But it looks like the coach agrees with you."

The punt team ran onto the field. It had started raining again, and the temperature was probably in the high thirties.

"Tavarez back to punt for Alta Mira," Howard announced.

"They've got Bennett back to return," Gordon said. "He hasn't done that before."

"Bennett deep to receive for Aspen Valley," Howard said into the mic.

The snap to Tavarez was perfect, but he bobbled the rain-slickened ball for a second and rushed his kick. It was a low line drive that shot downfield ahead of the punt coverage, bounced once, and came straight to Bennett, who caught it cleanly at the 14-yard-line in the middle of the field. He ran upfield, tacking to the right sideline, as the blockers and the coverage team converged on that side of the field.

Suddenly, at the 30-yard-line, he planted his right foot, spun left, and began sweeping around his blockers and the Alta Mira defenders. He turned the corner ahead of them and had a clear path to the end zone. Garcia and Brown pursued him, but lacked the angle or the speed to keep it from being an 86-yard touchdown return.

On the extra point attempt, the kicker managed to clear the offensive line this time, but hooked the ball off the left upright. The score was 12 7, and a minute later, that was how the game ended.

After the final gun, Howard wrapped up and thanked the crowd for turning out, before silencing his mic. He turned to Gordon.

"Well," he said, "we played our hearts out. That's all you can ask."

"Actually, it isn't," Gordon said. "You can ask for a win."

IT WAS RAINING HARDER as Gordon drove up the driveway to Elizabeth's place. The light was on inside (the main ranch house was dark), and it looked like a beacon in the storm. He parked in front, turned off the engine, and went over what he wanted to say, one more time.

Elizabeth opened the door as he got out of the car, and he kissed her in the doorway before going inside. They sat down on the couch.

"I heard the game on the radio," she said. "It was a good game, but all I could think of was how Bob would have called it."

"Yeah."

"It must have been freezing there."

"It was pretty cold."

"Need something to warm you up? I have brandy, or I can make hot chocolate."

"The chocolate sounds good, if it's not too much trouble."

"Not at all."

She returned with it a few minutes later, and he took a sip. Fortified, he started on what he had to say.

"Look, Elizabeth, I owe you an apology. At dinner tonight, when you said you were moving to San Francisco, well, it really took me by surprise, and I'm afraid I froze up."

"That's an understatement."

"I hope you didn't get the wrong idea. It's really exciting, and I'm really glad it's happening. I want it to happen. Please understand that."

A flicker of a smile crossed her face. He continued.

"When will you be moving?"

"I have to turn in grades for this semester Friday December 17. Sandy's going to ask for the weekend off, and if she gets it, she'll help me drive the U-Haul to the city on Saturday."

"So five weeks from now," he said.

"If you start the countdown tomorrow. Do you think you can be faithful until then?"

He was silent for several seconds.

"I don't know," he finally said. "Five weeks is an awful long time."

She smacked him with a pillow, and they both started laughing. She stopped first.

"One more crack like that, Gordon, and we're going back to Antioch Rules."

"No. No. *Anything* but that."

Saturday November 15

TODAY IS THE FINAL DAY OF TROUT SEASON on the streams of California. Gordon and I had been planning on seeing it out in style on the waterways of Plateau County, but that clearly isn't going to happen. There's a certain irony in what's happening to Gordon. The fisherman has become the fish, and the fish knows it's hooked good and proper. The expression on Gordon's face last night at dinner, when Elizabeth announced she's moving to San Francisco, was — well, priceless, especially given his usual poker face. I'd love to know what's going through his head right now, but he'll never tell me.

With all the stimulation from the game and the dinner repartee last night, I had a hard time falling asleep, but finally drifted off some time after midnight and woke up a little after six. It goes without saying that I had the place to myself, and I tried to enjoy the elbow room as I got up, shaved and showered. There was a little coffee pot on top of the dresser next to the TV set, and I made myself a two-cup pot after the shower. I was finishing the first cup when Gordon called and told me to meet him at Kemper's in half an hour.

It was still overcast, dark and cold when I stepped out of the front door of the hotel. The clock on the bank said 37 degrees, but it felt more like 27 as I slogged to Kemper's. It started raining just as I got there.

It was warm and smelled sweet inside, which was what I needed. I got a lemon Danish, along with my second cup of coffee of the morning, and got us a booth in one corner. In another corner, I could see Coach Geiser sipping a cup of coffee and reading the early edition of the *San Francisco Chronicle*. The place was half full, and from time to time, someone would go up to him with an attaboy about how well the team had played the night before. I doubt it was what he wanted to hear, but he seemed to be taking it as well as could be expected.

Elizabeth came in by herself a few minutes after I claimed the booth. When Gordon didn't immediately follow her into the establishment, I deduced they had driven down from her place in separate cars. Sure enough, he came in a few minutes later, took her order, and returned with pastries and coffee for two.

"Did you sleep all right, Sam?" he asked.

I decided he didn't want the long answer, so I said, "Yeah. Pretty well." I almost followed it with, "How about you," but realized the question would have been tactless.

"Things are beginning to break," he said in a soft voice. "They'll be looking at that car this morning."

"And while they're doing that," Elizabeth said, "Sandy and I will be going down to Blue Moon Ranch to have another talk with Alicia."

"Do you really think she'll drop the complaint?" Gordon said.

"I hope not. We need to keep her in a positive frame of mind, and after the team lost last night, she's probably going to be blaming herself."

"What for?" I asked. "She didn't do anything wrong."

"You and I know that, Sam," she said, "but we're not the ones who have to go back to that high school and face the other students. That wouldn't be easy for her if there were an open and shut case against Burnett and Jarrett. With Diane hitting a wall on the case, there'll be even more peer pressure on her. It's a heavy weight for a teenage girl."

Gordon's phone rang. I looked at my watch. It was nearly eight o'clock, later than I realized. The pervasive gloom outside made it seem as if the sun had not yet risen. A gust of wind came up and blew raindrops against the bakery window. I could only hear his end of the conversation, which consisted mainly of grunts and monosyllables. He ended the call in less than a minute and set his phone on the table.

"Chris says they're starting the examination of the car now," he said in a low voice. "We can come by the courthouse at 11:30 if we want an update on how it's going. You in, Sam?"

"Why not?" I said. "All my other engagements have been canceled."

We finished our food, and Elizabeth took off for her rendezvous with Alicia. Gordon and I started back to the hotel, but when we got there, he turned right, rather than left.

"Where are we going?" I asked.

"Just checking something," he said.

He drove to the school at the edge of town. Despite the rain and cold, the girls' soccer team was out practicing on the athletic field. John Armstrong, wearing a waterproof windbreaker and a baseball cap, was on the sideline shouting encouragement. I looked around quickly and saw that there were several cars in the parking lot, with moms waiting for their daughters, who were probably safe for the moment. I hadn't even realized I was holding my breath until I exhaled.

"Gives you pause, doesn't it?" Gordon said.

"A lot more than a pause," I said.

RAIN WAS FALLING INTERMITTENTLY, as it had all morning, when Gordon and Sam reached the courthouse. Because it was Saturday, and the office staff was home enjoying the weekend, Chris and Diane met with them in the sheriff's office.

"Did you find what you expected?" Gordon asked.

"I expected squat," Chris said. "We did better than expected. He's giving it one more look-see, but we have a pretty good outline."

Gordon nodded, and she continued.

"Either the CHP cleanup crew is careless or that car has hauled a bunch of shedding suspects in the last few days. We found six hairs in the back seat, and they appear to belong to two or three different people. No way of telling how long they've been there, but even though it's a long shot, we have to bust our budget and run DNA tests on them all. I'm still waiting to hear from Ponderosa if they even have a DNA sample on file for Tiffany. Wouldn't surprise me if they don't."

"So all you came up with was a remote possibility?" Gordon asked.

"That wasn't all we came up with. I was saving the best for last." She opened a desk drawer, removed a sealed plastic bag, and set it on the desktop. It contained a woman's ring with a stainless steel band and a purplish gem in a setting. "This was found under the driver's seat."

The men leaned forward.

"What is it?" Sam finally asked.

"It's an amethyst," Chris said. "That happens to be the birth stone for February. Tiffany Reese's DOB is 2/10/78."

No one said a word for a full minute. Diane picked up the baggie and looked at the ring.

"The amethyst has a long tradition in mythic lore," she said. "It's supposed to make the wearer clear-headed and quick-witted. I wonder if Tiffany was quick-witted enough to realize she was in trouble, and to try to leave a clue."

"We can hope," Chris said. "I'd love to go for a warrant to search Armstrong's house right now, but Diane says we don't have enough."

"Not nearly enough. The ring hasn't been definitely tied to Tiffany, and we don't know specifically what we're searching for. As galling as it is to be patient at a time like this, it's better than having the search overturned."

There was a rap on the glass door to the office, and Chris motioned Howard to come in. He opened the door and stood in the doorway.

"I have some news when you're free," he said.

"Is it about … ?"

He nodded.

"Come on in, then. We'll trust Gordon to keep it under his hat."

He retrieved a chair from a corner, placed it next to Gordon, and took a seat.

"I got hold of Barkis, the deputy commander in the Valley district where Armstrong worked before coming up here." Howard said.

"Was Barkis willing?" Gordon asked.

"Willing to help. We go back quite a ways, and he told me a lot about our Johnny Armstrong. Good reviews on the job, solid professional attitude, considered a bit of an eager beaver, but they usually grow out of that.

Interesting enough as far as it goes, but the real kicker was why he left the area to come here."

He looked around and saw that he had the full attention of all present.

"His wife left him." He looked around again.

"For another woman."

"That could knock you off the rails," Gordon said.

"Sounds like it did for him. Barkis said Armstrong was pretty worked up over it and after three months applied for a transfer. Plateau County was as far away as he could get."

After another uneasy silence, Gordon said, "I don't suppose you asked Barkis if there were any missing female college students while Armstrong was there."

"I may be a hick, Gordon, but I'm not stupid. I asked that very question, and Barkis said there was a female community college student who went missing and didn't fit the usual profile. She hasn't turned up yet. Only problem is, he can't say for sure whether she disappeared while Armstrong was still there or after he left. It was two and a half years ago. He said it would take him a while to look into it, having to deal with the police department, which handled the case, and it might be Monday or Tuesday before he had an answer for me."

"Everything's wait, wait, wait," Gordon said.

"That's the nature of law enforcement. Plodding and waiting," Howard said. "Oh, and one more thing. I checked into Armstrong's house, 214 West Fifth Street. It's a Pinelli."

The line drew vacant looks all around, and Howard continued.

"Bob's house was a Pinelli, too, Gordon. What do you remember as its key feature?"

"The windowless basement," Gordon muttered.

"That's right. Now if I recall correctly, it was Loretta James that handled the sale when Armstrong bought the place … "

"Honest to God, Howard," Chris said. "How do you know all this stuff?"

"Well," he said, "I always thought knowing what's going on in town was a big part of rural law enforcement. But then, I'm old school. Anyway, I got a call in to

Loretta to ask her if she remembers whether Armstrong specifically asked about the basement when he was looking. She's out showing some houses to a young couple and won't be done for a few hours. Plod and wait."

"Good work, Howard," Chris said. "And I mean that. Let me know when you find out more."

He took the hint and left.

When Howard was out of earshot, Gordon turned to Chris and Diane.

"All right," he said, "let me ask a question. You don't have enough to get a warrant to search Armstrong's house, right?"

Diane nodded.

"Well, four women have gone missing in the last five or six weeks," he continued. We know one was killed, and we've been assuming the others have, too, but what if they're still alive? What if they're being held captive in that Pinelli basement at Armstrong's house, maybe on the edge of death as we speak? Don't we owe it to them to go in now?"

"Sorry," Diane said. "If we're on the right track, we owe it to the victims and the public to nail this guy, and to do it in a way that no appellate court will argue with. Any search has to be airtight."

"Even if a couple of young women are languishing near death in that basement?"

"We don't know that, Gordon, and I think it's unlikely. And the wait may not be that long. If we can get a definite ID on that ring, with the right backup, I might have enough to ask for a warrant."

He sat back, clearly agitated. After a period of silence, he went on.

"I'm pretty torn up about this, and part of it is I want to see the son of a bitch who killed Bob get put away. Can I ask a hypothetical question?"

"If you want a hypothetical answer," Diane said.

"Let's suppose, hypothetically, that a private citizen were to break into Armstrong's house, and, just by chance, discover something horrifying and call it in to the sheriff's office. Would that give you grounds for going to the house and looking around?"

Sam turned to Gordon and said one word: "Clancy?"

Gordon nodded. "You see, I have a client, a professional athlete whose name you would probably recognize. He has a bodyguard named Clancy, who was a childhood friend. For the last three or four years, Clancy has been clean and sober and a model citizen, but before that — well, let's just say his life tended to revolve around drugs and theft. Now that he's gainfully employed, he came to me a few months ago and asked if I could help him set up a retirement plan.

"He wasn't starting with much, and my ordinary fee would have eaten a quarter of it, so I suggested he could pay me in kind. My fee was four lessons in how to pick a lock. For some reason, that's always fascinated me, and under his tutelage, I've gotten to be pretty good at it. I'm pretty sure I could get into Armstrong's house, and if I found nothing unusual, get out again without the entry being detected."

He sat back with a triumphant smile. Chris and Diane looked horrified. Diane spoke first.

"All right, for starters, I was in the ladies' room when you said that, and I never heard it. And I never said what I'm about to say. Speaking hypothetically, you're crazy, Gordon. To be perfectly frank about it, I think coming up with the Wheaties clue has gone to your head, and you need to stop thinking you can run the investigation by yourself. Oh, and by the way, if that hypothetical burglar got caught, he'd be lucky to get off with three months at the county prison farm — and that's with a squeaky clean record."

"Three months? I could do that standing on my head."

"A lot of criminal defendants say that, but they usually lose their positive outlook on life when the judge slams the gavel down and they're being led away to be fitted for an orange jumpsuit. Forget it. End of discussion."

Gordon turned to the sheriff.

"What do you think?"

Chris tapped the edge of her desk with a pencil three times.

"What she said. We're getting close. Promise me before you leave, Gordon, that you won't do it. You couldn't even try until dark. Armstrong is working swing shift tonight. By six o'clock, we might have a hit on the ring. Back off."

"All right," he finally said. "I'm abandoning the idea."

"Thank you," Chris and Diane said in unison.

"For now, anyway," he said under his breath.

AROUND TWO IN THE AFTERNOON, Gordon drove to Bob and Brenda's house. The sign on the bank showed that it was 42 degrees, which ended up being the day's high temperature. He made the short drive between rain showers, and entered the house perfectly dry.

A different woman, from the church, was with Brenda, and he wondered if Brenda ever got tired of company and just wanted to be alone with her thoughts. The woman went off to make coffee, and though he had drunk too much already, he welcomed the chance to be alone with Brenda.

"How are you doing?" he asked.

"OK under the circumstances. We're planning Monday's service now, and it gives me something to concentrate on."

"I guess that's good."

"But then I automatically want to run it by Bob, and I lose it."

"Could be a while before that stops."

"More than a while, I'm afraid. Can I ask you a question?"

He nodded.

"Our pastor was by this morning with a suggestion, and I just don't know. He's concerned that our church may be too small to hold the crowd. It seats 250, and it's never full on Sundays, but he thinks there may be a lot more people than that turning out for Bob's funeral. He said he's talked to the high school principal and they could hold the service in the gym at three o'clock Monday afternoon. I just worry that we may be putting on airs."

"How many people does the gym hold?"

"Eleven hundred, the pastor said. I can't imagine that many people would turn out. What do you think?"

Gordon didn't answer immediately, and when he did, he chose his words carefully.

"From everything I've seen and heard, Bob was well known, universally liked, and the fact that he died shockingly and suddenly is likely to make a lot of people want to come out and pay their respects. It's just my opinion, but I think even the gym might not be big enough."

"That's kind of you to say. Maybe I'll do it then. I have to decide by the end of this afternoon."

The coffee arrived, and the church woman retreated to the kitchen on another pretext.

"I'm changing gears emotionally," Brenda said. "Ever since Monday I've been in shock and denial, but now I'm getting angry. It seems like the sheriff isn't getting anywhere with the investigation, and I'm hearing grumbling from the people who are visiting. I know it's not easy, but ..."

"I think the sheriff is getting closer to something that can be acted on. But it has to be done right, or the killer could go free on a technicality. No one wants that."

"You've been talking to her. Isn't there something you could do? Bob had such a huge admiration for your ability to ..."

Gordon cut her off.

"Highly overrated, I'm afraid. Believe me, Brenda, I'm doing everything I can to help, but in the end, the sheriff has to do the real work."

They talked for half an hour, and Gordon thought Brenda seemed to be comforted by his visit, though it was hard to say. Before leaving, he asked her to show him Bob's basement room. He said he wanted to remember where he'd last seen Bob in the house, but the real reason was to acquaint himself with the layout of a Pinelli basement, just in case. He felt only slightly uneasy about the lie.

It was raining again when he left, and the drops that fell from the leaden sky were icy cold. The radio had said there might be snow that night, and it seemed entirely plausible. His phone rang as soon as he got into the Cherokee. It was Chris.

"Just wanted to let you know," she said. "Tiffany Reese's parents have taken off for the weekend, saying they needed to get away by themselves. No one seems to know where they went. It may be Monday before we have a chance to show them the ring."

He sighed. "Thanks for the professional courtesy."

"Don't mention it. And Gordon?"

"Yes."

"Don't get any ideas. Following procedure is the way to go on this."

"Thank you."

He put the phone in his pocket and stared straight ahead, through the fogged-up, rain-pelted windshield for five minutes. When he started the Cherokee, it took a minute for the defroster to restore visibility. By the time the vehicle was rolling, Brenda's plea and the delay in the investigation had settled his mind on the question of going to Armstrong's house that night.

THERE'S SOMETHING UNNERVING about spending a dreary, rainy afternoon in a dreary hotel room in a dreary small town, watching your best friend play with his burglary tools. Granted, it's not an experience most people are likely to have, but then most people don't have Gordon as a friend. I offered to help him out tonight, but when he said no, I let it drop. After our experience in Summit County four years ago, I've had my fill of life-threatening adventure.

I did, however, say a brief prayer of gratitude for the fact that Gordon had brought the tools up to the room and put them in his suitcase when he arrived in town last week. If they had been found in the Cherokee the morning Bob got shot, I'm guessing the average Plateau County sheriff's deputy would have believed in Clancy about as much as he would have believed in the Easter Bunny.

We were meeting Mademoiselle Macondray at Elizalde's at 5:45, which passes for a fashionable dinner hour in Alta Mira. At 5:35, we went downstairs, got into the Cherokee (after Gordon put his burglary kit under a jacket on the back seat) and started up Chaparral Boulevard. It was drizzling, and the sign on the bank gave the temperature as 33 degrees.

"Might snow tonight," I said conversationally.

"Might," Gordon said.

"So at the risk of being the skunk at the garden party, what if you break into the house and don't find anything?"

"I leave the house and lock it up."

At that point, I decided to wait until we got to the restaurant. Maybe she'd have more luck getting him to talk.

She did, but only a bit. It was a tense dinner, and when Gordon said midway through it that he'd need a couple of hours "to take care of some business," I could practically see her ears twitch. If she hadn't been talking about meeting with Alicia, and how she and Sandy were keeping her spirits up for now but didn't know how long they could keep her going, I don't know what we would have talked about.

When we'd finished eating, the waitress came by to ask about dessert. Elizabeth and I decided we could handle ice cream and coffee, but Gordon, after saying he had to tend to his "business," slipped me a hundred to pay for dinner and took his leave.

As soon as he walked out the front door of Elizalde's, she turned to me.

"All right, Sam. What's going on here?"

I looked at my watch while I tried to think how to answer her. The time was 7:02 p.m.

CHRIS WAS AT HER DESK, beginning to wade through three stacks of reports on the Jessica Milland murder, the shooting of Mountain Bob, and the Alicia Rios rape, when the call from the watchman came.

"Sheriff, this is Andy."

"What's up, Andy?"

"I got someone at the downstairs entrance who wants to see you."

"For God's sake, it's after hours on a Saturday night. Can't it wait until Monday?"

"That's what I asked, ma'am, but he says it can't."

"Did he tell you what it's about?"

"No, ma'am. Do you want me to ask him?"

She rolled her eyes. "Please."

She heard indistinct chatter in the background before Andy came on again.

"He says he's a witness, ma'am."

"Did he say what he's a witness to?"

"Hold on while I ask."

After a bit more background noise, "He says he thinks he saw the killer."

She pressed down so hard on the pencil she was holding that it snapped in half, a metaphor for her nerves.

"I don't suppose he happened to mention *which* killer?"

"No, but I can ask if you want."

She said nothing, and Andy didn't take the hint. Finally, through gritted teeth, she said, "Ask him."

A few seconds later, "He says the radio guy."

Chris had by this time begun to suspect that the visitor was a crank, but because no potential lead could be ignored, she sighed and said, "Send him up."

She stepped out of her office to see if, by chance, anyone else was around. Deputy Buzz Frazier, a second-year man, and the one who had traded banter with Howard when the aerial search was going on, was placing a stack of papers in the typist's basket.

"Deputy."

"Ma'am?"

"Are you doing anything now?"

"I was just about to clock out."

"Well, I hope you can use some overtime because I need you a bit longer. We've got someone coming up who says he saw Mountain Bob's killer."

Frazier looked puzzled. "Do you think it's for real, ma'am? I mean, why did he wait until now?"

"An excellent question, and one I'll be sure to ask. Grab your notebook, greet him when he comes in, and bring him into my office so we can find out."

The man who accompanied Frazier into her office a minute later didn't look familiar. He was the kind of stocky middle-aged man who could have been anywhere between 45 and 55, and whose straight hair might have been gray-sandy or sandy-gray. He introduced himself as Ed Mullin.

"All right, Mr. Mullin," Chris said. "You said you saw the killer of the radio DJ Mountain Bob Hastings, is that right?"

"I'm pretty sure."

"Well, what did he look like?"

"I don't know."

Frazier, sitting slightly behind the witness, broke into a smile, and Chris shot him a killing look.

"I see. You saw the killer, but you didn't see enough to describe him. Are you from around here, Mr. Mullin?"

"No. I make my home in Stockton, but I'm on the road a lot. That's how I saw it."

She sat up straighter, and lowered her voice to make it as soothing as possible. Even Frazier was paying more attention.

"Why don't you tell me in your own words, instead of me asking a lot of questions?"

"Yes, ma'am. Well, at 3 a.m. Monday morning, I picked up a load in Redding for delivery to Bozeman, Montana. I stopped for breakfast along the way, and was coming into Alta Mira a bit after seven o'clock. Can't say exactly."

"Go on."

"I was driving down the state highway, and just when I got to the radio station, some idiot in a pickup came flying out of the parking lot like a bat out of hell, if you'll pardon my language. These big rigs don't brake real fast, and I almost hit him. It beat me why he was in such a hurry. Nobody behind me and nobody coming the other way. He could have waited a couple of seconds and gotten on the road nice and easy."

He paused to nurse his resentment at the bad behavior.

"I said a couple of un-Christian things under my breath, but he just screamed on ahead of me, out of sight. I didn't think anything more about it until tonight. I stopped at Danny's Diner for dinner on the way back from Bozeman and picked up a copy of your local newspaper. There was a big story about the radio DJ being shot, and I realized it was right about the time that fella pulled out right in front of me, and I might have seen him."

"You said, 'seen him.' How certain are you that it was a man?"

"Pretty sure. I couldn't tell you much except that he looked young, but he was gone before I could see much more. He was driving a gray Ford Ranger, probably three or four years old."

"But you didn't get a good look at him?"

Mullin shook his head.

"Could you identify him?"

"No, ma'am. I don't believe I could."

She leaned back in her chair and tried to figure out how much to make of this. She was still sorting it out when Mullin spoke up.

"There's one thing you haven't asked, ma'am."

"What's that?" she said, as calmly as possible.

"About his license plate. I got that."

"Are you sure? You can remember it after almost a week?"

"Yes, ma'am. It was one of those personalized plates."

"What did it say?"

"It said SCR, space, CCH"

She wrote it on a pad, tore off the top sheet and handed it to the deputy.

"Buzz, run this right away."

He took the sheet, stood up and hesitated.

"No need for that, ma'am. I recognize the plate, but there must be some mistake. It belongs to Johnny Armstrong."

She said nothing for a minute, as that sank in.

"And what on earth does SCR CCH mean, deputy?"

"Soccer coach, ma'am."

The time was 7:29 p.m.

I HAD JUST PUT THE HUNDRED on the tray with the bill, and the waitress had gone off to get change. The nice thing about fishing trips to the mountains is that you can eat well and cheaply. It had only taken Elizabeth a little more than five minutes to worm the story of Gordon's escapade out of me. The woman has interrogation skills, and I don't think I'd like to be coming home late to her with a cock-and-bull story.

"So Gordon said to wait at the hotel?" she said.

"If you don't mind driving me."

"My pleasure."

The waitress returned with the change, and I left half of it as a tip. Elizabeth pulled a sweater over her shoulders.

"This is going to be exciting, Sam. I had a boyfriend who was a sociopath once — I mean, who hasn't? — but this is my first experience with a garden-variety burglar acting on the side of law enforcement. I can hardly wait to hear how it turns out."

She stood up. The clock on the wall read 7:33 p.m. as we walked out the door into the cold night.

GORDON SAT IN THE CHEROKEE with the engine and heater off, shivering slightly. Except for Chaparral Boulevard, the streets in Alta Mira didn't have lights, so the neighborhood was mostly cloaked in darkness. The front porch light of Armstrong's house was on, but the interior showed no sign of being lit. Gordon was trying to size up the situation as carefully as possible.

It appeared that the neighbors were home on all sides, but the blinds were drawn on all their windows. Even so, the front door would be too risky. He would have to get out of his vehicle, close the door quietly so as not to attract attention, move quickly to the back door, and hope he could get it open as fast as possible. Once inside, he'd use only his penlight until he got into the basement.

He looked at the other houses again. Everything seemed quiet. He realized that the moisture hitting his windshield now was from snowflakes and decided not to wait any longer.

Grabbing his tool kit in one hand, he opened the door, slipped out, and closed it as quietly as possible. Wearing dark jeans and a black windbreaker, he walked purposefully across the street, across Armstrong's lawn, and to the back door. He looked at the surrounding houses again, and all seemed quiet. He set his tools on the ground by the back door and turned off his phone. His nerves wouldn't have stood it ringing in the empty house.

But he hadn't seen that across the street, two venetian blind slats were slightly pried apart, and that the occupant of the house had been looking out. When Gordon disappeared around the back of the house, the two slats came together again.

The time was 7:46 p.m.

DIANE BRINKLEY had just opened a bottle of Chardonnay and poured herself half a glass when the phone rang. She felt she needed a splash of courage to tackle the stack of notes covering all the interviews in the rape case this week. She was sitting on the couch in front of a large fire, and, the ranch being at a higher elevation than Alta Mira, snow was falling steadily outside.

"This is Diane."

"It's Chris. We finally caught a break."

"Tell me."

Chris ran through Mullin's testimony. When she finished, Diane asked:

"Can you get a deposition?"

"Linda Britton will be here to take it in 15 minutes."

"If it's as you say, that should be more than enough to get a warrant to search Mr. Armstrong's house and work space for the gun that killed Mountain Bob. With any luck, you can be searching his house when he comes home from work after midnight."

"God, that's what I wanted to hear."

Diane was silent for a moment, then:

"Chris, you don't suppose Gordon is going to try anything, do you?"

"I forgot about that in all the excitement. I'll call him right away."

"Then I won't keep you a second longer. *Au revoir*, my dear, and fax that deposition the instant the ink is dry."

Diane corked the bottle of wine, took it to the refrigerator, and carried the half-glass, which would now have to last the evening, to the window. She loved watching the snow fall and intended to look at it until her thoughts were composed.

The time was 7:49 p.m.

I'D JUST BROUGHT OUR DRINKS to the table in the corner of the bar at the Danube Hotel when my phone rang. Even though it was Saturday night, none of the other three denizens of the establishment looked as if they were there to pick anyone up. They were sitting morosely at the bar, watching a college football game they probably wouldn't remember in two days, and they were ignoring us, which was fine by me. I didn't want Elizabeth to notice, but I was beginning to become concerned about Gordon's adventure. He's almost gotten himself killed twice (and me once, but I'm over it) trying to be an amateur sleuth. A man who puts himself in that sort of position is going to run out of luck sooner, rather than later.

I answered the phone. It was the sheriff, and she got right to the point.

"Sam, is Gordon with you?"

"No, he isn't."

"Are you alone?"

"Actually, I'm with a rather attractive woman."

"Say hi to Elizabeth for me, but listen, Sam, this is urgent. Please tell me Gordon didn't go to that house."

I paused for a few seconds before coming up with a clever and original response.

"Ummmmmm ..." I said.

"Oh, God. Do you have any way of reaching him?"

"Did you try his cell phone?"

"It went straight to voice mail. I think it's turned off."

"Then I'm out of ideas."

"All right, if you do hear from him, tell him I called and said something's come up, there's no need for him to go to that house, and if he's anywhere near it, get the hell out of there. Got that."

"I think so." In the background, on her end, I heard some squawking that could have been a police radio.

"Just a minute," she said. She was silent for several seconds while the squawking continued, and finally stopped. "Oh, shit. I've gotta go, Sam. If Gordon calls, keep him away from that house. And don't let him get a word in edgewise."

That wasn't what I needed to hear. As I set down my phone, I noticed that the time on the display was 7:54 p.m.

IT TOOK GORDON ONLY A MINUTE to quickly case the main floor of Armstrong's house. What he saw was not much. For a bachelor, Armstrong kept a tidy house, and a rather impersonal one. It was decorated in a Spartan style, and one of the few distinctive decorations was a photo of himself with a girls soccer team, taken in December of the previous year.

From his scrutiny of Bob's house earlier in the day, Gordon had determined that the door to the basement would be between the living room and kitchen, and it was. He began looking through his tool kit, then thought to try turning the doorknob first. It was unlocked. He took a deep breath and started down the stairs, keeping the thin beam of light on the stairs in front of him. When he got to the bottom, he knew, that if this house conformed to the pattern of Bob's, there would be a light switch on the wall at the right. The light in this underground room shouldn't be visible to the neighbors. It was silent as a tomb, and he guessed he'd been wrong about captives being held here.

He looked at the luminous dial of his watch, and it showed 7:57 p.m. He turned off the flashlight and began running his hand along the wall. He found the switch in less than 10 seconds and flipped it.

The first thing he saw when the light came on was a pair of malevolent eyes staring directly at him, only five feet away.

AFTER GETTING OFF THE PHONE with Sam, Chris sat at her desk, eyes closed, pinching the bridge of her nose with her left hand. In her 20-year law enforcement career, she had never faced a situation like this, and was not likely to again. The circumstances called for extreme care and judgment, yet she had only minutes, maybe even seconds, to figure out what to do.

She stood up and walked to the door of her office. There was a large window next to the door, which allowed her to see the entire sheriff's office. Assistant District Attorney Linda Britton had just walked through the door, and Deputy Frazier had risen to greet her. Like the tumblers falling into place on a lock, it came to the sheriff what she had to do.

She opened the door and barked, "Deputy!"

The time was 7:58 p.m.

THE BOBCAT whose gaze Gordon had encountered did not appear to have died peacefully. It was several seconds before Gordon could take his eyes off the animal and look around the room. What he saw was a bestiary of sorts. The head of an eight-point buck hung on one wall. A hawk, wings fully spread, was mounted on a stand. A three-foot-long rattlesnake, fully coiled, sat on a tabletop.

And Gordon flashed back to what Bob had said a week ago as they were leaving for Blue Moon Ranch:

"If you ever catch a fish you don't want to release, bring it to John Armstrong and he'll stuff it for you. He does a bit of taxidermy on the side, and his rates are very reasonable."

After all the buildup, after risking jail for committing a burglary, Gordon had discovered not a dungeon, not a torture chamber, but a man's home business. He felt unbearably foolish.

Exhaling, he looked around the room more carefully. There were two large tables, with what looked to be implements of the taxidermist's trade neatly atop them. There were a couple of animal heads and a handsome Brown Trout on the wall at the left. It all seemed perfectly normal.

And then he saw, along the back wall, a curious object. It seemed to be a container of some sort, about six feet long, with a curved top, resting on three sets of legs and wheels about three feet off the ground. It looked like an elongated, covered barbecue.

Or a coffin, he thought.

Having come this far, he decided he might as well check it out. He walked carefully across the cluttered room, taking care not to bump into anything, and stood in front of the container. It had a gauge of some sort on the right side, was connected to a plug that was in an outlet on the wall, and had two handles on its curved lid. He put his hands on the two handles and held them there several seconds.

"It's probably nothing," he told himself before lifting up.

Lying on her back, looking up at him was a young woman, about 18 to 20 years old. She was naked and had a tan line on one of her fingers. She looked real, but not quite real, and it took Gordon several seconds to realize why. She had the same stylized look as the other animals in the room, and had obviously gone through the same process they had.

Acting on instinct and reflex, he slammed down the doors, making what seemed like a thunderous noise. At the same time, he grabbed his throat and bent over in an attempt to keep down his nausea. It worked, and after about a minute, he stood up and reached into his pants pocket for his phone.

"I wouldn't do that, if I were you," said a man's voice behind him. "Now put your hands on top of your head and turn around slowly."

He did as directed, and saw Armstrong, in uniform, pointing a gun at him. Behind Armstrong, the clock on the wall showed the time as 8:03 p.m.

ELIZABETH WAS TAKING ADVANTAGE of our rendezvous to pump me for more information about Gordon. She was doing it pleasantly enough, but my heart wasn't really into it. I tried my best not to show it, but I was worried about him.

Finally, I tried a diversion.

"You realize," I said, "that Gordon is really into basketball. He played it well himself, and he still goes to a lot of games. Any woman who's serious about him is going to have to like basketball a lot — or at least learn to put up with it."

She took a sip of wine and smiled.

"Not a problem, Sam. I haven't told you — in fact, I haven't told Gordon yet because I haven't figured out how to bring it up properly — but I love basketball. I was

Illinois all-state and went to the University of Iowa on a basketball scholarship. The game is in my blood."

My head was spinning. Gordon has no idea what he's getting himself into, and I hardly knew what to make of it myself. Out of nervousness, I looked at my watch.

"Do you have to go somewhere, Sam?"

"No, no. Sorry. I didn't mean to be rude. It's just that Gordon should be coming back pretty soon."

"You don't think he's in any danger, do you?"

"I'm sure he's fine," I said with a straight face. My watch, when I had looked, showed the time as 8:04 p.m.

"THAT'S TIFFANY," Armstrong said. "She's just about ready now."

"You, you had her *stuffed*," Gordon said.

"Not stuffed, Gordon. That's ancient history. Freeze-dried, according to all modern specifications. You get a better result that way. I don't have much time to talk, but I want you where you can't make any sudden move. Lie down on the floor, on your back, with your hands clasped behind your head."

Gordon had no choice but to comply.

"I thought you were working tonight," he said after assuming the totally defenseless position.

"I am, but I clocked out early for dinner. You see, I've told my neighbors that if they ever see someone suspicious around my house, they should immediately call me on my cell phone. One of them just did. You weren't careful enough."

"But the sheriff must be coming, then."

Armstrong shook his head. "I told them to call *me*, not the sheriff. In a couple of minutes, when you're bleeding out, I'll go over and tell the neighbor that whoever it was must have gotten away, but thanks for calling me."

"Bleeding out?"

"I haven't had a chance to practice on a man yet, so in one way, it's good you came around. I even have a freeze-dry container ready for you. It was going to be for Jessica, but she misbehaved. Bitch. The one thing I never wanted to do was leave an actual body that could be found."

"You're not serious?"

"Oh, I couldn't be more serious. But I want to keep as much of you in good shape as possible, so I'll be shooting you in the lower abdomen. It'll take you a while to bleed to death, and it'll hurt like hell, but at least I'll be here to keep you company."

Gordon started to tell Armstrong that the sheriff was onto him, but stopped himself. It might give Armstrong an advantage in terms of cleaning up evidence, and it wouldn't help with the situation at hand. Gordon knew that he was looking death in the eye, and that the only consolation was that after killing him, Armstrong would soon be caught.

"How tall are you?" Armstrong asked.

"Six-four," Gordon said in a puzzled voice.

"Hmm. The container's only six feet long. I might have to cut your feet off to fit you in. But don't worry. I'll do it after you're dead. I don't want to hurt anyone unnecessarily."

Between the sheer terror of the situation and the mindset of the killer, Gordon was in a state of shock. He could think of nothing to say.

"I've only got an hour for dinner, so we have to get a move on. I'll give you 15 seconds to say a little prayer before I shoot. And don't worry if you forget to pray for something. You'll be conscious for a while before you go and can do add-ons." He looked at his watch. "Starting … now!"

Gordon closed his eyes. A jumble of unrelated thoughts were running through his head. He knew he was about to die, and he couldn't still his mind enough to let it happen peacefully.

The shot came sooner than expected, and he flinched. He was also angry, because he wanted to be looking Armstrong in the eye when he pulled the trigger. Perhaps it was the anger that kept him from realizing, for several seconds, that he had felt no pain and had heard a slight thump after the shot.

He opened his eyes and saw Chris Huntley, standing where Armstrong had been, a pistol in her hand.

He sat up and saw Armstrong lying on the floor, utterly motionless. The back of Armstrong's head was turned slightly toward Gordon, and he could see a bullet hole at the base of Armstrong's neck. He looked up at Chris.

"How …?"

"I found out from Sam that you were here, and then I heard on the police radio that Armstrong was in Alta Mira and clocking out for dinner. And since I had to talk to him anyway, I decided to come over and see if I could catch him having dinner at his house."

Gordon just looked at her.

"That's my story, and I'm sticking to it. Instead, I found this, and, well …"

"Thank you," Gordon said. "Thank you from the bottom of my heart. But, you must have come up behind him and had him dead to rights. Couldn't you have just told him to drop the gun instead of shooting him?"

Chris set her pistol on a nearby table and looked back at Gordon.

"Silly me," she said. "I didn't think of that."

Interlude: Thursday March 19, 1998

(From the Plateau Courier)

KYLE BURNETT, 18, all-state quarterback for the Alta Mira High School Eagles, pleaded no contest Tuesday in Plateau County Superior Court to a single misdemeanor count of statutory rape.

The unexpected plea brought an end to an investigation that has been the talk of the county since last November, when a cheerleader at the school alleged that he had gotten her drunk and raped her at a party.

Superior Court Judge Susan Jackson split the difference at sentencing. She rejected the prosecution's plea to require Burnett to register as a sex offender, saying it was too severe a penalty for a first-time offender in a disputed case.

But she also rejected defense attorney Owen Waterman's appeal for no jail time for Burnett. He was sentenced to 30 days at the county prison farm, to be served on weekends, and placed on probation for three years.

Judge Jackson also scheduled a hearing for Burnett in Family Court on April 6 to determine the amount of child support he will be required to pay.

On the courthouse steps following the hearing, Burnett's father, Lance Burnett, angrily denounced the proceeding.

"This case was a witch hunt, a farce, and a travesty of justice," he said, ignoring the attempts of his son's attorney to quiet him. "There's been an abuse of power here, and the sheriff and district attorney will pay for it at the polls in June."

Asked how the district attorney would pay at the polls in June when Deputy DA Diane Brinkley is running unopposed for the top spot, Burnett said, "There's still plenty of time to get a write-in campaign going."

Brinkley, who handled the case from the beginning of the investigation to its conclusion, saw matters otherwise.

"Mr. Burnett is very fortunate to have gotten off as easily as he did," she said. "From the beginning of the investigation, he lied about having sex with the victim, despite strong evidence. Only when she found she was pregnant, and DNA tests proved he was the father, did he change his story and claim he and she had consensual sex after school several days earlier.

"What's more," she continued, "he stood by *that* blatant lie, even though she had been at cheerleader practice until 5 p.m. that day and had been driven straight home by another member of the cheerleading squad.

"I don't know which is worse — what he did, or his non-stop lying about it. The only reason he didn't face felony charges was because of the victim's desire to get the matter behind her and move on."

The case first came to the attention of local authorities following a Nov. 1 party at the home of a prominent local resident, where numerous members of the football team were present. Reports have indicated that no adults were in the home at the time.

The girl who made the charge said that Burnett had urged liquor on her and given her several unusually strong drinks, which she didn't realize, due to her lack of experience with alcohol, were as strong as they were.

At one point, she passed out and was carried to a bedroom, where she claimed Burnett later came in and raped her.

The story made the rounds of the local rumor mill for nearly two weeks before the sheriff's office served a warrant on the home where the party was held and confiscated a video camera. The video has not been made public, and will not be under terms of the plea agreement, but reports from reliable sources indicate it corroborated at least part of the girl's story.

Because the girl was 17 at the time of the incident, any sex act with her, consensual or not, would qualify as statutory rape under California law. The law is rarely invoked in cases of consensual sex involving a teenager.

Following the seizure of the video, Alta Mira Head Football Coach Lloyd Geiser dismissed Burnett and a 17-year-old wide receiver from the team just before Alta

Mira's playoff game against Aspen Valley Nov. 14. The coach declined to comment on the *Courier's* question as to whether he had seen the video.

Deputy DA Brinkley said the full investigation showed the juvenile wide receiver had been guilty of "very poor judgment," but that there was insufficient evidence to prosecute him for any crime.

Burnett will report to the prison farm to begin serving his term next Friday, March 27. By checking in Friday afternoons and leaving after dinner Sunday, he will get credit for three days served each weekend and should complete his sentence the last weekend of May, just in time for his graduation from Alta Mira High Friday June 5.

Epilogue: Tuesday June 2, 1998

"I GRANT YOU IT WAS A LAME CHARGE under the circumstances," Diane Brinkley said to Gordon, "but I'll defend it as making the best of a bad situation. The victim was reluctant to testify and the evidence for forcible rape lacked a smoking gun. On statutory rape, we had Burnett dead to rights, and it got the case on the public record. That was something, at least."

They were sitting on the courthouse steps a bit after eight o'clock. The high temperature had been 88, and the sun, in a cloudless sky, was dropping closer to the tops of the mountains to the west. Cars were beginning to pull up to the courthouse for the traditional counting of votes in the local election.

"Do you think he learned his lesson?" Gordon finally said.

"Not at all. I really wanted him to have to register as a sex offender, so that would at least be on the record while he's in college. But Waterman refused to do a plea bargain with that provision or with jail time. We finally agreed that he would plead, and we would leave those issues for the judge to decide. I won one and lost one, and the one I lost was the one I really wanted. You never know what the judge is going to do."

"I grew up with one in the house."

"We knew Alicia was pregnant by the end of December, but it took more than two months to get a plea. Waterman tried to suppress the video and the DNA test and lost in both cases. Plus, I had to deal with the grand jury investigation into Armstrong's shooting. That took a long time."

"Thank you for not calling me as a witness."

"It was touch and go for a while. There was one grand juror who really wanted to indict you for burglary, and who was all over me for not prosecuting you. Finally, when he went on one of his rants, another juror turned to him and said, 'Let it go, Larry. The man was a friend of Bob's and he meant well, and no one got hurt.' I could see the other jurors were nodding, so I called for a vote, and it was 10-2 not to indict you."

"And Chris got a clean bill of health."

"Not only that — a commendation for bravery. Her race against Howard is going to be pretty close, and if she wins, it'll probably be because she shot Armstrong. When they found the other two bodies in the small room off the basement, the general sentiment was gratitude that she saved the county the cost of a trial or the embarrassment of a lynching."

"So it's over?"

"For us. It'll never be over for the families of Armstrong's victims. And it'll probably never be over for Alicia."

FOR AS LONG AS ANYONE CAN REMEMBER, it has been the custom in Plateau County for candidates and their supporters to come to the basement of the courthouse on election night. A large blackboard had been set up in a corner with local races printed on it. Chris and Howard were running for sheriff; a woman named Cummings was facing a man named Scribner for Boyd Winnett's supervisorial seat, and Diane Brinkley and one of the two female county supervisors were running unopposed.

At 8:30, a courier from the Elections Department came into the cafeteria and handed a folded sheet of paper to a fortyish woman standing by the blackboard. The woman opened the paper and began writing numbers after the names on the board. The first result was:

Honig: 523

Huntley: 479

Nearly everyone in the room applauded.

"That looks good for Chris," Diane said. "These are the absentee ballots, and they tend to be older, more conservative voters. I figured if Chris could hold him to 55 percent or less on the absentees, she'd have a real good shot. He got 52 percent."

"I don't see her around," Gordon said.

"She's waiting upstairs. She won't be coming down until either all the votes are counted or the result is clear."

"Then will you excuse me for a while? I see some familiar faces, and I'd like to say hello."

Diane smiled and nodded. Gordon saw Howard on the other side of the cafeteria and decided to start with him. He was standing with two older deputies and a half-dozen friends. He spotted Gordon walking up and extended his hand.

"Gordon. Long time, no see."

"I could say the same."

Howard looked around the room, taking it all in.

"Soak it up," he said to Gordon. "You may be witnessing the end of an era."

"You mean ...?"

"In the Sheriff's Department if Huntley wins, for sure. But I'm thinking of this," he waved his hand around the rooms.

"I'm sorry."

"Next month at budget hearings, the Elections Department is asking for new computers that will let them put election results on the internet. You won't have to leave the comfort of your home to find out what's happening, and no one will be coming to the courthouse anymore."

"That would be too bad."

"You really think so? I mean, I do, but I'm a dinosaur. I've been coming to the courthouse for election night for 40 years. The first time was in 1958, when I was 16. Plateau County voted Democrat for governor and senator that year. This year, it'll go Republican. Stick around 40 years, it could go the other way again. But the community will be broken up on election night."

"How do you feel about your race?"

"Too close to call. A year ago, I'd have won easy, but she's made some converts — especially the way she shot Armstrong when he was about to kill you. You sleeping all right yet, by the way?"

"It's getting better."

A flashbulb popped near them, and they turned to see a man with a camera several feet away, looking at them through the viewfinder.

"One more," he said, and fired off another shot.

He looked vaguely familiar, and after a few seconds, Gordon recognized him as Lovejoy, the man who'd been taking crime scene photographs when Jessica Milland was found.

"How are you, Mr. Gordon?" Lovejoy asked.

"Good, Lovejoy. And you?"

"Never better. I'm shooting this freelance for the *Courier*."

They were drifting away from Howard as they spoke, and Gordon reckoned they had gotten far enough for him to ask Lovejoy's opinion about the sheriff's race.

"Don't know," Lovejoy said. "I've been hearing a lot of different things about it, and I expect it'll be pretty close. I voted for the sheriff, though."

"Any particular reason — not that it's any of my business?"

"You remember that afternoon when they found Jessica Milland?"

"I'll never forget it."

"Well, you probably don't remember that when I started taking pictures of the crime scene, Sheriff Huntley jumped on me and told me to do it over."

"Actually, I do remember."

"I was a bit steamed about it that night. I'd been doing this for years and it had always been all right. But later, I got to thinking, and I realized it hadn't really been all right. It had been good enough for the people in charge, but they either didn't know there was a better way or didn't care enough to make me do it that way. And I started to think that maybe it was about time that we elected a sheriff who insists on doing things right and proper."

"Good for you," Gordon said.

Another cheer went up, and they turned to see the numbers on the blackboard had changed. For the sheriff's race, they now read:

Honig: 939

Huntley: 876

"Still anybody's race," Lovejoy said. "I've got to get more pictures. Maybe I'll catch you later."

Gordon milled around aimlessly for a while. Another result was posted, and Howard was still 60 votes ahead of Chris. If she's going to win, he thought, when do the numbers switch?

The cafeteria was getting stuffy. Gordon stepped into the hallway for some air, and a minute later saw a familiar figure heading his direction. He was six months older than the last time, and looked considerably more mature.

They shook hands like gentlemen.

"Good to see you, Harry. What's up?"

"I cast my first vote today. My 18th birthday was in March."

"Congratulations."

"I voted for the sheriff," he said. "How's she doing?"

"Neck and neck. Less than a hundred votes difference."

"Everyone's been saying it'll be close."

"You graduate Friday, right?"

Hooper nodded.

"What are you doing after that?"

"I didn't get any scholarship offers, but I showed some film to the coach at Sonoma State. He's going to let me walk on next fall."

"Then you have a chance."

"I have a chance. Say, I won't keep you very long. There's someone in the parking lot looking for you, and I think she's pretty serious about it."

Gordon smiled as Hooper walked into the cafeteria. A minute later, Brenda Hastings entered from the outside. The last time Gordon had seen her was the day of Bob's funeral, when he had delivered a eulogy in a post-traumatic trance. She had looked worn and haggard then, but now she looked more like her old self, though he thought he could see a certain sadness still in her eyes.

"Hey, you," he said.

"Hey, yourself. So it's finally happening."

"Finally happening."

"It's awfully good of you."

"I promised I would."

"The girls are really excited about it."

"Be sure to make them bring jackets. San Francisco can be cold and foggy in July."

"Eileen still thinks she can beat you at basketball."

"At the rate I'm aging, she might. I heard about your new job. Congratulations."

"Administrative assistant to the sheriff. It pays better than the bank, and you meet some interesting people. Plus, Howard told me last week he wants me to stay if he wins, so I feel it's a secure job now."

"I'm sure you're doing great at it."

"I've gotta go now. We'll talk more when it's closer to the visit."

As she walked toward the cafeteria entrance, he saw that she was still wearing her wedding ring, a sign that Bob couldn't be replaced in her heart — at least not yet.

There was another burst of applause from the cafeteria, and Gordon looked in the back door, from where he could see the blackboard. The latest results read:

Honig: 1,763

Huntley: 1,788

Chris had gone ahead for the first time.

The old connections and the tension of the race were getting to him. He walked outside to soak in the night air. It was completely dark now, and the temperature had dropped into the low 70s. Crickets were chirping. He walked around to the front of the courthouse, and as he passed a grassy area with a couple of picnic tables, he saw a pinpoint orange glow by a tree. A solitary man was contemplatively smoking a cigar, and Gordon thought he recognized him. He moved closer.

"Hi, Coach," he said.

"That you, Gordon?"

"The devil in the flesh."

"I heard you might be here for the election."

"You heard right."

"How's it going?"

"Chris — the sheriff — just went ahead for the first time. It's been close all night long."

"Pretty much as expected."

"So how are you?"

"As good as can be expected. I still have a job."

"You weren't worried, were you?"

"A lot of people weren't happy when I kicked Burnett and Jarrett off the team. When Burnett pleaded, though, that eased up a lot. Case really shook up the town."

"Do you think Burnett learned his lesson?"

"I'm afraid not. Five college teams have offered him a full scholarship. He's looking at two in Texas. I think he wants to get far away from here, but wherever he goes, there he'll be. I'll always remember him as one of my greatest successes as a player and as one of my worst failures in teaching character."

"If you had it to do over again," Gordon said, "is there anything you'd do differently?"

He took a puff of the cigar and exhaled slowly.

"If I had it to do over again, I'd give the ball to Hooper on fourth down."

GORDON TOOK A 20-MINUTE WALK to Chaparral Boulevard and back by a circuitous route. When he returned to the courthouse, the mood was still energetic, even though it was nearly 11 p.m. In the sheriff's race, the numbers read:

Honig: 2,916

Huntley: 2,972

He collared Diane Brinkley, standing alone against the back wall, clearly tight and nervous.

"It looks like she's going to make it, Gordon. The last votes just came in from Big Piney and Serendipity Valley. They should be posting them in 15 minutes or so."

"Jessica Milland's town," Gordon said.

"Figures to go our way. This is really amazing. Cummings beat Scribner, so three of our five county supervisors will be women. And if Chris wins, the Sheriff and District Attorney will be women, too."

"The daughters of Alta Mira are taking over the town," Gordon said.

"About time. Bet you don't have this many women in high office in progressive San Francisco."

"No, we do not."

Gordon checked his watch repeatedly over the next quarter hour. Finally, the Elections Office courier came in with another folded sheet of paper. The babble in the room grew to a higher level of excitement. As he looked toward the blackboard, waiting for the numbers to appear, he felt a pair of arms encircle his waist. He reached down and squeezed the feminine hand at the end of one arm.

The numbers went up on the board.

Honig: 3,179

Huntley: 3,308

The crowd in the cafeteria roared. Gordon tried to make himself heard over the din.

"You've been a long time," he said. "I was beginning to get worried about you."

"Sandy and I had a lot to catch up on," Elizabeth said. "So she really won."

"She really won."

"You haven't seen Brenda by any chance?"

"I did."

"Are the kids still coming to visit us next month?"

"Yes, they are."

"We'll show them a great time, won't we?"

"Yes, we will."

A new murmur of excitement began to ripple through the crowd. It appeared the sheriff was on her way to the cafeteria. A minute later, she walked through the door by the blackboard and stopped just inside the room. A spontaneous ovation broke out, and Chris looked happy, exhausted and shell-shocked. As the applause built, Diane came up to her, and the two women hugged each other in a tight embrace.

As they broke it off, Howard, standing across the room, crumpled a piece of paper in his hand, tossed it in the trash, straightened his tie, and walked toward Chris. As he reached her, he extended his hand, and she took it in both of hers. He said something, and she nodded. She looked now as if she were holding back tears.

"It's like watching two noble generals meet after the battle, and the loser hands over his sword," Elizabeth said.

"I hadn't thought of that, but now that you mention it ..."

"And have I been living in San Francisco too long, or did that hug between Diane and Chris have just a little too much passion in it?"

Another burst of applause gave Gordon a few seconds to formulate his answer.

"Actually," he said, "you haven't been living in San Francisco nearly long enough."

* * *

If you enjoyed this book, please continue reading for a preview of the fifth Quill Gordon novel, *I Scarce Can Die*, scheduled for release in late 2017.

I Scarce Can Die

A Quill Gordon Mystery

Rude Awakening

HE DIDN'T SO MUCH WAKE UP as come to, lying on the couch in the living room. It was dark outside, and he had a dry mouth, splitting headache and knot in the stomach — his body's way of reminding him he'd been blind drunk. He also needed to pee in the worst way.

He tried to look at his watch, but it wasn't on his wrist where it was supposed to be. Had he lost it in a bar somewhere? Had he taken it off when he got home? What happened when he got home, anyway? Had she made a scene again? She always did, never understood. But he loved her anyway.

There seemed to be a bit of light coming into the living room from somewhere. Maybe the kitchen. Maybe he'd gone in there and taken off his watch.

He started to get up, but groaned and slumped back on the couch. The need to pee was competing with the nausea, and the nausea had just won the first round. He knew he couldn't let it win, and after a minute forced himself up enough to see over the back of the couch.

The kitchen light cast some illumination on the wall he was looking at — enough for him to see the blood spatters.

He didn't immediately realize what they were. For a few seconds, he thought he was seeing spots before his eyes, in addition to everything else. Then his eyes drifted down to the body on the floor.

It was her, lying in a grotesque pose, utterly still. For some reason, he knew she was dead, just as he knew it was her, even though her face, smashed to a bloody pulp, was unrecognizable.

His entire body froze, going into a state of paralysis that lasted nearly two minutes.

What happened?

That was his first thought. The second was:

Did I do this?

I couldn't have, he thought. I was out drinking last night. What do I remember? Think, think. I remember playing darts at the Blue Badger and getting into the car, hoping there wouldn't be a Highway Patrol car or sheriff's deputy between there and home. That was, what, eleven o'clock?

After that, nothing.

Fighting the paralysis, he forced himself to get up, move around the couch and kneel by her body. There was no doubt it was her. He reached down to touch where her face had been, not even noticing that the cuff of his shirt picked up a smudge of blood.

A hammer was lying on the floor, a few feet from her body. He took it in his hand and stared at it. It looked like theirs, but it was a brand sold by the local hardware store, so he couldn't be sure. He could, however, be sure it was covered with blood. Her blood. It had to be.

Did I do this?

He asked himself the question again, and realized he couldn't be certain. Strain though he might, he could remember nothing after getting into the car.

I couldn't have done it, he thought. I loved her. I loved her no matter what, and she loved me.

Overcome with emotion suddenly, he began to cry — wracking, heaving sobs that jerked his torso in a way that further agitated his stomach and caused the nausea to overwhelm him.

He tried to get up, but found it impossible to stand up straight. Half-walking, half-crawling, he barely made it to the toilet before letting go. For five minutes, he leaned over the toilet bowl on his knees, alternately retching and sobbing, his entire body shaking. When he finished, gasping for breath, he realized he had wet his pants.

I need a drink.

Feeling better, but only marginally, he stood up and began the rounds of the house, looking for a bottle in all his usual hiding places.

He came up empty. He was sure there had to be a pint somewhere, but he couldn't find it. Damn her. Had she gotten to it first and thrown it out? Too late to do anything now. He'd have to take it from here without the comfort of alcohol. Or, more precisely, without the comfort of any more alcohol.

The nausea was coming on again, but he had to make the call first. He'd ended up in the kitchen, saw by the wall clock that it was just after 4 a.m., and picked up the phone. He heard a dial tone, which meant it hadn't been disconnected for non-payment.

With shaking fingers, he punched 4-1-1 on the keypad.

"Directory assistance," said the voice on the other end.

"Shit!" He slammed the receiver down. He didn't know if he could make it through another call without vomiting, but tried anyway.

"Nine-one-one," said a no-nonsense female voice on the other end. "What's your emergency?"

"She's dead," he blubbered into the receiver. "She's dead."

"Who's dead, sir, and what's your address?"

"My wife is dead, and I don't know what happened."

Opening, Shaughnessy Gallery

IN THE SECOND HALF OF AUGUST, it is not uncommon for San Francisco to experience a brief heat wave. For two to five days, the summer fog bank retreats well offshore, the temperatures climb into the high 80s or 90s, and for once, the tourists in shorts and T-shirts are properly attired. Then the fog — known to locals as God's air-conditioning — rolls in again, and life returns to normal.

It was the third day of such a heat wave, a Friday night. Shortly before seven o'clock, it was still 80 degrees outside, and the heat, trapped in the canyons created by the tall buildings, was stagnant and stifling. At Shaughnessy Gallery, two blocks off Union Square, a new exhibition was opening, "Sagebrush Sketches: Paintings by Elizabeth Macondray." The gallery was air-conditioned, and that fact, coupled with the large number of friends the painter had made during her short time in San Francisco, guaranteed a large turnout.

The crowd at the opening reception was building to its maximum level, the cheap wine was flowing freely, and the artist, looking lovely in a burgundy cocktail dress, was mingling freely and happily with the guests. She was a natural-born mingler and enjoyed working the room, talking to people, and, on this evening, taking compliments.

Quill Gordon, on the other hand, was no mingler. He stood off in a corner looking at a painting of cattle grazing in a pasture, with dry, stony mountains in the background. He was wearing a navy blazer from Cable Car Clothiers, tan dress slacks from Orvis, a powder blue button-down shirt from Nordstrom, a burgundy and light blue striped tie from Brooks Brothers, and Allen Edmonds loafers. His socks, a birthday present from the artist, were navy and peppered with images of the Quill Gordon trout fly. The navy matched his blazer, and the tan hackles of the trout fly went with his khakis. Standing a bit over six-four, in his late thirties and with a face more honest than handsome, he projected the image of a man lost in thought, who wanted to be left alone.

He was looking at the painting, titled "Serendipity Valley," trying to figure out what it was about the light that made it seem so right, even though it wasn't strictly accurate. It took him a while to register that a stunning redhead – late twenties, wavy hair, emerald dress – had appeared at his side.

"You're staring at that painting as if you know the place," she said.

"Actually, I do."

"Do you know the artist?"

He nodded, still looking at the painting.

"Do you know her from the college?"

Gordon looked across the room at Elizabeth, whose day job was teaching English at City College of San Francisco, happily chatting with four other people.

"No. I actually met her when she was living there," he said, gesturing to the painting.

"Oh, how nice. I just saw someone I have to say hello to. Catch you later." And she was off.

The people he was supposed to meet apparently hadn't arrived yet, and he decided to step outside for a breath of fresh air. Fresh was probably not an accurate description. The heat seemed to trap the vehicle exhaust between the buildings, and cooking odors from a Thai restaurant three doors down somehow made their way into the street. Next to the gallery was a small men's clothing store, with a window display of stunningly patterned ties and made-to-order shirts. He thought that with his long arms (he'd been a very good college basketball player) it might make sense to custom-order some shirts. He made a note to himself to come back next week.

"You already have enough clothes, Gordon," Elizabeth said, slipping up behind him. "They're both here now. Let me introduce you so I can get back to meeting with the guests."

"How's it going?"

"Wonderfully. They've sold three paintings in the first hour."

"Then you should probably raise the prices."

"Several people wanted to know if the two paintings on loan from the Quill Gordon collection were for sale."

"I hope you told them not at any price."

"I did. Come on, let's go."

She led him back into the gallery and through a door at the rear, into a narrow hallway. On the right was a unisex bathroom, and on the left was a closed door. Elizabeth rapped on it twice and was told to come in.

"Take it from here," she said. "I need to get back."

Gordon opened the door. It led into a cramped office, 8-by-8 feet, partially bisected by a four-foot desk. Behind the desk sat the redhead in the emerald dress and a stocky man in his early fifties with thick black hair, flecked with gray. They both rose.

"Melissa McConnell," the woman said, extending her hand. "Sorry I didn't get a chance to introduce myself earlier."

"And I'm Clarence Jefferson," the man said. "Pleased to make your acquaintance. We've heard a lot about you."

They sat down again, and Gordon sat in the room's remaining chair.

"I don't know how much Elizabeth has told you," Melissa said.

"A little," Gordon replied. "Why don't you just start at the beginning."

Melissa looked at Clarence, and he proceeded.

"Several years ago, I got involved with an organization called NGNC. That stands for Not Guilty Northern California. I teach sociology at City College, and I've always been interested in the way our criminal justice system works – or doesn't. NGNC looks into cases when the question of a wrongful conviction has been raised and all the ordinary appeals have failed. All the major law schools in the Bay Area have faculty who volunteer their services, and when it appears there's been a conviction of someone who is actually innocent, they petition for a writ of *habeas corpus* to overturn the conviction. It's a good cause, and I've enlisted several students and faculty members at the college to volunteer. One of them was Melissa." He looked at her. "Why don't you take it from here."

She nodded. "I went through the NGNC training program to learn how to conduct interviews and gather information. They get a lot of requests from people wanting their case looked into, and each one gets assigned to a volunteer for an initial investigation to determine if it's worth pursuing. At the end of last month, I got my first case, a man named Gary Baxter, who was convicted of killing his wife, Connie, two years ago in a place called Dutchtown. Have you ever been there?"

"Not really," Gordon said. "I drove by it or through it on the way back from a fishing trip a few years ago. About all I can remember is that it's pretty small and isolated – even for a town in the mountains."

"It was one of the original Gold Rush boomtowns, hard as it is to believe today. Anyway, Gary grew up there, graduated from high school, kicked around for a couple of years, then joined the Army. He served in Desert Storm, came back, married a woman he met at a community college, and kicked around some more at various jobs. The marriage was tempestuous, and his drinking was getting worse.

"Early in the morning on September 14, 1996, 911 got a call from him. He was barely coherent and kept babbling about Connie. A sheriff's deputy went over and found her lying in a pool of blood on the living room floor. There was a bloody hammer next to her, and her face and head had been smashed in pretty good. Gary reeked of piss and alcohol and said he'd just woken up from a bender with a fierce hangover when he saw her body lying on the floor."

"On the floor?" Gordon asked.

"He apparently passed out on the couch. Anyway, they took him down for questioning and started leaning on him about what he'd done. After a couple of hours, he finally broke down and said, 'I guess I must have done it.' That sealed his fate. The sheriff's department started putting together the case against him."

"But why did he confess if he didn't do it?" Gordon asked.

"It was hardly a full confession. He'd been saying all along that he didn't remember anything, but he finally broke down under pressure."

Clarence coughed. "Actually," he said, "there have been several cases of people who confessed to a crime and were later exonerated by DNA evidence. Generally, they were poor, had been in trouble with the law before, and didn't expect to get a fair break."

"Which is not a bad description of Gary Baxter," Melissa said. "Three DUIs and a number of visits from sheriff's deputies when he and his wife got into arguments. He was made to order as a fall guy."

"Maybe so," Gordon said, "but it sounds as if the case against him was pretty strong."

"The jury surely thought so," Clarence said. "They were out less than 45 minutes before finding him guilty of second-degree murder. It probably took them longer to pick a foreman than to reach a verdict."

"So why do you think he may not be guilty?"

"Three weeks ago," Melissa said, "I talked to him at Folsom Prison. He's starting to wonder if he really did it, but he can't remember a thing that happened after 11 o'clock the night she was killed. In prison he's gotten into Alcoholics Anonymous and developed a deep Christian faith. And when I talked to him – you'll probably laugh at this – I just couldn't believe he'd kill a defenseless person, let alone a woman."

Gordon said nothing for a moment. His father, a judge, had told him stories about women who had been emotionally seduced by prisoners, men who, when they wanted to be, could be charming and plausible.

"So you judged him by the look in his eye and trusted your instincts?" Gordon said.

"That makes it sound superficial," Melissa said. "But it's not far off the mark. There are a couple of other things, though. From his description of the trial, it sounds like some of the evidence might have been inconsistent."

"Do you have a transcript?"

"No, but his attorney would, and Gary can ask him to share it with you. Still, it comes down to two things that seem right in terms of his story."

Gordon spread his hands slightly, as if to say, "Go on."

"The first is that he's not swearing up and down that he's innocent. He honestly doesn't know."

"That was what impressed me," Clarence interjected. "I've dealt with a lot of ex-cons, and the ones who are still conning you are absolutely sure of themselves."

"And the second reason?" Gordon asked.

"Gary and Connie had a tempestuous marriage. They argued a lot, and the sheriff's deputies were called more than once. But Gary says he loved her, and that even though they had huge arguments, even though they shouted and threw things, he never laid a hand on her in anger. That's why he thinks he can't have done it."

"On the other hand, to play the devil's advocate, maybe he finally boiled over."

"Maybe, but I don't think so."

After a silence, Gordon spoke again.

"Something else I don't understand about this," he said. "I'd assume NGNC has its own people to look into cases, so why are you asking me to do it?"

"Good question. When I went back to the lead attorney to report on my interview, she shook her head at the end and said they couldn't take the case because Gary didn't insist on his innocence. With all the appeals coming into NGNC, they have to make decisions on which cases they take, and it's a hard and fast rule that they won't investigate the case of a prisoner who doesn't affirm his innocence."

"I can see you're puzzled," Clarence interjected. "We – Melissa and I – read his behavior as psychologically true. But NGNC doesn't want to represent someone unless he's all in. It makes sense from their perspective. They don't want to invest hundreds, thousands of hours on a case, and have the client suddenly back out."

"Makes sense, I suppose," Gordon said. "But if he's not sure he's innocent, why did he contact NGNC in the first place?"

"He didn't," Melissa said. "The request to look into his case came from a woman named Nell Quinn. She lives in a town about 12 miles up the road, and she's known Gary since they were both little kids. She doesn't believe he did it . . ."

"And she's in love with him," Gordon said.

"I didn't ask, but that was the impression I got, and it would have to be taken into consideration, certainly. I'm sure she'd be willing to talk to you."

"I'm sure she would, " Gordon said, "but let's cut to the chase. What, exactly, would you be asking me to do?"

"If NGNC could be presented with new evidence indicating innocence, they could still take up the case. If I had the time, I'd go up to Dutchtown for a couple of weeks and nose around, but classes are starting and I can't go at Christmas break because I have to be back east with my family. The earliest I could get there would be spring break, and only if nothing else came up. Time is of the essence; with each passing day, it gets tougher to compile accurate information. Elizabeth said you were planning a fishing trip in the next few weeks . . ."

"Probably the second half of October," Gordon said. "I'm still talking to my friend about times, but he's really slammed at work."

"That's a lot sooner than I could get there," Melissa said, "and a fishing trip would be a perfect cover for you to be in town while you're nosing around and asking questions."

"And if you're not going for almost two months," Clarence added, "it would give us some time to have Gary contact people and ask them to talk to you."

"What, exactly, would I be looking for?"

"Perhaps I can answer that," Clarence said. "In examining these cases over a period of years, NGNC and other innocence advocacy groups have found a number of common factors in wrongful convictions. There's bad faith and fraud by police and prosecutors, to be sure, but that's a small part of it. Most of the time, there's just a jumping to conclusions. The police see a couple of things early that point in one direction, it makes sense to them, so they start focusing on that and downplaying or ignoring the facts that don't fit their theory."

"Isn't the defense attorney supposed to challenge that?"

"Ideally, yes. In practice, it doesn't always work out that way. Incompetent defense counsel is also a major factor in wrongful convictions, and, in fact, one of the things we'd be asking you to do is look for that in the trial transcript."

"But I'm not an attorney."

"Granted. But you *could* be a juror. Look at the transcript and see if there's anything that you, as a juror, would have liked to have seen some elaboration on. Something where you didn't think the defense pressed hard enough."

"What else would I be looking for?"

"Some of the more common problems in these cases are bad eyewitness testimony, bad expert testimony, witnesses who weren't called when they should have been, questions that should have been asked but weren't."

Gordon exhaled with a whistle.

"That's an awful lot to turn up in a week or so," he said. "Especially if I want to get some fishing in, too."

"Look," Melissa said, "we're not asking you to be Perry Mason and produce a confession on the witness stand. Just nose around and tell us if you think there's enough there to justify further investigation. Right now, you're our best option. The question is, will you do it?"

Gordon said nothing for several seconds, trying to convey the impression that he was thinking about it. In reality, the matter had been settled when Elizabeth had first asked him to have this meeting. Unpromising as the case appeared, he felt he owed it to her to help her friends.

"All right," he finally said. "I'll do what I can."

"Thank you," she said. "Thank you so much."

"There's just one thing," he said.

"Yes?"

"What if I do my nosing around, as you call it, and everything I turn up points to Gary Baxter being guilty as charged?"

"I hope that doesn't happen," Melissa said. "But if it does, and we agree with you, we drop the case. And maybe Gary finally has closure."

AUTHOR'S NOTE

REX STOUT, American, 1886-1975, was the widely honored creator of the Nero Wolfe detective series, also a lifelong activist in civil liberties and peace issues. The Wolfe novels, set in New York City, were narrated by Wolfe's assistant, Archie Goodwin, who took a somewhat less than exalted view of his boss. Some critics, in fact, consider Archie, rather than Wolfe, to be Stout's great creation. In bringing Gordon's sidekick Sam Akers back after a two-book hiatus, I decided to enlarge Sam's role by having him play Archie to Gordon's Wolfe, hence the dedication at the beginning.

Gerald Nachman, used fictitiously in this book, is a real person, who graciously consented to his fictionalization. At the time the book takes place, 1997, Nachman was in fact working on a book that was published the following year with the title *Raised on Radio*. It is an absolutely delightful work, and I would highly recommend it to anyone who has the slightest interest in radio or American cultural history.

Finally, some advance readers have questioned whether someone convicted of statutory rape in California could avoid having to register as a sex offender. Such registration would be mandatory today, but at the time the book takes place, it was not, so the handling of that issue is entirely plausible as a reflection of the time in which the story occurred.

ACKNOWLEDGEMENTS

Many thanks to all who helped in the research and production of the book. This would include Gil Courtney and David Robles, who got me into the press box for a high school football game; former Chief of Police Terry Medina, who answered questions I didn't want on my internet search history; the U.S. Marine Corps Santa Cruz Recruiting Office for visual assistance with the book cover; Lauren Wilkins, my editor; Deborah Karas, the cover designer; and Melody Sharp, who keeps the website quillgordonmystery.com current each time a new book is published.

ABOUT THE AUTHOR

MICHAEL WALLACE is a native Californian, former editor of a daily newspaper, and longtime consultant in public relations and publications. He is a fly fisherman, a Rotarian, and an avid reader of mystery novels and stories. He currently lives along California's central coast and can be emailed at quillgordon@calcentral.com

Made in the USA
Las Vegas, NV
15 November 2021